Jacquelin Thomas is an [...]
author with more than fift[...]
not writing, she is busy catching up on her reading,
attending sporting events and spoiling her grandchildren.
Jacquelin and her family live in North Carolina.

Beth Cornelison began working in public relations
before pursuing her love of writing romance. She has won
numerous honours for her work, including a nomination
for the RWA *RITA*® Award for *The Christmas Stranger.*
She enjoys featuring her cats (or friends' pets) in her
stories and always has another book in the pipeline! She
currently lives in Louisiana with her husband, one son
and three spoiled cats. Contact her via her website,
bethcornelison.com

SAFE HOUSE SECURITY

JACQUELIN THOMAS

CAMERON MOUNTAIN REFUGE

BETH CORNELISON

MILLS & BOON

First Published in Great Britain 2024
by Mills & Boon, an imprint of HarperCollins*Publishers* Ltd
1 London Bridge Street, London, SE1 9GF

www.harpercollins.co.uk

HarperCollins*Publishers*
Macken House, 39/40 Mayor Street Upper,
Dublin 1, D01 C9W8, Ireland

ISBN: 978-0-263-32250-7

1024

This book contains FSC™ certified paper and other controlled sources to ensure responsible forest management.

For more information visit: www.harpercollins.co.uk/green

Printed and Bound in the UK using 100% Renewable Electricity at CPI Group (UK) Ltd, Croydon, CR0 4YY

SAFE HOUSE SECURITY

JACQUELIN THOMAS

Chapter One

Deputy Marshal Nova Bennett stepped out of the elevator and walked quickly to her boss's office. She'd received an urgent call from her supervisor, Roy Cohen, almost as soon as she'd arrived at work this morning. Nova didn't know what this was about, but whenever they discussed sensitive information, they did so within the confines of his office.

She took a deep breath before knocking and letting herself in.

"Juan DeSoto was found in the trunk of his car. Shot in the head," Roy said as soon as she stepped inside.

Filled with disappointment, Nova sighed and dropped into the nearest chair. With that news, what had started as a good day in the Witness Security Division of the US Marshals Service had taken a sudden turn. According to police reports, Juan had left his office five days ago and never returned home. Nova had been hoping for a better outcome for the missing brother of her latest witness, Mateo de Leon.

Mateo, whose real name was Manuel DeSoto, was close to his brother. He'd owned an accounting firm with offices in Los Angeles and Mexico, a perfect cover for laundering money. He was a prominent, trusted member of the Mancuso cartel, overseeing many of their financial transactions—until they discovered he was stealing from them. Poppy Mancuso, the head of the cartel, had ordered his death, and Mateo had since joined WITSEC. Nova had been his handler for the past eight months.

She tapped the oblong-shaped table before her, her nails beating a staccato rhythm with increasing intensity. Her eyes bored into Roy's as she said, "Mateo has been nothing but a thorn in our side since he entered WITSEC. Demanding a six-figure stipend, a mansion in an exclusive neighborhood, and all the country-club privileges. But now, with Juan's death, he might go over the edge. He was already angry with his brother for refusing to join him in the program."

Despite Mateo's constant complaining, she was his handler. And she'd wanted this case because of the connection to the Mancuso cartel. She wanted to help bring down the organization to avenge her father's murder. Her dad's killer, a lower-level hit man, had been arrested but died before he could stand trial. Nova would not be satisfied until Poppy Mancuso was arrested and imprisoned.

Her cell phone rang.

Recognizing the number, Nova said, "It's Mateo. I'd better take this..." She braced herself for what was to come.

As soon as she answered, the man on the other end yelled, "Johnny Boy had my brother killed! Juan didn't have nothing to do with this. The cartel...they just went and murdered him. As far as I'm concerned, it's an eye for an eye... I'm going to find Johnny Boy myself and make sure he pays for this."

John Boyd Raymond, also known as Johnny Boy, was Poppy's right hand. Before Mateo joined WITSEC, he'd placed a call to the DEA. He'd agreed to testify against Poppy and a few other prominent cartel members—including her top lieutenant—in exchange for protection for him and his wife. No doubt Johnny Boy was behind this murder, trying to lure Mateo out of hiding.

Nova heard sobbing in the background and spoke calmly. "Mateo, you can't do something reckless. I'm so sorry for your loss, but there's nothing you can do to help Juan now. You did everything you could to convince him to come to WITSEC, and he refused. Go comfort Arya. Your wife needs you."

"You expect for me just to let this go?" he demanded. "Juan was innocent. His murder must be avenged…" Mateo lapsed into Spanish as he continued to vent. "I gave up millions for this…"

Nova kept a gentle demeanor as she listened to Mateo's rant about seeking revenge for his brother's murder and how he'd given up everything to join witness protection. The news of Juan's death saddened her. She understood his grief and his desire for revenge.

"Arya's afraid for her parents, Nova," Mateo said. "And I don't know what to tell her. It's my fault that she's in this situation, but it's not like I can do anything about it. Johnny Boy and Poppy aren't gonna rest until they see me dead for betraying the cartel. I never shoulda gone to the DEA. I shoulda just kept my mouth shut and disappeared."

"You went to the DEA for help because you embezzled money from the cartel. They found out and were going to kill you," Nova stated, reminding him that it wasn't some selfless act on his part. "You wanted protection. You still *need* that protection, Mateo."

"I know that," he muttered, his tone filled with resignation.

Arya must have taken the phone from Mateo, because Nova heard her voice next.

"My parents need to be in witness protection." Her voice

faltered a moment. "That horrible Johnny Boy is going after Mateo's family. He'll kill my family next. My husband's told the DEA everything he knows about the cartel. Why hasn't the FBI or DEA—whoever—why haven't they arrested Johnny Boy and locked him up already? You all know that he's a murderer. I'm not understanding why he's still walking around free. Why are we living like…like this…? We're the ones in *prison*."

Nova clenched her jaw, trying to contain the small wave of frustration. Mateo was overcome with grief at the moment, but he couldn't forget his situation, she thought to herself, taking a deep breath to calm her nerves.

"You call this living?" Arya asked. "We gave up everything, while Johnny Boy is free to do whatever he pleases."

Johnny Boy had been a close friend of Poppy's for years. After her husband Raul's death, Poppy had taken over the Mancuso cartel, which was one of the largest importers of drugs smuggled into the United States through elaborate land and air distribution channels. She had handpicked Johnny Boy to control a large part of the cartel operations after her former lieutenant, Calderon, was arrested two years ago. Tall and dark-skinned with long dreadlocks, Johnny Boy was an unassuming man. However, his unremarkable appearance was deceptive. He was a skilled marksman with an uncanny ability to elude capture for the past ten years. He needed to be stopped.

"Arya, would you put Mateo back on the phone, please?" Nova asked.

After a pause, Mateo's voice came on the line. "Juan's death is on me, and there's nothing you can say to change that, Nova. It's up to *me* to make sure Johnny Boy and Poppy Mancuso pay for having him killed."

She listened with rising dismay before saying, "Mateo, I

can't keep you in WITSEC if you want to leave, but understand that we can't protect you if you abandon the program." Frankly, they couldn't let him walk. The DEA needed Mateo to testify in court against the cartel.

"My b-brother is dead, and I can't even attend his f-funeral." His voice broke.

"I'm sorry, Mateo."

"It bothers me that this is all my fault," he said again. "If I'd kept my mouth shut, then maybe Juan would still be alive."

"I know this isn't easy for you," she responded. She searched for something to say that might offer a small comfort to him.

"No, it's not. If it weren't for my wife, I'd go after Johnny Boy myself. But I'll let the law handle him." He released a sigh of resignation. He sounded much calmer. "I don't feel like going, but I better prepare my mind for my work shift. I'm due at my new job at three o'clock." Mateo paused momentarily, then added, "Nova, you don't have to worry. I'm not going to leave the program."

She expelled a breath. "I'm glad to hear it."

They finished their conversation and hung up.

"I'm not sure what they're mourning more—Juan or the money they had to give up," Nova said.

She stood up and walked around the table, navigating toward the door. "I'm thinking both. Mateo's a little calmer now, so I'm going to get myself a cup of tea, then try to clear some of the paperwork off my desk."

Nova stopped in the break room to make herbal tea, then walked to her work area. She sat down at her desk, eyeing the wood-framed photo of her father. A pain squeezed her heart as she thought of him. "I miss you so much," she whispered. She was thirty-three years old but still yearned for the haven her father's arms had once provided.

She placed a finger as if to stroke his grayish-blond hair. Special Agent II Easton Bennett was a man she'd always admired. He'd fallen in love with a Black woman and stood up to his parents when they voiced their disapproval. Her father didn't care. He loved her mother and had married her. It was her father's passion for his career that had inspired her to become a US marshal. He had been dedicated to his job, but it was that same dedication that ultimately led to his death at the hands of the cartel while protecting a witness.

She whispered to the face with deep-set blue eyes, "I wish I could talk to you, Daddy. I've got such a bad feeling about this… I know Mateo's going to do something stupid. Something that will get him killed." Mateo wasn't the sort of man who would let his brother's death go unanswered. She understood this particular feeling. Luis, the cartel member who'd murdered her father, died before his conviction, leaving Nova still hungering for justice.

She'd considered before that Mateo hadn't told Homeland Security and the DEA everything he knew about the cartel. A man like him, who wanted to be in control, might keep crucial information if he thought it would give him an edge. She felt terrible for his poor wife. Arya was innocent in all this. Now she was doomed to spend the rest of her life in witness protection.

Her Apple Watch notified her that it was time for movement.

Nova exited her desk and strolled outside her 9 x 9 cubby to a nearby window. She stared at the busy street down below, bustling with automobiles and people going about their business in all directions. This September weather was the perfect temperature. Not too hot or cool.

Nova had left Wisconsin two years ago in search of a place that wouldn't remind her so much of her father everywhere she went. She loved Charlotte, North Carolina, but she still missed him dearly.

Her heart filled with grief, Nova turned away from the window and returned to her desk.

She'd learned that her father's absence would follow her no matter where she went.

Nova gave herself a mental shake. She had a stack of paperwork that required her attention. Although focused on her tasks, she couldn't escape the ominous feeling swirling around in her gut.

If Mateo violated the rules of the program, then he risked having to leave WITSEC, and any criminal actions on his part could land him in prison. Nova often had to remind Mateo and Arya of the importance of this chance they'd been given.

It was an opportunity to stay alive—something the cartel would never offer them.

Los Angeles, CA

DEA SPECIAL AGENT RIVER RANDOLPH and his partner entered the federal building on East Temple Street. He and Kenny, along with a few other colleagues, had just concluded a knock-and-talk with a suspect and were returning to the office.

"I hope the rest of the day won't be as exciting as this morning," Kenny said as they strolled across the lobby.

River chuckled. "Can you believe that guy? He welcomes us into his house and then tries to run."

Earlier that morning, they'd met up with a team of ATF

agents and police officers in an empty warehouse fifteen minutes away from the suspect's home.

While the team remained out of sight, River and Kenny had brazenly walked up, knocked and asked if they could search the house. Surprisingly, Rico Alfaro had given them full access, claiming he had nothing to hide.

The man had no idea he'd been under surveillance for the past twenty-four hours.

Not long after, Rico Alfaro was apprehended and brought downtown in handcuffs. River's team had found massive quantities of chemicals in the garage, just as River had suspected. They'd also found stashes of cocaine, fentanyl and amphetamines in one of the bedrooms.

River felt a sense of purpose after the bust—the weight of his fallen partner's badge hung heavy on River's chest, a constant reminder of the vow he'd made to keep illegal substances off the streets. But now, with his partner's blood staining those very streets at the hands of the ruthless cartel, it was no longer just a sense of duty that fueled River. It was pure vengeance, a burning desire to bring down every member of that cartel and make them pay for what they had taken from him.

His new partner, Kenny Latham, was an experienced DEA criminal investigator, having worked in the field for more than fifteen years since River came to the agency. At forty-two, Kenny was the type of man who faithfully went to the gym three times a week to maintain his athletic build and never touched alcohol or cigarettes. It was something they had in common. River also worked out several times a week to keep in top physical shape for his job. Both men were over six feet tall, although Kenny was a few inches shorter than River.

They walked past an open area with potted plants and

chairs down a hallway to a room filled with desks grouped in clusters of four, surrounded by a wall of offices belonging to the superior agents.

River could hear the voice of a news reporter on television coming from one of the offices—the one with the open door. His attention was immediately drawn when he overheard the news of Juan DeSoto's death. River had recently inherited the file on Manuel DeSoto from his former coworker, who'd decided to leave the agency. Manuel DeSoto and his wife were in WITSEC as Mateo and Arya de Leon.

River stood at the door outside of his supervisor's office, knocked and waited for a response.

"Come in."

Special Agent in Charge Jared Rush was seated behind a large desk.

"I just heard the news about Juan DeSoto as I walked by," he said, strolling inside. He sank down in one of the visitor's chairs facing him.

"Yeah…certainly wasn't the outcome we were hoping for," Jared said. "I'd hoped we'd find the man alive."

River nodded in agreement. Mateo had handed over important evidence to the DEA—it was a shame Juan had lost his life because of it. "The cartel must be desperate to try and flesh out his brother this way."

River didn't doubt that Juan was murdered because of his brother's criminal dealings. He had reviewed several pages of notes on the man and his family. To their knowledge, Juan had been a law-abiding citizen with not so much as a speeding ticket; he'd attended church regularly and seemed devoted to his wife and children. Juan's death was meant to send a clear message to his brother. To silence him.

River's main concern now was whether Mateo would still be willing to testify against the cartel. If Mateo wavered in his decision, River's job was to convince him that testifying was still in his best interest. And if necessary, remind Mateo that he'd become a dead man when he decided to steal from Poppy Mancuso.

River would make a trip to Charlotte to see Mateo in a couple of days. Before exiting the office, he discussed a few final particulars about his trip with Jared. He was looking forward to meeting Mateo and Arya de Leon. Less so, their handler. River had stopped short when he'd learned the name of Mateo's case agent with the US Marshals.

Nova Bennett.

He shuddered inwardly at the thought that they had to interact and work another case together.

He'd read Mateo's dossier and understood the type of man he was. There wasn't much on his wife except that she denied knowing her husband's criminal deeds.

River didn't necessarily buy it as the gospel truth but decided to reserve judgment until after he met the woman. The previous agent had also noted that he believed Mateo was withholding information from the DEA. He knew more than what he'd shared with them.

Mateo had been distraught when he'd learned that he would have to turn over all the money he'd stolen to the DEA. The report said they'd recovered over three million dollars in cash hidden in his office's walls. There was nearly a hundred thousand more in two safes at his house. He'd called it his emergency fund. The man was furious when the DEA had seized his house, business and other properties.

They were a pair of high-maintenance witnesses... He wondered how Nova was faring with them. He shut that thought down. He would come face-to-face with her soon enough.

A flicker of apprehension coursed through him. It had

taken him eighteen months to erase the pain of a broken heart after she'd left.

He'd met Nova while working with her agency on a prior case nineteen months ago. When the two weeks of working together ended, River couldn't help but feel a sense of longing. They had shared countless laughs, inside jokes, and even a few blissful moments together.

He woke up one morning and was met with an empty bed and the realization that Nova had left without a word. All their memories now seemed bittersweet, knowing it was just a temporary passion fueled by late nights and adrenaline rushes until it became more profound.

River's heart ached as he remembered their stolen kisses and whispered confessions of love. River couldn't deny that what started as a fling had become genuine and meaningful. He had fallen hard and fast, and now he was left to pick up the pieces alone. But now he couldn't shake the emptiness that consumed him. As he went through the motions of his day, River couldn't help but think about Nova—the one woman he wanted desperately to forget.

He couldn't understand why Nova had disappeared without a word to him. Was it something he'd said or done? Had he imagined the connection they'd shared? Doubt crept into River's mind, clouding his memories with uncertainty. The more he dwelled on it, the more his heart sank.

His pride wouldn't allow him to chase after her. It had been easy to avoid further contact with the woman he never wanted to see again.

Until now.

THE NEXT AFTERNOON, Nova learned that another member of Mateo's family had been assassinated outside his home. She braced herself for the phone call she knew was coming.

As expected, Mateo was enraged and spouting threats.

"I'm coming out there tomorrow to see you and Arya." Perhaps she could better reassure them in person. She spent the next thirty minutes on the phone trying to calm them.

"My cousin was just murdered! Johnny Boy is gonna kill my entire family unless somebody does something to stop him. If DEA or Homeland Security don't do something, then I will."

From what Nova had learned of Johnny Boy, he was a ruthless foe and seemed fated for the drug trade. He was the son of Chilton Raymond, a drug kingpin in Jamaica, and had become involved in the family business at the age of thirteen. Johnny Boy had risen to prominence in the cartel quickly. However, he'd been forced to leave his birthplace when his father violated a pact with a Sinaloa cartel and was assassinated when Johnny Boy was eighteen years old.

Johnny Boy had come to the US to live with his uncle at age twenty. He and Poppy had connected at a party in Miami, and she'd introduced him to Raul Mancuso. Johnny Boy soon began working for the cartel, rising quickly through the ranks.

"We're taking the threats seriously, Mateo," Nova said. "However, family members not part of the program don't receive the same level of protection. Still, we're taking appropriate action to address and investigate any threats or concerns of your relatives."

"So, what does that mean?" Mateo asked. "Do they get some type of protection or not?"

"Various measures will be taken—surveillance, law enforcement intervention, and other protective measures to mitigate potential risks. I want you to know that the safety of your family members is a priority. Law enforcement will assess and respond to threats accordingly. I want you to know that their well-being is a top priority."

As she spoke those words, her mind raced with possible scenarios and plans to protect those under her care. She couldn't afford any mistakes or lapses in security, not when the lives of her witnesses were at stake. Nova was determined to do everything she could to keep everyone safe.

"As long as you stay put, he won't find you," she said. "Do not contact any of your family members, Mateo. This is what the cartel wants. They want you out of hiding."

"I hear you," he responded.

"Do you *really*?" Nova asked. She couldn't shake the dull ache of foreboding that had persisted since Juan's murder. "Don't do something stupid, Mateo." She felt like her words were falling on deaf ears.

It's gonna be a long day, Nova thought to herself after her conversation with Mateo ended.

Her phone rang for a second time, and her heart began to race as she saw the caller ID. The Los Angeles area code flooded her mind with memories of River.

"Hello," she answered cautiously.

"Nova, it's River," he said, his voice bringing back all the emotions she had tried to bury the past couple of years.

"River…hey…" she managed, her heart pounding. "What can I do for you?"

"I'm coming to Charlotte," he announced without preamble. "We need to discuss your witnesses. I'm sure you're aware that Juan DeSoto was killed. I need to speak with his brother. Make sure he's still going to testify."

"Another member of his family has been murdered. His cousin Julio. Neither he nor Juan had any cartel affiliations."

There was a pause on the line. "They're trying to get Mateo out of hiding," River responded.

"That's what I told him. I will try to get protection for his aunt and Juan's family. Have them moved to a safe house."

"Any other family members in Los Angeles?"

"No. The rest of his family is in South America," Nova stated. "When will you arrive?"

"Tomorrow."

"I'm… I'm planning to see Mateo and his wife in the morning." She hesitated, her heart racing at the thought of facing him again. Would he even want to see her? "I'll send you their address, and you can meet me there." Despite the excitement and nerves coursing through her, Nova couldn't deny that seeing him after all these years would bring up a mix of emotions—both longing and fear of the unresolved conflicts between them.

"That's all I need from you," he replied flatly.

She felt a twinge of disappointment at River's lack of emotion. Part of her wanted him to show some enthusiasm that they'd be working together again.

As the clock struck quitting time, Nova considered canceling out meeting up with her best friend, Jersey, at the Golden Pier, a popular spot in uptown Charlotte where local law enforcement went to unwind over drinks.

By the time she reached her car, Nova decided she needed to unwind. She needed to take her mind off the case for a bit.

Her friend met her at the door.

"Perfect timing," Nova said in greeting.

"Hectic day?" Jersey asked after they sat at a table near the bar area shaped like a boat.

Nodding, she responded, "It's been a trying few days, to say the least."

Nova ordered a glass of red wine, and her friend chose white.

While waiting for their drinks to arrive, she said, "I'm so

glad it's Friday." It didn't mean much that it was the week-end, because she'd be driving out to Burlington first thing in the morning to check on Mateo and Arya. But she needed the short reprieve.

"So am I," Jersey murmured as she released her long red-dish locs from the hair band that held them hostage. "I'm glad I'm not on call this weekend. I've had a busy week." Her friend was a homicide detective for the Charlotte-Meck-lenburg Police Department. "I wore my murder boots more than my heels."

"You're the only person I know who has murder boots," Nova said with a chuckle. "And bright yellow ones at that." Jersey always wore rain boots whenever she visited a crime scene.

"I'm not messing up a good pair of shoes while looking for evidence," Jersey responded. "I can just rinse off my boots and keep it moving."

A couple of middle-aged men sat at a table across the room. One worked with the Marshals Service, while the other was an assistant district attorney. The assistant DA made eye contact with them and gave a slight nod in greet-ing.

"What's up with you and Matt?" Nova asked in a low whisper as their drinks arrived. "He can't seem to take his eyes off you."

"He keeps telling me that he wants us to try again," Jer-sey answered, turning her face away from him to Nova.

"How do you feel about it?"

"I don't know." Jersey shrugged. "I still love him, but I'm just not sure we belong together. Sometimes it's best not to revisit the past."

Nova picked up the menu and opened it.

Jersey sipped her wine, then asked, "What about you? Have you met anyone interesting?"

"Not really."

"You're a borderline workaholic, Nova," Jersey stated.

"You're probably right," she responded with a slight shrug.

"What about that DEA agent, River?"

Nova gave a choked, desperate laugh. "What about *him*? It's been *two* years. I'm pretty sure by now he's found someone else and is incredibly happy." She tried to keep her expression bland, but she couldn't ignore the ache in her heart whenever she thought of him. She wouldn't tell Jersey just yet about the call they'd had—or the fact she'd see him tomorrow.

Jersey studied her for a moment before replying, "I can tell by the look on your face that you don't really mean that. Don't you think it's about time you and River had a conversation?"

Nova placed a hand over her face convulsively. "About *what*?"

"Well…the way y'all left things, for one."

"You just said that sometimes it's best not to revisit the past—I agree," Nova said smoothly.

"I was referring to *my* situation."

"I know that. But it can apply to my personal life as well."

Jersey's greenish-gray eyes rested on hers. "There's just one huge difference with you and River. Y'all left a lot unsaid on the table."

"I told you that things moved at an alarming pace between us, Jersey," she stated with a hint of sadness in her voice. "It was overwhelming and I couldn't keep up." She paused, her eyes clouded with memories. "We spent every waking moment together for two weeks straight. It was all-consuming and it scared me. I needed to take a step back and figure out what I really wanted."

"Maybe for you," she responded. "But how do you know that he feels the same way?"

"Jersey, I know you mean well, but what River and I had is over and done with," Nova stated. "I admit I could've handled things better with him, but I can't rewind the clock. Besides, I spoke with him earlier. He'll be in town tomorrow to discuss a case."

Jersey's eyebrows shot up in disbelief. "How was it? Talking to River after all this time?"

"It was just business," Nova responded. "He told me he was coming to Charlotte. I said okay."

Although Nova continued to put on a facade of nonchalance for her friend, she felt an acute sense of loss deep down.

She shoved that aside as they gave their food order to the server who'd come to their table.

Jersey stood up. "I'm going to talk to Matt for a few minutes. I'll be right back."

"Take your time," Nova said.

She glanced around, taking in her surroundings. The servers were dressed in nautical uniforms. Nova soaked in the laughter and the various conversations that danced upon each interval just a tad higher than the soft musical notes playing in the background. She studied the muted colors of the bottles behind the bar.

A platter of hot wings was delivered to their table.

Nova placed six on her plate but waited for Jersey to return to dive in.

"Sorry about that. I didn't mean to be gone so long," her friend said when she sat down ten minutes later.

"I was just about to get started without you."

"Well, I appreciate you." Jersey stabbed her fork into a wing, placing it on her plate. "Oh, I ordered us another glass of wine."

"Thanks," Nova said. She dipped a lemon-pepper drumette into ranch dressing, and the conversation turned to lighter topics.

After eating, Nova left the restaurant, heading home while Jersey stayed behind with Matt.

They are so getting back together, Nova thought to herself.

She tried but couldn't remember the last time she'd been on a date. Her focus for the last year and a half had been advancing her career. However, Nova was slowly realizing she was ready for a new career challenge.

There was a time when she didn't want anything other than to walk in her father's footsteps as a US marshal, but it hadn't been the same for her since Easton's death. She still wanted to go after the Mancuso cartel but had been thinking about switching law enforcement agencies to have a more active role in the fight against drug trafficking.

Nova glanced over at the clock on her nightstand. In a few hours, she would come face-to-face with River. Her heart raced as memories flooded her mind, the weight of regret pressing against her chest. She had always been a free spirit, drifting wherever the wind took her. And two years ago, when River had hinted that he wanted a future with her, she couldn't bear the thought of being tied down. It wasn't in her nature.

So, Nova ran.

But now she found herself questioning her choices. Had running away indeed been the right decision?

She sat in the middle of her bed, contemplating what to say when she saw him.

Nova had to prepare emotionally for facing him again. She didn't have a solid explanation for why'd she done a disappearing act. She cared deeply for River, and those feelings had scared her.

If someone asked her why, Nova couldn't provide an answer.

The clock ticked relentlessly, its sound echoing through the quiet room.

Nova couldn't understand why she struggled with commitment. The lingering doubt of what could have been if she hadn't run away that fateful night consumed her thoughts. It was a question that haunted her, even though she had accepted long ago that it would never be answered.

Deep down, Nova knew that the real reason for her reluctance stemmed from losing her father. His sudden passing had left a hole in her heart and a fear of getting too close to anyone else for fear of losing them, too. This realization only added to the weight of her doubts and fears, making it all the more difficult for her to let go and open up to love.

Chapter Two

Nova got up early to make the hour-and-forty-four-minute drive to the quaint town of Burlington. She was vigilant, making sure no one was following her. Not that she expected to be followed, but one couldn't be sure. She always took extra precautions whenever she went to a witness's house.

She exited off I-85 and took Freeman Mill Road to a small neighborhood near the Friendly Center.

Ten minutes later, Nova pulled into the driveway of a modest two-story house on a corner lot with two sizable, colorful rosebushes adorning the front.

She took a deep, calming breath before walking to the porch. Mateo and his wife were going to find a way to work her nerves.

Nova admired the two giant Boston ferns in hanging baskets before ringing the doorbell. Arya had gifted hands when it came to plants and flowers.

She found the door unlocked—the lock looked like it had been tampered with, putting her on instant alert.

Nova entered the house, hand on her duty weapon.

The tiny hairs on her neck stood to attention, and her pulse raced. Her internal warning system screamed, but she couldn't abandon her charges.

After thoroughly searching the main level and finding no one, she went upstairs, relieved she hadn't stumbled across their bodies.

Nova was about to walk into the master bedroom when she heard a sound behind her. She glimpsed a shadowed figure in her peripheral view. She prepared to defend herself when another masked intruder shoved her back into the hall. Taken by surprise, Nova managed to get her gun in hand, but before she could get a shot off, the intruder's gloved fist slammed into her face, making her eyes water.

He went for her gun and ripped it out of her hand.

Dizzy and disoriented, she used every ounce of strength to land a punch to the intruder's gut; the force of it loosened her gun from the man's grasp and sent it sliding across the floor.

Lightning flashed before her eyes as another fist hurtled into her. Nova fought off her assailant with her full might. She scratched, pummeled and kicked, then grabbed the lamp off a hall table and smashed it down on her attacker.

The second intruder hit her on the head with something, causing white-hot pain to flash through her brain before everything went black.

As River approached his destination, his heart began to race and his palms grew sweaty. He had avoided seeing Nova for the past eighteen months, but now he couldn't escape it. As he pulled into the driveway, his eyes landed on a black SUV. His thought was that it belonged to her.

Dread filled his stomach as he parked next to the vehicle. Seeing Nova again after all this time made him realize how much he had missed her, but also how much he feared her presence.

He took a deep breath and exhaled slowly before getting out to walk up the front steps.

River had barely touched the door when it swung open. Warning prickled at the back of his neck as he stepped over the threshold. He could practically hear his heart beating over the silence.

He pulled out his duty weapon, raising it at shoulder level as he cautiously entered the house.

River checked out the kitchen and dining area. Faded traces of sunlight penetrated through the large window along the opposite wall, casting shadows in the living room.

"Mateo?" he called out. "This is Special Agent River Randolph with the DEA. D eputy Marshal Bennett…?"

The sense that something was off felt even stronger now. River's eyes darted around, searching for the slightest movement. He moved deeper into the house, then walked back to the front door. He looked upward to the second-floor railing before making his way slowly up the stairs.

As he approached the landing, River saw Nova crumpled on the floor outside of a bedroom. Unconscious.

His heart leaped to his throat as he knelt to check her pulse. *Please let her be okay. She's got to be fine.* Her pulse beat faintly against his fingers. River called for paramedics and the police.

He examined Nova while waiting for the EMTs to arrive. He wanted to make sure she was still breathing. River couldn't bear the thought that she might be seriously wounded. Someone must have been here when she arrived.

After Nova was taken to the hospital, River stayed behind with the two police officers who were processing the house as a crime scene. He walked slowly through the house where Mateo and Arya had lived for the past several months, scanning his surroundings.

The living room looked fine, except for the bookcases. It looked like someone had rummaged through them, searching for something.

When he entered the master bedroom, River found the space in disarray. Items of women's clothing were strewn across a chair in one corner. Several drawers were left open, and it looked as though someone had rifled through them. The closet door was ajar, revealing empty hangers and abandoned shoeboxes.

He walked over and peered inside to get a closer look. There was only one piece of luggage inside. Indentations in the carpet showed there were at least two suitcases missing. *Looks like someone packed in a hurry*, he thought to himself.

There were signs of forced entry when they examined the back door. Someone had broken into the house, but he didn't think they'd found what they sought. When he found no vehicle in the garage, River was pretty sure that Mateo and Arya were on the run. And he wasn't happy about it.

He went back to the bedroom for a second, more thorough observation.

The room was in disarray, with drawers and cabinets left open as if someone had frantically searched for something. River knew it wasn't just a coincidence. The intruder must have been looking for something specific, and they likely heard Nova enter the house. They knocked her out and quickly disappeared, leaving behind a trail of destruction in their wake. It was clear that they were determined to find whatever it was they were after.

An hour later, River was at the hospital checking on Nova. He stood outside her room, silently debating whether to go inside. He'd been told her injury wasn't life-threatening, which was a relief to him. Despite how he felt about her, he didn't want any harm to come to her.

He peeked inside.

Nova lay on her side, buried under a couple of blankets.

River noted that she was more beautiful than he remembered. Lying in that hospital bed, a bandage on her forehead, Nova looked much younger than her thirty-three years. When they'd first met, she wore her hair in a cute pixie cut, which had grown out, reaching well past her shoulders. The warm brown tendrils and golden highlights complemented the glow of her honey complexion. Faint freckles were speckled across her nose.

Unexpected and disquieting thoughts raced through his mind; River's heart rate increased every time he pictured Nova's smile. His mouth tightened as he remembered how she'd treated him at the end of their assignment.

After a romantic evening filled with talk of a possible future together, River woke up to find himself alone. He had left his room foolishly searching for Nova, only to discover she'd already checked out of the hotel. She didn't even bother to leave a note behind. He'd witnessed firsthand the way she handled herself in dangerous situations, so River had never thought Nova was the type of woman who would run away.

Nova moaned softly, then shifted her position slightly.

River eased back toward the door.

She had hugely gotten under his skin, and when she'd left, she'd disappeared when he needed her the most. River shook his head as if to ward off the thought. It wasn't something he wanted to admit to himself.

NOVA OPENED HER eyes and looked around. She felt dizzy and weak but alert enough to recognize that she was in a hospital. Judging from the royal blue curtain that walled off the space, which was big enough for a bed and a chair, she was in the emergency department.

It took her a moment to remember what had happened. Her memory cleared from its foggy state—someone had jumped her. Maybe two people. Nova squeezed her eyes shut, trying to remember exactly what had taken place at the de Leon home.

Bracing herself against the pain, she placed a shaky hand on her face, which still throbbed with a dull ache. Her eyes were sensitive to the lighting in the room. She closed then opened them a few times, trying to adjust her gaze. She heard someone moaning softly in the bed next to her. Not only could she hear every groan and the private conversation between the patient and family member, but she could also smell the vomit.

The sickening odor caused Nova's stomach to churn in rebellion. She swallowed the sourness that threatened to come up and silently commanded the stirring in her belly to calm down.

Nova glimpsed a couple of nurses in light blue scrubs walking past her room. Wincing, she put a hand once again to her forehead.

Out of the corner of her eye, she glimpsed a slight curtain movement.

Nova's eyes widened as she spotted River walking toward her, his close-cropped hair perfectly framing his face. His almond-colored skin seemed to glow in the sunlight, highlighting every chiseled feature. Despite the pain that spiked through her head, she couldn't help but admire how handsome he still was, just like she remembered him. "River... what are you doing here?"

"I told you I was coming to Charlotte, remember?"

"I do," she responded after a moment.

"I found you unconscious at the house."

Nova blinked. "You brought me here?"

"No. I called the paramedics," River responded. "Did you happen to see who hit you?"

"Everything happened so fast. All I know is that there were two people in the house. I had one down, and the other hit me with something. I don't know what."

"Nova…how long have you known Mateo and his wife were thinking about running?"

River's accusatory tone made Nova sit up in bed. "Mateo was upset, but I'd hoped I'd convinced him to stay in the program. There were intruders in their home. There is the possibility that they might have been kidnapped." She winced from the throbbing ache of her head.

"I don't think so," River responded.

She peered over at him. "Why do you say that?"

"Kidnappers wouldn't have taken the time to pack clothes," he replied. "Two pieces of luggage are missing and so is the vehicle. It looks like they *ran* off before the intruder arrived."

"We have to find them," Nova said as she slipped from under the covers. "I'll initiate a search for the SUV."

"You're not going anywhere," he said. "The doctor hasn't released you."

"I can't just sit here either."

"Do you have any idea where Mateo might have gone?" River asked.

"I'd say Los Angeles. He was really upset over the deaths of his brother and cousin. He wants revenge. As for Arya, she most likely went to her parents' home in San Diego. She's been really worried about them. From what I understand, she and her mother were extremely close."

Nova's gut twisted with guilt. She should have been watching them more closely. They were her witnesses, under her protection, and now they were missing. Her heart raced with worry for their safety, knowing how consumed with rage one had been and how anxious the other was about her family. It was all too much, a constant nagging that kept Nova on edge, unable to relax until she found them safe and sound.

He shook his head no. "I don't think she's with her parents. Since Juan's death, I've had someone watching them, and there's been no sighting of Arya."

Mateo and Arya's disappearance made her head pound even worse. "I hope you're wrong about this."

"I've been wrong about many things, but this isn't one of them," River stated.

Nova stiffened. She had a feeling he was referring to his past relationship with her. But she was too weak to mount up a defense, so she let the comment slide for now. She and River had more pressing matters that required their full attention.

Chapter Three

River was all business with Nova. "You know that Mateo called the DEA after an attempt was made on his life," he said.

"Yeah." She nodded. Mateo knew how far the cartel would go to get to him and yet he'd fled.

"He embezzled money from them. They won't forget that. So, why do you think he'd risk leaving the program?" River asked. "Do you really think it's about revenge for Juan's and Julio's deaths?"

"Obviously, you think it's something more," Nova responded. "What's your theory?"

"I believe it's because Mateo had something he assumed was important enough to bargain with. I agree with the agent who did the original interview. He suspected that Mateo withheld crucial information from us. If this is true, then it's possible that he's out there trying to negotiate for his and Arya's life."

"Randolph called to update me on your condition." Roy Cohen's voice made them both look toward the entrance.

The appearance of her supervisor at the hospital caught her by surprise.

Something's wrong. She could tell by the grave expression on Roy's face. His pale complexion almost matched the yellowish-blond color of his hair.

"What's happened now?" she asked. "Has another one of Mateo's relatives been murdered?"

"Not a relative," Cohen answered, closing the curtain behind him. "This time it was Mateo."

Shock coursed through her body. "*What?* When?"

Cohen shook his head. "Mateo flew to Los Angeles last night.A nd now he's dead."

After she found her voice, Nova said, "That's why I drove to Burlington. I wanted to assess the situation. I knew Mateo was upset over Juan's death. I wanted to make sure he didn't do anything like leave the program."

"Airport surveillance shows that he was traveling alone."

"I can't believe this…" She muttered a string of profanity under her breath. "I told Mateo to stand down…" After a moment, she asked, "Where's my phone?"

"Nova, you need to rest," River said.

"I need my phone."

He handed it to her.

She immediately called Arya's number.

No answer.

Nova tried it several times over the next half hour.

Still no answer.

She left a message saying, "Arya, this is Deputy Marshal Bennett. I need you to return my call as soon as possible." She knew Arya was the anxious type, and Mateo's death would only make her anxiety worse.

She looked over at River. "There's a chance that Arya stayed behind but she's gone into hiding somewhere. I feel in my gut that she's in trouble."

"She is in just as much danger as Mateo was," he agreed. "Arya may actually have knowledge of what her husband did for the cartel, or the cartel suspects Mateo told her everything."

Nova folded her arms and said, "She told the last DEA agent assigned to the investigation that Mateo had kept her in the dark. She thought her husband was an accountant for high-profile clients—not that he was involved in something illegal. According to her, Arya only discovered the truth when he decided to go into the program."

"Mateo gave us copies of cartel files, but I strongly feel he didn't give us everything. The last agent who touched the file felt the same way. Mateo knew where most of the bodies were buried, so he knew way more than he told us."

"You seem pretty sure about this?" Cohen interjected.

"I've known Mateo for a few years. He came up a few times in other investigations. From what I know about him, that was his character. He was stealing from the cartel, so it's not beneath him to try to blackmail Johnny Boy and Poppy. Especially if he thought he could get enough money to stay alive."

"Okay, you might be right about Mateo, but that doesn't mean he told Arya anything. Mateo told me that he kept her from his business dealings with the cartel."

"Nova, she's the only person Mateo trusted," River stated.

She slowly swung her legs to the edge of the bed and braced herself for the head rush. "I need to see the doctor. I have to get out of here." Nova pressed the call button.

"You should try and rest for a while," River said.

"I agree," Cohen commented.

"I told you both that I'm good," she responded. "We have to find Arya."

When the nurse came, Nova told her, "I need to see the doctor. I'm ready to get out of here. I'm in the middle of an investigation."

"He'll be here as soon as he's done with another patient."

"Thank you," she replied.

The doctor walked into the room.

"I'll be outside," River said.

"You don't have to leave," Nova responded. "This shouldn't take long."

The doctor conducted a series of neurological and cognitive examinations and then ordered an MRI.

"Don't leave until I get back?" she told both men. Nova suddenly didn't want to be alone. Her anxiety level was always high whenever she had to undergo any medical assessments.

"Sure," River responded, while Cohen nodded in agreement.

After the MRI, Nova was returned to her room, and River was nowhere to be found.

Disappointment washed over her that he hadn't kept his word. It was soon blocked by the memory that she'd disappeared on him. Maybe this was some form of payback.

"He stepped out to make some phone calls," Cohen said.

River hadn't left. Her body sagged with relief as she eased back into the hospital bed. She didn't want to examine that reaction too closely. River was here for work—it was nothing personal.

"CAN I COME IN?" River asked from the doorway a few minutes later.

"Yeah. C'mon in…"

The doctor swept into the room behind River. "You have a concussion… We want to keep you overnight for observation."

Nova shook her head. "No. I need to go home."

"You have to physically and mentally rest to recover from

a concussion," the doctor said. "Although you have a minor concussion, if you try to return to your regular activities too early, there is a risk of another concussion. You should wait until all your symptoms are gone before resuming normal activities."

"How long can these symptoms last?"

"In many cases, symptoms of a minor concussion resolve within a few days to a couple of weeks," the doctor responded.

When he left the room, Nova eyed her supervisor and River. "Great. I'll be fine in a few days. I've always healed fast."

"Nova, you could've been killed," Cohen stated.

"I know. The good news is that I wasn't." She sighed in frustration. "I can't believe I have to stay here in this hospital."

"It's just one night," River responded.

Nova surprised him by asking, "Will you stay with me?"

He met her gaze before looking away. "I have to go back to the house and speak with the police."

River glimpsed a shadow of disappointment in her eyes before it disappeared.

"Oh. Okay," she said.

"I want to make sure I didn't miss anything earlier." He didn't know why but he felt the need to explain. "I'll come back here if it's not too late. In the meantime, you need to rest."

"What I really need is to get out of this hospital," Nova responded. "I'm so over it already."

River knew why she didn't like hospitals. They'd talked about it during the two weeks they'd spent together. He also despised this environment because it served as a constant reminder of vulnerability and mortality. Every sterile

smell, clinical beep and antiseptic surface reinforced his
discomfort. But pain of any kind was a sign of weakness,
as far as River was concerned. In the thirty-five years he'd
been in this world, he'd cried twice: when he realized his
mother never wanted him, and at the death of the woman
who did—his grandmother.

He knew Nova associated hospitals with her own fragil-
ity, stemming from witnessing the decline of her paternal
grandmother when she was sixteen.

Turning up her nose, Nova uttered, "The smells...the
white coats and scrubs..." She shuddered. "I just can't stand
being in here."

"Don't give the nurses a hard time." River walked toward
the curtain. "I'd better get out of here."

"Now you're the one running away," Nova muttered beneath her breath. Could she blame him? River had every
right to be skittish where she was concerned. But they would
have to put aside their feelings to work together.

BY THE TIME River returned to the hospital, Nova had been
moved into a private room for the night. He took the elevator to the fourth floor and stood outside her door until a
nurse asked, "Are you okay?"

"Yes, I'm fine," he responded. "She's resting, and I didn't
want to disturb her."

"She's been expecting you."

"The other visitor...is he still here?" River inquired.

The nurse shook her head no. "He left when she was
moved to this room."

River eased inside, careful not to disturb Nova.

She was asleep, almost buried under the thin bedcovers.

He'd never forgotten her mesmerizing brown eyes or the
way his body reacted when she locked gazes with him. Her

long lashes brushed the top of her cheeks, almost kissing the freckles sprinkled across the bridge of her nose.

Nova had come close to dying earlier. Although they hadn't been on speaking terms, River didn't want anything bad to happen to her.

A soft moan interrupted his thoughts. Nova shifted her position but didn't wake up.

Silently, River slid into the chair meant for visitors and suppressed a shiver as the antiseptic smell of the hospital surrounded him. He hated this place, with its sterile walls and constant reminders of death. It brought back painful memories of his grandmother's final days, fighting a losing battle against cancer. And now he was here again, by Nova's side.

He couldn't let himself get too close to her. But for now, he would stay by her side until she woke up and he could leave this place once again.

While she slept, River reviewed the information he had on her witnesses. He and Nova shared a common goal. They both wanted to find Arya de Leon. Her husband had been a valuable informant for the DEA, providing them with crucial information on drug trafficking operations. However, upon further investigation, they discovered that there were significant gaps in his reports.

Files from certain years were missing, and it appeared that large sums of money could not be traced or accounted for. This raised suspicions and cast doubt on the validity of his testimony. The DEA team knew they had to tread carefully as they delved deeper into this tangled web of deceit and illegal activities. It would mean a win for the agency if River could fill in the missing pieces. Not to mention his career.

His last two investigations had resulted in significant

busts. River felt he was on a winning streak and didn't want to lose focus. He wanted to prove something to himself and those who never thought he'd amount to much. It was too bad Mary, the woman who'd given him up at birth, was gone.

He had been a very angry kid and was constantly in trouble for fighting and skipping school. And then he'd been recruited to play for an AAU basketball team when he was fourteen. The coach had watched him playing street ball and thought he showed promise.

River had flourished under the tutelage of his coach/ mentor, eventually graduating with a 3.99 GPA. He'd attended college on an athletic scholarship, joining the DEA after graduation.

He and his former coach still kept in touch. The man was there for River when his grandmother passed away four years ago and again when Mary had died in March.

Nova turned from one side to the other, and River observed her for a moment, then looked away. He settled back against the cushion of the chair and closed his eyes. The events of the day were catching up with him.

NOVA SAT UP in bed, looking around. A smile tugged at her lips when she saw River across from her, sound asleep in what had to be the most uncomfortable chair.

Almost as if he'd felt her eyes on him, River woke up.

"Good morning," she said, trying to sound cheerful.

He brushed at his eyes. "G'morning. How are you feeling?"

"I still have a little bit of a headache, but other than that I feel fine." Nova gestured toward the chair he was sitting in. "How could you sleep in that?"

"It's more comfortable than it looks," River responded.

"The nurse told me it converts into a cot, but I hadn't planned on falling asleep."

Nova moved to the edge of the bed and then swung her legs outward. "I'm gonna take a shower. Hopefully, the doctor will come by soon, and I'll be able to get out of here."

She slowly made her way across the room.

In the bathroom, she stood close to the mirror, checking out the bruises on her forehead.

Nova removed the hospital gown and got into the shower.

The hot water didn't do much to soothe her aching body, but she hadn't expected otherwise. She just wanted a bath.

Two knocks reverberated through the bathroom door.

Nova turned off the water and then got out. "Yeah?"

"I was checking to make sure you're okay," River said through the door.

"I'm good."

"Okay."

Nova grabbed a towel and dried off.

She slipped on a T-shirt and a pair of leggings that were in the large handbag she had with her. Nova took a deep breath and then walked out of the bathroom.

"Do you know if my gun was recovered?" she asked.

"I have it," River responded.

Nova was relieved. "Thank you for keeping it safe."

She tried to hide her joy at being back in bed. She felt accomplished in not having to ask River for help. If they were on better terms, it was possible Nova wouldn't feel the way she did.

He hadn't been rude to her, but he was very distant. Even now, they sat in the room in a pregnant silence, waiting for the doctor to arrive.

River got up and walked over to the window, looking out.

"How long do you intend to be in town?" Nova asked.

"Until I speak with Arya."

"I'm not sure she'll be of much help to you, River. She had nothing to do with anything," she responded, keeping her voice low.

Their conversation came to a halt when the doctor entered the room.

An hour later, Nova was released from the hospital.

"Thanks for having my car brought here," she said as River held the door open for her.

"Are you sure you can drive yourself back to Charlotte?" he asked. "You can ride with me."

"I'm good," Nova responded. "The headache is pretty much gone now. No dizziness or double vision. I'll be fine."

"I'll be following you. If you need help, just pull to the side of the road."

"Thank you, but I'm sure I'll be okay."

Nova didn't drive off right away. Her head was consumed with thoughts of Arya and her safety, trying to come up with ideas of where she could have gone. So far, nothing had come back on the license tag.

She was acutely aware that River was sitting patiently in his vehicle waiting.

When it looked as if he were about to get out of his car, Nova started the car and left the hospital parking lot.

He followed her to I-40.

Three and a half miles later, they took the exit to I-85 South. Nova noticed that River stayed at least two cars behind her. It was as if he was sending the message that he intended to keep her at arm's length.

Nova felt the stirrings of guilt and regret over how she had walked out of River's life without so much as a word to him. At the time, she didn't know what to say to the man she'd fallen in love with but hardly knew. She'd panicked, and the only thing she could think to do was run away.

Nova assumed he must have had regrets, too, because she'd never heard from River afterward. His lack of communication validated her belief that she'd made the right decision. Still, she was bothered by the remoteness she'd glimpsed in his gaze earlier.

Could he forget what we shared so easily?

Swallowing her apprehension, Nova chewed on her bottom lip as she drove. As much as she wanted to forget, she couldn't. The first time she and River had made love was forever etched in her mind. It was when Nova realized she'd fallen in love with him. That realization had shaken her to the very core.

The intensity of her feelings for River scared her, forcing Nova to flee despite knowing she couldn't move on with someone else. The truth was that he wasn't a man who could be easily replaced.

Now he could barely look at or stand around her. Not that Nova could blame him, given how she'd left things between them.

I should have written River a note or something. He deserved better from me.

She couldn't undo what had transpired between them. Nova considered it a waste of time to dwell on something she could not change.

She wondered if he'd met a woman who loved him freely and without reservation. The thought didn't sit well with her, but she couldn't blame River. After all, she was the one who'd chosen to walk away.

An hour and forty-five minutes later, Nova walked into her town house. She'd half expected River to follow her all the way home or at least call to see if she was okay.

Silence. He didn't call or come by.

He's really over me.

Nova choked down her disappointment. Forcing River from her mind, she navigated to her home office. Seated at her desk, Nova placed a quick call to check in with her supervisor. She pulled out a bottle of Tylenol from the side drawer and tossed one in her mouth, followed by sips of room-temperature bottled water.

Nova settled back in her chair, waiting a few minutes for the pain to subside.

A photograph fell out when she picked up the folder lying on her desk.

It was of Mateo and his wife.

Nova admired the locket Arya always wore around her neck. It was a lovely piece of jewelry. Her mother had one that was given to her by her grandmother, but she hardly ever wore it.

Nova pushed away from her desk and stood up.

She walked over to a painting and removed it to reveal a built-in safe. She opened it and tossed the file inside. She kept all the physical files on her witnesses locked up for security. The copies on her computer were all encrypted as well.

She thought back to what River had said about Arya. Nova had to find her before the cartel did.

Chapter Four

There had always been an undeniable magnetism between River and Nova, which probably explained why he was sitting in his rental car down the street from her town house. River wanted to make sure she'd arrived home safely. But he didn't want her to know that he cared this much about her well-being.

He hated seeing her again. It had taken him two years to get her out of his system. River certainly didn't want to work with her, but he had no choice. She was Arya's handler, and he needed her assistance finding the woman. He didn't doubt that Nova would do whatever she could to keep Arya safe and in WITSEC.

After an hour passed, River felt she'd pretty much settled in for the rest of the day, so he headed to his hotel. He had only planned to be in town long enough to talk to Mateo, but now that he was dead and his wife missing... River's stay would be extended. He knew Nova had initiated a trace on the vehicle owned by Mateo and Arya. In the meantime, he decided to comb the file once more.

He spent the afternoon watching hours of video taken during Mateo's interrogation. Outside of handling finances and laundering money for the cartel, Mateo had also assisted in securing stash houses where thousands of kilograms of cocaine were unloaded from tanker trucks and then reloaded with weapons and money headed to and from California, Mexico and Arizona. During his involvement with the Mancuso cartel, he had extensive knowledge of shipments of cocaine, fentanyl and other drugs worth several billions of dollars.

Mateo had been a valuable asset for the DEA; the wealth of information and evidence he had against John Boyd Raymond made him a coveted witness. The notorious criminal sat atop the FBI's Ten Most Wanted Fugitives list, hunted by every law enforcement agency in the country. But for the DEA, it was personal. They were determined to bring Johnny Boy to justice for the cold-blooded murder of two of their agents. For River, one of the fallen agents had been like a brother, fueling his burning desire for vengeance and driving him to do whatever it took to see Johnny Boy behind bars.

River ordered room service and then made a phone call to his partner.

"Hey, Kenny. Thanks for the information on Pablo and Ramona Lozano." He'd had his partner help with the surveillance of Arya's parents, and so far, there had been little movement from the couple. "Do me a favor and keep them under surveillance for a few more days. Their daughter may show up there. Let me know as soon as she does."

"How is Nova doing?"

"She's fine," River responded. He'd called Kenny to update him after Nova was taken to the hospital. "No real damage done. She's at home now."

"Did you two get a chance to talk things over?"

"About the witness…yes, we did."

"You know that's not what I was talking about," Kenny

responded. "You and Nova need to have a conversation about what happened."

"I told you that what Nova and I had is long over. I'm not about to rehash the past. The only thing between us now is our dead witness's missing wife."

"If you say so..."

"I do," River stated. "Hey, look... I need to get back to work. I'll check in with you tomorrow."

He disconnected with Kenny and called Nova, unsure why he couldn't shake the worry that clung to him. "I just wanted to make sure you're all right and see if you needed anything."

"I'm fine." Her calm voice reassured him, but he could hear the exhaustion. "I ate something and took my medication."

"Okay," River said, trying to sound casual. "Call or text me if you need me to pick up dinner or something."

"I will. Thanks."

After hanging up, he stretched out on the bed, his body feeling out of sync with the time difference. As he lay there, thoughts of Nova filled his mind. He tried to find comfort in shifting from one side to the other, but it was useless.

Giving up on sleep after an hour of restlessness, River sat up in bed and propped himself against the pillows. He returned to reviewing the files on Mateo, but they couldn't distract him from the nagging thoughts about Nova and their complicated past.

CLAD IN A sports bra and a pair of leggings, Nova sat down on the edge of her king-size bed. She pulled her golden-brown hair into a high ponytail before sliding under the covers. The headache was now a dull throb.

At 3:07 p.m. her phone rang, the ringtone identifying the caller as her best friend.

She sat up in bed to take the call. "Hey, Jersey..."

"You all right?" she asked. "River told me what happened."

"River called *you*?" Nova couldn't believe it.

"Yeah. I was listed as your emergency contact. He had called the precinct the day everything happened and left a message for me. I was working a case and didn't call him back until a few minutes ago. He told me you were home now. How are you feeling?"

"I'm good," Nova responded.

"Girl, what happened?"

"I went to check on my witness, and someone clocked me good," she responded. "River was meeting me there. He found me unconscious."

"Thank goodness he showed up in time," Jersey said. "I think it's interesting that you are working together again."

Nova didn't respond.

"Do you need anything? I just got off work, but I can pick up something for you to eat."

"River called not too long ago asking if I needed anything. I told him I was good. I can always have something delivered."

"That was sweet of him."

"Yeah. Don't read too much into it, Jersey."

"Well, reach out if you change your mind. I can run out and pick you up something."

"I probably won't be bothering you," Nova said. "I'm going to take a nap."

"Check in with me when you wake up."

"Okay," Nova responded.

As she settled under her soft, fluffy comforter, Nova

reached over and placed her smartphone on the nightstand. She sighed in relief, hoping that the darkness and stillness of the room would help ease her pounding headache.

Just as she closed her eyes, the shrill ringtone of her work phone broke through the silence. Her hand darted to grab it.

"Deputy Marshal Bennett speaking," she answered professionally. But all she heard on the other end was silence.

"Who is this?" Nova asked, growing suspicious and slightly irritated.

Still, no response came from the other end, just an eerie quiet that sent a chill down her spine. "Arya?"

The caller hung up.

Nova bolted upright and called the office to ask one of the techs to trace the call.

She released a short sigh of frustration, abandoning the idea of a nap. She couldn't afford to be down right now.

Headache or not, she was going back to work.

The only reason she'd tried to rest was because her boss had insisted. Her gut instinct told her that Arya had been the caller.

"Where are you, Arya?" she whispered.

Rubbing her temples, Nova reached for her phone and dialed the office to check on the progress of the trace. As she listened to the ringing, her mind wandered back to the missing woman.

"Deputy Marshal Bennett, we managed to trace the call." An agent's voice crackled through the receiver, snapping Nova back to reality. Her heart raced as she leaned forward, anticipation filling her. "It's from a burner phone."

"Where did it come from?"

"It's strange. The call was traced back to an abandoned house in Concord."

So, Arya's still in North Carolina.

"Send the location to my phone, please."

"Sending now."

Without hesitation, Nova got out of bed. She slipped a hoodie over her head and grabbed her keys, determined to find Arya and bring her back into the safety of WITSEC.

Chapter Five

As Nova approached the abandoned house, her heart quickened with unease. The air was thick and still, almost as if it held its breath in anticipation. In the distance, she could hear the faint whispers of the trees rustling in the wind, adding to the ominous atmosphere.

She scanned the wooded area, searching for any signs of life, but there was nothing—no cars on the street, no movement behind the windows.

Taking a deep breath, Nova exited her car and stepped onto the cracked pavement. With each step closer to the house, she could feel a strange energy enveloping her, making her skin prickle with goose bumps. She'd considered calling River, but decided to venture out alone. Her thoughts were centered on Arya and finding her.

The front door hung open, the lock broken and swinging on its hinges. She couldn't tell if someone had forced it open or if time had slowly eroded its strength.

Cautiously, she entered the darkened interior. "Arya?" she called out softly. "It's me, Nova. Please don't be scared. I want to help you. I can take you somewhere safe." Her voice echoed through the empty halls, but there was no response except for the creaking of floorboards beneath her feet.

As Nova ventured farther into the house, the atmosphere grew even more suffocating. The air seemed to thicken, making it harder to breathe. The dying light from the outside filtered through the cracks in the boarded-up windows, casting eerie shadows on the peeling wallpaper.

With each step, Nova's apprehension deepened and her temples throbbed. A shiver danced down her spine, and she wrapped her arms around herself for comfort, though it offered little solace.

The silence was deafening, broken only by the distant howl of a neighborhood dog. As Nova ascended the creaky staircase, she felt a strange pull drawing her toward a particular room. The door stood slightly ajar, inviting her inside like a siren's call.

Summoning every ounce of courage, Nova placed her hand on her weapon before pushing open the door.

Evidence of recent occupancy was scattered about the bedroom. A brand-new sleeping bag lay crumpled on the floor, still bearing the crisp folds from its packaging. Empty fast-food containers and their greasy remnants were strewn on the dusty window seat, along with a roll of toilet paper and depleted water bottles. It was clear that someone had slept here, but they were long gone now.

This current setting before Nova was a stark contrast to the woman she had come to know. Arya de Leon was all about five-star hotels, often clutching the locket she wore around her neck at the thought of staying anywhere less extravagant.

Her gaze drifted back to the sleeping bag, and she strode over to it. With a nudge from her shoe, the cover was thrown open, revealing a cell phone inside. Nova was confident that it was the one used to call her earlier.

She hesitated for a moment, her mind racing with questions. Was it Arya who had left the phone here? And why?

Nova's curiosity got the better of her, compelling her to pick up the device. As she held it in her hand, the weight of intrigue settled upon her.

The screen flickered to life, displaying a simple text message: Find me.

RIVER WAS CAUGHT off guard when Nova reached out to him. He had offered to help with errands or bring food but never expected to actually hear from her.

"I heard from Arya," she announced.

"When?"

"She called me a couple of hours ago but didn't say anything."

"How did you know it was her?" he asked. "How can you be sure?"

"I wasn't until now," Nova responded. "I had a trace put on the number, which led to an old abandoned house in Concord. I followed the trail and—"

"You did *what*?" River's mind was abuzz as he took in the news. Nova had risked her safety and well-being to find answers, and he couldn't shake off his worry for her.

"I checked out the house and found the cell phone. There was a message on it that said, 'Find me.'"

"Nova, where are you right now?"

"I'm in my car at a gas station. I'm heading home when I hang up with you."

"Be safe."

"River, I'm fine. I feel fine."

As Nova promised to head back home, River couldn't shake off the conflicting emotions swirling inside him—relief and concern for Nova despite everything that had happened between them. He shouldn't care as much as he did.

As the minutes ticked by, River found himself pacing restlessly. Their shared history weighed heavily on his shoulders. Nova had vanished from his life once before, leaving him heartbroken and confused. The wounds from their past were still raw, yet she had managed to stir up a whirlwind of emotions within him once more.

A gentle breeze blew through the open balcony door, rustling the drapes and bringing a momentary respite to River's racing mind. As he gazed at the bustling city life below, nostalgia washed over him, reminding him of the two beautiful weeks he'd spent in Nova's embrace.

His mind strayed to Nova's mention of the message that was on the phone.

Find me.

The urgency in Arya's message echoed in his head, but a flicker of doubt crept in. Why flee again without speaking to Nova if she wanted to be found? Was that message really from Arya, or was something more insidious at play?

FIND ME.

With Mateo dead, Arya was now in the wind on her own. Nova considered that perhaps she was scared the intruder was on her trail, which may be why she continued to run. Nova couldn't rest until Arya was back safely. With the weight of her father's legacy on her shoulders, she couldn't afford to fail.

She had driven to the office to speak with Cohen and to drop off the phone after speaking with River. He agreed to send a team of agents to the abandoned house.

She planned to return to the Burlington house with River to attempt to retrace Arya's steps, searching for clues that could lead Nova to her whereabouts. She intended to scour the house, meticulously examining every corner, hoping to find a hidden message or hint pointing them in the right direction.

"We will find you," she vowed. Her father had never lost a witness, and she wouldn't either. This would not be her legacy.

Nova couldn't shake off the concern in River's voice during their brief phone call, but she couldn't afford to dwell on it either. Her priority was Arya and making sure she was safe. Yet a small part of her was grateful for his genuine worry despite their tension.

In solitude, Nova realized that it may not have been the most sensible choice to venture off to an abandoned house alone. But her determination to find Arya had driven her to take the risk. Unfortunately, she'd returned home without any luck in her search. She felt both aggravated and anxious for Arya's well-being.

As the sun continued dipping below the horizon, casting long shadows across the quiet street, the weight of Nova's unsuccessful search for Arya bore down on her shoulders, exacerbating her frustration and unease. The abandoned house loomed in her mind, haunting her thoughts with unanswered questions.

How did Arya come across the empty home? Why did she stay in North Carolina instead of seeking refuge with her parents? A m I reading his all wrong?

What if it was something more?

Her phone rang, cutting off her thoughts.

"I hope you're at home resting," River said when she answered.

"I am," Nova confirmed. "At least, my body is resting. My mind is busy trying to figure out this phone message.

Cohen's sending agents to watch the abandoned house. I'd like you and me to return to Mateo and Arya's home in the morning. I want us to conduct our own search."

"Sounds like a plan," River said. "Anything on her vehicle?"

"Not yet."

"Do you want to meet me at my hotel?"

"Just come to the Marshals office. I'll be there in the morning."

"Do you still have the phone?"

"No, I took it to the office. I want it checked for prints."

"I guess I'll see you in the morning."

"See you then," she murmured.

They hung up.

Nova had gotten out of bed and walked through her house while talking to him, checking locks and arming the security system. Arya was still at the forefront of her mind.

She had to find her before the cartel did, no matter what it took. Nothing would stop Nova from keeping Arya safe.

THE EARLY MORNING sun cast a soft glow over the quiet suburban neighborhood as Nova and River parked their vehicle discreetly down the street from the de Leons' residence. The house, surrounded by neatly trimmed hedges and a white picket fence, appeared calm and unassuming.

As Nova approached the porch, she noticed the once lush and vibrant ferns drooping and wilting from neglect. The leaves hung limply, their once bright green color faded to a dull, sickly shade. It was as if the plants were crying out for help. Nova made a mental note to give them the care and attention they deserved before they left the house.

She adjusted the strap of her holster as she approached the front door. River followed closely behind. They exchanged a quick nod before Nova knocked on the door, the sound echoing through the stillness of the morning.

No answer.

She pushed away the thought of what had happened the last time she was here. Nova's instincts kicked in, and she reached into her pocket for the spare key.

With a swift turn, the door creaked open, revealing a dimly lit living room.

The air inside was tense as they stepped into the house.

Nova swept her surroundings, her eyes scanning for any signs of disturbance or anything that seemed out of place.

They moved through the house methodically, checking every room for any clues or indications of where Arya might have gone. Nova examined the study, rifling through papers and files. River focused on the kitchen, checking the refrigerator and cabinets for any signs of sudden departure.

As they explored, a sense of urgency grew. The unanswered questions fueled their determination to find Arya before it was too late.

Nova halted in front of a corkboard behind the desk, covered with pictures and notes. She traced her finger over a recent photograph of Arya, reminding herself of the stakes involved.

River discovered a plastic bag hidden between packages of meat in the freezer. "Nova, take a look at this," he called, holding up a small notebook he found inside.

The notebook contained cryptic notes and coded messages, hinting at Mateo's attempts to stay one step ahead of the cartel and law enforcement.

Nova's eyes narrowed as she scanned the pages, noting the dates and realizing that Mateo had been preparing for something all along.

"He never intended to stay in WITSEC," she told River. "He had money stashed in several banks in other countries."

"Looks like he never intended to testify. He and Arya were going to leave the country."

"We really need to find her," Nova said, determination flashing in her eyes.

With newfound purpose, Nova and River continued their search, determined to unravel the mystery surrounding Arya de Leon's disappearance and bring her back to safety.

The morning sun climbed higher in the sky, casting a determined light on their path as they pursued the elusive trail that would lead them to Arya's whereabouts.

LATER IN THE DAY, River went to the local DEA agency to check out a few things and to reconnect with a friend he'd met years ago when they attended college.

"I heard you were in town," Taylor said. "I was out yesterday when you called."

"They told me that you called in sick. You all right?"

"Yep, I'm great. My son was the one who was sick. He's getting over a stomach virus. My wife had to be in court yesterday, so I had to stay home and clean up the messes from both ends. Man, I'm traumatized."

River chuckled. "Poor you…"

Shaking his head, Taylor said, "You don't know the half of it."

They walked into the break room for coffee.

"So, what brings you to Charlotte? And where is your partner?"

"Kenny's back home working our investigation on that end," River said. "I came here because one of my witnesses is dead and another is missing."

"Any leads?"

"Not very many, but we're exploring all of them. I need a space to work."

"There's an empty desk behind me," Taylor offered. "You can plug in your computer there."

"Thanks."

River added copies of the information they found at the house to his file. He called his partner and discussed his findings. He and Nova weren't sure whether Arya was still in town, but there was no doubt that she would turn up in San Diego at some point.

Sunlight filtered through the blinds and lent an air of secrecy to his solitary pursuit. Every document, every line of text he scrutinized brought him closer to uncovering Mateo's slipup.

As time ticked by, River's anticipation ignited like a flame in the depths of his chest. A strong sense of determination coursed through his veins, driving him to unravel and destroy Mateo's intricate schemes of corruption. Despite the fact that their key witness was deceased, his information could still shed light on the inner workings of the drug cartel.

As River carefully examined the financial records, a peculiar pattern emerged. It seemed that Mateo had unknowingly left a trail—an intricate breadcrumb trail leading straight to his betrayal.

River's eyes widened with astonishment as he connected the dots, realizing that Mateo's slipup was not just a simple miscalculation but a meticulously calculated move to divert attention from his true motives.

As he delved deeper into the financial records, River's analytical mind pieced together the irregularities that had initially caught his attention. It was a web of intricate transactions, money funneled through various shell companies and offshore accounts. The path seemed convoluted at first, but patterns emerged; hidden beneath the facade of legitimate business dealings lay a complex network of bribery and embezzlement.

Still, there were gaps in the information. There were more, perhaps critical details on the cartel's business dealings that Mateo hadn't shared. The cartel's operations extended far beyond what he had revealed, and River was determined to uncover the truth.

He leaned back in his chair, his mind racing with possibilities. He reached for his coffee, taking a slow sip as he considered his next move.

Some of the handwritten entries were written by someone else. River assumed that Arya was the writer. Although he hadn't met them, his gut told him that the only person Mateo would've trusted with this information was his wife. If his theory was correct, then this was proof that Arya knew of her husband's relationship with the cartel.

He pulled out his phone and tapped out a message, fingers moving rapidly over the screen.

Can you meet me in thirty minutes? River sent the text to Nova, hoping she would agree to see him.

Sure. My place okay? came the reply.

Yes. He slipped his phone into his jeans pocket.

River took his time gathering his notes, making sure they were organized. He spent a few more minutes catching up with Taylor before heading out to his car.

River knew that Nova had more information about Arya than he did. He depended on her knowledge; they would have to work together to find the missing woman.

The lingering recollections of their ill-fated romance, the repercussions from their previous joint assignment, weighed heavily in the atmosphere, forming an uneasy knot in River's stomach. He desperately wanted to keep things strictly professional.

River pulled into the driveway and turned off the car's engine.

Nova was waiting for him by the front door, and she stepped aside to let him enter the foyer. "What's going on?" she asked.

"I just finished going through Mateo's file," River replied. "He gave us some useful information, but as I followed the trail, I'm convinced that he didn't give us everything. Considering his position, every financial transaction was done with his knowledge."

"I believe you," Nova said. "Their house had been searched—someone was looking for something. Apparently, they didn't find anything on Mateo when they killed him."

"He could've stored it somewhere safe, or he gave it to Arya," River stated. "I also found some handwritten entries that I believe were written by a woman."

"You think it was Arya?"

He nodded. "I do."

Nova eyed him. "Either way, she's not safe."

Their gazes locked, both understanding the urgency and danger that surrounded them. "That's why we have to find her," River declared, determination evident in his voice.

"Right now, all we have is a cell phone," Nova stated.

"What about the place where you found the phone?" River asked. "I would think that's where we'll find clues. The first of which is the phone—she knew you'd be able to trace the location. That's most likely why she called you and stayed on the line."

"The house was searched and nothing else was found," she announced. "The sleeping bag was taken into evidence, along with the food containers. There wasn't anything else there."

"There's only one way to find out for sure," River said. "Up for a drive?"

"Always. But it's going to be dark soon."

"I have a couple of flashlights."

Nova's cell rang.

She answered it.

He heard her utter a word of profanity. The call wasn't good news.

She ended the call, saying, "Arya's SUV was just found in a Target parking lot. They searched the stores in the shopping center. She's nowhere to be found."

Inside the car, River asked, "How is your head?"

"I'm good," Nova answered.

They parked down the street from the house in Concord and waited.

"How did she even find this place?" he wondered aloud.

"I have no idea," Nova responded. "I can't imagine her staying behind in North Carolina."

"Maybe that was part of Mateo's plan," he suggested.

She nodded in agreement. "So, what do you think? Should we head inside?"

"Let's do it."

The air was heavy with anticipation as they approached the dilapidated structure. The moon's feeble glow offered little visibility, casting eerie shadows upon each broken windowpane.

To River, the house stood as a forgotten relic of a bygone era, its secrets buried within its decaying walls.

Nova led him up to the bedroom on the second floor. "This is where I found the phone."

The sleeping bag was gone, but the rotting remains of old

take-out containers filled the room with a sour odor. She wrinkled her nose in disgust.

River glanced around the room with observant eyes. The walls were cracked and peeling, with remnants of old wallpaper clinging on for dear life.

"I told you that there's nothing here," Nova uttered in frustration. "Right now, all we have is a message on a phone."

"It's a start," he said. "Were there any other calls made?"

"No. It only had my number."

"Then she must have another burner," River suggested. "My partner is still surveilling her parents' home. No sighting of Arya as of yet."

Nova eyed him. "What do you think about flying out to San Diego? I think we should speak to Pablo and Ramona Lozano in person. There's a chance that Arya's on her way there. We'll check flights, but my gut tells me that she will most likely travel by car."

River hesitated a brief second before replying, "I understand your drive to see this through, but you need to consult with your doctor first. Changes in air pressure and cabin conditions during a flight could affect you after the concussion."

"I can't just sit around and wait for something to happen!" Nova snapped, her hands clenching into fists at her sides.

"I'm not saying you can't travel," River reassured her, his voice firm but gentle. "But we need to be cautious."

"I understand your concern, River," Nova said through gritted teeth, trying to rein in her impatience. "But Arya needs our help."

River watched Nova fidget with the hem of her linen shirt, a determined furrow in her brow. He could sense the familiar blaze of determination burning within her, but he also knew that caution was necessary in this situation. With Arya still on the loose, pushing Nova to take it easy was impossible.

Chapter Six

Nova wasn't interested in seeing her doctor. She was more than capable of taking care of herself. She didn't want someone telling her that she was grounded because she'd had a minor concussion. She intended to be on the plane with River heading to San Diego despite this. Arya had been missing for three days now, and Nova couldn't bear the thought of the woman being out there alone and in danger.

As she packed her bag with essentials for the journey, Nova felt a mix of anticipation and anxiety. She knew that finding Arya wouldn't be an easy task, but she was willing to go to any lengths to bring her home safely.

River, always the voice of reason, watched Nova with concern. "Are you sure about this?" he asked, his brow furrowing. "Your health is important, too, you know."

"I'll be fine." She brushed off his worries with a dismissive wave of her hand. "Besides, we can't just sit around and wait for something to happen. Arya needs us."

He openly studied her.

"I'm fine, River. You need to go back to the hotel and pack," Nova stated. "I want to be on the first flight out tomorrow." She sat down on the sofa and picked up her cell phone. "I need to call Cohen."

After speaking with her supervisor and assuring him that she was fine, he backed River's suggestion to see her doctor.

She hung up and scheduled a video visit with her physician. Thirty minutes later, they discussed her travel plans.

"No headaches," Nova said. "No problem with my vision. I feel good."

When the appointment ended, River approached her cautiously, worry evident in his eyes. "Your health is more important than finding Arya right this moment. I'll be searching for her and we can get other agents on this case."

Nova looked up at him, a fire burning in her eyes. "You don't understand," she replied, her voice laced with determination. "Arya is my witness. I'm responsible for her. I can't just sit back and do nothing while she's out there, possibly in danger. I have to find her."

"All right." He nodded resignedly. "Your doctor didn't have a problem with it, and I can't stop you. Just promise me that you won't push yourself too hard."

Nova paused for a moment, contemplating River's words. She realized that he was right. She couldn't let her determination blind her to the importance of her well-being. Taking a deep breath, she said, "I promise," her voice softer now, filled with gratitude for his concern. "I won't push myself too hard, and I'll make sure to look after myself as we search for Arya."

River prepared to leave.

"I'll see you tomorrow at the airport," Nova said.

He stepped out, and she watched him get into the rental and disappear from the city streets.

As night fell, Nova was consumed by a whirlwind of emotions. The weight of uncertainty pressed down on her chest, but she refused to let it deter her from finding Arya.

She knew that time was of the essence, and every moment spent apart was another moment Arya could be in danger.

RIVER ARRIVED BACK at his hotel room shortly after 9:00 p.m. He and Taylor had eaten dinner across the street from the DEA agency on Randolph Road.

He was about to shower when his phone began to vibrate. He picked it up off the marble counter. "Hello."

He walked out of the bathroom and sat down on the edge of the bed.

"Hey, big brother."

A smile tugged at his lips. Despite his feelings about their mother, he shared a special bond with his sister. "Bonnie, how are you?"

"I'm okay. I'd like to know what's going on with you. I haven't heard a word from you since Mama's funeral."

River sank into a nearby chair. "I've been busy with work."

"She's been gone almost six months."

His jaw tightened. "I know."

"Do you think you'll ever forgive her?"

"I forgave Mary a long time ago, Bonnie." River had always addressed his mother by her first name. Mary was more like a sister. No, not even that. Mary was more of an acquaintance.

"She was sixteen when she had you, River. At that time, Mama didn't know anything about being a mother."

"I've heard it all before and I'm fine," he responded. "You don't have to worry about me."

"But I do worry. I know you feel like Mama abandoned you. I know she didn't raise you, but you were always in her heart."

"That's exactly what she did. None of it matters now."

River didn't want to talk about the effect his mother's rejection had had on him.

He was the result of his teen mother's relationship with an older boy who went off to college and never returned home. She'd never told anyone his name—just moved on with her life and without her son.

He swallowed hard, forcing down the bitterness that threatened to spill out.

"After Mama got married and had me, she wanted to get you, but Grandma wouldn't let her take you. She told Mama that you were more her son than anyone else's."

That was a lie. He'd heard his grandmother practically beg her daughter to raise him with his sister. Mary had flat out refused. She'd told her mother that she didn't want a boy, but River didn't want to hurt Bonnie with the truth. His sister adored Mary. "Bonnie, all I can say is that the damage was done long before then. Look, I can't unfeel the way I felt growing up without Mary's love. Like I said earlier...it doesn't matter anymore."

"I miss you, River."

"When I can get some free time, I'll make a trip to Sacramento to visit with you," he said.

"I hope you mean it."

"Bonnie, I mean every word. I'll call you and check in next week. I promise." Despite his feelings for their mother, River never let them affect his relationship with Bonnie, who was eight years younger. He loved his sister beyond measure.

He buried his emotions deep within himself, pushing away any thoughts of Mary and Nova. The painful rejections from both women still lingered in his mind, but River had a mission to focus on.

Finding Arya de Leon was his top priority, no matter how

much his heart ached for the love he had lost. He couldn't afford to let these distractions hinder him, not when so much was at stake.

River pushed aside the pain and focused solely on the task at hand, determined to succeed no matter the cost.

THE NEXT MORNING, Nova continued to try to contact Arya several times at the cell number she'd been issued by WIT-SEC. She arrived at the airport and met River at their gate, hoping that Arya had gone to her parents' house and they could speak to her soon. However, when Nova had called the Lozanos last evening, Pablo and Ramona denied their daughter was there. They both claimed they hadn't spoken to her in years.

The steady hum of airport activity surrounded Nova as she stared at her laptop screen, her eyes skimming words without registering their meaning. Frustration gnawed at her, a relentless companion echoing the turmoil within. She couldn't shake the feeling that the threads of Arya's disappearance were slipping through her fingers like grains of sand.

Beside her, River's silence mirrored the weight of the unsaid.

An electric current seemed to crackle between them, unspoken and undeniable. As Nova's fingers grazed the rough surface of her laptop, she could feel River's intense gaze piercing through her, causing her jaw to clench with unease. With a quick snap, she shut out the outside world, wanting desperately to escape the heavy tension that hung in the air. But even in this momentary respite, she couldn't shake off the powerful pull that River had on her.

Their boarding announcement echoed through the intercom, and Nova stood up, her movements precise, purposeful toward the gate agent. This journey held more than the promise of flight—it was a pursuit of answers.

The agent, indifferent to the weight of their mission, processed the documents with routine efficiency.

As they took their seats on the plane, the engines hummed to life, drowning out the doubts in Nova's mind. Leaning back, she glanced at River, their eyes locking in a silent pact. The aircraft taxied down the runway, hurtling them further into their investigation.

The plane transported Nova and River into the unknown, leaving their unresolved tension in the air like the turbulence that awaited them.

THE SCENT LINGERED, a ghost haunting River's senses with every breath. If only she hadn't worn that perfume. It wrapped around him like a relentless adversary, an uninvited companion on this mission. River's attempts to ignore it proved futile, each whiff a reminder of a vulnerability he wasn't prepared to acknowledge.

In the cramped confines of the plane, River fought to regain control. He couldn't afford distraction, not now. Not when the stakes were so high.

As Nova excused herself to make a phone call, River took a moment to collect himself. Leaning back in his seat, he closed his eyes.

"I can't let her affect me this way," he muttered, a vow to steel himself against the unseen forces at play. "I'm in control."

But as the minutes ticked away, doubts crept in like shadows. Was he truly in control, or was it a facade he clung to for pride? The truth whispered in the recesses of his mind, a nagging reminder that emotions were not easily subdued. As the flight wore on, the plane's hum became a backdrop to the internal struggle within River. He opened his eyes, glancing toward the empty seat beside him where Nova would soon return. The air still carried faint traces of her presence, a reminder that she held an inexplicable sway over him.

A sense of vulnerability gnawed at him. In this clandestine battle of wills, it became evident that the only person in control was Nova. The realization settled over him and River grappled with the unsettling truth—he was navigating uncharted territory. The compass of his emotions pointed directly toward her.

If only she hadn't worn that perfume. It was the one he remembered on her from their two weeks together, when he'd felt the rush of falling for her. He'd been so certain that feeling would last. After the heart-wrenching pain and betrayal he'd experienced the first time, River knew he couldn't risk opening his heart to Nova again. The thought of being vulnerable and potentially getting hurt once more was enough to send shivers down his spine. He couldn't bear the thought of going through that kind of agony again, and losing her a second time would surely break him beyond repair. No, it was safer for him to keep his heart guarded, even if it meant sacrificing the possibility of a future with Nova.

I can't let her affect me this way, he thought silently. *I won't let her do this to me. I'm in control.*

Was he, really? Because the way River felt right now... The only person in control was Nova.

Chapter Seven

Nova didn't relish having to endure the cloud of uneasiness surrounding them for the next five and a half hours. They had all this quiet time together to clear the air... It was time to tell him exactly how she felt. She cleared her throat. "I know things between us are strained, but I thought we could coexist. We're working a case. This isn't some social outing. We're supposed to be a *team* on this investigation. I don't have a problem working with you, but can you say the same about me? Because if you can't, then you need to just have the case reassigned to another agent."

"That won't be necessary," River responded. "I can manage my feelings while working with you, Nova."

"I apologize," she said. "I guess I'm letting my personal feelings affect my judgment and it was unprofessional. It won't happen again." Nova rubbed the right side of her temple, trying to massage away the hint of a headache. It was a subtle reminder that she'd suffered a concussion.

"I'm sorry if I haven't been my professional self either," he said.

Nova nodded, satisfied with where they'd left things. She took an aspirin and checked her emails. Then she settled in her seat and closed her eyes as she waited for the pill to work its magic.

"I don't remember you ever being this quiet."

She opened her eyes and looked at River. "I have a lot on my mind."

"Is this the first witness to do a disappearing act on you?"

"Yeah," she said. "And hopefully my last. I know that most of the people in the program are criminals and that they often struggle with what they perceive as mundane living. Some have difficulty leaving their previous life behind and often return to old habits. I know now that I was right to be concerned about Mateo."

"From everything I've learned about him, Mateo was a greedy man," River said. "He wouldn't have been happy with a simple life in some small town."

Nova couldn't disagree because River spoke the truth. Mateo was an intelligent man who'd decided to apply his accounting expertise to aid the cartel in cheating the government of tax dollars and helped them launder drug money.

She'd been a case agent for Mateo for the past eight months. Before that, Nova had worked a six-month protection detail for a federal judge who had been receiving death threats.

She stole a peek at River, who seemed interested in an in-flight movie. She pulled her iPad out and opened a book to read. She almost released an audible sigh of relief when the headache finally surrendered to nothingness.

THEY WALKED IN silence through airport exit doors to pick up their rental—Nova had chosen an SUV—and drove out of the parking lot ten minutes later.

"It's been quite a while since I was here in San Diego,"

she said, programming the Lozanos' address into her GPS. "Probably five years or so."

"I came down for a conference a couple of months ago," River responded.

Pointing to her left, Nova asked, "Hey, are you still crazy about In-N-Out?"

His expression suddenly became animated as he said, "I *love* In-N-Out. You know that's my spot."

Grinning, Nova maneuvered the vehicle into the drive-through line. They'd skipped breakfast and might as well eat on the way. They placed their orders and then pulled out into traffic again.

"How much do Arya's parents know about her situation?" River asked when they'd finished eating.

"They were allowed to say goodbye before they went into the program. So, they know she's in WITSEC. From day one, it was made clear that she wasn't to have any contact with them."

"That knowledge alone could get them killed," River said.

"I know."

He glimpsed the worried expression on Nova's face.

Glancing over at him, she said, "I hate that this is happening on my watch."

"Don't take it personally."

"It's hard not to do so," she retorted. "They got on my nerves more than once, but I wanted to see them thrive in this new life. Not everyone gets a second chance, you know…"

River nodded in agreement. "They have to want it for themselves, Nova."

"I know you're right." Her mind was working overtime as she tried to figure out Arya's next move.

"We're going to find her."

Nova gave him a grateful smile as she tried to ignore the cold knot in her stomach.

RIVER SAW NOVA massaging her right temple. "Do you have a headache? Why don't you let me drive?"

"No, I'm good. We're almost to our destination."

Five minutes later, Nova pulled into the neighborhood. She put the vehicle in Park at the top of the street and turned off the ignition. Her eyes bounced around, searching.

He glanced around, too.

"Who are you looking for?" she asked.

"I wanted to see if one of our guys was still on surveillance," River responded. "Must have taken a break."

Nova finished off her bottled water.

He pointed straight ahead. "That's the house over there."

"There aren't any lights on," she observed aloud as she looked in the direction he was pointing. "You think they go to bed this early?"

"Nope," River stated. "The last time they were spotted was about a day ago. No one has been in or out since then. My partner said that they don't venture out much."

Nova got out of the car and slipped on a Kevlar vest.

"What are you doing?" he asked.

"I can't explain it, but I have a bad feeling about this. I felt this same way in Burlington." She already had her weapon in hand. She wasn't going to let anyone jump her a second time. "We need to make sure they're okay."

River followed suit, putting on his own vest, then walked behind her as she approached the back of the house. "Look at the back door," Nova said in a loud whisper. "Someone broke in."

She tried the knob, turning it gently. "It's unlocked."

Nova pulled out her phone and called the police before going inside.

They entered the house gingerly.

River tried a light switch.

Nothing.

Nova found the darkness thick and claustrophobic. It was like a hand closing around her throat. She pulled out a miniature flashlight.

"The power's been cut off," he said.

With her flashlight, Nova's eyes bounced around her surroundings. When she walked into the living room, she said, "I seriously doubt that Mr. and Mrs. Lozano left their house looking like this. We can safely assume that this house has been ransacked."

River nodded in agreement. "It looks like a crime scene."

"Do you think they've been kidnapped?" she asked.

He pointed upstairs. "It's possible. There's a packed suitcase up there that was probably left by mistake. They have security cameras in place throughout the house but the wires have been cut. I noticed it when I checked the garage."

"That's just great..." Nova walked back into the living room and was about to ascend the staircase.

A knock sounded on the front door.

"Is it the police?" Nova asked.

"Naw, it looks like he might be a neighbor," River said, peeking out of the front window.

"I came to see what's going on over here," a middle-aged man with a trim beard said when Nova opened the door.

She showed him her badge. "You took great risk coming over here after noting strangers in the house," she chided. "What if I weren't law enforcement? You could've been killed."

"I thought you were the police," he replied. "The people

that own this place left town. Pablo called and told me that they were going away for a couple of weeks. He sounded scared." He looked past River. "What's going on over here?"

"Looks like there might have been a break-in," Nova said. "Did you happen to see anyone else near the house?"

"I never saw anyone outside of Pablo and Ramona, other than Yolanda, their housekeeper."

Nova and River exchanged looks. "I'm sorry, but I have to go back inside," he said. "Thank you for your help."

"Jerry Spotswood. That's my name." The man stepped off the porch and River swung the door closed.

Nova rushed up the stairs with River following close behind.

They proceeded cautiously through the house, their senses heightened by the ominous atmosphere that clung to the air.

With a shared nod, they approached the door of a room, the creaking floorboards beneath their feet betraying their presence. Pushing the door open slowly, they revealed a dimly lit guest bedroom. The space was a tableau of horror.

Their eyes fell upon Yolanda, her lifeless body slumped in the corner. Blood pooled around her, staining the white carpet a dark red. Nova and River entered, their guns drawn as they cautiously scanned the area for an intruder.

Then Nova rushed to Yolanda's side, checking for a pulse she knew wasn't there. Her heart sank as she realized they were too late.

Turning to River, she could see the same anger and determination she felt in his eyes. An innocent woman was dead, but they would not rest until they found those responsible.

As they combed through the room for evidence, Nova noticed a glint of metal under Yolanda's hand. Pulling back the woman's fingers, she discovered a small piece of jewelry engraved with a strange symbol.

River's voice broke through her thoughts. "We need to call this in. The killers can't be far."

But Nova couldn't shake the image of Yolanda's terror-filled eyes from her mind. She vowed to get justice for the woman, no matter what it took. "They didn't have to kill her."

"Johnny Boy doesn't believe in leaving witnesses behind," River responded, pulling out his phone. "I need to call my partner. I don't know what happened here, so I'm hoping he can help me make sense of this."

In the living room, she looked at the photos lining the walls and the mantel over the fireplace, paying close attention to the picturesque details. There were several framed photos of a house with mountains in the backdrop. Nova grabbed a few. She hoped they might explain where Arya and her parents may be hiding.

"Jerry lives across the street," River said. "I had Kenny check him out. He's been living there for the past ten years. As far as we can tell, he has no cartel connections."

"Was he able to explain what happened with the surveillance?" Nova asked.

"There was a disconnect. The team was taken off prematurely. My supervisor isn't happy right now. This is on us."

"It looks like Arya's parents packed in a hurry to me," Nova observed as she continued looking around. "But why? Is it because she warned them, or were they hurrying to get to her?"

"It could be both," River responded.

"But killing her parents won't force Arya out of hiding," Nova said.

"But it could *silence* her forever," he said. "It could make her too afraid to ever speak against them."

She nodded in agreement.

Nova could sense the frustration written all over River's face. She understood that it was weighing on him that the surveillance team had been abruptly removed from Arya's parents and now the housekeeper had been killed.

They heard the shrill scream of sirens in the distance.

Nova and River stood on the corner, watching the flashing lights approach. Whirring sirens grew louder, piercing the calm suburban ambience like a discordant melody.

Moments later, Jerry appeared, hastily jogging toward them with his trusty flashlight. His face etched with concern, he seemed to age before their eyes. His neatly trimmed beard was now disheveled, and sweat glistened on his furrowed brow.

Jerry abruptly stopped beside Nova and River. "What in the world is going on? I've been patrolling these streets for years—nothing has ever happened in this neighborhood... Well, just some teens wreaking havoc."

Nova laid a gentle hand on Jerry's trembling shoulder. "Yolanda's dead."

He gasped in shock. "I never heard a thing."

Minutes ticked by like hours as they waited in silence.

The flashing lights of the approaching police cars grew brighter, casting an eerie glow upon the once peaceful street. Neighbors began peering out the windows and leaving their houses, drawn by the commotion.

"This neighborhood will never be the same," Jerry uttered.

"I THINK WE should hang back and watch the house to see if someone comes back tonight," River said after the police and CSI team left. He wanted to catch the perpetrator who had taken an innocent life, but he also knew that the surveillance team had probably been pulled due to budget cuts. Should they take a chance and stay back to see if anyone returned to the crime scene? "It's a long shot, but that's all we have right now." He stood outside the vehicle, watching.

Nova nodded in agreement. "Let's do it."

It was after 10:00 p.m. It was just dark enough on the street to provide some cover for the surveillance. River had positioned the rental car well away from the house but close enough to see if anyone drove up. The view was excellent but discreet enough for them to keep from being seen.

Now and then, they caught movement in one of the windows at Jerry's house. He was watching the empty home as well.

"I still don't believe Arya knows anything about her husband's business dealings."

"Nova, she may not be as innocent as you'd like to think," River said, not understanding why she had so much faith in Mateo's wife. "I watched Arya's interview, and her answers sounded rehearsed to me, but I don't know the woman."

"Arya was probably nervous," Nova explained. "Her whole life was changing in a short period."

He opened the driver's-side door for Nova.

"Thanks," she murmured.

River walked to the other side of the car and got in.

"Do you really think Arya's parents plan to return to this house?" Nova asked.

"I'm not sure, but you'd think by now they know something's wrong," River responded. "Like the fact that their alarm isn't working. I'm sure the alarm company has tried to reach them. If they're not running, why not come home?"

"We can assume that Arya warned them, which is why

they left town. We need to find them all. I don't want any more bodies turning up."

"I don't want that either," he said. River hoped that Arya's parents would be found alive and well.

Staring out the driver's window, Nova stated, "I really hope Arya's with her parents. If she isn't, then I don't know where to begin looking for her." She wanted to roll down the window so the breeze could wrap itself around her like a soft shawl on a cool evening. "We didn't really have any reason to think they were in danger. With Mateo dead, I can't figure why they'd want Arya or her parents."

He looked over at her. "The cartel isn't going to give up."

"I know," she responded with a sigh.

"Nova, whatever happens…this isn't on you," River said.

"That's what everyone says, but the facts are that Mateo and Arya went missing on my watch. I was responsible for them. If something worse happens and fingers are pointed, they'll be at *me*."

He could tell that Nova was taking this to heart. She was great at her job and dedicated to keeping her witnesses safe. River didn't want to see her begin to doubt herself. *That's when p ople start to make mistakes.*

Chapter Eight

Nova was becoming antsy just sitting in the car doing nothing. Her mind was all over the place. If Arya wasn't in San Diego, then where could she be?

Anywhere.

She bit her bottom lip, trying to remember if Arya had ever mentioned anything that would explain her whereabouts. The woman had often griped about living in North Carolina and openly expressed her desire to return to her life in Los Angeles.

"Do you think she would risk returning to LA like her husband did?" Nova posed the question.

River replied, "It's worth considering. At this point, we can't rule out any possibilities."

"I know a couple of people we should talk to—they might be able to help us," Nova said. "There's Kaleb Stone, a close friend of my father's. The night my dad was killed, he stepped in to provide security for a cartel witness determined to return home. He was on his way to the safe house... My dad had been shot... He was dead by the time Kaleb arrived."

"I actually know Kaleb. The last time I saw him was right after he left the Marshals."

"He opened his own security firm after he left."

"So, what happened to the witness?" River asked.

"He married her," Nova responded with a chuckle. "After she testified against Calderon and a few other high-ranking members of the cartel."

"Are you talking about the Homeland Security agent who was shot at with her partner a few years ago? Everybody thought she'd died, too."

"Yeah."

"So, she left WITSEC to go back to LA?"

Nova nodded. "There was a leak in the Milwaukee office. It was a mess, but after that, the Marshals changed some of the protocols regarding witness security. But now I'm wondering if we have a leak here. I'm still trying to figure out how they found the house in Burlington."

River settled back in his seat. "We are aware that Poppy and Johnny Boy were using bribery and blackmail to control individuals within various levels of law enforcement and the government. But there is a chance they obtained information by killing Mateo. His body was found without any identification, so it's possible they had accomplices visit his house."

"That's why I think we should talk to Kaleb and Rylee. They've been investigating the Mancuso cartel for the past two years," Nova said. "Since we're here in California, it won't hurt to meet with them."

"I'm open to it," River said. "Without Mateo alive to testify and if Arya doesn't have any information…my case against the cartel will fall apart. I don't want that to happen on my watch."

Nova placed a call to Kaleb Stone. "Hey, it's me. I'm in San Diego."

"Nova, hi. How long will you be here?"

"A few days," she responded. "If you and Rylee aren't busy, I'd love for you two to come down. I want your feedback on a case I'm working with the DEA. It's concerning the Mancuso cartel."

"Rylee and I can fly down there tomorrow morning. I'll text you once I make the flight arrangements."

"Thanks a lot, Kaleb."

"I'll see you tomorrow."

Nova hung up, saying, "They're flying down in the morning to see us." She glanced around, then said, "I don't know about you, but I'm not looking forward to sleeping in this car."

"A couple of agents should be arriving soon to take over surveillance," River said. "We can head to the hotel when they get here."

The mention of a hotel reminded Nova of a similar situation two years ago. They'd been tracking a fugitive. The more time they'd spent together, the harder they'd found it to ignore their growing attraction, so they gave in to their feelings. Two weeks later, Nova had walked out of his life the day after they'd apprehended the guy.

"You okay?" he asked, cutting into her thoughts.

"Huh. Y. eah, I'm good."

After the agents arrived, River had a brief discussion with them before he and Nova left the area. "There's a hotel not too far from here," he announced.

"That's fine," Nova replied. "As long as they have a comfy bed, I can sleep anywhere."

"I only stay at a certain hotel brand," River said.

She smiled. "You sound like Mateo and his wife."

River eyed her. "Are you saying that you don't have a favorite chain?"

"I do, but I'm also open to staying elsewhere."

They settled on any hotel under the Marriott brand.

Nova pulled into the first one that came up on the GPS. "This is the Mission Valley location."

"I'm fine with that," River said. "I've stayed here once before. It's very nice inside."

"I'm good with clean and comfortable," she said. "After a few hours' sleep, I'll be ready to return to work."

RIVER'S STOMACH COMPLAINED loudly enough to garner Nova's attention. "Sorry about that," he said.

She gave a tiny smile. "You're not alone. I'm hungry, too."

They got out of the car after pulling into the hotel parking lot. River grabbed their luggage and followed behind Nova.

Inside the hotel, they checked into separate rooms.

"I'm going to grab a bite to eat," River announced in the elevator. "When I get back, we can try to create some type of timeline leading up to Arya's disappearance."

"I need to eat as well. Why don't we order room service?" Nova suggested. "This way, we can keep working over dinner."

He didn't respond as thoughts ran through his head. Room service… How many room service meals had they enjoyed two years ago? Intimate dinners that had led to him telling her things about his past, about his feelings, that he shouldn't have…

At River's hesitation, she said, "C'mon… It's just a meal. We should be mature enough to eat together."

He chided himself for reading too much into the situation. Nova wasn't trying to make dinner more than it appeared to be—she just wanted to continue working while they ate. River couldn't deny that it was the best use of their time. "We can do that," he relented.

Nova unlocked her door and held it open for him to enter.

"Where's the menu?" River asked, leaving his suitcase near the door. He placed hers right outside the closet.

She pointed to a thin binder on the desk. "It's over there." After they flipped through, Nova called to place their order. While they waited, she let her mind drift back to the Lozanos and where they could be. Had they lied when they'd said Arya hadn't contacted them recently? If she had, she could've put the cartel on her parents' trail.

A knock at the door interrupted her thoughts. She answered and took the meals from the hotel server. "The food's here," Nova announced as she brought them in. "Perfect timing, because I'm starving."

She placed a covered plate in front of River. "I can't believe you were so hungry and then you just ordered a salad and bread."

"It's late," he responded. "I don't sleep well after a heavy meal."

"Heavy or not, I'm going to enjoy my grilled salmon burger and fries. I'm not gonna feel guilty about it."

River chuckled. "I hear you. Enjoy your meal."

A mischievous grin on her face, Nova held out a french fry to him, saying, "Here. I know you want one."

"What are you trying to do?" He gave her a sidelong glance. "Tempt me?"

"I just remember how much you love a good fry."

"I'll pass," River said.

Nova's smile disappeared and she dropped her gaze to her plate.

The air in the room had abruptly become stuffy.

"You wanted to discuss the case," he said. River loaded salad onto his fork, clearly not wanting to lose focus.

She cleared her throat softly. "Yeah. Where do you want to start?"

"From the beginning. Has Arya ever mentioned a place she loved visiting? When a witness runs, they may go to someplace familiar to them."

"She wanted to be relocated to New York or Chicago—we decided they were the wrong places to send them." Nova stuck her french fry into a puddle of ketchup. "We felt the smaller the town, the better for them."

"Her parents travel a lot," River said. "They could be anywhere."

Nova nodded. "We should check hotels. They have to sleep sometime."

River chewed, considering, and she spotted the bread-crumbs that had gathered near the corner of his mouth. Without thinking, she reached out to brush them away. The action took her back to a time when he welcomed her touch.

He jerked his head back as if stung.

"Crumbs," she murmured. "Sorry."

River wiped his mouth with a napkin.

Embarrassed, Nova concentrated on her food and waited for the moment of awkwardness to become a thing of the past. She hoped River didn't get the wrong idea. It had been a stupid move on her part, although it wasn't planned.

Her phone emitted a sound, notifying her of an incoming text.

Nova read it, then said, "Kaleb and Rylee should be arriving sometime after nine."

He nodded, and they continued their meal in silence. As the evening wore on, River rose from his seat. "I'm gonna turn in."

Nova wasn't ready for him to leave, but she refrained from voicing any objections as he quietly exited her room. They remained in a fragile space, the unspoken tension hovering between them.

Sitting on the sofa, Nova was caught in the present moment, no longer dwelling on the past. Eleven o'clock arrived, triggering memories of a night that weighed heavily on her conscience.

After a night of shared intimacy and whispered confessions, River had uttered those three powerful words, "I love you." Nova's smile had concealed the turmoil within, but his words had brought a sudden rush of panic. She'd sprung out of bed, fabricating an excuse about her mother needing assistance.

Fifteen minutes later, she'd returned, feigning calmness. River, ever observant, had asked about her mother. She'd assured him everything was fine, inviting him back into their shared embrace. But as they made love again, a shadow of unease had crept over Nova.

In the quiet aftermath, she'd slipped out of bed, tiptoed out of the room with her clothes and left without a trace. The memory now propelled her to River's door. She needed to confront the ghosts of the past to explain why she had vanished that night and left California for Charlotte.

Nova paused in the hallway outside his room to take several calming breaths. She inhaled deeply and exhaled slowly, then knocked on his door, hoping to bridge the gap between the present and the unresolved fragments of their shared history. At least if they discussed it, this would end the tension that was their constant companion.

"Has something happened?" River asked when he opened the door. He looked instantly concerned.

"No," she quickly assured him. "I… I need to talk to you."

His eyebrows rose in surprise. "About what?"

"About *us*."

River shook his head, the dim light casting shadows on

his face. "No... There's nothing to talk about, Nova. Besides, it's late and I'm exhausted."

"I just need to explain myself..."

"Nova, you leaving me like that... It was a cowardly move." His voice was laced with anger. "And after everything we'd been through."

Her heart swelled with pain and fear, her past mistakes coming back to haunt her. She desperately wanted to make things right with him before it was too late.

River's next words rang in her ears: "It's eighteen months too late."

Nova felt dizzy as tears threatened to spill from her eyes. "I... I didn't want to fall in love," she whispered, her voice trembling. "I'd just lost my father... Then I met you. Back then, I wasn't sure if it was a way to avoid dealing with my grief or if it was something more. I was confused, hurting, and just not in the right mental state for a relationship. I came here to say that I'm sorry for hurting you."

Nova turned away, suddenly needing space. She felt the weight of his gaze on her body as she walked away, fighting back the tears in her eyes.

As she went back to her room in silence, Nova tried to steady her breathing and calm the racing of her heart. She knew that River was right—they couldn't change the past. But she couldn't help feeling disappointed.

She lay in bed, feeling an emptiness in her chest where love should have been.

Chapter Nine

River couldn't believe Nova suddenly wanted to have a conversation. There was a time when he would have welcomed a discussion, but it was much too late for that now. It had taken him a long time to get over her. He wasn't about to let her dredge up that pain again.

He had never been the type of person who had scores of women chasing after him. River had always been considered the nerdy type. It didn't bother him to be called a nerd. He wore that label with pride.

Before Nova, there had only been one girl whom he'd dated for four years. While he cared for her, River had never been in love until the day Nova walked into his life. The time they spent together was one of the happiest in his life.

Until he woke up to find her gone without saying goodbye. Without saying anything.

River's pride wouldn't let him contact her once he returned to Charlotte. He spent much of his time chasing criminals. He didn't have any interest in pursuing women. He desired a simple, uncomplicated relationship. He'd dated a couple of women after Nova, but not for long. No one made River feel the way she had. No woman had come close. But that was another time and place.

River decided to call his sister. He didn't want to sit there in his room being pitiful or feeling sorry for himself. He wanted pleasant conversation.

When Bonnie answered, he said, "Hey, sis. I'm calling to check in as promised."

"I'm glad to hear from you. Are you traveling?"

"Yes," he responded.

"Any chance you'll be coming to Sacramento?"

"Not right now," River said. "I'm in the middle of an investigation."

"Oh."

He heard the disappointment in her voice. "You know the plane flies both ways. Why don't you come visit me?"

"I'd love that."

"Send me some dates and I'll fly you to LA. There's this new restaurant in Marina del Rey that I know you'll love."

"I can't wait," Bonnie said. "I need a vacation, too."

She'd spent the past two years taking care of their mother. Now that Mary was gone, Bonnie had returned to the hospital as a nurse.

"I mean it," River said. "Look at your calendar and get back to me. We'll spend some time together after I close this case I'm working on."

"I will," Bonnie responded. "Looking forward to it."

They talked for a few minutes more before hanging up.

The weight of the recent events pressed heavily on River's shoulders. The murder of Mateo, the agency's star witness against the Mancuso cartel, and the disappearance of Mateo's wife had thrown a meticulously built case into chaos. It was a setback that demanded a recalibration of his approach.

River stared at his notes, mapping out the intricate connections he had painstakingly pieced together. The photos of Mateo and his wife seemed to mock him, their faces a haunting reminder of the cost of this relentless pursuit.

His mind raced, searching for a thread to pull, a lead to follow. A flicker of determination sparked as River reached for his phone. Dialing, he waited for the familiar voice on the other end.

"Kenny, it's me. Did you manage to persuade Rico Alfaro to give up his supplier?"

"He claims he's willing to take the fall. My gut tells me he's been in cahoots with the Mancuso cartel."

River released a sigh of frustration. "We need to convince him that we'll go as far as putting the word on the street that he's a snitch."

His partner's agreement resonated through the line, and River hung up, his mind racing with possibilities. He needed to revisit every lead, every contact and every piece of intelligence they had gathered. He couldn't afford to overlook anything, not if he wanted to salvage what remained of the case and bring Johnny Boy to justice for Mateo and the deaths of his friend Jason and another agent.

River and Special Agent Jason Turner's friendship was forged in the face of danger and a shared purpose. They had stood side by side, confronting the ruthless Mancuso cartel, and with each mission they completed together, their bond grew stronger. From the moment they were introduced in the dimly lit corridors of DEA headquarters, there was an instant connection—a recognition that they were cut from the same cloth, driven by an unyielding determination to bring justice to those who sought to spread fear and chaos.

Their friendship went beyond mere camaraderie; they were like brothers, not only because of their shared experiences but also due to a deep mutual respect and trust. Jason had been there for River during his darkest moments, offering unwavering support and encouragement when the weight of their mission threatened to crush him. And River had returned the favor, standing by Jason's side and willing to sacrifice his life to protect his friend from harm.

But then came the day when tragedy struck, shattering their world and leaving River to pick up the pieces. Jason's death at the hands of the Mancuso cartel was a devastating blow, one that left River consumed with grief and anger. The loss of his friend was like an open wound, a constant reminder of the dangers they faced and the ruthless enemies they were fighting against.

In the aftermath of Jason's death, the stakes were higher than ever before. The Mancuso cartel operated without consequence, their power spreading like a disease through society. But River refused to let his friend's sacrifice be in vain. He clung to hope that he would find a thread that would unravel the cartel's empire and bring an end to their reign of terror. For Jason's sake, he would stop at nothing to put an end to the Mancuso cartel's tyranny.

After a shower, River sat in a chair, his legs propped on the ottoman, watching television. His thoughts drifted back to Nova. He wondered what she was doing right now.

River felt terrible for how he'd reacted when she came to his room; it was an unexpected move on Nova's part—one he had never seen coming.

He hadn't changed his mind about sending her away. It had been the right thing to do. River couldn't afford to lose concentration on the job he had to do.

THE FOLLOWING DAY, Nova ate breakfast alone in her room. She hadn't bothered to check in with River because she'd had enough of his attitude. Besides, she didn't want him getting any closer to her. It would only make things more dangerous for them both.

Nova took a deep breath and then a sip of herbal tea. She had a job to do, which required her complete focus.

Shortly after 8:30, the phone in her room rang.

Sighing softly, Nova answered it. "Hello…"

"Good morning. I was checking to see if you're awake," River said.

"Actually, I've been up for a couple of hours. I just finished eating breakfast."

"So did I," he responded. "What time are you expecting Kaleb and his wife?"

"Within the hour. Their plane landed thirty minutes ago."

"I'll come to your room whenever they get here," River said.

Nova didn't reply.

"Did you hear what I said?"

"I heard you," she uttered. "I'll ring your room."

Nova hung up before River could respond.

Deep down, she really didn't have a right to be angry with him. River was entitled to his feelings. Nova wasn't the type of person who carried grudges for years. She chose to either settle them or purge them. Her parents had always told her that life was too short to hold on to bad feelings.

When Kaleb and Rylee arrived, Nova called River. "Hey, they're here."

He was at her door within minutes.

"River, oh man… It's good to see you," Kaleb said when he entered the room. "It's been a long time."

"It sure has," he remarked. "*Kaleb Stone*. I hear you're a married man now."

"Happily married man," he said. "This is my wife, Rylee."

River shook her hand. "It's nice to meet you."

Nova watched River interact with Kaleb. He was smiling, his body more at ease. She wished he were that way around her.

She indicated the small kitchenette. "We can sit over there."

They gathered around the table to discuss the de Leon investigation.

Rylee sat beside her, saying, "Nova, I hope you know how much your father meant to me. I really hate that he lost his life trying to keep me safe."

"My dad died doing what he loved," she responded.

"How is your mother?" Kaleb asked.

Nova smiled. "She's great. Mom keeps busy by volunteering at church and a shelter for homeless women and children."

"Do you have any leads on Mateo's wife?" Rylee asked.

"Not really," Nova answered. "Her parents live in the area, so River and I flew out here to see if she was with them."

Kaleb looked at River. "What's the DEA's part in this?"

"We're hoping that Arya de Leon might have information critical to our investigation. We know Mateo didn't give us everything he had on the Mancuso cartel. I think it was because he was hoping for some type of leverage. He might have been planning to negotiate with Johnny Boy or Poppy for his life, or he was going to try to blackmail them. All this is speculation until we find Arya."

"If what you suspect is true," Kaleb said, "if Mateo gave evidence to his wife for safekeeping…that information could possibly help us dismantle the cartel."

River nodded in agreement. "Exactly." Especially now that their key witness was dead.

Nova knew that Rylee and Kaleb wanted to tear down the cartel just as much as she and River did.

"We're willing to lend our assistance and resources to you both," Rylee said.

Nova smiled. "Thanks."

"I was told by a CI that Manuel DeSoto… Mateo…tried to blackmail Poppy before he disappeared into WITSEC," Rylee said. "He claimed to have copies of deeds and information on all the properties and businesses owned by the cartel. He offered to sell it to her for ten million dollars. He said he'd go away, and they'd never hear from him again."

Nova nodded, familiar with the intel. "Apparently, Poppy didn't believe him," Nova responded. "That was such a stupid move on his part."

Shaking his head, River interjected, "Mateo only narrowly escaped when Johnny Boy discovered he'd been skimming money off the top. If Johnny Boy was the one targeting Mateo's family, Mateo might have sought him out for revenge."

She nodded, though she didn't spare him a glance. She didn't want to give Kaleb and Rylee the impression of tension between them.

"What happens when you find Arya?" Kaleb asked. "Are you putting her back in the program under a new alias?"

"I just need to find her," Nova responded with a slight shrug.

She suddenly felt like she needed some air. She stood up and walked over to the balcony. She opened the sliding glass door and stepped outside.

"Nova, you look troubled," Kaleb said when he joined her on the balcony.

"I keep thinking about Mateo and Arya. I can't help but feel as if I failed them somehow."

"Nova, Mateo's death isn't on you. He took it upon himself to leave WITSEC. He knew the risks, regardless of his reason."

She looked over at Kaleb. "River told me the same thing. But the reality is that Mateo was under my protection. I should've put him under twenty-four-hour security because I knew he was beginning to spiral out of control. I went out to see him, but it was too late."

"You didn't do anything wrong. At the time, he wasn't under a high-threat situation, Nova. There wasn't a need for additional security. Look, I know all too well how it feels to lose a witness. It's not a good feeling," Kaleb said. "I don't know if your dad ever told you, but that's why I left the Marshals."

She studied him. "He didn't."

"My witness left the program just like Mateo," he said. "It's what got him killed, but I took his death personally. I didn't want to lose another one, even if it was caused by their own actions."

"I'm beginning to feel the same way. After we find Arya, I'm not sure I'll stay with the agency. I joined the Marshals because I wanted to work with my dad…" Nova paused momentarily, saying, "I'm not going to lose Arya."

"We'll do everything possible to help you find her."

"Kaleb, I'm so glad you're here."

"Me, too." He placed an arm around her. "I want you to know that Easton would be so proud of you. I bet he's looking down at you with a big grin."

She glanced up at him. "I hope so. How is Nate?" Nova asked.

"My brother is doing well. I've been trying to convince him to leave Wisconsin and join me in Los Angeles. He's not trying to hear it."

She laughed. "How do *you* like living in California?"

"It's fine. I'm happy anywhere Rylee is," Kaleb responded.

"Kaleb, that's a nice thing to say," Nova responded, masking the pain in her voice. "I can see how genuinely happy you are with Rylee." She couldn't help but think of her short time with River and how it had left a lasting imprint on her heart. Despite trying to move on, memories of their time together haunted her.

"I'm surprised some man hasn't snatched you up yet."

"One-track mind," Nova stated. "I've been focused on my career. Besides, the badge intimidates some of the men I've dated. I'll probably end up with someone in law enforcement. They seem to be the only people who understand me."

Kaleb smiled. "I used to feel that way, too."

"And you ended up marrying someone in the field."

"That wasn't the deciding factor, though," he responded. "I would've married Rylee no matter what."

"That's great. Maybe one day I'll get lucky enough to find my Mr. Right. I'm not really in any hurry, though."

"You just have to be open to loving and being loved, Nova."

She smiled. "I hear you."

Nova really wanted to share her life with someone special. It was just that she hadn't met him yet. Well…she'd blown it with the man who'd come close. He would always hold a special place in her heart. She definitely had regrets. Nova wished now that she'd handled things differently.

Her chance with River had come and gone. No point in dwelling on the past. Life was meant to be lived looking ahead and not in the rearview mirror.

RIVER EYED NOVA'S interaction with Kaleb from across the room and wondered what they could be discussing. He'd never seen her like this. From the moment he'd met her, River had quickly learned that Nova was always sure of herself and liked to be in control. The woman outside with Kaleb seemed reflective and doubtful. He wondered what could have made her so upset.

"How long have you known Nova?" Rylee asked, cutting into his musings.

"A couple of years," River answered, trying to sound nonchalant. "We worked on a case together. I hadn't talked to her since. Until now."

"I see. Nova's father was my handler when I was in WIT-SEC," Rylee said. "My relationship with her actually developed after Kaleb and I got married."

She leaned down to open her laptop. "Have you conducted a property search?"

"I checked for listings under Mateo's and Arya's names. Nothing came up."

Rylee sat down at the table. "I'll run her parents' names and those of other known relatives. Maybe we'll get a hit. Arya could be hiding in one of the family properties."

Nova approached, trailed by Kaleb, and said, "I took some photographs from the Lozano house. Maybe we can find out where they were taken. There's nothing but dates written on the back of the pictures."

"I'll scan them and send them to the tech at HSI," Rylee said.

"It's worth a try," Nova agreed as she laid them on the table. "River and I have already conducted a property search. We have a list of places to check out. One of which is a house given to Ramona Lozano by her brother before he died," Nova said. "It's in Oceanside. I need to change out of these sweatpants. Then I'll be ready to leave."

River thought she looked nice in the tank top and navy sweats but decided to keep his opinion to himself.

"Kaleb, you can join me in my room while Nova gets dressed," River said. "I need to grab something before we go.

"I had no idea that you were with Homeland Security," River said as he and Kaleb walked across the hall to his room. "I thought you were done with this life."

"I thought so, too," he responded. "My brother and I were partners in a private security firm. I sold my shares to him after Rylee and I got married."

"Did you join HSI because of your wife?" River inquired.

"Partly. While I was trying to keep Rylee safe, it made me realize just how much I missed being part of the action.

"How long have you been working the Mancuso cartel investigation?" Kaleb asked.

"Not long. I inherited the case from another agent who left the job. I think it was given to me because of my recent investigation into the Torres cartel. But I have personal reasons for wanting this case—a close friend of mine was murdered at the hands of Johnny Boy."

"The Torres cartel… That was *you*?" Kaleb asked. "That was a huge bust. Great job, River."

"It was a team effort coordinated with HSI, ATF and LAPD."

"Still, it was good work. Man, don't sell yourself short."

"Thanks," River replied.

He wanted to ask about Nova but decided against it. Kaleb wasn't aware of their past and River thought it best not to bring up the subject. *Keep he focus on the job.*

Chapter Ten

"Kaleb looks happier than I've ever seen him," Nova said. She'd freshened up and was back in the kitchenette with Rylee. "I have to say that you two are so good for each other."

Rylee smiled. "I've never loved anyone as much as I love him."

"Did you fall in love with him while he protected you?"

"The first thing I noticed about Kaleb was those piercing gray eyes. We were initially attracted to one another, but at the time, our main focus was keeping me alive and out of the cartel's reach."

"I love a happy ending," Nova said.

"You sound like a romantic."

"Not at all," she responded. "When things get serious… I run." To be honest, there was only one man she'd run from. It was hard to put into words what was going on in her head back then. She'd just lost her father and felt like she couldn't catch her breath.

"Have you ever tried to figure out why?" Rylee asked.

"I don't know."

"Sounds like you panic."

Nova nodded. "The excitement of this intense connection clashed with the heaviness of my sorrow and left me feeling lost, like I was spiraling out of control. I didn't know which way was up, and every emotion seemed to blur together into a confusing mess. In the middle of all that chaos, it hit me—I hadn't really taken the time to grieve for my dad properly. His loss was this gaping hole in my heart, and instead of facing it, I let myself get swept away by the whirlwind romance. I was scared, Rylee, scared that I was losing myself in the middle of it all. I really messed things up between us and I don't know how to fix it."

"What happened?"

"I made the toughest decision I've ever had to make—I ran away. No words…no note…nothing."

"No…" Rylee offered a sympathetic look.

"Yeah, and I regret the way I left," Nova admitted, a wave of sadness flowing through her. "I should've stayed there and talked to him. I should've told him what I was feeling at the time."

"How long has it been?"

"Eighteen months."

"Do you still see him, or can you get in contact with him?" Rylee inquired.

"I've run into him recently," Nova said.

"I'm assuming it didn't go very well."

"There's a lot of tension between us." She turned to check her reflection in the mirror before saying, "I guess we'd better get going."

Rylee nodded, standing up. "Nova, I have a feeling everything will work out between you and River."

Turning to face Rylee, she asked, "How did you know I was talking about River?"

"Girl, you can cut the tension between you two with a knife."

"Really?"

"Yes." Rylee grinned. "But things will get better between you."

Nova picked up her black tote. As they walked to the front door, she said, "Rylee, I really hope you're right about me and River. I miss his friendship."

"Is that all?"

"No, but it's all I can expect from him now, and even that's asking a lot."

River and Kaleb were in the hallway waiting.

Nova met River's gaze; then she looked away almost immediately. He was such a handsome man. Her eyes traveled down to the white polo shirt and jeans he wore.

Ten minutes later, they were walking through the parking deck to the SUV.

They made the forty-five-minute drive to Oceanside.

While Nova sat in the back seat chatting with Rylee, Kaleb and River talked about how they met and the case that brought them together.

Nova watched the passing streets and immediately fell in love with the area's laid-back vibe. She especially liked the quaint little homes. Nestled in the coastal town was the military base Camp Pendleton. Her father had once been stationed there when he was in the Marines. Nova had been too young then to remember anything now about the base or the area.

The Lozano house wasn't too far from the Oceanside Pier. The exterior was painted in soothing shades of seafoam and aqua. From where they were parked, they could see the patio featured a firepit, lounge furniture and a grill. Nova imagined it was the perfect spot for evenings with family and friends to sit back and chill, watching picturesque sunsets, toasting marshmallows or making s'mores.

Her attention shifted to the house as they sat in the car

across from the corner property, watching as a middle-aged woman walked out to retrieve the rest of the bags from the trunk of a car.

"Somebody's home. Possibly the housekeeper," Nova suggested.

River removed his sunglasses. "Judging from the groceries… Pablo Lozano and his wife must be here, too, and they're planning to stay a while."

Nova released the breath she'd been holding. "I think it's best I speak to the parents alone," she said. "River, you might intimidate them."

"Why don't I go with you?" Rylee suggested. "Two women won't seem so threatening."

Kaleb nodded in agreement.

She exited the car, and she and Rylee walked to the door. Rylee rang the bell. "Here goes…"

"Hello," Nova said when the woman they'd seen earlier opened the door.

She and Rylee showed their badges and introduced themselves before Nova added, "We're looking for Mr. and Mrs. Lozano."

"They're not here," the housekeeper responded. "They left yesterday. They're traveling, and I don't know when they'll return."

"Do you happen to know where they went?" Nova inquired, wondering about the groceries.

The woman shook her head. "No, they didn't tell me anything. Just that they would be out of town for a few weeks. Mrs. Lozano said it was a much-needed vacation." She smiled gently before adding, "They haven't traveled much since they lost their daughter."

Rylee nodded. "Do they always leave without telling you where they're going?" she asked.

"They tell me only what they want me to know."

"Someone broke into the house in San Diego," Rylee stated. "Whoever it was killed the housekeeper."

The woman gasped. "Yolanda…"

"Yes," Nova confirmed. "We noticed the bags of groceries you brought into the house. It's a lot for a house no one currently lives in."

She looked from Rylee to Nova. "What do y'all want with Mr. and Mrs. Lozano? These are good people."

"Here is my card," Nova said. "I just want to make sure they're safe."

"Wait here…"

The housekeeper left for a moment before returning with a photo in hand. "I'm not sure where it is, but I think it might be in North Carolina. The Lozano family used to go there every summer. It belongs to one of Mrs. Lozano's cousins."

Nova's face lit up with a smile. "Thank you." The photo was different from the ones they'd found.

The photograph showed a beautiful, large lakefront home with white exteriors and a charming stone pathway leading up to the front door. The house was surrounded by lush green trees and a sprawling lawn that faded into the crystal blue lake in the background. There was a glimpse of a wooden dock extending from the backyard toward the water, lined with cozy lounge chairs and a small boat tied to its side. The clear blue sky and fluffy white clouds above completed the picturesque scene.

She climbed back into the car, unsure if they were getting closer or falling behind in their investigation.

RIVER PEERED AT NOVA, who sat in the back seat with Rylee. He'd been trying not to stare all morning. He yearned to unpin her hair, allowing it to flow free around her face, but quickly forced the image out of his mind. The only thing between them now was their missing witness and her parents.

"I emailed a copy of that new photograph to one of the techs at HSI," Rylee told the group. "Hopefully, they'll be able to narrow down the location for us."

Nova looked up at River, saying, "The housekeeper thinks Arya's parents are in North Carolina."

"Where?"

"She didn't know for sure, but we're thinking this is where this picture may have been taken."

River said, "That's great if it's in North Carolina, but it's a long shot. That backdrop could be anywhere."

"If it were just the beach, I might agree with you," Nova stated as she studied the photograph. "But look at those mountains… This house sits on a lake."

While waiting for the light to turn green, she handed the picture to River.

"I think you might be right," he said after returning it to her. He tried not to focus too much on the feeling of his fingers brushing hers as he'd passed the picture back. "Now we need some luck to find the exact location."

"Sounds so simple, doesn't it?" Nova smiled.

"Hopefully, my tech person will call back with some good news," Rylee said.

The traffic light switched to green, and they continued down the road, the anticipation palpable in the air. The journey to uncover Arya's parents' whereabouts had become a puzzle, and each piece could lead them closer to the missing woman.

AS THE CAR rolled forward, Nova couldn't shake the sense of urgency that propelled them back to the East Coast, chasing elusive answers against North Carolina's landscape.

When they returned to the hotel, Rylee said, "I've been charged with putting together a multiagency task force. My team will be in this area for a meeting with the San Diego police and I asked them to stop by. They should be arriving within the hour."

"That's great," Nova said. "I'm looking forward to meeting them." She sat down and opened up her laptop. "While we're waiting for an address on that property, I'm going to go back through the phone records of Arya's parents. I want to see which relatives they have been in contact with. It looks like they may be trying to cover their tracks."

"It will help keep them alive," Kaleb said.

"But for how long?" River responded.

That was Nova's concern as well. Her heart raced as she realized the gravity of Johnny Boy's actions. The men he sent were ruthless and calculating, experts in hunting down their targets. She knew they would stop at nothing to find their intended victims, leaving a trail of destruction in their wake.

Fifty minutes later, there was a knock on the door.

"They're here," Rylee announced.

As Rylee introduced each team member, Nova took a moment to observe them individually.

Sabra Gomez stood with an air of authority, her dark hair pulled back in a tight bun and dressed professionally in a white button-up shirt and black blazer. Next to her was Tauren Gray, whose mixed heritage could be seen in his rich cream-colored skin and serious expression. He mentioned that he and River had trained together at the DEA Academy in Quantico.

Maisie Wells, on loan from LAPD, exuded confidence with her twist-out hairstyle and regal posture. Rolle Livingston from ATF had a neat ponytail that showed off his defined features, and FBI agent Harper Arness's short hair gave off a professional vibe.

Finally, there was HSI agent Seth Majors, who commanded attention with his tall stature and commanding presence, framed by clean-shaven dark brown skin and closely cropped black hair.

"Wow," Nova murmured. "Looks like you've put together quite a team."

"I wanted you all to meet because we share a common interest," Rylee stated. "We're currently focused on the Mancuso cartel."

"We heard the DEA lost a witness recently," Tauren said.

Nodding, River responded, "He was mine."

When everyone was seated, Nova said, "I was his case agent in witness protection, and now his wife is missing. We think she's gone into hiding. She's in danger."

"There's been some chatter about a missing package," Sabra said. "Maybe this is what they've been talking about. But something else is going on that they seem to consider more urgent. We've decoded some of the conversations originating in Mexico and discovered that the cartel has several tractor trailers leaving the Arizona/Mexico border. They're said to be carrying *lettuce*. In this instance, lettuce refers to cocaine. Several hundred kilos."

Nova knew that the codes and lingo used by drug traffickers were only limited by the imagination. Kilos had often been referred to as batteries, oranges, melons…

"Johnny Boy has been on a pretty good run," Rylee stated. "It's time we stop him."

"How does this man manage to keep eluding arrests?" Harper asked. "Even Calderon was apprehended eventually."

"Because he's smarter than Calderon ever was." Nova's jaw clenched as she replied, her eyes burning with determination. "Johnny Boy knows how to stay under the radar, never getting too comfortable or predictable." She couldn't help but secretly hope that he would slip up, a glimmer of desperation creeping into her tone. They needed a break from this endless game of cat and mouse.

Rolle interjected, "We all know he has a pretty good system going. His life is like a shell game. Johnny Boy has several body doubles, just like Raul Mancuso did. Ninety percent of the time, no one knows where he or the doubles are. The difference between Raul and Johnny Boy is that he didn't hire these look-alikes to fool the Mexican and US governments—they're in place to fool the people closest to him."

Nova said, "According to Manuel DeSoto, outside of Poppy, only a few people can speak to Johnny Boy in person—and the families of those with that privilege live in luxury at Johnny Boy's expense. It's how he rewards their loyalty."

"Naw…it's not a reward. That's all about power," Rolle stated. "Johnny Boy wants the people around him to know that not only are their lives in his hands, but their family's lives are, too."

River nodded in agreement. "My witness told the DEA that Johnny Boy had one of his lieutenants killed because the man brought a personal phone to a dinner hosted by him. He's always been paranoid about anything that might be a tracking device, a recorder or a camera. The only known picture of Johnny Boy was taken when he was nineteen and booked for a murder in Jamaica. He sat in jail for about a week. During that time, all the witnesses to that murder ended up dead, so he was released. They couldn't go forward without a witness, and his alibi was solid. Johnny Boy disappeared after that."

"How do we know that the man arrested in Jamaica wasn't one of Johnny Boy's doubles?" Harper asked. "Maybe the real Johnny Boy murdered the witnesses. Think about it... His fingerprints disappeared... If it wasn't for my witness, we wouldn't have what information we have now. Johnny Boy is still pretty much a shadow."

"I have a man in custody right now... Rico Alfaro...but he's not saying a word," River announced. "He fears Johnny Boy more than doing life in prison."

"He can't elude us forever," Rylee stated. "We will dismantle his routes truck by truck—come down hard on his people until someone is willing to talk."

"What will y'all do with this new information you've decoded?" River asked.

Nova wondered the same thing, but he'd beat her to it.

"The team is heading to Arizona this afternoon. They'll connect with local ATF and DEA agents to assist with intercepting the trucks," Rylee responded. "We just scored a win when we seized fifty pounds of cocaine in a shipment of what was supposed to be packs of coconut flour a few days ago, and we're hoping for another."

"Johnny Boy might be in Arizona then," River said. "I heard he likes to be nearby if there's a problem. He wants to know the person responsible for any mistakes."

"If this is true, then he isn't focused on Arya," Nova responded.

River eyed her. "That's because he's got people out there searching for her. Trust me...he's not letting up."

Seth checked his watch. "We need to pick up Max."

"Who is Max?" she asked.

"Oh yes, we have another team member," Rylee announced. "Max. He is Seth's K-9 partner."

"What kind of dog?" Nova wanted to know.

"He's a Belgian Malinois," Seth answered. "He's six years old and the best partner I've ever had. Max is a dual-purpose dog trained for patrol and narcotics."

"Where's Max now?" she asked.

"He's getting some much-needed grooming," Seth stated. "My sister owns a shop down here, so we dropped Max off before coming here."

After a few more minutes of discussion, Rylee's team left the hotel.

"I wanted you all to meet because I hope that we'll continue to work together in this war against the drug cartels," Rylee stated.

"What did you have in mind when you mentioned working together?" Nova asked.

"I meant that I'd like for you and River to join the team. Nova, you'd have to relocate to Los Angeles. I'll understand if this is not something you're interested in doing right now."

She glanced over at River. He seemed as surprised as she was by Rylee's offer. Nova didn't know what he would decide, but she knew what she would do—she wanted a change. Relocating wasn't a problem because Nova loved the West Coast and could see herself living here full-time.

It would also place her and River in the same city. She didn't know how he would feel about it, but it didn't matter because this was about her career. She wouldn't let their past get in the way of her aspirations.

Chapter Eleven

River's eyebrows rose in surprise over Rylee's job offer.

He was even more shocked when Nova said, "I'd be interested in joining. I've been trying to figure out my next move after Arya is safe, and I really believe this is it."

Rylee smiled. "That's great. We can talk about this in detail after we find Arya."

River sat quietly, observing the women as they talked. He was stunned by the idea of Nova moving to Los Angeles. While the task force sounded interesting and like a great opportunity, he loved his job and wasn't looking for a change. He wasn't opposed to helping if needed, but he was finally up for a promotion he'd been wanting—now wasn't the time to leave.

He personally didn't think it was a good idea for Nova to relocate to Los Angeles. It was too close for his comfort. It was a big enough city to keep them from running into one another. However, because they were both in law enforcement, he and Nova were bound to move within the same circles.

I can't make Nova's career moves about me. No point in worrying about something that might not happen.

The sound of her laughter was like a siren's call, luring

him back to the warmth and comfort of their past love. But as he watched Nova laughing with Kaleb, River couldn't help but feel a twinge of fear in his heart. A fear that if he let her back into his life, she would once again leave him broken and alone. The familiar excitement at the sound of her laugh quickly dissipated as he remembered the pain and heartache she had caused before. He knew deep down that letting her back in meant risking his heart all over again, and he wasn't sure if he could survive another shattering blow.

He couldn't deny that Nova still had an effect on him, although he'd never admit this truth aloud to anyone. River struggled with admitting it to himself.

Nova walked over to where he was sitting. "What did you think of Rylee's team?"

"I've known Tauren a long time, but the others… They were cool," he responded.

She nodded. "I thought they were an impressive group of people."

Nova didn't spare him so much as a glance when she walked past, crossing the room to where Rylee was sitting. They were looking at something on the laptop computer.

River got up to make a phone call. He strode to the door, opened it and walked across the hall. The case he was calling about was in his room. Although his focus was on finding Arya, he still continued investigating the other assigned cases.

He had to return to Nova's room afterward. They were going to discuss the next course of action to find the Lozanos and Arya. He also placed a call to local police to send someone to check out one other house in San Diego that belonged to Arya's grandparents. It was currently listed for sale.

When River returned to Nova's room, he was met by her

frosty stare. Working in a tense environment wasn't good for either of them. If they weren't careful, this tension between them could turn into something more toxic.

River didn't want that, and he was sure Nova didn't either.

"HEY, NOVA... I don't want to get into your business, but are things cool between you and River?" Kaleb inquired while they were sitting in chairs on the balcony. They had taken a short break.

Nova had come out to watch the sun go down. She wanted to experience a California sunset.

"Why do you ask that?" She wondered if Rylee had mentioned their earlier conversation to him.

"I noticed that you two don't seem to have much to say to one another outside of your investigation. Things between you seem kinda strained."

"Rylee mentioned the same thing earlier," Nova stated. "You might as well know what happened... Eighteen months ago, River and I worked on a case together. We spent two wonderful weeks together. Things between us started happening so fast that I could barely breathe and panicked. Kaleb...he made me feel things I'd never felt before. I didn't know what to do, so I left without saying anything to him."

"And now?"

"As you can see...he's not exactly fond of me." Her heart ached at the very thought, but she wasn't going to let it show.

"You know that River's responding out of hurt, Nova. If he really didn't want anything to do with you, I doubt he'd be here."

"That's the irony. I was actually trying to save him from heartache, but maybe he needs more time to erase the pain."

"Have you tried to talk to River about what happened?" he asked.

Nova shook her head as terrible regrets assailed her. "He's done a really great job of discouraging any personal conversation. You know Dad used to be the one who gave me relationship advice. I wish I could talk to him about this."

Kaleb embraced her. "I'm sorry Easton's not here, but you can always come to me, Nova. I'll do the best I can. Your dad was my go-to person for relationship advice as well."

"I feel like I've failed him in some way," she said. "He never lost a witness. I knew Mateo and Arya were headstrong. I should have…"

"Don't torture yourself like this. It doesn't do you any good."

Water welled up in her eyes and overflowed, rolling down her cheeks.

Nova pulled a tissue out of her pocket and wiped away her tears. She clenched her jaw to kill the sob in her throat. "I don't know why I'm getting so emotional."

"Our jobs are stressful, and you're still grieving. Sometimes, we all need to sit down and have a good cry."

With a deep breath, she forced herself to head back to work, trying to impose an iron control on her emotions.

Kaleb excused himself and went inside to speak with his wife.

"Are you okay?" River asked when she walked back inside. "You looked like you were crying."

Nova was surprised by his question. "I'm good. I just had an emotional moment over my dad."

"I know you must miss him very much. Are you up to discuss a plan of action? If not, we can do it later."

"No…of course. We can do it now."

Nova grabbed a water bottle and a snack bag of peanuts from a basket in the kitchenette, taking them to the table.

Rylee stepped away from them when her phone rang.

"We found it," she said after hanging up. "The house in the photo is in the Lake Glenville area. Another relative."

"Arya never once mentioned that she had family in North Carolina," Nova stated. "We never would've been placed there. She intentionally withheld that information. I know that she and Mateo vacationed there for the past two years." Shaking her head, she uttered, "Those two…"

River looked up from his file.

"That's probably where Arya's been all this time," she said. "She may have felt it was the safest place to go."

He agreed. "Lake Glenville is about three and a half hours from Charlotte."

"We should book seats on the next flight to Atlanta," River said. "It's two and a half hours from Lake Glenville."

Nova agreed.

Kaleb and Rylee prepared to head back to the airport.

"It was so good seeing you and Kaleb," Nova said. "Thanks for everything."

Rylee stood with her hand on the doorknob. "I'll be in touch within the next week or so regarding the task force."

"Great! Because I'm really looking forward to hearing more about it," Nova responded. "I'm ready for something new."

"We're booked on a flight leaving tonight at seven," River announced.

Rylee said, "Kaleb and I want to take you to dinner before you head to the airport."

"Fine by me," Nova responded with a smile.

She glanced over at River, who said, "Sure."

Nova quickly packed her suitcase because they were heading to the airport right after they finished eating. River went back to his own room to do the same.

After checking out and putting the luggage in the SUV, they decided to eat at the restaurant in the hotel.

"This is a nice place," Rylee said.

Nova glanced around. "Yes, it is…"

She was saddened by Kaleb and Rylee's leaving. They were the perfect buffer between her and River. She wasn't looking forward to being alone with him again.

"I GUESS THIS wasn't a completely wasted trip," River stated shortly after the plane took off. "Unfortunately, Yolanda was an innocent victim in all this."

Nova agreed. "We probably wouldn't have found out about the house in North Carolina otherwise."

"I hate to put a negative spin on this, but there's a chance that Arya or her parents might not be at this house either."

"I know, River," she said. "But we'll cross that bridge when we get to it." Nova felt the tension rising between them like a thick fog, suffocating and uncomfortable. They were being very careful to keep space from each other even though they were seated beside one another.

"So, you're thinking about leaving the Marshals?" River asked, his voice laced with skepticism.

Nova gave him an icy stare. "I've given it serious thought… What about you?"

His response was a dismissive shake of his head. "Not interested. I'm happy where I am."

She clenched her jaw, struggling to keep her emotions in check. They needed to talk about what had happened in their past, no matter how painful it may be. But last time she'd tried, it hadn't gone well.

Nova sighed, feeling frustrated and unheard. "I just hate all this tension between us," she finally said, her voice low and strained.

River's expression softened slightly. "I didn't mean for things to turn out this way. I don't think I've been rude to you."

"You haven't exactly been warm and fuzzy either," Nova retorted, her tone sharp with hurt.

"I never meant to hurt you," River answered, his words genuine but guarded. "I just don't want things to get out of hand."

Nova's heart sank at his admission. So, he didn't trust himself around her. She couldn't blame him after what had happened between them.

"Just so we're clear," she said, keeping her gaze fixed ahead. "I am capable of keeping my distance and staying professional."

"I know that."

The comment ended things on a bittersweet note, both silently agreeing to put aside their issues for the sake of the investigation. But as River pulled out a bag of potato chips and offered some to her, Nova couldn't help but feel a sense of unease and sadness linger between them. Would they ever be able to repair their fractured relationship fully?

Only time would tell. She shook her head at his offer of a snack.

"You sure you don't want any?" River asked. "Because I've seen you staring them down. I'm pretty sure I heard your stomach growling, too."

Nova knew he was trying to lighten the mood. She decided to accept his peace offering. "It was probably your stomach you heard. Considering you only ordered a salad at dinner," she teased.

"C'mon… It's been a while since we shared a bag of potato chips."

"It's been a minute," she responded while settling back in her seat, her unease slowly dissipating.

Nova eyed the bag of chips again, then reached inside.

"I knew you couldn't resist." River smiled.

Giving him a mock roll of her eyes, she took the bag out of his hand.

"I can't believe that you're really thinking about leaving the Queen City," he stated. "When we met, you talked about how much you loved Charlotte."

She nodded. "I do love it there, but I want a more productive role in helping to take down the Mancuso cartel. They're responsible for my father's death. I want to make sure he didn't die in vain."

His eyes widened in surprise. "You never told me that. I don't think you ever mentioned how he died."

"I didn't want to focus on the tragedies in my life back then," Nova responded. "My dad and I... We were close. Losing him is harder than I ever imagined it would be. I feel like there's a hole in my heart."

"I understand," he responded. "I felt that way when I lost my grandmother."

"I have his text messages saved. I read them when I need to talk to him."

He smiled. "I think about all the conversations I used to have with my grandmother. There are times when I can almost hear her voice."

As they talked about the people they'd lost, Nova sank deeper into her seat while trying to stifle a yawn.

"Why don't you try and get a nap in?" River suggested. "We will hit the ground running as soon as we land."

"I really hope we find them this time," she murmured.

"We haven't lost yet."

"We haven't exactly gotten anywhere either." She paused

a moment, then said, "River, don't mind me. You know I'm not a pessimist. This whole thing with Mateo and Arya..." Nova gave herself a mental shake. "You know what... I'm good."

"I know you're frustrated," River said. "I am, too. It's an unspoken part of our job description."

She gave a short chuckle as she stuck a pair of AirPods in her ears and selected a playlist to enjoy. She resolved to let the music revitalize her spirit. When the plane landed, they had to move quickly. They couldn't afford to waste any time heading to Lake Glenville. She hoped fervently that Pablo and Ramona Lozano would be at the house along with Arya.

RIVER TOOK WHAT he considered a power nap during the final hour of the flight. Turned out it was what he needed, because he felt rejuvenated by the time the plane landed in Atlanta.

They rented a car and drove to Lake Glenville, the coastal town located eight miles from Cashiers, NC, in a mountain rainforest.

"It's beautiful up here," Nova said, looking out the passenger-side window.

"It looks like the perfect place to visit if you're a lover of the outdoors," River remarked. He wasn't, so while the landscape was indeed a beauty, it wasn't his thing.

Nova took a sip of her water. "I remember you saying that you weren't the camping or fishing type."

"I'm not. I love the beach, but I've never cared much for the mountains."

She chuckled. "I'm not either. I'll take the beach any day. I did read that there are three waterfalls here."

They made a left turn into a quaint neighborhood. Following the directions of the GPS, River turned right on the first street they approached.

"This is the house that was in the photograph." Nova's voice was a velvet murmur as River slowly passed the home. "It's the one with the dark blue shutters."

River felt his heart race and swallowed hard. "Yes, that's it."

They parked down the street.

"I'm thinking we watch the house for a bit instead of just rushing up to the door," River said. "If they're in there, we don't want to spook them."

"After what they've been through, don't you think seeing a strange car in the neighborhood with two people sitting in it might spook them more?" Nova responded. "I think it's better for us to get out and talk to them."

Shrugging, River said, "Okay. We'll try it your way. Do you think we should wear our vests?"

"Not this time."

They got out of the car and made their way up to the house.

Nova rang the doorbell a few minutes later. She released a soft sigh of relief when the door opened a sliver and Ramona Lozano peered through the crack.

Looking from River to Nova, she asked, "May I help you?"

"Mrs. Lozano, I'm Deputy Marshal Nova Bennett. Your daughter may have mentioned me." She held up her badge. "Is your husband home with you?"

The thin woman looked as if she were about to faint. She ran trembling fingers through her short hair. "Yes, he is. Is he in some kind of trouble?"

"No, he isn't."

Her brow furrowed. "Then why are you looking for him?"

Nova glanced over at River, then back at Ramona. "You know I'm not here about Pablo. I've been searching for the two of you and your daughter. You all could be in danger." She identified Arya by the name she was given at birth.

Nervous, Ramona glanced away. "I'm afraid I don't know where she is. I—"

"Look, I know she's been in contact with you, Mrs. Lozano," Nova interjected. "I'm sure you've heard by now that Yolanda was murdered in your home. The people after you are not playing games. You're all in grave danger, and I'm here to help."

The woman released a shaky breath. "Ava called to warn us that we were in danger, but I haven't heard from her since then, and I don't know where she is."

"Mrs. Lozano, I only want to keep your daughter safe."

Clutching her necklace as if it were a lifeline, Ramona responded, "If I hear from her, I'll let you know if you leave your number with me. All I want is for Ava to come home to us. We miss her terribly. I don't know what that dreadful husband of hers has gotten her into…"

"I want you to know that I'll do everything in my power to keep Arya safe," Nova reassured her. "But I need to find her first."

Ramona gestured for them to enter. "You can search the house, but she's not here." River accepted her invitation to verify that they were alone in the home while Nova sat down in the living room with Ramona.

"Ava said she couldn't tell us where she was—only that we had to leave California," Ramona explained. "We heard about Mateo's family, and then Mateo… Her father and I did as she asked. We left our home and came here." Clutching the gold cross around her neck, Ramona sighed. "Poor Yolanda. I told her that she should visit her family in Mexico. But she wanted to help. We knew someone might be watching the house, and we didn't want anyone to know we'd left. She thought she'd be safe."

"They were either looking for you and your husband… or trying to find your daughter. Don't you see that *we* can protect all of you?" Nova paused momentarily, then added, "If you do hear from her, tell Arya I found her message and I'm on her side."

"I will," Ramona responded. "Thank you."

"My daughter told us to leave and go where nobody would find us," Pablo said when he and River joined them in the living room. "We figured we'd be safe here."

"It wasn't easy locating you," Nova stated. "I must confess that I took some of your photos, and they led us here. Are you sure you can't give us a clue as to where we should look for your daughter?"

"I can't help you," Ramona said, averting her gaze. "I'm sorry."

Nova understood the fear and desperation that gripped the Lozano family. She respected Ramona's decision to keep quiet, even though it made their task more challenging. Her heart went out to them, but without more concrete information, finding Arya would be like searching for a needle in a haystack.

Chapter Twelve

They walked back to the car and got inside.

"It's obvious that Ramona Lozano isn't going to tell us anything because she wants to protect her daughter," Nova said. She was frustrated and needed to vent. "I thought telling them about Yolanda's murder might scare her into telling us where to find Arya, but she's sticking to her story."

"You don't seem convinced," River said.

"I'm not sure what to believe," she responded. "Arya was worried enough to warn them to leave their home… Surely, she'd check in. She'd want to know that they're safe. At least, that's what I would do."

He nodded. "I agree. So, what do you want to do?"

"We should hang around and see if they suddenly have visitors."

They sat there for the next couple of hours.

"There hasn't been any movement coming or going," River said. "There's a café two blocks from the neighborhood. Why don't we pick up something to eat?"

Nodding, Nova said, "Works for me."

They made the trip in silence and River pulled back into the neighborhood. "What's weighing so heavily on your mind?" River asked as they returned to their surveillance spot and started to eat in the car. "You look like you're trying to figure something out. I can almost hear your brain working."

"I was thinking about Mateo," Nova explained. "I think he wanted money to disappear, and this was the only way he thought he'd be able to get it. Unfortunately, now Arya has a target on her back."

"From what I know of Johnny Boy, he'd eliminate Mateo's wife and her entire family to play it safe."

"My gut tells me that Ramona knows where Arya's hiding," Nova said, pulling her hair into a ponytail. "I wish I could get her to trust me."

Glancing around, River said, "Everything seems normal around here. No perceived threats in the area—that's a good thing."

"It is, but I'd feel better if we just sit for a while longer to see if anything happens."

"I don't have a problem with that," he said with a slight shrug.

Nova swallowed hard. She was quickly becoming tired of the runaround. She didn't mind the chase if she were getting results. Right now, she didn't see anything but disappointment. They needed to find Arya, and soon.

RIVER AND NOVA continued to watch the house after dark, but nothing seemed amiss.

Nova pulled out a small bottle and spritzed some of the liquid on her neck.

"Arya's endgame is to be reunited with her parents," he said while trying to ignore the tantalizing scent of her fragrance. She'd opened a window and her scent now wafted to him. "We just have to figure out how they're going to make that happen."

Nova craned her neck and stared at the house. "I really thought they'd pack a suitcase and take off as soon as we left. Maybe Ramona was telling the truth. Maybe she doesn't know where Arya's hiding."

"The day's not over yet." A few more minutes passed in silence and he tried to think of a conversation starter while they were sitting there in the vehicle. There were so many things River wanted to say to her, and much he didn't want to say. His emotions were conflicted since Nova had come back into his life. It brought back memories of Mary and the way she'd rejected him. The trauma of that experience shaped the man River had become, especially when it came to love.

Nova would never know how hard it was for River to be vulnerable enough to share what he was feeling with her. She'd made him feel safe and then she destroyed that safety. After their relationship ended, River had vowed to never show such vulnerability to anyone ever again. He viewed love as a weakness—one that could be easily exploited.

He chided himself for going down that path. They were on assignment, and making sure the witness and her parents remained unharmed was the priority. Right now, nothing else mattered.

River eyed the license plate of a black truck that passed them.

Nothing was remarkable about it, but it held his attention for the moment. He watched to see if the vehicle slowed as it neared the Lozanos' house.

It kept moving without slowing down.

"Something wrong?" Nova asked.

"No. Just checking out the truck that just passed by. It wasn't anything."

The tags were local. River kept looking to see if it passed

by again, but it didn't. Nothing to send off any red flags, but his experienced senses were on alert.

NOVA STRUGGLED TO maintain a professional front, but keeping her mind off the handsome River was a challenge. She wondered how he could be both sexy and frustrating simultaneously. Those kissable lips of his reminded Nova of their time together in the past. Memories that she didn't want to dredge up. Memories she regarded as precious.

They were only precious to her, Nova realized.

The garage door to the Lozano house went up, cutting into her thoughts.

She glanced at the clock. It was one o'clock in the morning.

Pablo walked briskly, carrying a travel bag to the SUV. Ramona followed behind.

Nova nudged River, who'd seen it, too.

"Looks like Arya's parents are about to leave."

"Let's find out where they're going," River said as he started the vehicle.

Nova nodded. "Pull in front of the driveway so they can't leave."

The black truck that cut them off came out of nowhere. River made an abrupt stop to avoid a collision. Nova's body was pushed back and then thrown forward. Her instincts immediately sounded the alarm in her mind. Trouble loomed on the horizon.

"That's the same black truck that passed earlier." River's voice was tense, carrying the weight of recognition. "I remember the license plate. It's an ambush."

Nova's heart raced, and she drew in a deep breath, attempting to steady the nervous energy that flooded her. Anxiety surged as she mentally mapped out the potential outcomes. There was no avoiding it; they had to face this danger head-on.

In a swift, practiced motion, Nova slipped on a vest before emerging from the shelter of the SUV.

"US Marshals," she yelled with authority as she swung open the passenger-side door. "Get out of the truck with your hands up."

On the opposite side of the vehicle, River stood, gun drawn, moving cautiously toward the driver's side of the suspicious truck.

Nova repeated her command, scanning their surroundings, and that was when she noticed another truck strategically parked in front of the Lozano home, effectively blocking any chance of escape.

Pablo and Ramona Lozano were trapped.

The only thought on Nova's mind was finding a way to reach Arya's parents and get them to safety.

Just then, the passenger-side door of the vehicle that cut them off suddenly swung open, and a dark-skinned man with dreadlocks leaped out, brandishing a weapon aimed directly at her.

Instinct took over, and Nova fired off a shot with precision, hitting her target.

River swiftly closed the distance between them, pulling her to safety just as another assailant opened fire in her direction. He responded in kind, unleashing a round of gunfire.

The driver of the black truck, undeterred by the chaos, seized the opportunity to escape, accelerating around the other car with reckless speed.

Shots echoed through the air from the other vehicle before the driver shifted to Reverse and backed down the street.

River aimed and fired his weapon at the SUV.

Nova cautiously made her way to the bleeding man on the ground. She kicked his gun out of reach, then knelt to see if he was dead.

The Lozanos' SUV was bullet-ridden, its metallic frame reflecting the faint glow of a single light bulb hanging from the ceiling. The passenger-side door hung open at an awkward angle, revealing torn upholstery and shattered glass.

Nova felt lightheaded. "Nooo!"

Ramona lay motionless on the cold concrete floor beside the vehicle, her chest rising and falling in shallow breaths. Pablo's lifeless body was sprawled out in front of the car, his limbs twisted at unnatural angles and blood staining the ground beneath him. The unmistakable scent of gunpowder lingered in the air, a grim reminder of the violence that had taken place.

She rushed toward them.

River ran behind her.

"Pablo Lozano is dead," he said, kneeling beside his body with his fingers over the pulse point.

Ignoring the tightening in her stomach, Nova checked on Ramona. "She's still alive." She pulled out her cell phone. "But she needs to get to a hospital." Nova called the shooting in and requested an ambulance.

Ramona opened her eyes. Her voice barely above a whisper, she said, "Please h-help…my d-dau…my daughter." She arched her back, winced and closed her eyes, probably trying to block out the pain.

"Mrs. Lozano, don't try to talk. The paramedics are on the way," Nova said "They should be here soon." She sent up a quick prayer, asking God to keep the woman alive. She didn't want Arya to lose both parents. One was devastating enough.

"Ava.M   iami.G   PS…"

"I'm going to do everything I can to help her."

"My h-husband…" Ramona murmured before losing consciousness.

Nova heard the wailing of a siren in the distance and released a short sigh of relief. She'd done what she could to help Ramona and now it was up to the medics.

While they waited for the EMTs, she peered inside the Lozanos' SUV.

Nova checked the GPS, took a photo of the address input for Miami. "So, you were planning to meet up with Arya," she whispered. "I knew you weren't telling me everything."

Police officers quickly arrived on the scene, followed by an ambulance.

River went over to talk to the police while she stayed with Ramona.

"She's been shot," Nova told the paramedic, ignoring the officers who were going over the details of what had happened with River. "One bullet grazed her arm and the other one…it's below her right breast. She's unconscious."

They placed the injured woman on a backboard and transported her to the ambulance.

"C'mon," Nova said. "We're going to Miami. That's where they were headed."

"You think Arya's there?"

She nodded. "Before she lost consciousness, Ramona asked me to help Arya and said the address was in the GPS."

Something flickered in River's eyes but disappeared as quickly as it had come, leaving Nova to wonder what he could be thinking.

"What is it?" she asked.

"I'm just wondering why she chose Miami."

"I don't know," Nova said. "But I'm calling the Marshals and having her mother placed under round-the-clock security."

River nodded, wrapping up with the police while Nova called Cohen to update him. When she disconnected, she and River made their way back to their vehicle.

"Miami... I find it interesting that Arya would go there since there's tension between the Mancuso and Mali cartels in Miami," River said. "Johnny Boy's been trying to establish a firm presence down there."

She'd heard something about that. "The Mali cartel hijacked and burned more than a dozen stash houses belonging to the Mancuso cartel in Florida a year ago," Nova said. "The fighting between the two organizations was so bad that they had to impose a curfew in certain areas. There's definitely bad blood between those two."

"Maybe that's what Mateo had planned all along," River said. "If negotiating with Poppy and Johnny Boy didn't work, then it's possible he intended to sell information to the Mali cartel for protection."

"Only he didn't count on being murdered."

River nodded in agreement. "Exactly."

"He never learned his lesson," Nova said. "Let's hope Arya does."

Chapter Thirteen

Nova sent up a silent prayer for Ramona Lozano. She'd already called the Marshals office in Miami, giving them the address for Arya's known location and requesting round-the-clock protection. She and River would get there as soon as they could, and when they finally found her, Nova planned to be the one to convince her to come back into the program. One question lingered in her mind. "How did they find Arya's parents?"

"I don't know, but I'm glad we were there," River responded. "If we hadn't been, Arya's mother might be in the morgue with her husband."

"She's not out of the woods yet," Nova pointed out.

Her phone rang, and she answered quickly.

"The marshals are at the hospital," she announced after ending the call. "At least we know Ramona's safe. She's under twenty-four-hour security. As soon as she's stable enough, she'll be taken someplace safe to recuperate." Nova paused briefly, then said, "Looks like you've been right all along. The cartel must consider Arya a huge threat. There has to be a reason why. They must see her as more than a potential loose end."

River nodded. He made a call, then got off the phone,

saying, "She's been assigned to a Victim Witness Coordinator. I'm expecting a callback from the federal prosecutor."

Nova couldn't help but express her disgust at such a heinous act. "Arya's going to be devastated over her father's death, but hopefully, the news about her mother will be a brighter note."

"My partner is going to meet us in Miami," River announced.

She grinned. "I'm surprised Kenny is still putting up with you."

River gave her a sidelong glance. "Did you really just say that?"

"The two of you fuss like an old married couple," Nova said. "Did y'all ever check into couples counseling like I suggested?"

He chuckled. "Whatever…"

IN THE DRIVER'S SEAT, Nova glanced over at River, who seemed deep in thought. She could tell from his body language that her nearness brought him discomfort. He always seemed to stand with his arms crossed as if to protect himself. Whenever River had his laptop out, he carried it close to his chest like a physical barrier. Even now, he sat with his back so straight that Nova couldn't imagine he was relaxed in that position. She tried a couple of times to strike up a conversation, but River gave her one-word responses.

They were both exhausted, so it didn't bother her that he wasn't being very talkative. However, Nova desperately wanted to bridge the gap that had formed between them. She was at a loss on how to do so. It was her fault that their relationship had crumbled, and she couldn't shake off the weight of guilt.

Despite everything, she knew that their priority right

now was protecting the witness from the deadly drug cartel. If only they weren't in this dangerous situation, she could focus on repairing their broken bond.

As they crossed into Florida, Nova welcomed the short break. Her mind and body were drained from constantly being on high alert.

River offered to take over driving for the rest of the journey to Miami, and Nova didn't protest. Part of her wanted to stay awake and keep an eye on things, but exhaustion eventually caught up, and she drifted off for a quick nap.

Nova woke up to River softly humming a tune beside her. Blinking away the remnants of sleep, she looked out the window and saw they were parked in front of a small roadside café. The warm Florida sun was casting a golden glow over everything, lending an air of tranquility to the scene.

Stretching her limbs, Nova took a deep breath and turned to River. "How long have we been here?"

River glanced at her with a smile. "Just about half an hour. You seemed so peaceful—I didn't want to wake you."

Nova nodded gratefully, her heart swelling with affection for him. She realized that despite their strained relationship, there was still an unspoken connection between them.

"I feel refreshed. I can take over if you'd like to get some sleep." Nova glanced at the clock. "You haven't been to sleep since we left North Carolina."

"Let's grab something to eat, and I'll see how I feel after," he responded.

Stepping out of the car, Nova couldn't help but notice the way River's hand grazed against hers. It sent a thrilling rush through her body, but she pushed those feelings aside as they entered the café. She needed to focus on Arya and avoid getting lost in this unexpected attraction. The more time they spent together, the more Nova's resolve wavered, torn between duty and desire.

RIVER WAS DOING everything he could to maintain a professional distance around Nova. But after her statement, he realized it wouldn't be as easy as he'd imagined.

Memories of the last time they'd worked together came flooding back. River tried to force them back into the deep recesses of his mind. There wouldn't be a repeat of what had happened two years ago. River vowed he wouldn't succumb to the weakness he felt whenever Nova was in his presence. His self-control was much stronger now, built up by the heartbreak she'd inflicted upon him.

Nova wanted to move forward as if nothing had happened, but it wasn't that easy for River.

He glanced over at her. She was on the phone. She'd periodically checked in on Ramona Lozano to learn her prognosis. The last time she'd called the hospital, Ramona was in surgery.

"How is she?" he asked when she hung up.

"She's out of surgery and is expected to recover fully," Nova responded. "At least I'll be able to tell Arya that her mother will be okay despite her father's death."

River met her gaze. "I'm really sorry about your father."

"I miss him a great deal. My mom and I are also very close, but I am... I was a daddy's girl for sure. He was my hero."

"Is your mom still in Wisconsin?" River asked.

"Yeah," she answered, giving a slight nod. "She'll never leave Milwaukee. Since I left, she's visited me several times, but she loves her hometown. I tried to convince her to move to Charlotte." Nova turned in her seat. "I know you were very close to your grandmother."

"Adelaide was my heart." Memories of his time with her floated to the forefront of River's mind. "She didn't miss any of my games when I was growing up. She was the team mom… She hosted a lot of the meals…"

"She sounds wonderful," Nova said. "I didn't know my paternal grandparents—they disowned my dad for marrying a Black woman. But my mother's parents… Bessie and Isaiah Chapman… They gave me so much love that I don't feel I missed out on having the other set in my life."

"You can't miss what you never had," River responded. "That's what people say, but it's not true. I missed the love of a mother."

"I—"

He cut her off. "Let's change the subject." River hadn't meant to show more of his vulnerability, and he wouldn't open up to her about his relationship with his mother. They had crossed into a red zone. He had to get them back on course.

"Sure," Nova said.

River relaxed his body. They were once again in the safe zone, and he wouldn't stray from it again.

Chapter Fourteen

Nova moved her body into a more comfortable position. They were less than twenty minutes away from their destination. "Arya rented this place under her mother's name," she said, closing the laptop.

"I'm not so sure that was a smart move," River responded. "Since the cartel went after her parents."

"I emailed my supervisor about her mother. I'm hoping we can get Ramona into the program with Arya."

They took the exit SW 11th Lane, where the house was located.

River received a call from his partner.

"Kenny's already there," River announced when he ended the call. "Arya's in the house alone. She's expecting us.

"Nice location," River said as they passed through the small community of luxury homes.

Staring out the window, Nova said, "Mateo and Arya sure love the finer things in life. I thought she was going to faint when I took them to their house in Burlington. She kept saying it was much too small. They had a square-footage requirement of at least six thousand square feet."

"Okaay... What kinds of jobs did they have in the program?" River asked with a chuckle.

"She worked in a dental office," Nova said. "She was the office manager. Her husband worked second shift at a medical-supply warehouse. Their incomes wouldn't have supported the type of housing they desired."

"We're here," River announced.

A pair of Arya's signature rosebushes led up to the porch.

Nova and River exited the vehicle and walked up the steps of the two-story house to the front door, which opened before they could knock.

Arya was standing in the doorway, immaculate from head to toe, but her eyes were lined with shadows, and she looked as though she hadn't slept in days. "Finally," she breathed as she guided them into the house. "I was beginning to worry you wouldn't find me." She led them into the living room.

"You didn't make it easy for me to find you," Nova began. "I found out from your mother."

"I thought my parents would be here by now. Do you know if they left already? They aren't answering their phones."

"Something's happened…" Nova began.

"What?" Her eyes grew large, and her voice trembled with fear.

"Arya, you might want to sit down."

But Arya refused, shaking her head frantically. "Nooo… Just tell me."

Nova took a deep breath and spoke the words that would shatter her world. "Someone from the cartel showed up at the house in Lake Glenville," she said gently. "Arya, they shot your parents."

She began crying.

"I'm so sorry. We couldn't save your father, but your mom is alive. Ramona's in a hospital under guard."

"It's all my fault," Arya sobbed. "I never should've involved them. Mateo told me to warn them and have them go to the vacation house and stay there until I was safe in Miami, and they could follow. But the day I left Burlington, I returned to the house because I'd forgotten something—I could see that someone had broken in, so I left."

"How did you end up at that abandoned house in Concord?"

She dropped down on the love seat. "Mateo found it. It's where I was supposed to stay until he returned." Nova and River sat across from her as she continued, "We were going to leave the country, but when I never heard back from him, I knew something must have gone wrong. I had a bad feeling... I knew he'd been killed. I didn't know what to do, so I called you. Then I was too scared to tell you where I was, so I left the phone behind." Arya shook her head. "I don't know how the cartel could track my parents down—they were careful in covering their tracks."

"They must have put some tracking software on the car or maybe they hacked your parents' phones," Nova suggested.

"If so, then it definitely won't be hard for them to find me, too," Arya said. "I spoke with my parents at least three or four times since leaving Burlington. It was because I didn't want them to worry." She chewed on her bottom lip. "Nova, I've really made a mess of things. Now my father is dead." She started crying again.

Nova leaned forward. "None of this is your fault."

Arya stood and paced across the hardwood floors. "Nova, I need to see my mother."

Nova shook her head. "I'm sorry, but it's unsafe for you to go there. The doctor will keep me updated on her progress."

"What if they try to kill her while she's at the hospital?"

"That won't happen."

"Why not?" Arya asked, knitting her trembling fingers together.

"Because they believe that she died along with your father," River interjected. "Your mother is being moved to a secure location under a temporary assumed name. US marshals are guarding her. Arya, she's safe."

Tears rolled down her cheeks. "I can't even bury my father."

"Your father will be cremated," Nova said. "Meanwhile, I'm working to get your mother into the program with you."

Arya appeared surprised. "You're not kicking me out?"

Shaking her head, Nova responded, "I'm giving you a second chance, but this time you will have to comply with the rules of WITSEC, and if you're holding on to evidence the DEA can use, you *must* turn in everything to Special Agent Randolph."

Arya averted her gaze. "I don't have anything. Mateo took it with him when he went to LA."

The hitch of her voice told Nova the woman was lying. Why?

"Arya, those are the terms," Nova stated. "It's not negotiable. We both know that Mateo was too smart to carry anything on him."

"I can't give you what I don't have. You can search my things for yourself." A lone tear ran down her cheek. "I wasn't involved in my husband's business. I just want a few minutes to myself to mourn the loss of my father. Can you give me that?"

Nova nodded. "Sure."

"I'll be in my bedroom."

"That went better than I thought it would," Nova said when she and River were alone in the living room. "She denies any prior knowledge of Mateo's business with the cartel."

"She knows more than she's telling us," River stated. "It's possible the information could also be somewhere in a bank, but I doubt it. Mateo didn't trust banks. He told the DEA how he'd hidden money in the walls of his office and the bottom of his freezer."

"Most likely, he was hiding that money from the cartel since he was stealing from them," Nova responded. "Didn't he turn over his computer to the DEA?"

"Yes," River responded with a nod. "Mateo was a smart man. I wouldn't be surprised if he had another computer hidden somewhere."

Kenny walked into the house after surveilling the perimeter of the property just as Nova said, "I'm going to check on Arya. I need to make sure she isn't trying to escape out the window."

"I don't think you have to worry about her," Kenny replied. "When I arrived, she appeared relieved. I believe she is grateful for the company and support during this situation."

"How is she?" River asked when Nova returned from checking on Arya. Kenny had picked up dinner for them from a popular chicken eatery.

"She says she's not hungry. Right now, she's still very emotional," she said. "Mateo and her father dead, her mother in the hospital, and the stress of being on the run. It's a lot to have to deal with. I was able to convince her to lie down and try to rest. She's worried that if the cartel was able to find her parents, they might be headed here."

"It's possible."

"I know," Nova responded.

"Does she have her cell phone?"

"Kenny took it from her," Nova said. "He turned it off."

"That's good to hear," River responded.

"He's camped outside her door right now," she stated. "I volunteered to take the next watch."

They found a movie to watch on television.

Nova stretched and tried to get comfortable. She snuggled up in one corner of the sofa.

When River glanced over at her, she was fast asleep. He'd known she wasn't going to last too much longer.

Smiling, he gave her a gentle nudge. "Why don't you go to one of the guest rooms? You're tired."

She sat up. "No, I'm good."

"No, you're not," River said. "Nova, you're exhausted."

She wiped her face with the backs of her hands. "I told Kenny that I'd keep watch so he could get some sleep."

"I can hold it down for now."

"Okay, but I just need a couple of hours," Nova stated.

Pointing toward the first-floor guest bedroom, River urged, "Go get in bed."

She refused. "No, I'll stay out here. Besides, I'm much too comfortable to move right now."

Grinning, he handed her a throw.

Nova smiled at him. "Thank you."

River settled back, keeping a watchful eye on their surroundings, as Nova drifted into a well-deserved rest on the sofa, the glow of the television casting a soft light on the room.

The night unfolded in a hushed ambience, punctuated by the occasional distant sounds of the city. He found a moment of respite, even amid uncertainty and danger.

NOVA WOKE UP with a start. She looked around, asking, "What time is it?"

"Almost two a.m.," River answered from across the room. He was in the dining area, working on his laptop.

"Oh, wow.I. didn't mean to sleep so long."

"It's fine. You needed to get some rest, Nova. You're not a robot."

"Neither are you, River." Standing, Nova said, "I'll keep watch now. It's time for you to get some sleep."

He didn't argue. "I'm going to take a shower first. Wake me at six."

"Will do," she responded. "Where's Kenny?"

"He was in the kitchen a few minutes ago," River said. "He may be upstairs."

River opened the door to the first-floor bedroom and went inside, heading straight to the bathroom.

From where she sat, Nova could hear the steady downpour of water hammering the ceramic tiles inside the glass-enclosed shower.

She got up and navigated to the kitchen, needing something else to focus on than a wet, naked River Randolph. The hinges on the pantry door whined as she opened the door. She wasn't looking for anything specific but found cases of bottled water, various snacks, pasta and spaghetti sauce. In the refrigerator, Nova saw an assortment of cheeses, pepperoni, sausages and other meats.

Before she even turned around, Nova knew he was there. River was standing in the doorway, dressed in nothing but a pair of gray sweatpants. His look was so electrifying that it sent a tremor through her.

"Looking for a late-night snack?" he asked.

"Naw," Nova responded, averting her eyes. "I was just being nosy. What about you? I thought you were going to bed."

"I just came to get a bottle of water."

She retrieved one from the fridge and tossed it to him.

"Thanks," he said.

"Good night."

"What are you about to do?"

She swallowed tightly. "I'm going upstairs to check on Arya. I'll take the position outside her room."

He nodded. "I'm going outside to check the perimeter before I turn in."

Nova went upstairs and peeked in on Arya, who appeared to be sleeping soundly. Satisfied, she sat in the chair outside the room with her iPad. Might as well catch up on some reading, she decided.

She couldn't fully concentrate because of the handsome man in the room below. Seeing him in those gray sweatpants had struck a vibrant chord with her. She hadn't wanted to tear her attention from River but had forced herself to do so. Arya wasn't entirely out of danger yet.

Chapter Fifteen

"Where's our witness?" River asked the following day when he walked out of the bedroom. Although he hadn't slept eight hours, he felt completely rested in half the time.

"Probably still in bed," Nova responded as she removed four slices of bread from a toaster. "I haven't seen her at all this morning."

She walked the short distance to the fridge and retrieved the butter. "Kenny was down here a moment ago."

"You've got it smelling good in here."

She glanced over her shoulder at River. "You sound like you're surprised. I've been cooking since I was twelve. I'm a foodie, so I had to learn how to cook."

He held up his hands in mock surrender. "I didn't say a word…"

Nova went halfway up the stairs, then shouted, "Arya, if you intend to eat, you'd better come on down while everything is hot."

Arya entered the kitchen, saying, "I prefer to have breakfast in bed. I'm in mourning."

"I'll fix you a plate. You can take it upstairs if you want."

"I'm tired of tasteless food." She picked up a bagel. "I bought them like four days ago. Why can't we go to a real restaurant?" Arya whined.

"Because you're in hiding," Nova responded. "You're not out of danger yet."

"I'm so sick of this. This isn't how my life is supposed to go."

Nova shrugged. "Then you should've chosen a different one."

She glared at Nova. "Why did the feds take all our money? Why couldn't they leave us with at least a million?"

River could tell that Nova was struggling to keep her temper in check.

"It wasn't *your* money," River stated.

Arya rolled her eyes. "Mateo told me we would one day have our life back. He said we'd be rich again. That we could live anywhere in the world—it was our choice. We were going to buy a luxury yacht and live on it. Nobody would've been able to find us because we'd sail around the world... This just isn't fair."

"You should be grateful that you're still aboveground," Nova said. "Your life is in danger, Arya. We're not concerned with your social status. And while we're here, we're not your servants. We are here to keep you safe. Try to remember that."

Pouting, Arya rolled her eyes heavenward. She put a piece of toast on her plate, then stuck her fork into a sausage. "It would be nice to have an omelet now and then."

"Feel free to make one," Nova said with a grin to lighten the mood. "If you're cooking, I'll take one with spinach and tomatoes. Arya makes the best veggie omelets."

"I'm just saying... I feel like I'm owed something, Nova. I lost my husband because he went to the DEA for help, and now he's *dead*."

River opened his mouth to speak, but Nova touched his arm. When he met her gaze, she gave a shake of her head.

It was her telling him to take it easy on Arya.

After breakfast, they settled in the living room with Kenny posted at a window upstairs. Nova sat beside Arya on the leather couch while River sat in a chair across from them.

"I'm telling you that my husband wouldn't have given me any files or documents. Maybe he stored them in a safe somewhere, but only he would have the key."

They'd been trying to find out what the de Leons could be hiding but were getting nowhere. River decided to choose a different line of questioning. "I'm curious. What made you decide to come to Miami?"

Shrugging, Arya responded, "I don't know... I just thought I'd be safe here."

"In a city run by the Mali cartel?"

"Has nothing to do with me. I don't belong to any cartel."

She tried to keep her expression neutral, but River didn't miss the way she fidgeted on the couch.

"Your husband was a prominent figure in the Mancuso cartel. Was he going to switch sides?"

Arya shrugged once more. "I don't know."

River eyed her. "I decided to look into your mother's family, and one of your uncles was an attorney for the Mali family."

He heard Nova's soft gasp of surprise. He hadn't yet shared this piece of information with her. River had only found out that morning. He'd decided to look when he recalled that the owner of the property in North Carolina had a Florida mailing address.

"I don't know anything about that," Arya responded, her hands folded in her lap. "I mean, my uncle was a lawyer. He had his own law firm. No idea who his clients were."

"I have a feeling that Mateo knew all about him."

"My uncle died a long time ago." She met his gaze. "I

want to help you, but whatever my husband knew died with him, I'm afraid."

"Do you expect us to believe you had no help getting to Miami?" River demanded.

"I followed Mateo's instructions. That's all."

"Did you contact anyone outside of your parents?" River pressed.

Arya shook her head no. "Just the rental agency."

"Using your mother's identification," Nova said.

"It's all I had to work with. I don't have pay stubs or a job anymore. I needed a place to stay."

"Why don't we take a break?" Nova suggested.

River sighed, feeling frustrated with the lack of progress in his interrogation. He glanced at Nova, noting the sympathy in her eyes. She had always been compassionate and willing to give people the benefit of the doubt. But River knew better. He had seen firsthand the deceit and manipulation rampant in the criminal world.

Gesturing for Nova to follow him out of the room, he stepped into the foyer. Nova joined him, and they leaned against the wall, the air tense as their gazes locked in a silent conversation.

"We're not getting anywhere with her," River finally said with frustration. "She's hiding something. I can feel it."

"AGENT RANDOLPH THINKS I'm lying," Arya said when Nova returned to the living room alone.

"Are you?" Nova inquired, fixing her with a penetrating gaze.

"No, I'm not," she retorted with a mixture of frustration and desperation.

"He's not the only one you have to convince," Nova stated, her tone indicating the gravity of the situation.

"What do you mean?" Arya's eyes widened with curiosity and a hint of fear.

"Johnny Boy. He knows your death was a lie… He's coming for you."

Arya's face lost color as she stammered, "Th-that's why I think it's time to leave Miami. Nova, just let me get a ticket to someplace far away. I'll disappear for good."

Nova shook her head, a heavy sense of responsibility settling on her shoulders. "He will hunt you down unless you help us put him in prison."

"Johnny Boy is unstoppable!" Arya exclaimed, her fear palpable. "Can't you see that?"

"We can't let fear dictate our choices. If you run, he wins. We need to stand up to him, expose the truth and make sure he pays for what he's done."

Arya looked torn, caught between the terror of facing Johnny Boy and the uncertainty of trusting Nova and the team to protect her. The gravity of their choices weighed heavily on them both, their fates entwined in this dangerous game that could only have one outcome—life or death.

Nova found River in the kitchen.

"How did it go?" he asked.

"She's scared."

"She doesn't trust that we can protect her," River stated. "We'll have to remind her that she and Mateo were safe until they left WITSEC. Johnny Boy knew exactly how to get Mateo to leave the program. Arya is not safe on her own."

"I agree." Nova sighed. "But how do we get her to trust us?"

SHORTLY AFTER MIDNIGHT, a vehicle parked across the street.

"There's a black SUV outside," Nova yelled from the home office. She watched with growing concern. "The doors are opening, and two guys just got out. River, they're *armed*."

"I'll get Arya," he said while taking the stairs two at a time.

Kenny went out the door leading to the back of the house. They were likely going to attack from both the back and front of the house.

Nova stood at the window, studying the men even as she slipped on a Kevlar vest. They didn't look familiar. The taller of the two was dressed in a black sweat suit, the expression on his face threatening. The other wore a black knit cap and leather jacket. He seemed intent on hiding his face.

River ran to the porch armed and ready while Nova went to the front window with her Glock pointed at the two men. River ordered them to halt.

Instead, the first assailant took aim.

The quiet street soon erupted in a deafening noise. Bright muzzle flashes and the sound of automatic gunfire filled the neighborhood, the bullets causing a couple of the windows to explode.

Nova ducked for cover, then fired at the would-be intruders, hitting the tall one. He collapsed on the sidewalk.

From the side of the house, Kenny took a shot at the other and wounded him in the arm. The man dropped his gun and stood with his good hand up in the air. Kenny approached to make an arrest.

Nova ushered Arya, who was in a Kevlar vest as well, downstairs and through the door leading to the garage. Her adrenaline was high, and she was ready to take on any threat.

She heard rather than saw the garage door going up.

Kenny gestured for them to leave. "Get out of here," he said. "I will take care of this." She slid into the vehicle beside Arya in the back seat while River got into the driver's seat.

"Arya, get down on the floor," Nova said.

The cartel gunman now lay on the ground with his hands stretched out. Kenny stood over him with his gun still in hand.

Arya was crying. She glanced over her shoulder and said, "How did they find me?"

"I wiped the address off the GPS in your parents' car, so I don't know, but I can promise you that they won't be able to find you again," Nova responded. "We're going off the grid."

River glanced into the rearview mirror at her as they drove away. "What do you have in mind?"

"I'm going to call Kaleb and Rylee. We could use their help."

"We need to change cars, too," he said.

She punched in a phone number.

They passed two police cars speeding toward the house.

"Kaleb, I need a favor," Nova said when he answered. "I need a safe place to take Arya de Leon. Someplace outside of Miami. She's been compromised." They could lie low and regroup using one of the houses that wasn't even on the Marshals' radar.

"Rylee's going to send Rolle to meet you in Jacksonville," he responded. "We'll let you know the address within the hour."

Nova looked over her shoulder at Arya. She sat in her seat, staring out the window blankly.

Maybe the poor woman is in shock.

"It's going to be a long night," River said.

"I'm glad we're all here to experience it still," she replied with a smile.

"I don't want to die," Arya said. Anguish colored the tone of her words.

"We're going to make sure that doesn't happen," River stated. "We want you to live out the rest of your life without fear."

"I think I will always be afraid."

Nova was struck by how helpless Arya looked right now, and compassion washed over her.

She pulled a cap out of her backpack and held it out to Arya. "Put this on and keep your head low. I wouldn't put it past Poppy or Johnny Boy to have someone monitoring street cameras."

Arya twisted her long hair into a tight bun and secured it with a black scrunchie that was on her wrist. She put the cap on her head, then slipped on a pair of dark sunglasses.

Satisfied, Nova looked to the front.

"What about Kenny? He's going to meet up with us, right?"

River nodded. "I'll send him the location as soon as we get it."

THEY MADE IT safely to Jacksonville.

"We're supposed to meet Rolle at an IHOP off Stanton Road," Nova stated. She released a soft sigh of relief when they arrived. Rolle was there waiting for them as prearranged.

"Good to see y'all," he said when Nova got out of the SUV. "We're switching vehicles, so I'll take the keys to your SUV."

River handed them over. "Here you go. What are we driving?"

"This," Rolle responded while pointing to the car parked next to the SUV.

"Wow…nice…" River walked around the gray Mercedes G 550.

Rolle looked at Nova and asked, "You have the address for the safe house in Alabama?"

"Yeah," she responded.

"Then you're all set. Oh…" He pulled an envelope out of his pocket. "Kaleb sent this. He said that none of you should use credit cards. *Cash only*."

Nova opened the envelope to reveal two thousand dollars in denominations of hundreds, fifties and twenties.

"Thanks for your help," River said.

"No problem. I was in Atlanta to visit my mom. Rylee called and I got on the first flight down here."

"Sorry for disrupting your vacation," Nova said.

"It's all good. I'm flying back home in a couple of hours. I had a day with my mom, so I'm good for another six months."

Nova glanced at River as they walked toward the car. "Why don't you get some rest and let me drive?"

He shook his head. "I'm good," he said before getting in and starting the car.

Nova sat down on the passenger side. "You just want to get behind the wheel of this Benz. I remember you telling me this was your dream car."

He chuckled. "I just thought you might want a break from driving."

"I'll take over in a couple of hours," she responded, settling into her seat and closing her eyes. "Wake me when you want me to take over."

"We're less than eight hours from Birmingham. I can make it."

"Good," Arya uttered. "I'm beginning to feel claustrophobic being in a car for so long."

Although Nova didn't voice it, Arya had more serious concerns than being cooped up in a car. The cartel had no intentions of giving up their search for her.

Chapter Sixteen

"Are you sure this is the right place?" River asked. He stared at the stunning brick home nestled in the prestigious Greystone neighborhood.

"This is the exact address that Kaleb gave me. 5430 Rosemont Circle in Birmingham."

"This house is gorgeous," Arya murmured. "*See*, this is the kind of place I should have in WITSEC."

"Not gonna happen," Nova responded with a chuckle. "The only way you get this type of house—you'll need a high salary to afford this lifestyle."

"Why couldn't I keep some of the money Mateo—"

Nova dismissed her words with a slight wave of her hand. "You already know the answer to that."

Arya sighed. "It isn't fair."

Kenny pulled up, parked and got out. River entered the house ahead of everyone and turned off the alarm. The main level featured a large gourmet kitchen with Corian countertops, a double oven, an eat-in area and a formal dining room. He navigated to the door leading to a screened-in porch with an open deck. The house was gated all around and separated from the other houses behind them by trees. He was pleased to see there were cameras and motion lights.

He joined Arya and Nova in the great room.

Nova pointed toward a hallway. "The master suite is over there," she told the men. "It has dual vanities, a jetted tub and a huge shower. Kaleb texted me some details on the way over."

"That's the room I want," Arya said.

River, Kenny and Nova all looked at her.

"No?"

"No," Nova stated. "Pick a room upstairs."

Listening to the interchange, River knew she was correct. Arya would be safer up there than on the main floor.

"This really sucks," Arya grumbled.

"I'll check out the second level," River said.

"I want to check out the grounds," Kenny stated.

River nodded and followed Nova and Arya upstairs, where they found four bedrooms, each with its own bathroom.

Arya chose the largest one, which came as no surprise.

"How long will we be here?" she asked.

"As long as necessary," Nova answered. "We're waiting on a new ID for you and a new location."

"And my mom will be able to come with me?" she asked.

"We're working out the details," Nova responded.

"Can't I go someplace exotic? I've had enough of small towns. I stand out like a sore thumb. I don't believe it's safe for me."

River returned downstairs and conducted a quick search of the kitchen to see if he had everything he needed in terms of cookware.

"What are you doing?" Nova asked when she strolled into the kitchen.

"I'm making dinner tonight," he announced. "Just checking to see if we have the cookware."

"Write down what you need and Kenny or I will pick it up," she offered.

River recalled the last time he'd made dinner for Nova. It was their last night together. He'd taken her to a restaurant owned by a friend of his. The restaurant was closed on Mondays, so they were the only people inside. She'd kept him company while he prepared their meals.

River forced his thoughts back to the present. This wasn't some romantic gesture on his part. He cleared his throat softly, then said, "Kaleb really came through with this house. It's a nice place."

She nodded. "He did. I already hate having to leave it."

He could feel her watching him as he typed up a shopping list for Kenny.

After a moment, she said, "I need to check in with my supervisor. Then I'm gonna check on Arya."

"I'll let you know when dinner is ready."

NOVA FOUND ARYA sitting on the edge of a king-size bed. Grief was etched all over her tear-streaked face.

"How are you holding up?" she asked.

The woman inhaled deeply. "I'm trying to put on a brave front, but I really miss my old life. I miss my father and Mateo. I. 'm scared all the time."

"We will do everything possible to make sure that you and your mother stay safe."

"Mateo told me he was going to fix everything so that the cartel would leave us alone."

"Did he tell you how he was going to accomplish this?" Nova inquired.

Arya hesitated, then said, "Agent Randolph was right. Mateo went to California to try and negotiate with the cartel. He said that if that didn't work, then he planned to give the Mali cartel information on the Mancuso operations in exchange for money and protection… I had a bad feeling about it, but Mateo… He just wouldn't listen to me."

"Why didn't you call me? I could've tried to talk some sense into Mateo."

"Because he made me promise not to say anything. He said we'd be gone before you realized it. Mateo said he had a plan." Arya started to cry again. "I—I t-told him not to trust those p-people. When he didn't respond to my texts or calls, I called my mother to tell her and Papi to go to the house on Lake Glenville. I thought they'd be safe there since no one knew about it."

"The cartel may have been listening to your mother's calls," Nova said.

Arya wiped her face before asking, "Can you call the hospital to check on my mother?"

"I can do that." Nova picked up her phone, connected with the nurse in charge of Ramona's care and spoke to her for a few minutes.

"Your mother is resting, and she's doing great," Nova said when she ended the call.

Arya released an audible sigh of relief. "Thank goodness." There was a brief pause before she spoke again. "Special Agent Randolph… He's very handsome, don't you think?"

"Let's focus on what's really important," Nova said. "Like telling him everything you know about the cartel."

RIVER HAD NOVA sample the chicken enchiladas after retrieving them from the oven.

"I'm impressed," she said. "Where did you learn to cook like this?"

"Trial and error," River responded. "Along with several cookbooks."

"Well, the enchiladas are delicious."

Nova helped him prepare the plates and carried them to the table.

After Kenny blessed the food, Arya sliced into her chicken enchilada and stuck a forkful in her mouth. "This is really good. Have you ever considered that maybe you're in the wrong line of work?"

"Cooking is a way to relieve stress. I'd never want to make it a career," River said. "I love my job with the DEA."

Wiping her mouth on a napkin, Arya said, "I was furious when Mateo told me he worked for the cartel. I always thought he should be working for some huge corporation. He was very intelligent. He could've worked anywhere he wanted."

"You really didn't know anything about Johnny Boy or Poppy Mancuso until you went into witness protection?" River asked.

Averting her gaze, Arya responded, "I didn't. Mateo didn't take me around his clients or business associates."

He glanced over at Nova, then turned to Arya again. "Your husband mentioned pulling all-nighters in his interview. You were never suspicious when he didn't come home? Most accounting jobs are Monday through Friday, and while some accountants work late, it's usually during tax season, and they aren't in the office all night long."

"Of course I was," Arya answered. "I thought he was having an affair. We fought about it all the time." She picked up her napkin and wiped her mouth again. "Can we change the subject, please? I don't want to talk about this anymore. Not right now."

River picked up his water glass and took a long sip. Arya's body language indicated that she wasn't being completely honest with him.

He was also finding it hard to keep his emotions at bay.

It had been a long time since he'd been around Nova, and River wasn't prepared for how she made him feel.

Just being here in this room with her sent a course of electricity within him. River tried to shake off this feeling of being so alive, but he failed miserably. The part he thought had died rose in him suddenly and refused to be ignored.

After they finished their meal, Kenny volunteered to clean the kitchen and, surprisingly, Arya offered to help him.

When they were done and had gone upstairs, River and Nova settled in the loft.

"Kenny's going to come up and relieve you at midnight," River announced. "I'm probably going to crash. I'm tired."

"You should," she responded with a smile. "Thank you again for such a delicious dinner. It was a lot better than the pizza I thought we'd be eating tonight."

River met her gaze and couldn't look away, feeling that there was a deeper significance to the visual interchange. He pulled Nova toward him and kissed her, surprising them both. Heat sparked in the pit of his stomach and ignited into an overwhelming desire.

He kissed her a second time; his tongue traced the soft fullness of Nova's lips. His mouth covered hers hungrily until he released her, saying, "I'm sorry. I never should've done that. I have no idea what came over me."

Nova chuckled. "If we'd had wine, we could blame it on that."

"I suppose we could pretend that the kiss never happened," River suggested.

She gave a stiff nod. "Yeah, we could do that."

His senses reeled as if short-circuited, but he tried to display an outward calm despite the physical reactions to his desire for Nova. "Maybe we should get back to the reason why we're here."

She agreed.

"I really didn't mean to ravish you like that."

Nova placed two fingers to his mouth and said, "We're fine, River. I have no illusions that the kisses meant anything to you."

"That's not…"

"Good night, River. I'll see you in the morning."

Instead of going to bed like he'd planned, River went down to the office.

He checked the security camera footage displayed on the monitor. He was sure they were safe and hadn't been found, but he intended to stay cautious.

He checked every area more than once.

After conducting a walk-through to make sure the windows and exterior doors were securely locked, River turned on the alarm system before going to the great room. He sank down on the sofa to watch television. He kept the TV volume low.

River felt himself drift off and forced his eyes open. He got up, went to the office, then checked the security cameras once more before navigating to the bedroom to shower.

Afterward, he considered going upstairs to check on the women but pushed the thought away. He didn't want to face Nova just yet. River had given in to his emotions earlier, but it couldn't happen again. He didn't want a repeat of the last time they were together.

Chapter Seventeen

Positioned in the loft across from where Arya lay sleeping, Nova remembered the kisses she'd shared with River over and over in her mind for most of her watch.

She squirmed uncomfortably in the chair she was sitting in. Her back was starting to ache, and every now and then there was numbness in her legs.

Nova stood up and stretched.

She thought she heard movement below and crept over to the railing, looking down. She watched as River strode to the narrow window beside the door and peered outside. He'd changed into a pair of light gray sweats. The socks on his feet cushioned the sound as he walked across the marble floor.

She descended the stairs, whispering loudly, "Is everything okay?"

River turned to face her and said, "I thought I saw lights through the trees. It looked like the vehicle was coming here, but then it turned around. Nobody's out there."

Alarmed, Nova walked over to a window and glanced out. "Are you sure?" Kaleb's brother, Nate, owned the safe house and the adjacent properties on both sides. She was confident that the cartel couldn't have discovered their location.

River nodded. "I am."

She relaxed. "That's good to hear."

"Why don't you go back up there and get some sleep?"

"I'm good," she said while trying to stifle another bout of yawns. "You were supposed to be resting."

"I wasn't as sleepy as I thought," River said. "If you want, you can take the master suite down here and I'll keep watch."

"Kenny should be up taking over shortly."

Nova was touched by his concern but didn't allow herself to think it could be something more. What they'd shared two years ago had been nice. She cherished the memories of their time together, but the reality was that they would both do their jobs, and when Arya and her mother were safe, she and River would say their farewells and that would be the end of it.

"You really need to get some rest," Nova said.

"I will at some point." He smiled, and she couldn't deny the sudden warmth she felt being on the receiving end of that smile. "Good night, Nova."

"Good night."

"I HAVE SOMETHING to tell you both," Arya announced when she came downstairs the next morning.

"What is it?" Nova asked as she poured herself a cup of herbal tea.

"I think it's time I told you the truth," she said, settling across from Nova at the breakfast table. "It's true. Mateo had enough stuff on the cartel to cause some serious damage."

Nova nodded. "What made you change your mind?"

"It finally sunk in that Johnny Boy isn't going to stop until he finds me."

Nova rested her hands on the table. "I'm not going to let that happen, Arya."

River and Kenny joined them a few minutes later.

"Arya wants to talk to you both," Nova stated.

She nodded. "I know all of you will do what you can to keep me safe, but Johnny Boy means to kill me. At least you'll know everything if that happens."

"I meant what I said," Nova told her. "We are going to protect you with everything we have."

Despite the danger seemingly all around them, this was the very thing that Nova had trained for—she was willing to risk her life to save Arya. She'd followed her father's path to become a marshal because it was admirable work. Nova also thought it took courage to enter the witness protection program—having to be separated from loved ones, often living in strange cities, then having to lie to everyone and look over a shoulder for the rest of the individual's life. Arya was doing the right thing.

Nova took a sip of her tea. "The best chance for being safe is following my instructions, Arya. And by telling River everything you know."

Arya carefully opened the silver locket hanging from her neck and extracted a small, black micro SD card. She held it out to River with a determined look in her eyes.

Nova couldn't believe it—all the evidence to bring down the cartel was in his hands.

"It's all there. Some of the information you already have, but there was a whole lot more that my husband didn't give the DEA all those times he met with them."

"I knew it," River exclaimed.

Nova left Arya alone in the room with River and Kenny. She went to the office and eyed the quad split screen, checking the multiple security cameras on the property. Although she was confident that they wouldn't have any unwanted visitors, Nova wanted to be prepared if there were any signs of suspicious activity on the property. Her Glock was loaded and ready.

She made another call to the hospital requesting an update on Ramona Lozano.

"Mrs. Lozano's wounds are healing nicely," Nova was told.

Arya's mother had been moved to another location, which would be safer for her. "Have there been any calls asking about her?"

"No, ma'am."

"That's good to hear."

Nova found a couple of articles online about the deaths of Pablo and Ramona Lozano. She printed them. She wanted to prepare Arya before she found them herself.

RIVER SLIPPED THE SD card into his laptop while Arya picked up an apple and took a bite out of it. He'd spent the past hour being filled in on what Arya knew and now he wanted to dive into the evidence. His eyes widened as he realized that all the evidence they needed against the powerful cartel was contained on that small card.

As he scrolled through the files, Arya said, "You now have everything, Special Agent Randolph. More financial records, lists of properties owned by the cartel—even drug shipments."

"Mateo kept meticulous records," he said. River was relieved to have this information and someone else who could testify.

"So, what do you think?" Nova asked when River entered the office an hour later. "Can you use any of what she gave you?"

"We have some solid and damaging evidence," he answered. "I can see why Mateo tried to blackmail Poppy. This information could potentially topple a huge part of her dynasty. However, it's going to be a challenge getting to her since she's hiding on a private island near Ecuador and there is no extradition to the United States."

"I believed Arya when she told me that Mateo kept her out of the loop. She lied to me."

"She was protecting her husband."

"I'm beginning to think she knew all along that Mateo worked for the Mancuso cartel."

"I've always believed that," River said.

"Where is she?" Nova asked.

"She's still in the dining room with Kenny."

"I checked in with the hospital. Her mother's doing well."

"You should tell her," River said. "I need to make some phone calls. Mind if I sit in here?"

Nova pushed away from the desk. "It's all yours. By the way, I checked the security cameras—nothing unusual." She placed a hand on her weapon.

"Keep an eye on Arya," River said. "I'll be out shortly."

Nova left the office.

He called his supervisor first, then the federal prosecutor to update. "I have great news. I have the rest of the information DeSoto didn't turn over to us earlier. I'll email everything over to you in a few minutes."

River was grateful to Nova. He knew that she was part of the reason Arya had agreed to come forward.

Chapter Eighteen

After Arya went to bed, Nova and River sat down on the stairs.

She'd been wanting to have another conversation with him, but thought it best to wait for an opening. He gave her that when he said, "I keep thinking about the night you came to my hotel room. You could've talked to me about your feelings, Nova. You didn't have to run away. Your silence and absence spoke volumes."

"I realize that I handled things wrong," she responded. She wanted to be completely honest with River. "When we first got together, I didn't think either of us was looking for anything serious."

"So, you were just in it to have a good time—nothing more?"

She looked over at him. "I'm not saying that at all, River."

"Then exactly what are you saying?"

"We lived over three thousand miles apart. I really didn't have any preconceived notions about what was going on between us. I knew that neither one of us wanted a relationship that might interfere with our jobs—remember we talked about that? It's probably why I honestly never expected you to make any type of declaration. Especially so soon."

"To be honest, I surprised myself when I said it," River confessed. "I have to admit that I never expected things between us to become so passionate. It scared me, too, but I was willing to take a chance with you. I thought you felt the same way."

"That's why I regret leaving. I wish more than anything that I'd just talked to you that night."

"I wish you had," he responded. "I've had to deal with rejection all of my life and it's not been easy for me to trust someone with my heart." River wished he could rescind the words that had just come out of his mouth. He hadn't meant to share his personal pain with her. Not like this. He didn't want her pity.

She reached over and took his hand in her own. "I'm really sorry."

River gave a slight shrug. "You don't have to apologize."

"Yes, I do," Nova insisted. "You deserved better than what I gave you."

"I appreciate that you didn't lie about your feelings."

"You must know that I cared deeply for you, River. And since we're being honest… I didn't realize just how much until after I left."

He gave a wry smile. "It's all in the past now."

Nova swallowed hard, then said, "I've really missed talking to you."

River eyed her. "Same here."

"Do you think we can try being friends?" she asked.

"Sure. If that's what you want."

She nodded. "I'd really like that."

His cell phone rang. "I need to take this call." River stood up and walked down the stairs.

NOVA SAT THERE wondering if he was going to come back upstairs. When ten minutes passed, she got up and moved to the loft.

At some point, she must have fallen asleep, because when Nova woke up, it was around 2:00 a.m. Kenny was seated in a chair across from her. He was watching something on his phone.

He glanced over at her and smiled.

Nova got up and checked on Arya, then crept down the staircase. She was hungry.

She was surprised to find that River was still up.

"When I finally got off the call, you were asleep," he said.

"I'm really glad we had a conversation," Nova responded while looking for something to snack on. "I know it doesn't change anything."

"It doesn't change things, but we don't have all that tension between us any longer." He opened the refrigerator. "There's some fruit, cheese and crackers."

"You must be snacky, too."

"I had an apple. I finished it just before you came down."

Leaning against the counter, Nova asked, "River, what did you mean when you said you've been dealing with rejection all your life?"

His expression became unreadable. "It's nothing."

"Please don't do that. *Talk to me.*"

"My mother never wanted me," he announced. "After I was born, she left me with her mother. She was only sixteen at the time, so my grandmother raised me. She got married when she was twenty, but even before that... I don't remember having a real relationship with Mary—that was her name. I think back then she was like a sister to me."

Nova's heart broke at the thought of River having to grow up feeling rejected by his mother. She couldn't imagine what that was like. "And you two were in the same house?"

River nodded. "There were a few times when she'd help me with my schoolwork... She'd buy me a toy every now and then, but that was it. After she got married, Mary and her husband had a baby girl. They loved Bonnie dearly. I think Mary always wanted a girl."

"She never came back for you?" Nova asked.

"No. I was never in Mary's heart. I was only an inconvenience to her."

"Did her husband know that she was your mother?"

"My grandmother told him. He welcomed me, but Mary told him that her mother refused to part with me."

Nova hurt for River. "I'm so sorry."

His gaze downcast, he shrugged in nonchalance. "It's fine. I had a wonderful grandmother and she loved me until the day she died."

Nova reached for his hand, which had settled near hers, then thought better of making contact. They were still in a fragile state. "But I'm sure it hurts that your mother rejected you. Is she still alive?"

"Mary died about six months ago."

"Did you attend her funeral?"

"I did, but only because Bonnie said she needed me to be there with her," River responded.

"You and your sister have a good relationship, then?" Nova inquired.

"Yes, we do. I'm thankful that Mary didn't try to discourage my getting to know Bonnie. I love my sister."

They walked across the hall to check the security cameras.

"So far, so good," she murmured. "I spoke with Sabra earlier, and from what she's gathered from cartel conversations, Johnny Boy is furious with his men for losing the package." Sabra was a tech on the task force Rylee had put together, and her intel had been helpful.

"That's pretty much what I expected," he responded.

"That SD card Arya handed over is a definite threat to his organization. I feel good knowing that he's most likely losing sleep over this."

"I'm with you there," Nova said. "Every time I think of Calderon in prison for the rest of his life plus one hundred and thirty-five years…it makes me really happy. Although he didn't actually shoot my father, he is still responsible. I wonder how he feels about being so easily replaced by Johnny Boy as Poppy's right hand."

"You have a right to your feelings, Nova." River paused a moment, then asked, "Are you wanting to leave the Marshals because of your father?"

"That's a part of it."

River wrapped his arms around her, drawing her closer in his embrace. With her body pressed to his like this, he felt blood coursing through his veins like an awakened river.

Their eyes locked as their breathing came in unison.

Nova tried to ignore the aching in her limbs and the pulsing knot that had formed in her stomach.

Without a word, River swept her up, weightless, into his arms.

He carried her to the first-floor bedroom, where he eased her down onto the bed.

He unbuttoned her blouse, but before River could go any further, he abruptly pulled away, saying, "I'm sorry. I can't do this to myself a second time."

His rejection was like a bucket of cold water, washing over Nova and cooling her ardor.

"It's okay," she said while buttoning up her top. "I understand."

But the truth was that she didn't understand at all.

Nova looked up at him, noting his pain-filled gaze. "You're just not ready."

"You are such a beautiful woman. I..."

"It's okay." She shrugged. "Why don't we just keep this at friendship?"

He nodded. "I'm sorry."

"Stop apologizing, River. It's not necessary." Nova wanted him to know that he didn't need to protect himself from her. Not this time. "I've always cared about you."

"Let's not do this..."

"We're supposed to be having an honest conversation." She really wanted him to hear her heart through her words.

"And I'm speaking in truth."

"So am I," Nova said. "I just need you to listen and hear me."

"I can't do this right now," he responded. "I'm sorry."

He walked out of the bedroom.

"No," she whispered, "I'm sorry."

River woke up from a dream about Nova that had quickly become erotic. He turned from one side to the other, trying to escape thoughts of her, but it wasn't meant to be. She was still heavy on his mind.

He had thoroughly enjoyed spending time with her in the early morning hours. For a moment, River had been able to forget that so much time had passed between them. It felt like old times.

Nova never did anything to try to impress him—she was comfortable in her own skin, which was a quality he greatly admired.

When River thought of how he'd reacted last night, he felt like a heel for running out on her. He should have just explained that he felt it was best to have a platonic relationship. He never should have gotten involved with her on a personal level. From the moment River saw her that first time, he'd known that his life would never be the same.

"I should have kept it business between us," he whispered. "From the very beginning."

It was too late then and it was too late now.

River was still in love with her.

Chapter Nineteen

Nova hoped to avoid River, but he opened the door to the room he'd slept in just as she walked by.

"Good morning," she said, not looking at him. "I'm glad you finally got some sleep."

"I'm sorry about last night."

She shrugged in nonchalance. "Forget about it. I have." Nova wasn't about to let him know how much his rejection hurt.

His eyebrows arched a fraction at her words. The air suddenly felt thick with tension between them as they went downstairs.

River followed her into the kitchen and tried to make small talk, but Nova didn't have much to say.

"Nova…"

"I mean it," she interjected. "Let's just forget about it."

"It's not that easy for me," he responded.

"That sounds like a *you* problem," she said, walking over to the refrigerator and retrieving the carton of eggs. She was embarrassed and just needed some distance.

River left the kitchen without another word.

Nova was relieved because she needed some time alone

to process her feelings. She could no longer deny that she was falling in love with him.

She cooked several slices of bacon, scrambled six eggs and made four slices of toast. When everything was ready, she went upstairs.

Nova ran into Arya coming out of her bedroom. "I was just coming to tell you that breakfast is ready."

She stopped by the office. "Breakfast is ready," she told River and Kenny.

Ten minutes later, they all sat at the table, eating in silence.

River was the first to finish his food.

Pushing away from the table, he said, "I'll be in the office if you need me."

She nodded, then reached for her glass of orange juice and took a sip. Kenny left a moment later.

"Nova, I'm sorry for lying to you after everything you've done to keep me safe," Arya said when they were alone. "Mateo really thought he could get the cartel to back off. He went to Los Angeles to meet with Poppy. He figured she'd do anything to get that information back."

Wiping her mouth, Nova said, "Like I told you before, you should've come to me. If you had, I would've done everything I could to keep him safe, even if it meant holding him in custody."

Arya leaned back in her seat. "I have to live with the choices I've made for the rest of my life. I've lost two important men in my life. I pray I don't lose my mother. I don't think I could bear it."

"If there's anything else that you know about the cartel, you should tell River and Kenny."

"I will," she responded. "Because there is more."

Stunned, Nova met her gaze. "Are you telling me that you're still withholding evidence?"

"I've given him all the files. I just didn't tell him everything that I know yesterday."

"This isn't a game, Arya."

"I know that."

Nova called out for River and Kenny to join them.

"What's going on?" they asked in unison.

Arya appeared slightly embarrassed before admitting, "I need to tell you—"

"If you're going to confess that you knew he was working for the cartel, I figured as much," River interjected.

Kenny put his phone on the table. He was recording the conversation.

"I've always known about my husband's relationship with members of the cartel..." She glanced over at Nova before adding, "That's because I urged him to work for them."

Nova's mouth dropped open. She hadn't expected to hear anything close to this.

"You have to understand..." Arya continued. "My parents weren't supportive when my husband and I married. They didn't think he was good enough for me and refused to give us any financial support. We were so poor at the time, and I didn't want to live that way. I knew my uncle worked for the Mali cartel and I wanted what my cousin had... Glitz and glamour...fancy parties and private jets. I wanted it all."

Arya clasped her hands together and hid them in the folds of her ruffled maxi skirt. "My husband was a small-time drug dealer when we met in college. My friend connected him with her boyfriend and soon he was working for the Mancuso cartel. After he graduated, he moved up the ranks and started handling the money." She paused a moment, then said, "My background is also in accounting, although

I also had a real estate license. On occasion, I'd help him reconcile the books, usually around the end of the year. I'd also help him find opportunities to launder the money."

Floored, Nova glanced over at River, who said, "What you're telling me is that you also worked for the cartel."

"Yes," she responded. "I found property for them. The cartel owns a building on Front Street in Los Angeles. It used to be a clothing store. There's nothing there now, but according to the paperwork filed at the end of the fiscal year, it's bringing in over a hundred thousand in sales each month."

"Are you telling us that they're laundering money through a store that's closed?" River asked.

Arya nodded, then said, "That's not the only one. They have several businesses like that—empty storefronts that show a profit on the books. They buy lots of commercial properties. Houses, too. They also have several legitimate businesses. A nightclub on Sunset Boulevard, a couple of hair salons and beauty-supply stores. They own several shell corporations, but the largest is Grupo Worldwide Holdings Inc."

Nova sat there listening to the woman she'd believed to be an innocent victim in all this.

"Have you ever been around Johnny Boy?" River inquired.

"Once," she responded. "And I'm sure it was really him. Not one of the fake Johnnys."

"Why do you say that?" he asked.

"Because he had a tattoo of his father on his chest with the initials *CR* below it. Six months before they discovered we were stealing from them, we were invited to a pool party at one of his houses. The host was supposed to be Johnny Boy. Only he wasn't the host. He was just another guest.

At least, he pretended to be one. I'd drunk a lot and had to go to the bathroom, and when I came out, I glimpsed this guy in one of the bedrooms with some girl. He didn't have on a shirt. That's when I saw the tattoo. It's pretty large."

"Did he see you?" Nova asked.

"I don't think so. I got out of there as quickly as I could, because if he had, I'd probably be dead already."

"Why didn't you tell us any of this before?" River asked.

"Because Mateo was trying to keep me safe," she responded. "I hope you get Johnny Boy. *I hop he dies.*"

"Is there anything else you can tell us?" Nova inquired.

"I've told you everything. The rest is on that SD card." Arya paused a moment, then said, "I never even told Mateo about seeing that tattoo. I couldn't risk anyone finding out that I could identify Johnny Boy. I want to stay far away from these people—they've destroyed my life." She looked at River. "I don't want to have to testify."

"We can request anonymity," he responded. "If granted, none of the defendants will know who you are."

"If you can really do that, then I will testify to what I know," Arya said, "but I'm hoping that with the information and evidence you have in hand, you won't need me at all."

"I can't make any promises. I will need to speak with the federal prosecutor about all this."

"I understand."

"Arya, we will do everything we can to ensure you're safe," River said.

Arya glanced at Nova. "I hope you'll be able to get my mom into the program with me. If she's with me…we can completely disappear together." Arya stretched, asking to retreat to her bedroom for some rest. River nodded.

After she left, Nova said, "If Arya never told Mateo about

the tattoo, then Johnny Boy may have no idea that anyone outside of his small circle knows about it."

"I'm glad she finally decided to come clean." River shook his head. "I had no idea just how involved she was. She worked for the cartel."

"Makes sense to me why they're after her," Kenny said.

Kaleb called Nova later that afternoon. "We've heard some chatter. Johnny Boy isn't a happy man these days. He wants his lost package found. He's now offering bonuses to the person who finds it."

"Arya knows too much. She can also identify Johnny Boy. She's going to need round-the-clock security until his arrest."

Kaleb agreed.

The next few days went much the same. Cohen gave his approval to keep Arya in Birmingham for now. After breakfast, Arya rehearsed her new backstory in the WIT-SEC program; they took an hour and a half for lunch, then more practice to perfect her new identity. After dinner, Arya spent an hour or so with River and Kenny, discussing her time in the cartel.

Nova thought about how much she would miss working with the Marshals Service, but she was super excited about the next chapter in her career. Her eyes strayed to River.

If only she had someone to share it with.

River went outside after Arya went upstairs to her room after dinner one night.

Nova found him sitting on the patio half an hour later. They hadn't talked about what had almost happened a few nights ago or how it made her feel.

"I realized something from the other night," she said. "I fully understand how you must have felt when I left without saying anything to you. I want to apologize for that, River."

He met her gaze. "Apology accepted."

He was still peering at her intently. Nova saw the heart-rending tenderness of his gaze. She secretly hoped that River would ask her to stay outside a while longer, but he didn't, much to her disappointment.

"I'll see you tomorrow morning," she said.

"G'night."

Nova tried to swallow the lump lingering in her throat.

She was falling in love with a man who would never be able to return that love. The thought shattered her heart into a million little pieces.

RIVER STOOD OUTSIDE the room Nova was in. He'd been there for almost ten minutes before finally deciding to knock.

She opened the door, then stepped aside to let him enter.

"Tomorrow, Arya and I will travel to meet with the marshals transporting her mother," Nova announced. "Her documents will arrive in the morning. I don't want to prolong this any longer."

River nodded in understanding. "She won't be in your custody after that."

"I know. I might even miss her."

They stood staring at one another with longing. There was no denying that they shared an intense physical awareness of each other.

Without warning, River pulled Nova into his arms, kissing her. He held her snugly.

"I'm so glad you're here."

He gazed down at her with tenderness. "I will be here for as long as you need me."

Parting her lips, Nova raised herself to meet his kiss.

His lips pressed against hers, then gently covered her mouth. River showered her with kisses around her lips and along her jaw. As he roused her passion, his own grew stronger.

This time, it was Nova who slowly pulled away. She took him by the hand and led him over to the edge of the bed.

They sat down.

"Being around Kaleb and Rylee reminds me of how much I'm lacking when it comes to love," Nova said. "I've never admitted this to anyone, but I get lonely sometimes."

"So do I," River confessed. "Growing up, I used sports to take my mind off how lonely I felt. Now I use work."

His closeness was so male, so bracing.

River stroked her cheek. "What are you thinking about?"

"You want the truth?" she asked.

He nodded.

"I was thinking about how long it's been since I've been this close to a man. How long it's been since I've kissed a man or made love." She raised her eyes to meet his. "It's been a while."

"Same here," River murmured.

"I'm not trying to seduce you," she said quickly. "I meant what I said about us being friends."

"I was thinking about hanging around in Charlotte for a few more days when we get there. I can change my plane ticket. That is if you don't mind showing a friend around the city."

She broke into a grin. "I don't mind at all."

He reluctantly and quietly made his way to the door and eased it open. "Good night."

It was getting harder and harder to walk away from Nova.

Chapter Twenty

Nova's mission was a simple, protective security detail: take Arya to the checkpoint, hand her off to the next set of marshals who would settle her in her new location, and head back to Charlotte.

They were nearly in Tennessee—Nova had accompanied another marshal in moving Arya securely to the handover point. "How is everything going?" River asked when she called to check in while at a gas station.

"It's going. I've considered taping Arya's mouth up a few times," she admitted. "We're about thirty minutes away from the destination."

He chuckled. "Exercise patience, beautiful."

"I'm trying," Nova said. "After the handoff, I'm heading straight to the airport. I'll get home close to six."

"I'll see you then."

His words brought a smile to her lips. "Same here."

When she hung up, Arya said, "I knew something was going on between you and Special Agent Randolph."

Nova didn't respond. She slid back into the passenger seat, next to the marshal who was transporting them.

When they passed the sign welcoming them to White Water, Tennessee, Arya said, "I don't think anybody will ever think to look for me here. I've never even heard of this place. It looks kinda depressing."

"That's the idea," she responded. "We don't want anyone to find you."

"What is there to do in White Water? And where is there to shop to find *real* clothes? I'm not a Target kind of girl."

"The town is close to Memphis," Nova responded. "It's a thirty-minute drive. But, Arya, you really must be careful. You can't forget for one minute that Johnny Boy wants to silence you permanently."

"That's good to know about Memphis." Arya looked out of the passenger window. "As for that murderous Johnny Boy.I. hope somebody kills him."

"Thanks to you, we now have a good shot at finding the man."

"I wish I didn't have to have another handler."

Nova hated having to turn her charge over to someone else, but it was for the best. "You'll be fine, and I think you'll really like him," Nova reassured her. "Just follow the rules... You and your mom will be safe."

Arya nodded. "It's been a painful lesson to learn."

Nova glanced over at the marshal who was driving them, and smiled. She truly hoped Arya was serious.

"I appreciate you letting me pick out my new name. I've always loved the name Ariel. *Ariel Ramos.* I love it."

"Glad to hear it," she replied with a smile.

"Will my mother be there when we arrive? Sorry... I mean my aunt Rosa."

Nova looked out the front passenger window. She'd been checking periodically to make sure they hadn't picked up a tail. "If not, she should be arriving shortly."

"I can't wait to see her."

Nova released the breath she was holding when they arrived at the designated meeting location. She opened the door. "Stay inside," she told Arya. Hand on her duty weapon, she walked around to check the perimeter.

Deputy Marshal Hightower, who'd driven them, remained near the vehicle.

They were the first to arrive.

Nova walked back to the SUV and got back inside. "They should be arriving soon."

"You don't think anything happened to them?" Arya asked.

"Nothing outside of traffic, maybe."

An SUV like the one they were in pulled up a few minutes later.

Arya reached for the door handle. "Why aren't we getting out?"

"Just wait," Nova uttered.

Hightower got out of the vehicle first and walked over to talk to the driver of the other SUV.

"You can get out now," she confirmed.

Nova escorted Arya over to the waiting vehicle, which held Ramona. Nova's eyes watered at the emotional reunion between mother and daughter, who would now live as aunt and niece.

When they were back in the SUV, she said, "Drop me off at the airport in Memphis, please."

Nova eagerly anticipated going back home and reuniting with River. She was thankful for the opportunity to mend their friendship, but she wasn't expecting too much. After all, she was the one who had left. But she'd apologized for the past. Now it was up to River to take the next step.

DESPITE HER RESERVE, Nova threw herself into River's arms the moment he arrived at her house. "I'm so happy to see you."

She'd called him as soon as her plane landed, then rushed home to shower before his arrival.

"Same here," he responded, sweeping her into his arms. His mouth covered hers hungrily.

Nova gave herself freely to the passion of his kiss before stepping out of his embrace to say, "Let's get business out of the way first. Your witness and her mother are safe and secure in their new location." She handed him a business card from her pocket. "Here is the contact of her new case agent. For the next two weeks, they'll have twenty-four-hour security and stay in a safe house before moving to their new home."

"Thank you," he said.

"Where's Kenny?" she asked.

"Hanging out with some of the local DEA agents. He wanted to enjoy himself before his flight back to LA."

Nova chuckled. "I'm sure. It feels good to breathe finally," she said. "I like Arya, but I'm thrilled that someone else is responsible for her. She's more cunning than I ever thought."

"I agree."

"And right now, she's the only person who can potentially identify Johnny Boy."

Nova poured two glasses of red wine, then handed one to River.

After preparing plates laden with cheese, crackers, pepperoni and hot-and-spicy chorizo, they sat down on the sofa.

"I don't feel like I can fully relax until Johnny Boy's off the streets," Nova said. "Poppy will still be out there somewhere, though. Once I close out this WITSEC case, I'm turning in my resignation and going after them both."

River took a sip of wine, then bit into a cracker covered with cheese and pepperoni. "You'll be a great asset to Rylee's team."

"I think so," Nova responded.

River's phone rang.

"You've got to be kidding me…" she muttered, sitting up. "Tell Kenny he has terrible timing."

"It's not him," he responded.

Nova nodded and gave him some privacy. She went to her office and quickly checked her email.

River appeared in the doorway moments later. "Johnny Boy's been located. Kenny and I have to catch an early flight to Arizona in the morning."

She couldn't contain her excitement. "Where is he?"

"He's hidden in some remote hideaway between Arizona and the Mexican border," River stated. "Kenny and I will participate in his capture as part of the Native American Targeted Investigation of Violent Enterprises Task Force. They're called NATIVE for short."

Nova knew of the group. Her father had first told her of the elite group of Native American trackers working within US Immigration and Customs Enforcement. The team patrolled their portion of the border between Arizona and Mexico in the fight against drug and human trafficking. "You'll be working with the Shadow Wolves, then," Nova said.

"You know about them?"

"My dad told me about them. Have you worked with them before?"

"I have," River said. "One of their team members, Ray Redhorse, is a good friend of mine."

"How do you know that it's really Johnny Boy?"

"We don't, but it's the only credible lead we have, so we're going to pursue it," he responded. "Thanks to Arya, we should be able to verify if it's him or not."

"I'm going with you," Nova announced. "I want to be

there when you take Johnny Boy down. He killed my witness."

"Nova…"

"Don't try to stop me, River. This is important to me."

After a moment, he nodded. "Clear it with Cohen. You will have to follow my lead."

"I can do that," she agreed. "Just let me go up and grab my bag. I keep one packed and ready to go."

As they headed out the door fifteen minutes later, Nova couldn't shake the dull sense of foreboding she felt.

"YOU JUST GETTING BACK?" River asked Kenny when he answered the door to his hotel room.

"Yep." He glanced over at Nova and grinned. "You tagging along?"

"I intend to do my part in taking down Johnny Boy," she responded. "It got personal when he killed Mateo."

Kenny nodded in understanding. "I feel you."

River quickly packed his travel bag, then set it on the floor across from the king-size bed. He was glad to have Nova along on this operation. She was calm under pressure and a great shot. He trusted her instincts.

But there was more.

For so long, River had believed he didn't deserve love, but Nova made him feel otherwise. Maybe once this was over… He stopped the thought from forming. He didn't like making too many plans when he was about to go on an operation like this. River wasn't worried about the outcome—he had confidence in his abilities and the team he was working with. But he knew all too well how things could go left in the blink of an eye.

He preferred to take it day by day.

Catching Johnny Boy would be a massive victory for

the DEA and his career. River looked forward to the day
he could look the drug trafficker in the face. There would
be one less threat on the streets. He was smart enough to
know that another would rise for each one they took down,
but River would never stop fighting.

He glanced over at Nova. "Let's get out of here."

Downstairs in the lobby they waited for Kenny, who was
still packing.

Fifteen minutes later, they were headed to the airport.

The drive was filled with a tense silence. River could feel
the weight of their mission hanging in the air, suffocating
any casual conversation they might have had. Nova stared
out the window, seemingly lost in her own thoughts, while
Kenny fiddled with the radio, searching for a distraction.

As they arrived at the airport, the atmosphere shifted.
Energy crackled around them as travelers hurried by, oblivi-
ous to the dangerous game River and his team were about
to play.

They made their way through security without incident,
blending seamlessly into the bustling crowd.

River couldn't help but steal glances at Nova as they navigated through the maze of corridors. Something about her
drew him in—the way she carried herself with unshakable
determination, her unwavering loyalty to their cause. But
it was more than that. Her presence offered him hope amid
the darkness they were about to face.

They reached the gate just as their flight was boarding.
River watched as the flight attendants checked tickets and
passengers shuffled onto the plane. He could feel the anticipation building within him, knowing that this mission held
the key to everything they had been fighting for.

River noticed a subtle shift in Nova's demeanor as they
handed their tickets to the flight attendant. Her usually

steely gaze softened, a flicker of vulnerability betraying her facade of strength. It was at that moment that he realized she was just as weighed down by the gravity of their task as he was.

The team settled into their seats.

River glanced out the window, catching a glimpse of his reflection in the glass. His face, worn with determination and sacrifice, revealed the toll of this impending fight on him. He wondered if there would ever be a time when he could be free and wouldn't have to bear the world's weight on his shoulders.

As the plane taxied down the runway, Nova turned to River, and their eyes locked briefly, a silent understanding passing between them.

They were in this together, no matter what lay ahead.

THE ENGINES DRONED ON, drowning out the noise of the doubts and fears that echoed within Nova's mind. The plane accelerated, and soon, they were airborne. The turbulence rattled the cabin, but she found solace in the chaos. It reminded her that even amid uncertainty and upheaval, she could still find her footing.

With each passing minute, their destination grew closer. They were heading into the heart of darkness, where victory awaited them or… Nova couldn't shake the feeling that this mission was different from all the others they had undertaken before.

She leaned closer to him, her voice barely audible over the whir of the engines. "River, this isn't going to be an easy fight. So far, Johnny Boy has been two steps ahead of us."

He turned to face her, his eyes filled with conviction. "I know," River replied, his voice steady, although laced with concern. "But we've trained for this. And I've got you watching my back. I'm not worried."

Nova nodded, taking comfort in his unyielding confidence. River had a way of grounding her, reminding her that they were stronger together than apart. She squeezed his hand, their fingers intertwining in a silent promise to face whatever awaited them.

The once turbulent skies began to clear as the plane pierced through the dense clouds. The sun's golden rays spilled into the cabin, casting a warm glow that breathed life into Nova's troubled soul. It was as if the Lord offered His blessings for the mission ahead.

She was excited to meet the Shadow Wolves team, a group of elite operatives chosen for their unparalleled expertise in covert operations. Each member had their unique skills and backgrounds, but together they formed a formidable force, ready to face any challenge that came their way.

They landed two hours later.

A DEA agent based in Arizona picked them up and transported them to the base of their operations. The Shadow Wolves contingent and agents from the DEA and ATF awaited them.

"Are Redhorse and his team sure it's Johnny Boy?" Kenny asked in a low voice.

"As sure as any of us can be," River replied. "He was sighted in Sells, Arizona. Ray told me he could sneak into an area where cartel members were supposed to be on watch— instead, they were sleeping. He said he got close enough to get a pretty good look at the man. He believes that it's Johnny Boy. Not some look-alike."

"You're saying that he was basically in the cartel's camp, and nobody saw him?" Nova questioned. "He'd have to be a *ghost*. Johnny Boy's too paranoid to sleep that deep."

"Ray's team nicknamed him Fade because of his uncanny ability to become a part of the scene without being detected," River said. "It means ghost or spirit, so you're right. I wouldn't be surprised if he slipped a sleeping aid in their coffee or something."

"Regardless, that's impressive," she responded.

"Wait until you see the Shadow Wolves in action," River said. "They can look at desert vegetation and tell how recently a twig has been broken, a blade of grass trampled by a human, or how many smugglers there are and which direction they were headed. I guess it's because they grew up comfortable with nature and know how to hear silent things and see the invisible in the desert."

"Wow," she murmured. "They have some serious tracking skills."

"Passed down from the elders, according to Ray," River said.

Nova looked up at him. "What about modern technology?"

"They have night-vision goggles, but it's been a while since I was on a task force with the Shadow Wolves," River answered. "What equipment they had back then didn't come close to the high-dollar toys the cartel can afford. But regardless of expensive technology, there still needs to be a person in the field. This is what the Shadow Wolves do well. They rely on traditional methods of tracking."

The room designated for the briefing was dimly lit, the air carrying a tangible air of anticipation. Nova fell into step behind River and Kenny as they made their way to a table situated in the middle, flanked by other law enforcement officials. The atmosphere buzzed with a mix of hushed conversations as everyone prepared for the critical briefing.

As Nova took her seat, she stole a glance at River. The

presence of two additional US marshals entering the room brought a reassuring sense of unity. Cohen, her supervisor, had worked his magic with some last-minute negotiations to secure permission for Nova's involvement. Her father's collaboration with the local agency had played a crucial role several times in the past. Still, Nova's proven performance during the prior investigation with River had truly tipped the scales in her favor.

The dynamics of the room shifted subtly as the briefing commenced. Maps were spread across the whiteboard, detailing the intricate web of the upcoming operation. The plan unfolded like a chessboard, each move considered, calculated and executed with precision.

Nova's attention remained focused, her mind absorbing the details and contingencies. The room became a hive of activity, with agents discussing tactics, sharing intelligence and preparing for the challenges ahead. The collective expertise in the room allowed for a well-coordinated effort, a symphony of skills coming together for a common purpose.

One by one, the agents filed out of the room, each grabbing their tactical gear and checking their weapons before heading off to complete their final preparations.

Chapter Twenty-One

Nova stared out the window, taking in the rugged, mountainous landscape dotted with mesquite trees and cacti, as she, River and Kenny headed to the cartel's known location in the desert. The muted browns, yellows and greens were interrupted by occasional pops of vibrant red desert flowers. In the distance, a few humble buildings could be seen, signaling the location of tribal lands.

"I can see why the cartel would choose this terrain near the border," Kenny said. "It's wide-open land."

"It's desert," River responded. "Since Calderon's arrest, nearly half of the Mancuso drugs are now coming through Mexico and across the international boundary through the Tohono O'odham reservation."

They arrived at their destination twenty-five minutes later.

A muscular man approached and River conducted introductions between Nova, Kenny and Ray Redhorse.

Ray introduced his team. "We have another member," he said. "Ben Chee...he's out following a *sign*."

"What type of sign?" Nova asked.

"We use a technique called *cutting for sign*. Cutting is

how we search for and evaluate a sign. This includes footprints, tire tracks, thread or clothing."

Nova listened with interest. "River said that you were able to sneak into a cartel camp once, and nobody saw you."

Nodding, Ray replied, "I'd been tracking them for a few hours. I waited until they made camp and fell asleep. Their spotter didn't even see me."

"You really are a ghost," Kenny said.

Nova nodded in agreement. She was in awe of Ray Redhorse and glad to have the Shadow Wolves accompanying them on this operation.

Ray chuckled. "I just try very hard not to get caught."

"The last time I was here, Ray made this incredible jackrabbit stew," River said. "I'd never tasted any rabbit and wasn't interested in trying it, but he talked me into it. He cooked it over an open fire, which had a smoky flavor. It was *delicious*."

"I told River he'd starve if he didn't eat it," Ray responded with a chuckle.

"You made something else… It tasted like asparagus."

"Oh, the buds from a cholla cactus."

"The man is a ghost and can cook," Nova stated. "Now I'm really impressed."

"You haven't seen nothing yet," River responded.

RAY REDHORSE DROVE his truck slowly, with River, Nova and Kenny riding along. He kept his window open and carefully examined the ground as he drove.

"Anyone coming north had to travel this path," he explained.

Ray suddenly stopped and got out of the truck. He crouched down to study what seemed to be scrapes in the sand. "Looks like they tied carpet strips to their shoes. They're trying to hide their footprints."

"How long ago?" River asked.

"Most likely late yesterday." Ray pointed to a print. "See that groove? A rat probably made it during the night. The traffickers could be far away by now."

Kenny sighed. "We missed them."

"This desert is huge," Ray said. "Traffickers don't rely on a specific route. They have a labyrinth of routes to utilize. The cartel uses spotters in the mountains to warn traffickers when to change their route."

"So, then we take out the *eyes*," River stated.

"The cartel will send a replacement," Ray responded. "We can take them down all day, but like ants...they'll just keep replacing them."

They all got back into the truck.

Ray drove down another path.

Fresh tire tracks shimmered in the sunlight, while older footprints overlapped with insect trails.

The three men got out of the truck a second time.

Ray fingered a burlap fiber snagged by the thorns on mesquite bushes. He held it to his nose, sniffing it. "This came from a bag filled with marijuana."

They scanned the area before climbing back into the vehicle. Ray drove around the mesquite bushes. "It's getting worse out here. Lately, we've had some problems with machine gun–wielding thieves lying in wait to steal drugs from the traffickers," he said. "And a couple of cartels fighting over ownership of certain routes."

"I see you have your friend with you," River said, referring to Ray's M4 ssault rifle.

"I never leave home without it."

River glanced over at Nova. "How are you feeling about all this?"

"All I can think about is capturing Johnny Boy and his many minions. The Mancuso cartel robbed me of my father and a witness. I want to take down as many of them as possible."

"I understand," River responded. "They took out two DEA agents... One of them was like a brother to me."

The fire burning in her eyes mirrored his own. River knew they were kindred spirits fueled by a desire for retribution and justice. They both wanted nothing more than to dismantle the Mancuso cartel piece by piece.

"Nova," he said solemnly, "we will get Johnny Boy."

She nodded in agreement, her face etched with determination.

It was close to two o'clock when the joint task force spotted a ramshackle shack hidden amid the rocky terrain of the Arizona desert.

The air was thick with tension as they cautiously advanced, their weapons drawn and senses on high alert.

"All right, move in," barked Ray Redhorse, his voice terse with urgency.

With practiced precision, the team spread out, each member taking up a strategic position around the weathered structure.

River cautiously pushed it open.

Nova scanned the area, determined to see everything and everybody.

As they stepped inside, the pungent aroma of marijuana assaulted her senses, mingling with the musty scent of decay that permeated the air. Stacks of crates lined the walls while the floor beneath their feet was littered with discarded debris.

"Spread out and search the premises," ordered Ray, his eyes scanning the room for any signs of movement.

They heard a noise outside.

Two men tried to escape, from the sound of it, but had been apprehended.

"This is just the beginning," Ray declared, his voice resonating with determination.

As the sun began to dip below the horizon, their mission had been a success. They had taken down several scouting locations and captured those involved in trafficking.

But there was one crucial element missing.

Johnny Boy.

The team had been on the lookout for him, with no luck. However, their persistence paid off when they uncovered a massive stash of marijuana linked to the notorious Mancuso cartel. One of the men decided to talk after the agents seized 3,400 pounds of marijuana from the shack he was guarding.

"*Puedo ayudarle*...eh... I can help you," the scout repeated nervously, his eyes darting between each agent in the room. "I know where Johnny Boy is hiding."

Those words caught River's attention. "Where is he?"

The scout fidgeted nervously, knowing this was his only shot at survival. "*Acuerdo*...deal.I. want deal."

River stepped closer, his gaze never wavering from the scout's face. "Speak quickly," he commanded. "Tell us everything you know about Johnny Boy and maybe we can offer you a chance at redemption."

The scout hesitated for a moment, his mind racing as he weighed his options. It was evident that fear wrestled with his desire to escape the clutches of the cartel. Finally, he gave in to his desperation and whispered, "Okay. I'll tell you..."

AFTER MIDNIGHT, River and a team of DEA agents and police officers were on the road to the small town of Pima,
Arizona. The scout had given up Johnny Boy's location—
a community in the desert outside of town. The Shadow
Wolves had remained behind at the arrest site to continue
monitoring movement in the desert.

"Wow...look at this place," said Nova when they arrived
at their destination. "There's a grid-tied solar system, a
greenhouse...all miles away from the nearest neighbor."

River glanced around. This was the perfect place to hide
because it was so secluded. The three-story house was situated on eight or nine acres. There were orchards with apple,
peach, apricot, pomegranate and pear trees. Nearby was a
large fenced garden area and a metal shop warehouse. He'd
heard that Johnny Boy was vegan and preferred to grow
his own food.

His gaze returned to the home with the elaborate entry.
"It's a beauty. It'll be a shame to have to shoot up this house
if it comes to that."

They were a safe distance away from the property, waiting for the command to infiltrate.

"What do you think a place like this would cost?" Nova
asked.

"At least a couple million," River responded. "The floor
plan showed an Olympic-sized pool, a tennis court and a
basketball court. There's also a hair salon and barbershop
on-site. The guy has everything he needs."

"I'm surprised there's no guardhouse or men on roofs
with guns," Kenny interjected.

"My guess is that he's trying to blend in around here,"
River stated. "The guns are in the house and that building
over there...trust me."

He and other law enforcement fanned out around the

house and perimeter as they set out to capture and arrest Johnny Boy. There was still the chance that he might have fled already like a thief in the night, but River pushed the thought away.

We have to make sure we have every avenue covered.

River and the team crept to the porch steps of the house. Nova flanked him on the right.

He glanced over his shoulder, ensuring everyone was in position before gesturing to the officer to his right who was holding the ram waist-high.

River instructed the others to assume their positions, then gave the door a hard knock and yelled, "This is the DEA. *Op n up.*"

No response.

River repeated the order sharply.

Again, nothing from inside.

He signaled to the officer standing behind him, then moved out of the way.

The officer drew the ram back, then swung it toward the door.

It didn't open.

He struck the door again, getting the same result.

River had enough experience to realize that the door was most likely barricaded on the inside. He also knew that they'd lost the element of surprise. Whoever was in the house had time in which to prepare a defense.

The officer repeatedly battered the door, forcing it to give way. It would open a few inches, but then immediately slam shut.

River swallowed his unease and stood directly in front of the entrance. He was able to steal a glance into the house for a split second, brief snapshots of figures moving about. He soon realized he was seeing a person—no, it was two people.

The officer slammed the ram once more.

River caught sight of a man with a shotgun aimed directly at the door.

"Gun," he yelled, ducking and pushing the officer out of the way just as a loud noise erupted from the interior of the house, leaving a hole in the door. Another round of bullets tore through the wood, forcing River to jump off the porch and into a cluster of bushes for cover. He glanced around, searching for Nova. She was safe, having taken cover behind a nearby tree.

He looked back at the house and caught a real glimpse of Johnny Boy—just as gunfire rang out all around him.

River felt a flash of raw pain and knew he'd been hit. Still, he drew his weapon and began firing into the house.

Out the corner of his eye, he saw one of the agents run to the left corner of the house. Another moved quickly to the right.

River touched his left side. His fingers were covered with warm blood. The wound throbbed as he felt blood spread across the front of his shirt.

I'm losing too much.

River tried to speak but couldn't think clearly. Everything started to spin, moving him toward a cloud of darkness.

In the distance, he heard someone saying, "We have an agent down..."

Nova rushed to his side. "We have to get you out of here. Hang on, River."

"Ken..." River managed.

"I'm right here," his partner uttered.

"No... Nova..." Every word took effort and all of River's strength.

"Don't try to talk," she responded. *"I'm here."*

Burning pain ripped through him.

"Where's the ambulance?" Kenny yelled. *"Call* them again."

River heard another round of gunfire nearby.

"Stay with him, Nova." Crouched low, his partner took off toward the side of the house.

A circle of darkness swirled around River, growing larger each minute until he couldn't see anything else. Waves of pain washed over him. He groaned with each wave.

Just before he was carried away on a sea of unconsciousness, River heard the loud shrill of sirens.

Chapter Twenty-Two

The journey from the perilous scene to hospital was a blur for Nova. As the medical team rushed River into surgery, she found herself directed to the waiting area, the weight of worry settling heavily on her shoulders.

The setting was different but it still reminded Nova of the night her father was killed by a cartel member.

"I can't lose him," she whispered, her words a silent prayer as she sat amid the sterile stillness of the hospital waiting room, every passing moment an agonizing eternity.

Time stretched until the door swung open, and a doctor entered.

His solemn expression carried the gravity of the situation, but his words brought a glimmer of hope. "Agent Randolph's surgery was a success. They were able to remove the bullets. Thankfully, no major areas suffered any real damage. He should be waking up anytime now. He'll be moved into his room after that."

Nova's sigh of relief was audible, the tension releasing from her like a held breath. "I'm relieved to hear it," she acknowledged, gratitude welling up as she realized that River had emerged from the brink of danger.

When Nova was finally allowed to see him, River lay sleeping, surrounded by the quiet hum of medical equipment.

She pulled a chair beside his bed and sat down, her gaze never leaving his face. The harsh fluorescent lights of the hospital room felt softer in these quiet moments, and Nova waited patiently for him to wake up, in a silent vigil by his side.

The steady beep of the heart monitor filled the room, a reassuring rhythm as she watched over River and hoped that he would awaken soon.

The room became a sanctuary of quiet anticipation. In this space, the echoes of worry were replaced by the promise of recovery and an unspoken bond forged between them.

RIVER OPENED HIS EYES, blinked several times, then opened them again. No doubt he was still feeling woozy from the anesthesia.

"Hey, you…" she said, relief and happiness flowing through her.

He turned his head. "Nova…"

"I'm here," she responded with a tiny smile. "You really scared me out there."

"I'll be fine," River said. Still feeling groggy, he closed his eyes. He opened them a few minutes later. "I'm sorry if I drifted off."

"You're good," Nova said. "Don't try to stay awake for me. I'm not going anywhere."

"Did we get Johnny Boy?"

Nova didn't want to be the one to tell River about the trafficker's escape. In the rush of the shoot-out, her only goal had been getting River the help he needed. But Kenny had called to fill her in that they hadn't made an arrest. "Kenny is on his way. He should be here soon."

When the nurse entered the room, Nova stood up. "I'm going to the cafeteria to get something to drink. I'll be right back."

"You don't have to leave," River said.

"I know. Don't worry. Not going far at all."

Nova walked out of the room just as Kenny stepped off the elevator.

"River just asked about Johnny Boy," she said, meeting him halfway. "I think you should be the one to tell him what happened."

He nodded, looking exhausted. "After all River's been through, I wish I could give him some much better news."

"The nurse is in the room with him right now," Nova stated.

"How are you holding up?" Kenny inquired.

"I'm relieved that he's still alive."

"Me, too." Kenny passed her, heading to River's room.

As she made her way to the elevator, Nova glanced up to see a tall man with long dreadlocks, a bouquet in hand, weaving through the corridors. His movements seemed purposeful, and a chill crept up Nova's spine.

Johnny Boy.

Instinct kicked in, and she followed him discreetly. He was so intent on his purpose that he never once looked in her direction. She was grateful her badge was hidden inside her pocket and that she'd removed the jacket that would've identified her as law enforcement.

Nova's eyes never left the bouquet, trying to see if it concealed potential danger.

The man moved with an eerie calmness, scanning room numbers with predatory intent. The dreadlocks swung with every measured step.

Nova's heart pounded as he drew closer to River's room.

When he produced what appeared to be a weapon from beneath the flowers, determination eclipsed her fear, and she stepped forward, calling out his name.

"Johnny Boy!"

He turned sharply, eyes narrowing as he saw Nova.

In that tense moment, the bouquet became a weapon. He threw it at her and fired a shot.

Nova's instincts propelled her into action; she lunged for cover. The bullet missed, leaving only the echo of gunfire in the hospital hallway.

Amid shocked screams, her eyes quickly bounced around to see if anyone had been shot.

Dropping the flowers to the ground without hesitation, Johnny Boy made a break for the stairwell, his hurried steps resonating in the hallway.

Nova, fueled by adrenaline and fierce determination, sprinted after him. The hospital staff, caught off guard by the sudden chaos, looked on in shock.

As Johnny Boy reached the second floor, Nova closed the gap.

Hospital security, alerted by the commotion, sprang into action. Responding to the urgency, they swiftly intervened, creating a human barricade at the bottom of the staircase.

Johnny Boy's escape route thwarted, Nova cornered him, her eyes locking on to his as she took aim.

"Drop the weapon!" she ordered.

His eyes darted around, taking in his situation.

The armed security closed in, acting in synchronized precision.

Smirking, Johnny Boy did as she instructed, then held up his hands in surrender.

Nova stood breathless, her gaze fixed on the man in custody. She was thrilled to see him in handcuffs.

When he was taken away, the hospital gradually returned to its usual hushed atmosphere, the threat extinguished, but the echoes of the confrontation lingered in the air.

"What happened?" Kenny asked when Nova returned to River's hospital room. "I heard gunshots."

"Johnny Boy was here," she announced. "I think he was planning to take out River."

"Where is he now?"

"In police custody. I called Special Agent Scott. I'm going to meet him at the precinct, but I wanted to check on River first."

"He's still groggy from the anesthesia and pain meds. I expect he'll probably be out until morning."

River opened his eyes just as Nova approached the hospital bed.

Nova could tell he was struggling to stay awake. "Stop fighting it. Go to sleep, River."

"No. I. need to talk to Kenny."

"Here I am, partner."

She planted a kiss on his cheek. "I have to go."

He took her hand in his. "You will be back, though?"

"Yes. I'll get back as soon as I can."

"HEY, BUDDY," Kenny said when River woke up a second time. "You don't look so great."

"Just tell me that my getting shot was worth it," he responded. "Is Johnny Boy in jail?"

"He's in custody now." Kenny paused momentarily, then said, "He came to the hospital. Nova saw him and interrupted his plan."

"I thought I heard gunshots. Was I dreaming, or did that happen?" River asked.

"Naw, it was real. Right out in the hallway. Luckily, no one was hurt. Nova's on her way to the precinct now."

Nova's genuine concern, her quick actions in saving him, melted the final wall around River's heart. *Once I fully recover,s he and must sit down and alk.*

It was still a struggle for him to stay awake. "I need to close my eyes for a bit."

"You go right ahead," Kenny said. "I need to make some phone calls."

He fell back to sleep as he heard the door shut.

Chapter Twenty-Three

Nova wore a huge grin on her face as she exited the police precinct in the early morning hours.

The man captured at the hospital was not just another doppelgänger. The tattoo on his chest left no room for doubt—he was indeed John Boyd Raymond. His fingerprints had regrown, providing further evidence of his true identity. She silently thanked Arya for informing them about the tattoo and its significance.

Johnny Boy's arrogance was astonishing. He sat there smirking and laughing at them, unfazed that he was in custody or that he would be doing serious time for all the many crimes he'd committed.

He flat out refused to entertain any conversation, repeatedly saying, *"Lawyer."*

She'd left the interrogation room in frustration, wanting to get back to River.

She was looking forward to sharing the news that Johnny Boy had been arrested. He was Poppy's number one—his being in custody would shake up the cartel.

A sense of foreboding washed over her.

Maybe Johnny Boy didn't seem worried because he

had a backup plan. There was a chance that River was still in danger.

Upon her return to the hospital, a palpable urgency to secure River's safety gripped Nova. Approaching the front desk with resolute determination, she flashed her badge and asserted, "I need Agent Randolph moved to another room immediately." Her tone conveyed a seriousness that couldn't be ignored.

The nurse behind the desk, eyes a mix of concern and fear, nodded in response. "Yes, ma'am."

Nova headed to his current room, passing a man with a cell phone to his ear, positioned a few feet away from the nurses' station. He was dressed in a pair of jeans and a Western-style shirt with cowboy boots. She homed in on him as she quickly approached River's room.

Both Kenny and River looked at her when she entered.

"What's wrong?" he asked.

"I requested to have you moved." Nova paused a heart-beat, then continued, "Johnny Boy's been arrested, but I'm not convinced that you're out of danger."

River nodded, looking less groggy than the last time she'd seen him. "See if it can be arranged for me to be flown to a hospital in Los Angeles."

A nurse came in to check his wounds and change his bandages, putting a temporary halt to their conversation.

"Has anyone been asking about me?" River asked.

"Not that I know of," the nurse replied. "Just so you know…we were instructed not to confirm that you're a pa-tient here."

"That's great," Nova said. She showed her badge, then added, "I want the names of any nurses or doctors who will be caring for River. They are to be the *only* ones to come into his room."

"I'm working a double shift, so it will be me until seven a.m. tomorrow morning."

"I won't be leaving your side," Nova announced.

Kenny chuckled. "I had a feeling you'd say that. Can't say I'm surprised at all."

The rest of the morning passed without incident, and Kenny left the room to pick up some lunch for him and Nova.

She got up to go to the bathroom, leaving the door open just a tad in case River called for her.

Just after she washed her hands, Nova heard the door to the room open and close.

The nurse had checked on River at noon. The doctor wasn't expected to come back for another round until later in the evening.

Nova eased to the door and peeked into the room.

A lone figure moved stealthily toward the bed.

It was the man she'd seen earlier. Somehow, he'd been able to sneak into the room. He must have been watching the room and assumed River was alone after Kenny left.

Nova quickly assessed the situation. This man was bigger and stronger, but she wasn't about to leave River vulnerable to his attack. She fervently prayed that her boxing and self-defense lessons were about to pay off.

Using her foot, Nova eased the door open wider.

The man turned around, surprise evident on his face.

Nova saw the needle in his hand and wished she hadn't left her gun in her tote beside the bed.

He gave her a menacing look, then lunged at her.

Nova dodged and shoved the man off balance, forcing him to drop the syringe.

But it wasn't enough. He recovered, then sent a punch in her direction.

Agony tore through her as Nova took a hard hit to her right shoulder.

She cocked back her uninjured arm and threw a jab as hard as she could. It connected with his jaw. Kicking out, Nova connected her foot into the man's knee, bringing him down.

Nova squeezed her eyes closed as she tried to breathe through the pain ripping from her shoulder and down her arm. The tendons in her left hand were on fire, but Nova wasn't about to let up. She punched the attacker's face again, then a third time.

In the distance, she heard River talking, but she couldn't understand what he was saying.

She had no sense of time or place as she put all her energy into knocking the man unconscious. Nova had no awareness of when Kenny rushed in with hospital security.

Someone—she didn't know who—pulled her off the man.

The room was soon filled with hospital staff. Some were checking on River while others placed the man on a gurney, handcuffed him and pushed him out of the room.

"Nova," River called out. "You okay?"

Kenny assisted her over to the chair. "You should let them look at your shoulder."

"I'm good," she said. "He landed a solid punch. I'll be sore for a few days but that's about it." Her gaze was on River. She evaluated him, making sure he was okay. Satisfied that River was safe, Nova lowered her eyes, searching the floor. "Kenny, over there… He came in here with a syringe."

Kenny slipped on a pair of gloves from a nearby counter before picking it up. "I'll send this to our lab."

Nova's eyes traveled back to where River lay in bed. "You sure you're okay?" he asked again.

She nodded. "I'm good."

But the truth was that she was anything but okay. Nova could have very easily taken that man's life to save River. But this time it had nothing to do with her sense of duty as a law enforcement officer. It was different because she was protecting the man she loved.

RIVER WAS MOVED into a new room with twenty-four-hour security. The doctor felt he was too weak to be moved to a hospital in California.

Nova hardly left his side for the next two days. River was concerned that she wasn't getting enough rest.

"You should go with Bonnie to the hotel," he told her. His sister had arrived this morning. He was glad that she and Nova were getting along so well.

"I'm good. Don't you start worrying about me," Nova assured him. "Focus on getting better so we can get you home."

She sank into the visitor chair. "I can tell you're feeling much better. You're starting to get bossy."

He tried to laugh but it hurt.

They talked for a little while until River noticed she could barely keep her eyes open. Ten minutes later, she was sound asleep.

River eased out of bed and held on to the portable IV stand for support. He crossed the short distance to the bathroom.

His business done, he made his way back to bed, sagging with relief when he eased his body under the covers.

Bonnie had tried to convince him to use the portable urinal for another day or so, but his pride just wouldn't let him. He'd argued that he needed to move around to regain his strength. Right now, he was out of breath and in extreme pain. The medication helped to take the edge off, but the sheer effort it took for him to get out of bed and go to the bathroom—it almost wasn't worth it.

River felt bad that he hadn't helped Nova fend off the attacker who'd come into his room, but she'd managed well. He could only press the call button and hope someone would arrive in time. He'd tried to pull the chair closer to the bed in hopes of getting to the gun he knew was inside the tote.

He knew that Nova had had the same goal—she'd wanted to retrieve her weapon but couldn't. Still, she'd managed to subdue the man.

River had done a silent assessment of his own, making sure she wasn't seriously hurt. He caught her wincing every now and then, but Nova had refused to be examined. She kept telling the nurse and the doctor that she was fine. He felt that was because she didn't want to leave his side—she was in what he called *guard* mode.

Later that evening, River signaled to his sister and Kenny to give him a moment alone with Nova.

"Kenny, we haven't had a chance to talk," Bonnie said. "Why don't you take me to dinner? I don't mean to the cafeteria either."

"I'd love that, actually," he responded with a grin.

"Did I miss something?" Nova asked when she and River were alone.

"Kenny met my sister a few years ago," he responded. "As far as I know, it's not been anything outside of harmless flirting here and there."

"Oh, okay."

"Nova...you saved my life. Thank you."

"I was just doing my job." She shook her head. "No, that's not true. River, all I saw was that the man I loved more than life itself was in danger. He was going to kill you and I had to stop him."

He couldn't help but feel a swell of pride and love for her in that moment. She saw him as the man she loved with all her heart. And in that instant, as his life hung in the balance, she risked everything to protect him. He couldn't believe how lucky he was to have someone like her by his side, willing to sacrifice herself for his safety.

"I wondered what was going on in your mind. I'd never seen you filled with such rage. Kenny had to pick you up to keep you from punching the man to death. He deserved it, as far as I'm concerned."

"I'd do it again," Nova said smoothly.

He gestured for her to sit on the bed beside him.

"You're supposed to be resting."

"What's the plan? I know you're working on something in that brain of yours."

"As soon as you're strong enough to fly, I'm taking you to Los Angeles to continue your recovery."

River nodded in approval. "Sounds good to me."

"I meant to check to see if he had any ID on him."

"Kenny most likely took care of all that," River said. "I'm just glad nobody else got hurt." He paused a moment, then added, "I wish you'd let someone check out your shoulder. I know it's bothering you."

Nova eyed him. "I'm good. My shoulder is a bit sore and my hand's swollen but not broken. That's it."

"You'd tell me the truth, wouldn't you?"

"Yeah."

River took her left hand in his. "I heard what you said, Nova. I would prefer to have that discussion when I'm not under the influence of pain meds."

She smiled. "I can wait."

FIFTEEN DAYS LATER, River was out of the hospital and home. Nova had finally convinced him to take a nap. He'd been up most of the morning after a follow-up visit to the doctor. Her gaze traveled her surroundings. The dove-gray walls and deep navy-colored drapes provided a rich backdrop while soft music floated throughout the house. River had a fantastic view of palm trees, the beach and the Pacific Ocean.

He had contemporary furnishings. The dining area was large enough for a table of six and overflowed in the open great room. She especially loved the teal-and-silver color scheme of the kitchen.

"Did you decorate this place by yourself?" Nova asked when he woke up an hour later.

He nodded. "Yeah, I did."

"You have a really nice home."

"Thanks. When are you going to start looking for a place out here?"

"I don't know," Nova responded. "Right now, I just want to make sure your recovery goes well. I must confess that I have zero nursing skills, but I'll make sure your bandages and the area around the wound are kept clean and dry. The doctor says you're healing nicely."

He smiled. "You'd probably do a better job than I would."

Nova rearranged his pillows so River could sit propped up.

"Thanks," he said.

"Your doctor said you could use an ice pack on the bandage to help with swelling. Do you have one?"

Nodding, River replied, "There's one in the freezer."

She picked up her iPad. "Let me check my notes. I want to make sure I'm not missing anything."

"Nova, you can relax." River chuckled. "You're doing great."

She released a short sigh. "Are you in any pain?"

He shook his head no. "I'm fine."

River patted the empty space beside him. "Sit down and talk to me."

"You should get some rest," Nova stated.

"I will."

"When you were shot…it reminded me of the night I lost my father." Her eyes teared up. "I'd never been so scared."

River took her hand in his own. "When I thought I was dying, all I could think of that night was you and how much I wanted to see that beautiful smile of yours. I was filled with so many regrets. I promised I'd make some changes if I was given the chance."

"Like what?" Nova asked.

"I've spent most of my life afraid to give my love to anyone for fear of rejection. Then I met you."

"And I broke your heart."

"That's all in the past," River said. "Back then, it might not have worked out. I think we were both trying to sort out our individual issues. Now we're older and wiser…"

"I'd like to think so," Nova responded.

"Back then, I thought we had something. Then I realized that you weren't ready for a relationship. I do believe that you cared for me, but I also believe that you aren't ready to make a commitment."

"I panicked, River, but that's all changed now," Nova said. "I want to be with you. Can't you see that?" She kissed him. "What we have is worth fighting for," she whispered.

His voice cracked with emotion as he asked her, "But can you handle the tough times that come with love? Will you stay and fight when things get difficult?"

She tightened her grip on his hand and looked into his eyes. "I already proved it when I risked my life to save yours," she said firmly.

He needed to hear it from her own lips that she was willing to stay and fight for their love.

Nova met his gaze. "You know that I love you. I'm not afraid anymore. River, I'm so sorry for the pain I caused. I would rather cut off my own hand before I ever hurt you again."

When he didn't respond, she said, "River, I'm the only woman for you."

"That you are," he confirmed. "I've never met anyone who makes me feel what you do. There was a time when I wanted to forget you, but I couldn't. My heart wouldn't let me. *You* wouldn't let me."

"Then I need to hear *you* say that you're ready to give me a second chance."

"I'm ready to take another chance at love…" River said. "With you."

Epilogue

Six months had passed since Nova decided to relocate to Los Angeles, leaving Charlotte behind and embracing a new chapter in her career with Rylee's task force, whose sole focus was targeting high-level drug cartel organizations such as the Mancuso cartel. She felt a sense of freedom that she never had with the Marshals.

She found herself thriving in the fast-paced environment, fueled by the adrenaline of her work and the camaraderie of her fellow agents.

Amid the chaos of their demanding jobs, Nova found solace in the arms of River. Their relationship had blossomed in the months since her arrival, growing stronger with each passing day as they navigated the highs and lows of their shared journey. Together, they forged a bond built on trust, respect and a deep-seated love that defied the odds.

The sound of Kaleb's voice cut into her musings.

"We received intel that Poppy has a new number one," Kaleb stated. "They're being very secretive about this one."

"Well, it's only a matter of time before we find out who he is," Rylee responded confidently.

"Nova, I know that this is never going to bring your father back, but it might help," Kaleb said after the meeting ended.

"It won't, but I'd still like to make as many of the Mancuso cartel members pay for what they've done," she responded.

"I'm alive because of Easton," Rylee stated. "If I have anything to say about it, we'll keep chipping away at Poppy's organization until we get to her."

Grinning, Nova shot back, "I'm here for it all."

"That's it for now. Operation Reckoning is live…"

* * * * *

CAMERON
MOUNTAIN REFUGE

BETH CORNELISON

For Patience

Prologue

The water was rising, along with her panic. She was trapped, and soon she would drown. She banged on the window, desp rately trying to get free. To save herself. To save her friends. But she couldn't get out. The water gurgled higher...to her chin, her mouth, her nose. Suffocating. Lungs burning.T hey wouldᵢ ll die.A nd t was her fault.

Then a giant bee appeared at her window. With his face. Gloating. Sneering. Buzzing. Buzzing. Buzzing.

Jessica Harkney woke with a gasp, her heart racing. Gulping air. She cut a quick glance around her, disoriented. Confused. He'd been there. But where was he now? The buzzing continued...

Clarity slapped her. Nightmare. Again. How long would the same replay of that awful night haunt her dreams? And did she deserve to be free of the nocturnal torture?

The buzzing sounded again as her phone vibrated on her nightstand. Taking a calming breath, she answered the call—her boss—and glimpsed at the time.

Damn! She was late. She tossed back her bedcovers.

"Sorry!" she said immediately. "Horrid night. And I... overslept."

After spending most of the night staring wide-eyed at her

ceiling, a parade of worries and regrets tumbling through her head, she'd drifted off around 4:00 a.m., turned off her alarm when it chimed at 6:00 a.m.—and remembered nothing else but the nightmare until now. Eight thirty.

"I was worried about you since…you're usually so punctual," her boss, Carolyn, replied.

And because your life has been such a traumatic mess lately. The words, while unspoken, hovered in her boss's tone.

Raking her raven hair out of her eyes, Jessica groaned. "I know. I—I'll be there in forty minutes."

"Can you make it thirty?" her boss said, firmly but without an edge. "We have a meeting with John Billings at ten, and we need to prep."

Grimacing, Jessica flew to the bathroom, took the world's fastest shower, threw on the clothes she'd laid out last night, whizzed through the kitchen to start her Keurig brewing a cup of coffee, dumped a messy pile of cat kibble in her cat's food bowl, grabbed a banana and a bagel, stuffed her phone in her purse and unplugged her laptop from the charger.

"See you tonight, Pluto! Be good!" she called to her buff-colored feline as she raced out to the garage, feeling like a juggler. She had her bagel in her mouth, her laptop under one arm, the banana under the other, her purse over her shoulder, her shoes in her left hand, her coffee in the right. Opening the door to her rental car with her pinky, she set the coffee in the drink holder and tossed everything but the bagel on the passenger-side seat. Sliding behind the steering wheel, she took a bite of the bagel, then set the rest on top of the dashboard. After she cranked the car engine, she slipped her high-heeled pumps on her feet and strapped on her seat belt.

Only when she reached up to the visor to push the garage remote did she realize her mistake. She hadn't replaced the door opener yet since the accident. With a shudder for the unpleasant reminder of her recent trauma and a grunt at the inconvenience, she unbuckled her seat belt again and climbed out. As she rounded the back end of the rental car, waving away the stink of exhaust, a figure stepped from behind the open storage room door.

She screamed and stumbled backward, away from the man who approached her. When she recognized him, her jaw hardened, and heat coursed through her veins. "How did you get in here? What do you want?" she snarled, then flapped a dismissive hand. "Never mind that. Just...get out!"

"Not until we talk. You owe me that much, Jessie. I saved your life." He took a decisive step, blocking her path back to the open car door. Her purse. Her phone.

She gritted her teeth in frustration. "How many times do I have to tell you, I don't want anything to do with you. Stay away from me!"

"Look, Jessie, stop being so stubborn. I love you! If you weren't so defensive, you'd see—"

When he took a step toward her, she slipped off a shoe and threw it at his head.

"I said stay away from me!" She backed up again, knowing she needed her phone. "I'm calling the police."

His eyes narrowed with menace. "No cops. Just talk to me. I will keep coming back until you see that you love me the way I love you."

With quick steps, she rushed to the passenger side of the rental car and jerked the door handle. Locked. Damn it! Another wave of panic swooped through her. She glanced around for something with which to defend herself. Her tennis racket was on the wall behind him, but she wanted something bigger, heavier. More lethal.

When she turned and darted toward her garden tools, propped against the far wall, he surged up behind her. She seized a shovel as he wrapped an arm around her waist. With a thrust, he threw her to the ground. The shovel clanged down beside her. As she scrambled to get up, he kicked her in the temple, and she saw stars. Blinking, trying to shake off the blow, Jessica rolled to her belly. As she rose to her hands and knees, she put her hand on the shovel's handle. She angled a woozy and wary glance up at him. "Get out."

He glared back, growling through gritted teeth. "You made me do that. If you hadn't—"

She swung the shovel at him, hitting him far too weakly in her injured state to do more than anger him.

He grabbed the shovel, yanked it from her grip and tossed it out of her reach. Then leaning over her, he grabbed a fistful of her hair and bent her head back. "Now you're going to be sorry."

She sucked in a breath, coughing on the collecting exhaust from the idling rental car, then spit in his face.

His face suffused with color, the veins on his forehead bulging. He swiped the spittle off with his free arm, then shoved her down again. His foot connected once, twice with her ribs. Pain juddered through her. With trembling arms, she tried to crawl away from his abuse, but he stomped on her hand. Yelping in pain, she balled herself in fetal position and wrapped her arms around the back of her head, her only thought now of protecting her most tender and vulnerable places.

He kicked her again in the side. The hip. An unprotected part of her head. He stepped back, coughing. Then, getting on his hands and knees, he stuck his face in hers. In a sibilant tone, he whispered, "A restraining order? You thought you could get rid of me? Not a chance. Learn this lesson. Don't piss me off, Jessie."

She heard him grunt as he got back on his feet, heard him stomp across the concrete floor, heard the side door to her garage open and close. And then the only sound was the rumbling purr of the rental car's engine as it filled her garage with poisonous gas.

Chapter One

Two months earlier

"You kill me!" Jessica said, holding her sides as she laughed. "You did not say that to his face!"

"I did," her best friend, Tina Putnam, née Coleman, assured her. "The twerp deserved it. This is the third woman he's broken up with since January! He's forty-three years old, for crying out loud. What's he waiting for?" She sipped her margarita, then shaking her head, added, "God knows I love my brother, but he's hopeless when it comes to women. I've never seen a man so adverse to commitment. And other than his apparent allergy to responsibility and marriage, Gage really is a good guy."

Jessica smiled as she nodded her agreement. Gage was good folk, as the Southernism went.

Across the table of the Charlotte, North Carolina, Mexican restaurant, Holly Teale arched an eyebrow. "And he's sexy as hell, too."

Tina sputtered and coughed as she took another slurp of her margarita. She wiped her mouth with her napkin and chuckled. "I wouldn't know about that. He's my brother!"

"Well, he's not my brother, and if I weren't married—I'd

hit that." Sara Callen gave her shoulders a little waggle as she lifted her beer and drank.

"You're not involved with anyone at the moment, Jessica." Holly twirled a lock of her red curls around one finger and gave Jessica a meaningful glance. "What do you think? A little wham-bam-thank-you-ma'am with Tina's brother?"

Jessica pulled a face and shook her head. "Good grief, no! I've known Gage as long as I've known Tina."

"So?" Holly said.

"So…it would be too weird. He's practically *my* brother." Jessica shoved her last bites of enchilada around her plate and shook her head. "Besides, I've sworn off men. This one—" she hooked her thumb toward Tina "—convinced me to try another dating app." She rolled her eyes. "Let's just say, it didn't go well. Of the three men I did finally go out with, after playing text-tag with several, one proved to be married and looking for some extracurricular activity—"

Her friends gave the appropriate groans and wrinkled noses.

"One was, well, how to say this politely—"

"Boring as hell," Tina supplied for her.

Jessica pointed at her friend. "That. He spent the whole night talking about his coin collection and going metal detecting on Saturdays. I mean, I have nothing against coin collecting in principle, but by dessert, I wanted to hit him over the head with his metal detector and run screaming from the Dairy Queen where he'd taken me for our meal."

Holly and Sara chortled. "Dairy Queen for a first date? I love me some DQ, but my God, for a first date?"

"He never once asked what I do, or if I had children, or if I had hobbies…" Jessica shook her head. "Then most recently I went out with a guy that seemed okay at first, but the more we talked, the longer the date lasted, I just got this strange vibe off him."

"What kind of strange vibe?" Holly asked, fishing a tortilla chip out of the basket in the middle of the table and crunching down on it.

Jessica twisted her mouth as she thought. "Hard to say exactly. He seemed genuinely interested in me, and he wasn't bad-looking. Early forties, blond and had all his hair, good build, stylish glasses and pleasant enough face. We talked about the usual get-to-know-you stuff. Movies. Jobs. Books. Travels. And we had a lot in common." She paused. "Maybe too much. Everything I liked or I said interested me, he said he loved, too. All the same music and movies and podcasts. It was..." She paused, gazing out the restaurant window as she reflected on the odd date. "*Too* perfect."

"Trying too hard to find things in common?" Sara asked. "Needy..."

"Maybe. He acted confident and self-assured, but again, it was...too much."

"How so?" Holly asked.

"Hmm." Jessica, the designated driver for the evening, sipped her iced tea. "He was rather...annoying in his certainty that we were a good match, and that we would be having many more dates in the future. For instance, when I told him I enjoyed canoeing and kayaking, he said, 'Well, we'll be sure to go boating this summer. Nothing better than a day on the water.'"

"This summer? It's March, and he was already planning your dates for this summer?" Tina asked, giving Jessica an incredulous look.

"Right? So that was weird. But like I said, he was pretty nice, and we did, apparently, have a lot in common, so—"

"You saw him again," Holly guessed correctly.

"Twice more," Tina said, holding up two fingers for emphasis. "I told her she should listen to her instincts if he gave her a funny feeling, but..."

Jessica pulled a face as she glanced at Tina. "But Henry was so persistent, and since I couldn't give a good reason *not* to go out, I just...gave him a second chance. Then a third."

"And the other dates? How was—Henry, you say?—then?" Holly's eyes lit with intrigue, and she leaned forward, her expression eager.

"The same. No...even weirder, I think. Cloyingly agreeable. Arrogantly assured of our destiny. But also polite and good at conversation and a good tipper."

"Well, that's always a positive sign," Holly said. "My mama always said you can tell a lot about a person's character by the way they treat servers in a restaurant."

All four women bobbed their heads in agreement, and Jessica sighed.

"But... I couldn't shake the vibe that something was off with him," Jessica continued, the uneasy sense returning as she described the events of the last week. "So when he asked for a fourth date...well, he didn't as much ask as *assume*, saying he'd 'be by my house on Friday at seven to pick me up.'"

"That's nervy," Sara said, sounding affronted on Jessica's behalf.

"My thoughts exactly. I told him I would be busy and couldn't go out Friday, and he demanded to know what I had planned."

Her friends issued more grunts of disdain.

"I told him it wasn't his business, which clearly irritated him, and when he continued to insist I tell him why I wouldn't see him on Friday, I told him I no longer wanted to see him. He didn't give up, though. He continued to call and text every day. After a few days, I had to block him to make it stop."

"Good riddance. He sounds too controlling and overbearing," Tina said, patting Jessica's arm.

"Except…he still showed up that Friday at my house expecting to take me to dinner."

"What!" Holly gasped, her expression aghast.

"I, of course, refused to go out with him, which didn't go over well. He got loud and hostile." Jessica paused to sip her tea, remembering the confrontation. "It was…ugly. He called me names, got in my face, then—get this—he told me he *forgave me* for my rudeness, and that I should get my coat. We were still going to dinner."

Her friends exchanged incredulous looks.

"Are you serious?" Holly asked.

"What a jerk!" Sara said.

Jessica nodded. "I told him to leave, or I would call the police. That didn't go over well, either, but when I got my phone and started dialing, he took off."

"Like a roach running for cover when the lights are turned on," Tina added, one dark eyebrow arched in disgust.

"I hope you still reported him to the cops." Holly's eyes were dark with concern.

Jessica shrugged. "No. I think he got the message. But I deleted the dating app from my phone. Like I said, I'm done with men. I'm fine on my own. And I have my posse." She raised her tea glass to each of her friends, smiling at them one at a time.

"Hear! Hear!"

"That's right!"

"Darn tootin'!"

The four clinked glasses, and as Sara finished taking a

sip of her drink, she sputtered a laugh. "Holly Teale, did you just say *darn tootin'*?"

Jessica chuckled. "She did."

Holly raised her hands, looking innocent. "What's wrong with that? My grandma used to say that."

"Exactly. Your *grandma*!" Sara lifted an eyebrow as another round of tipsy giggles erupted around the table.

Jessica sipped her tea, glancing around the restaurant, aware she and her friends were being rather loud.

And her gaze landed on a fair-haired man at the bar who was glaring boldly at her. Her stomach swooped, and she felt the cold drain of blood from her face. She set her glass down with a thump and muttered a bad word.

She stared down at their table, focused her energy on trying to calm her swirling gut. Lord, but she'd eaten too much, and this rush of anxiety was not mixing well with her spicy meal.

"Jessica?" Tina touched her arm and angled her head in concern. "Something wrong?"

"I always thought it was just an expression," Jessica muttered.

"Huh?"

"Speak of the devil, and he will appear," Jessica said. She lifted her gaze to the bar again to discover the devil had risen from his seat and was headed over to their table.

"What? Who?" Holly asked, then pivoted in her seat to see what Jessica was looking at.

"The guy I was just telling you about," Jessica said, panic rising. "Henry. He's here! He's coming ov—"

"Well, well, well. Imagine meeting you here," Henry said in a singsong tone, something cold behind his green eyes. He bent and gave Jessica a kiss on the check. "How are you doing, sweetheart?"

Scowling, Jessica swiped her cheek with her palm. "I'm not your sweetheart. What are you doing here?"

He raised both hands. "Getting dinner and a drink, of course." He grabbed a chair from the next table and pulled it up, saying, "Y'all seem to be having a great time. May I join you?"

"No," Jessica said firmly, her heart pounding in her ears. Locking her elbow, she placed a hand on his chest to discourage him pulling closer to the table. "You need to leave."

Her friends exchanged wary glances.

When Henry only pulled a lopsided and sardonic smile, a chill crept through her. He took the hand she'd braced on his chest and held it between his. "Jessie, honey, I know you're still mad about last week. I said some things I shouldn't have, but so did you. You provoked me. Let's let bygones be bygones and start over."

She yanked her hand from his and stood. "I mean it, Henry! You need to leave. Now."

He folded his arms over his chest and shook his head, grinning at her like she was a petulant child. "Not until we work this out."

Now Tina shoved her chair back and rose to her feet. "I'm getting the manager."

As Tina disappeared toward the front of the restaurant, Holly pulled out her phone. "Forget the manager, I'm calling the cops. He kissed you against your will. I believe that qualifies as battery."

While she appreciated her friends' defense of her, she motioned for Holly to stand down. She preferred to get rid of Henry without a scene, with minimal hullabaloo. If she could.

Holly frowned at Jessica, but she put her phone back on the table.

"Look," Henry said, his tone indicating he thought he was being reasonable and more than fair. "If your friends don't want me here, we can go somewhere and be alone. A movie? Bowling? Whatever you want."

"Hey, are you deaf? She said she wants you to leave!" Holly said, her back stiff and her hand still resting on her phone. "Get lost, pal!"

"Shut up, bitch!" Henry snapped, his eyes blazing. "This doesn't concern you."

Sara gasped. "Hey! You wanna take it down a notch? Jessica asked nicely for you to leave, and I think you—"

Henry shoved his face right in Sara's, snarling, "I don't much care what you think." He waited a beat, his grin malevolent before jabbing her with a finger in the chest and adding, "Bitch."

Jessica saw red. "Get away from her!"

Henry turned back to Jessica as if startled by the dark timbre of her voice. "Are you talking to me in that tone?"

"I am. You can't think I'd stand by mildly while you verbally assault my friends?"

He just snorted dismissively.

Jessica gritted her teeth. "Leave now, and I will let this go. But if you don't walk away right now—"

His shoulders squared. "Don't threaten me. You won't like what happens next, Jessie."

She didn't bother correcting him on his use of the nickname she'd despised since her mother's first loser boyfriend used it on her. She simply wanted Henry gone. Instead, she glanced back toward Holly and said, "Okay, call the cops."

But at that moment, Tina returned with the restaurant manager, and Henry raised both hands as he rose from the chair and took a step back from their table. "It's cool. I'm going." He hesitated, giving Jessica a direct look. "But I'll see you again, Jessie." He blew her a kiss as he strode across the restaurant floor and out the door.

GAGE COLEMAN STOOD to the side of the locked window and smashed the panes with his axe. When no flames leaped out, he nodded to Cal Rodgers and turned on the headlamp on his headgear. He climbed through the broken window, into the bedroom saturated by dense smoke. Despite his protective turnout gear, he felt the intense heat of the flames devouring the other end of the burning house.

"Madeline? Honey, where are you?" he called, searching for the five-year-old girl still trapped in the house. "I know you're scared, but I'm here to help you." He felt blindly and moved slowly across the floor, his feet occasionally kicking an unseen toy or other obstacle. Using the beam of his headlamp, he made out a closet door, sitting partially open. He entered the closet, searching the floor, behind the stacked boxes, under the dirty clothes.

"Madeline?" Nothing. No answer.

Cal Rodgers wiggled through the open window, his headlamp flashing in the small room, and he aimed his hand toward the door. "I'll check the bathroom."

Gage nodded and felt his way to the single bed. Getting on his hands and knees, he peered underneath. No Madeline.

But a pair of eyes reflected his headlamp.

His priority was the little girl, but he wouldn't walk away from a pet. Lying flatter to stretch an arm to the far corner where the eyes blinked back at him, he grabbed the scruff of the cat and dragged it out.

The feline was unmoving, either from shock or unconscious from smoke inhalation. He cuddled the cat to his chest and moved quickly to the window. "Smith!" he shouted to the first man he saw. "Come get this cat."

His coworker rushed over and took the limp animal. Gage didn't stay to see what Eddie Smith did with the feline. He had a child to find.

"Madeline!" he heard Rodgers calling as he searched the en suite bathroom, and Gage added his voice.

"Where are you, Madeline? Can you call to us?"

He completed his search of the girl's room with no results and headed out into the hallway. "Come on, Madeline. Don't be scared," he called, knowing children were often as frightened of the big men in turnout gear and face shields as of the fire. "I'll get you out and take you to your mommy and daddy." The smoke was thicker here, and so black he couldn't see even a foot in front of him. "Mad—"

His foot connected with something, and he crouched to determine what was in his path. A small, dark-haired girl in a white nightgown was crumpled on the floor. "Rodgers, I've got her!"

Gage scooped the child in his arms and heard her whimper. *Thank God,s he was alive!*

Turning back toward the bedroom, he carried Madeline through her bedroom and handed her out to Rodgers, who'd already crawled back out the window.

As he turned to climb out the window, his headlamp flashed across the rumpled covers of the girl's bed, and he spotted a colorful lump. A gut impulse sent him back to the bed, where he grabbed the item. Without pausing further, he turned and hurried out the window. Only once he was standing in the yard did he lift his face shield and study what he'd brought out. A ragged and obviously well-loved stuffed unicorn stared up at him with unblinking black-thread eyes.

Gage's heart thumped wistfully, remembering his sister Tina's favorite stuffed animal, a frog with a wide mouth, that had gone to college with his sister and still held a spot of pride on her spare bedroom shelf.

He scanned the area until he found where EMTs were treating the little girl. Carrying the pink-and-yellow toy to the child, he knelt beside the girl's mother, who clutched Madeline's hand as she sobbed tears of relief.

Madeline's dark brown eyes were open—definitely a good sign—and she wore a clear plastic breathing cup over her mouth and nose that fed her lungs oxygen. The child's gaze turned to him, then dropped to the unicorn. Her eyes widened.

"Hey, Madeline." Gage held out the toy, thinking how much the girl with her long black hair and dark eyes reminded him of someone else—a woman he'd cherished most of his life. If he'd followed his heart instead of his head years ago, he might have a daughter who looked like Madeline, thanks to the woman's genes. "I thought you might miss your friend."

Nodding, the little girl reached for the doll and hugged it to her chest.

Madeline's mother turned to him with a teary smile and rasped, "Thank you! You've no idea how much Beanie means to her."

He grinned and tugged on the unicorn's yarn mane. "Is that her name? Beanie?"

The woman shook her head. "No. The unicorn is Crystal. She's also treasured. I mean our cat."

Gage followed the woman's gaze to the driveway, where her husband held a sooty white cat for another child to pet.

"You're the one who saved Madeline...and Beanie. Aren't you?" she asked, clutching his arm.

Gage was uneasy with the hero worship in the mother's eyes, but he bobbed a nod. "Yes, ma'am."

"How can I ever thank you?"

He stood and shook his head. "Just doing my job, ma'am. Knowing Madeline's all right is all the thanks I need."

As he hurried back toward the fire truck to lend a hand with the hose, he cast a last glance at Madeline hugging her unicorn and thought again of Tina and her frog. He was still close to his younger sister, who lived just a few miles from his apartment. They'd been close enough in age that they'd shared a lot of the same friends in high school. In fact, they still maintained many of those same friendships today, some twenty-odd years later.

Hanging with the girls tonight. TTYL! Tina had texted him earlier that night.

The girls. Which meant at that very moment, his sister was enjoying a fun night out with *her*. His ebony haired, brown-eyed missed opportunity. Jessica Harkney.

Chapter Two

Jessica's body shook in the wake of the adrenaline, anger and embarrassment the confrontation with Henry had caused. She could feel the eyes of the other restaurant patrons on her, heard the low murmur of Tina's and Holly's voices as they discussed the events with the manager.

"You okay, sweetie?" Sara rubbed a hand on her back, and Jessica jolted.

Nodding, she sent Sara a warm smile. She had to shake off the incident. She would not rent Henry Blythe space in her head. Nor would she let him and his brutish shenanigans ruin the night for her and her friends. Before he'd shown up, they'd been having fun, letting off steam, enjoying the sort of girlfriend bonding that healed the soul. Henry would not steal that from her.

With a deep inhale and a cleansing exhale, Jessica shook her hands out as if physically flicking the menace of the man from her fingers. "I say we've earned dessert." Jessica flagged a passing waitress. "Can we have an order of flan, some sopaipillas and one tres leches cake with four forks please?"

Holly blinked at her. "Who has room for dessert?"

Jessica shrugged. "Maybe no one, but I'm feeling rebellious. I usually want dessert but feel guilty ordering it, as if it's too indulgent, too expensive, breaking my never-ending diet. But to hell with guilt and restrictions! Life was meant to be lived!"

Tina laughed and raised her glass. "I'll drink to that! Bring on the carbs!"

With the continued good humor of her friends, the rich flavor of the desserts, and another half hour of distracting conversation and uplifting giggles, Jessica could almost put Henry's interruption of their night behind her.

But as the four of them walked out of the restaurant and piled into Jessica's small sedan, the spring night had a bite. A chill that had nothing to do with the weather crept through her as they crossed the dark parking lot. Maybe the eerie sensation was due to lingering echoes of Henry's confrontation. Or maybe the prickly nip on her neck was just her own heightened awareness of her surroundings, thanks to the personal safety training her ex-husband had insisted she take early in their marriage. She couldn't say what hovered in the humid North Carolina night, humming like cicadas in July, but Jessica paused before climbing in the driver's seat to take her friends home. She scanned the parking lot, the side street, the shadows behind the dumpster where a stray cat scuttled into the tall grass.

Seeing nothing to concern her, she shook her head and slipped behind the steering wheel.

"Home, please, Winston," Holly teased with a fake accent, collapsing in the back seat in a fit of drunken giggles with Sara. Jessica rolled her eyes and grinned. The four of them each had a different chauffeur name that was dusted off when they took their turn as the designated driver for girls' night. Sara was Geoffrey. Holly was Hubert. Tina was Lyle. Complete foolishness. Completely random, but the sort of silly private jokes that were the stuff of yearslong friendships.

Jessica pulled out of the parking lot, turning toward the state highway that would take Holly home first. Holly lived outside of town in the same farmhouse her grandparents had bought seventy years earlier, raised chickens as a hobby and kept the financial books for her parents' dairy farm in lieu of rent on the house.

"Can I get some eggs when we get to your house?" Tina asked, turning her head to look to the back seat at Holly. She raised a hand to shade her eyes and squinted. "Jeez, dude. Easy on the brights."

Jessica, too, raised a hand to block the glare as a truck with its high beams on pulled close to her back bumper, the headlights glowing brightly in her side and rearview mirrors.

"Sure. I'll trade you eggs for your brother's phone number," Holly replied.

"Wha— Seriously? That again?" Tina twisted back to face forward. "What is y'all's fascination with my big brother? There is a reason he's never married, ladies. He's a man-child."

Jessica winced and tapped her brakes to try to get the truck to back off. "That's harsh. He's not that bad."

Tina shrugged. "Well, he is a commitment-phobe. A confirmed bachelor with the housekeeping skills of a teenage boy. You know that's true, Jessica. You ladies deserve better in a spouse."

The truck behind her revved its engine and continued to hover close behind Jessica's car. Irritation at the tailgater spiked. Had the truck followed her out of the restaurant parking lot?

"Oh, you misunderstand," Holly said, leaning toward the

front seat. "I don't want to marry him. I just want to play with him. Have any of his past girlfriends mentioned to you how he is in bed?"

Sara shrieked with laughter, making Jessica jolt. She shook off the start and, pressing a hand to her thumping heart, joined the chuckling.

Tina stuck her fingers in her ears. "La la la la la, not listening to this kind of talk about my brother. *My brother, y'all!* Just stop!"

"Come on, Tina, you have to admit—"

The truck behind them tapped Jessica's back bumper, jolting the car and cutting Holly's reply short. The four women gasped or muttered a curse in surprise and alarm. Against her better judgment, Jessica sped up a little, assuming the guy was simply bothered by her careful, not-quite-the-limit speed.

"What is it with jerks tonight? Is there a full moon?" Tina asked.

With a roar of his engine, the truck resumed its position tailgating Jessica.

"I'm calling the cops for real this time," Sara said, and the back seat lit with the glow of her cell phone. "Yes, my name is Sara Callen. My friends and I are driving home from a restaurant, and we're being harassed by an overly aggressive driver in a pickup truck." Sara gave their location on the highway and the direction they were traveling, sounding far more clear-minded and professional than Jessica figured she would have been after four potent margaritas.

The truck bumped them again, and Jessica heard Sara cuss. "I dropped my phone."

The snick of Sara unbuckling her seat belt filtered to Jessica from the back seat. A flicker of worry licked Jessica.

"Stay buckled, everyone. I'm gonna pull over so this creep can pass, but…just in case—"

"Yeah, I'm back," Sara said to the emergency operator. "Right, a reckless driver. Can't tell what color it is. He has his brights on, blinding us. He's bumpin' us intentionally."

At the first wide spot on the edge of the road, Jessica pulled over, and the truck passed them and roared away. She exhaled her relief, glad to be rid of the menace.

"Okay, never mind. My friend let 'im pass, and he drove away," Sara reported to the operator. "No, sorry. No tag numbers, but the truck was some light shade. Gray or white maybe. Possibly tan. Hard to tell in the dark."

Jessica took a moment to wipe her damp palms on her jeans and glance over at Tina.

Her bestie gave her a crooked smile. "You okay?"

Jessica nodded. "Just wondering why some people have to be such jerks."

Tina blinked. "As you look at me?" She snorted as she laughed. "Are you trying to tell me something?"

Tina's teasing helped soothe Jessica's ruffled nerves. She was good about that—calming her, encouraging her, sympathizing with her, sharing a grumble when needed. She swatted playfully at her friend. "Of course not. You're not a jerk." Then with a wry grin, she added, "Not usually, anyway."

"Unh!" Tina grunted in mock affront.

"Yeah, thanks," Sara said, presumably to the emergency operator. "Bye." Then louder, "She said to call back if we see the truck again, and especially if we get any more identifying information. Tag numbers, make or model of the truck."

"I think it was a Chevy," Holly said.

Tina shook her head. "Naw, pretty sure it was a Ford."

As she pulled back onto the highway, Jessica turned on the air-conditioning. Despite the cool spring night, she'd broken out in a sweat. Adrenaline after the run-in with the aggressive truck? Perimenopause? Could be either or both.

Stupid hormones reminding her she was getting older. Her son was finishing his second year of college, for cripes' sake! Sure, she'd been barely twenty-two years old when Eric was born, barely more than a kid herself, but she couldn't believe how quickly Eric had turned from a cuddly toddler to a precocious grade-schooler to a legal driver and now a sophomore at the University of North Carolina.

The cool air did its job, and a couple of minutes later she turned the air conditioner off again. Tina gave her a knowing grin.

"Shut up," Jessica mumbled.

Tina raised both hands. "I didn't say anything. I'm sure my days of hot flashes are coming."

They reached a stretch of road that passed through a more rural landscape, leaving the shopping plazas and fast-food restaurants of town behind. The road narrowed and became darker thanks to the absence of streetlights and the neon glow of businesses' signs. Though night had fallen, Jessica knew the gently rolling hills were marked with woods and streams and dotted with occasional ponds where Eric and his friends had gone fishing throughout his youth.

Jessica angled a quick glance toward Tina. "Did you see the prom pictures Kathy posted on Facebook of—"

Her question was interrupted by the roar of a souped-up engine. Despite the highway's double-line, no-passing zone, the owner of the loud engine passed Jessica and cut in front of her, nearly clipping her front fender. She braked to avoid the truck, her heart beating triple time against her ribs. "Jeez, man! What the—?"

"That's the same truck from before!" Sara cried from the back seat.

"Seriously?" Jessica asked. "But—"

"It is." Tina pointed at the bumper of the light-colored truck. "I remember that bumper sticker." She pointed at a red, white and blue decal on the tailgate of the truck declaring support for a candidate from a past state election.

Jessica's gut swooped as she focused on the sticker. A flash of recognition curled through her, and bile rose in her throat. "That's Henry's truck!"

"Henry, the jerk from restaurant?" Tina asked, though her tone said she knew what the answer would be.

Jessica nodded, trying to find her voice amid her shock... and concern. "Pretty sure. He had a silver truck and a sticker like that. I remember thinking how we had different taste in political candidates. At the time, I wrote it off as no big deal."

"But the truck from before passed us, so how..." Holly sighed, then started again. "Good God. Did he circle around somehow to find us again or pull off to lie in wait until we passed him? That's...creepy!"

Jessica swallowed hard, trying not to get overwrought. "Maybe it's just—"

The truck's driver slammed on the brakes, and Jessica reacted just in time to avoid rear-ending him. Accelerating again, the truck pulled away, and Jessica followed warily. "He toying with us. The SOB!"

Tina turned to the back seat. "Sara, call 911 again. Tell them to send the cops."

"Way ahead of you, girl," she said, then, "I called earlier about an aggressive driver. Well, he's back." She gave the highway number again and a mile marker.

"Should we pull over somewhere and wait for the cops?" Tina asked.

"And make ourselves an easier target for him to harass

us?" Holly replied. "We'll be at my house in a couple more miles, then y'all can come inside until—"

"Look out!" Tina shouted.

As they came around a blind curve where the road crossed a bridge over a small river, the silver truck sat blocking the lane. Jessica had no time to stop. Instead, she cut the wheel hard to the right. An angled guardrail appeared in her headlights.

She tried to correct her path. Too late. Her friends screamed. The left side of car went up the guardrail like a ramp. Momentum, loss of traction, angle. Somehow, someway, the car careened up. Briefly airborne. Landed with a jolt, upright.

In the middle of the river.

Chapter Three

Gage and his fire company had only been back at the firehouse long enough to strip out of their bunker gear and start a conversation about dinner when the alarm sounded again. Suspected car accident. A 911 call that ended unexpectedly after reports of an unruly and harassing driver.

"Seriously?" Smith said. "But I'm starving!"

"Come on, rookie," Gage called, tossing the young firefighter△ a protein bar from the box he'd been raiding when the alarm sounded. "Duty calls. This is what you signed up for."

The men hustled out to the truck bay to don their gear again and load the engine, moving faster than their tired bodies preferred. But haste was required. Every second counted and could be the difference between saving a life... or not.

WATER WAS RISING fast in the car's cabin, creeping closer to her mouth, her nose. Soon she'd not be able to breathe. To speak.

Other than the gurgle of water, the sawing of her frightened breaths, the car was chillingly silent.

"Tina?" Her friend slumped forward against her seat belt,

head lolling. She angled the rearview mirror to check on her friends in the back seat, but it was too dark to see anything. "Sara! Holly! We have to get out!"

Jessica turned her attention to escaping the car. She could only help her friends if she survived herself. When she tried to roll down the window, nothing happened. The waterlogged electrical system was useless. The thread of terror twisted tighter. She pounded the side window with her fist, trying to break the glass, to escape the death trap her car had become. The rising water had reached her neck.

Get out! Get out! *Get out!*

Drawing a shuddering breath, she battled to keep panic at bay. The only way she'd survive was to keep her wits. She unbuckled her seat belt, then Tina's. She tried to shake Tina awake. "Please, Tina! Wake up! We have to get out."

The clock was ticking. *Save yourself.*

The thought caused a sharp, guilty ache to slash through her.

She'd seen the YouTube videos about surviving various deadly scenarios. She'd just never imagined she'd have to use the information, had never purchased a rescue hammer for her map pocket. Now, glancing around her as the lake's muddy water burbled higher, she tried to come up with something, anything that would break the safety glass of her window. She needed something heavy with a sharp tip that would deliver a high impact, concentrated blow to break the safety glass.

Nothing. She thought of nothing heavier than the ballpoint pen she kept clipped to her visor. She tried her elbow. Pain juddered through her arm. Still the glass held.

Could she call 911? Her phone had been in her purse on the floor of the front seat when the car went in the water. Who knew where it was now. The thing was almost certainly nonfunctional after being submerged in the lake water. She prayed Sara's call had been enough to have help sent.

Contorting herself awkwardly as the river water reached her chin, she slipped off her shoe to whack at the glass with the high heel. But the resistance of the high water made it impossible to get a full, hard swing.

Images of her son, Eric, her beautiful boy, her pride and joy, flashed in her mind. A stinging grief squeezed her chest as she imagined the police contacting him at his college dorm to tell him she'd perished in a car crash. Had she fussed at him the last time they spoke? Told him she loved him more than anything?

She pushed with her feet, struggling now to keep her nose above the surface. A ragged sob tripped from her. She yanked the door handle and drove her shoulder into the driver's door. Even knowing that the weight and pressure of the lake's water against the door would make it humanly impossible to push it open, she had nothing to lose in trying.

But the door didn't budge and wouldn't until the water had filled the car completely and equalized the pressure on each side—at which point she'd have been under water holding her breath for how long? The notion terrified her.

She heard a whimper and jerked her gaze toward Tina. Her friend had raised her head, wide eyes taking in their situation. A dark trickle of blood seeped from a gash on her forehead.

"Try to stay calm," she called to Tina. "I'm trying to get us out."

"Jessica!" Tina cried, groping for her arm, her grip squeezing.

Could she kick the window out? Worth a shot, but maneuvering in the tight confines of her front seat as water pooled higher was not a simple task. As she twisted slightly on the driver's seat, wiggling her legs out from under the steering wheel, a movement outside her window startled her. She gasped, inhaling a mouth full of water that made her cough, sputter. The glow of her headlights illuminated the lake where a man had swum into the river. Her initial relief, her joy at being rescued, chilled when she recognized his face. *Henry.*

A flash of rage swept through her. The accident was his fault. His erratic, reckless driving was the reason she and her friends were trapped, about to drown.

He had something in his hand, and he banged it on her window once. Twice. Jessica took a large gulp of air, just before his third strike broke the glass. A gush of river water poured in and filled the interior of her sedan. Henry reached in and grabbed her arm, but she fought him. Turning to Tina, she tried to grasp her friend under her arms, tried to drag her from the seat. But Henry's grip on her was stronger, and he hauled her through the window. Jessica kicked, both fighting Henry and to propel herself to the surface.

The river's current was surprisingly swift, enough to tug her downstream. She gasped air and tried to swim back to the car, back to help Tina, Sara and Holly. Henry blocked her, grabbed her shirt and dragged her toward shore.

"Stop!" she choked out as her head bobbed above the water. "Let go!" She slapped at his hands, but she couldn't tread water, battle the current and free herself from him all at once.

"I'm saving your life, you ungrateful bitch!" He found purchase on the muddy riverbed, walked toward the bank, tugging her by her shirt until she, too, could stand. She twisted and pried at his hands, struggling to free her blouse from his grip. When he clung stubbornly, making her stumble as he hauled her closer toward shore, she ducked and shimmied until the blouse slipped off over her head.

He growled his frustration, then shouted, "What are you doing? Do you want to drown?"

Jessica faced the submerged car, heaving deep, ragged breaths as she calculated the best way to rescue her friends.

Moving well upstream of the car along the slippery mudbank, Jessica wasted no time diving back into the river. Though her arms trembled with fatigue, she swam out to her car and grabbed the car frame where her window had been. Jagged glass cut her hand, but she clung on. She tried to swim down into the car to find Tina, but the current was too strong. She almost lost her grip on the slick car.

Over the roar of adrenaline in her ears, the wail of a siren reached her. She spied the flash of red and blue lights on the surrounding trees. Help had come. She just prayed they were in time to save her friends.

As GAGE'S COMPANY arrived at the vehicle accident, he lit the headlamp he strapped on and grabbed an additional spotlight. Jumping from the engine even before it had come to a full stop, he shone his spotlight around the area, assessing the scene alongside the other firefighters. The glint of metal in his flashlight beam caught his attention. Along with the panicked plea of a woman.

"Help!" she screamed. "My friends are still in the car!"

The car in question was submerged in the river's tricky eddies, and the woman clung precariously to the roof of the car, barely visible above the muddy water line.

Gage raced to retrieve rope, a personal flotation vest with carabineers and a lead line, as did his coworkers. The station chief barked directions as they organized themselves for the rescue. "Coleman, Rodgers, you're going in. Barksdale, Smith, anchor the rescue line. Someone ask dispatch how far out the ambulance is!"

Adrenaline pumping, Gage hooked the straps of his safety vest at his sternum, then clipped his lead to the main line in deft movements. Barksdale had crossed the highway bridge with the heavy rope that would be secured on the opposite shore, giving the men in the water a steady line to hold, to tie off to as they worked in the current.

"Ready?" Gage called to the men tying off the line. He secured a headlamp, shoved on his gloves for better grip in the water and got the signal from his captain when the throw line was anchored.

He hurried to the edge of the river, stopping only long enough to clip onto the anchor line before he waded in. Beside him, Cal Rodgers did likewise. When the water level reached his waist and the water pulled at him, he pushed off with his feet and swam. He fought the current as he scissor-kicked and pulled with his arms, steering himself to the vehicle. The beam of his headlamp bobbed in the darkness as he half swam and half dragged himself to the vehicle. The car wasn't far from the bank of the river, and the water was not more than five feet deep. But if someone was trapped inside, that was more than enough to fill the interior and drown the trapped occupant in little time.

His first attention went to the woman clinging to the edge of the roof where the driver's window had been broken out. As he neared the car, she tried to duck under the water and go back inside the car. The current quickly caught her, and her grip faltered. Instead of wiggling into the car, she was swept back up and across the roof of the vehicle. She screamed as she scrabbled for a handhold, finding none and coughing on the water that filled her mouth.

"I got her!" Gage called to Cal. "Check the car!" He just

reached her and hooked his arm around the woman's waist in the nick of time. The men on the bank immediately tightened the slack in his safety rope to keep them from drifting. He dropped another rope, tied in a lasso, over her head and settled it under her arms. "I got you, ma'am. Reel us in!"

The woman sputtered again as water splashed in her face, then rasped, "No! Have to…friends in car!"

"We'll get them next," he said, "I need you to be still. Don't fight me." His headlamp swept across her face, and recognition jolted through Gage. "Jessica?"

Her head tipped up, her terrified gaze finding his. "G—" Water splashed into her mouth, and she choked. Coughing and retching, she flailed an arm toward the car.

"Easy now, I have you. Hold on to me." Renewing his focus, Gage pulled at the anchor rope and, hand over hand, pulled them through the river back to shore.

When they reached the bank, Captain Remis helped him get Jessica up to high ground and wrap her in a blanket. Already she was shivering from the cold water, from adrenaline. Shock was a real possibility. When she swiped water from her eyes and pushed her dripping hair back from her eyes, she smeared blood on her face.

"You're bleeding somewhere. Let me check you for injuries." Gage tried not to think about the fact that he knew his patient, his sister's best friend. He'd spent numerous game nights with Jessica, shared holiday meals with her after her divorce—and had kept his attraction to her a closely held secret.

He took hold of Jessica's wrists to turn up her palms, which bore small, seeping cuts. She shook her head violently as she coughed and tried to drag air into her lungs.

"What's wrong?" he asked Jessica as he flagged Captain

Remis with a raised hand. "I need the medical kit. How far out is the ambulance?"

"G-Gage," she rasped, between coughs. "T-Ti—" She rolled away from him abruptly, onto her hands and knees, and vomited in the grass. When she sat back on her heels, she raised a bleak look to him.

"Hey, it's okay. I see worse almost every day." He smiled, trying to comfort her.

"No." She shook her head again, then scooted a short distance away from the mess, her gaze on the river. She dragged in a sob and muttered, "I couldn't get— I tried to—"

"Jessica." He put an arm around her, pulling her into a hug, knowing he needed to get back to work, but wanting only to hold her. Damn, she'd had a close call tonight. The idea was too unsettling to consider. "You're safe now. You're okay."

She wiggled loose from his embrace and clutched at his life vest. "Gage, listen!" Her expression was haggard, distraught.

Jessica. Car accident. His last text from Tina.

Hanging with the girls tonight. TTYL!

A chill of foreboding settled in his bones.

Tears filled Jessica's eyes, even as she confirmed his dread. "Tina, Holly and Sara are still in the car!"

Chapter Four

Horror punched Gage in the gut, stealing his breath. *Tina!*

His brain screamed, "Save her!" while his body sat frozen, numb for precious seconds, grappling with Jessica's revelation.

Clutching his vest, she shook him. "Gage! Did you hear me?" Her voice was still thin and strangled, but the urgency in her tone was clear. "You have to get them out!"

With a hard blink, he shook himself from his shock and shoved to his feet. He staggered toward the riverbank, his wet clothes and equipment slowing him, tripping him. He reached for the anchor line to clip himself back on, his hands shaking. *Tina!*

Take care of your little sister and your mom. You're the man of the house now. His father's request, spoken days before cancer claimed his life, rang like a dissonant bell in Gage's head.

"I'm going back out," he told Smith, who frowned at him.

"Not yet," Smith said. "Rodgers and Barksdale are still out there. Three passengers inside."

"I know!" Gage shouted, his voice louder than he meant. "One is my sister! The others are her friends. I know them!"

Captain Remis approached. "What's going on, Coleman?"

Gage flung a finger toward the submerged car. "I have to go back out. My sister is trapped in there!"

"Your sister?" Remis scowled. "No. You're sitting this one out. We'll get her, but I need people I know won't take unnecessary risks—"

"Screw that!" Gage shoved past his boss. "Do *not* sideline me. That's my sister out there!"

A shout from the water reached them, and Cal Rodgers appeared with a limp woman in his arms. "Two more in the car! Coleman, get out here!"

Gage helped Smith pull Rodgers to shore, one arm around his rescue, the other clinging to the rope.

From behind Gage, a newly arrived team of rescuers rushed past. EMTs from one of two ambulances scuttled down the riverbank along with the second fire truck's crew. The second fire company deployed their swift water rescue equipment and more men into the water. Police officers brought blankets. In the buzz of activity, Gage wound his way through uniforms to reach Rodgers and the petite woman he recognized instantly as Tina. He fell on his knees beside his sister and slapped at her cheek.

"Tina!" He felt her neck for a pulse, but his own hand was shaking too hard to be helpful. "Tina, can you hear me? It's Gage. I'm here, Tina. Talk to me."

Rodgers gave him a sympathetic look before pushing him out of the way and rolling Tina to her side. Water poured from her mouth and nose. Again, Rodgers blocked him when Gage tried to get closer. "Move back, man. I've got this. Let me work."

Gage gritted his teeth, but gave way, knowing his partner was in a better mind space to help Tina. He rose on shaky legs, watching Cal administer first aid, check her pulse.

"She's alive. I've got a pulse," he told Gage. "Over here!"

Rodgers called to the arriving EMTs, before bending to pinch his sister's nose and give Tina a breath.

Gage stumbled back a step, allowing the medical team to surround Tina, and glanced back up the hill to the spot where he'd left Jessica.

She stared back at him with wide, sad eyes, her hands holding the blanket closed at her throat. From the shadows of the woods beyond her, a man approached her, bending to talk to her. Jessica whipped a startled gaze to the man, then shrank back from him. "No! Get away from me!"

Prickles of alarm sluiced through Gage, and he fought free of the ropes still attached to Tina and Rodgers. As he jogged back toward Jessica, weighted down by his soaked uniform, he watched the man stick his face in hers. Jessica screamed and crab-crawled backward.

"Hey!" Gage yelled, his tone an angry warning.

The man stood, glanced back at Gage, then set off at a run down the highway. Gage itched to chase the guy, but his first concern was Jessica. Tina.

"Are you all right? Who was that guy?" He crouched beside Jessica, his headlamp casting her already pale face in a silver circle.

She squinted against the light and turned her head. She was breathing too shallowly, too fast. "He…he tried…"

Reaching up, he flicked off the power to his headlamp. He placed a hand on her knee and squeezed. "You're hyperventilating, Jess. Take slow breaths."

She lifted her eyes to him now that the blinding beam was doused. Her throat worked as she swallowed, and the blanket fell off her shoulder as she stuck her hand out to grab his. She cast a tense glance to the highway where emergency vehicles crowded the road and light bars strobed in a dizzying array of reds, golds and blues. "Is he gone?"

"The guy who was just talking to you? Yeah. He disappeared that way—" Gage pointed down the highway away from the fleet of rescue vehicles "—when I headed up here. You know him? Who is he?"

"The accident... He—" Jessica drew a shaky breath. "He caused the accident." She held his gaze, her dark brown eyes drilling him. "Gage, he did it on purpose."

GAGE'S BROW FURROWED. He blinked, the thick fringe of his eyelashes, spiked from the river water, framing his gray eyes. "What do you mean?"

Jessica opened her mouth to explain, but a knot of emotion choked her. She shook her head. There'd be a time and place to explain later. But at that moment, she could only think about her friends. She shook her head, then shifted her gaze to the rescue efforts behind him. "Is Tina...?"

His hand tightened on hers, and, still in a squat, he pivoted on his toe to check on the cluster of men surrounding his sister. "Alive." His voice was choked. "She had a pulse anyway."

Jessica let a whimper roll from her chest. "What about Holly and S-Sara? Have they—" Her voice cracked and tears stung her eyes.

"I don't know," Gage said, his tone low and sympathetic, trembling slightly with his own pain. "Let me go see what I can find out. I.I. need to get back to work."

When Gage tried to stand, tried to free his fingers from her grasp, she clutched tighter, reluctant to let him go. "Gage!"

He narrowed his eyes as he faced her again. Tiny laugh lines—could she call them that in such a horrid, stressful time as this?—formed at the corners of his eyes, his mouth. "Yeah?"

Stay with me.I 'm scared.I don't want to be alone.

Another voice in her head, one she'd nurtured since she'd first recognized her mother's mistakes and weaknesses, silenced the fearful pleas that leaped to her tongue. She released him and balled her hands in her lap, inhaling deeply. Finally, sensing Gage's impatience to get back to his rescue duties, back to his sister, she settled on "I—I'm sorry."

The tilt of his head, the twitch of his mouth said he wasn't sure what she was apologizing for, but he must've decided against asking. "I'll be back in a minute."

As he trotted away, he shouted to the EMTs and pointed out where she sat in the night's shadows.

Jessica pulled the blanket closed at her neck again and shivered. She cast an uneasy glance around, looking for Henry, certain he was somewhere just out of sight, watching her. The hiss of his hot whisper in her ear moments earlier replayed in her mind. *You have only yourself to blame. I don't like being ignored or dissed! Don't disrespect me like that ever again,J essie!*

She shook her head and waved a hand by her ear as if the memory could be batted away like a bothersome bee. The commotion of the rescue team in the river refocused her attention, and Jessica caught her breath. Only her car roof was visible as the men, attached to a spiderweb of ropes, worked to pull her friends from the car.

How long had they been underwater? Had they even survived the initial crash in the river? Had Sara still been unbuckled? Renewed grief and guilt scraped through her. Though Henry's reckless behavior had been the catalyst, she'd been behind the wheel. Her driving choices and reactions had sent the car into the river. If she'd turned the wheel left instead of right, if she'd pulled to the shoulder and stopped, if she'd stomped the brake or let her car rear end the truck—

If, i f, i f only...

The litany of doubts and unused alternatives spun in her head as she stared through the darkness at the spots of light from the teams' headlamps and flashlights. Then someone turn on a giant spotlight, and the horrific scene was lit in all its tragic glory.

A woman with a medical kit that looked like Eric's fishing tackle box arrived and squatted beside her. The EMT introduced herself as Tracy, and as the medic began checking Jessica's pulse and the reactiveness of her pupils to a penlight, she asked the expected questions. Did Jessica know her name and where she was? Was she in pain anywhere? Had she lost consciousness?

Jessica answered each query numbly, but her attention remained on the rescue effort. She leaned to the right to gaze over Tracy's shoulder to follow the activity at the river. Two men carried a litter to the waiting open bay of an ambulance. Another pair of rescuers huddled over another of her friends on the shoreline, administering CPR. More men were still in the water, fighting the current to pull her third friend from her car. *Please, G od, p lease let them be okay!*

"Can you walk to the ambulance?" Tracy asked. "You should go to the hospital to get a more thorough exam by a doctor. I think you inhaled some water, and that gash on your head may mean you have a concussion."

"I—I think so."

Tracy put a shoulder under Jessica's arm and helped her stand. Knees wobbling, she staggered toward the road and the waiting ambulances. As she passed the stretcher where the rescuers had resettled a woman, she glimpsed red hair. Holly.

The man attending Holly squeezed what looked like a clear plastic football, manually pumping air into the mask over Holly's mouth and nose. Bag-valve-mask ventilation, she'd heard it called on the medical dramas she watched on TV.

Jessica shrugged away from Tracy's support and shoved her way to Holly's side, grabbing her friend's hand. "Holly! Holly, it's Jessica! Can you hear me?"

"Stand aside, please, ma'am," one of the men said. "We need room to work."

"Holly, fight! You can do it! Breathe, Hol!" Jessica called as Tracy tugged her away from the stretcher. She stumbled back and watched the EMTs load Holly's stretcher in the back of one of the ambulances.

Tracy steered her to the back of a different ambulance where, moments later, Tina was brought up on a stretcher, pale and unresponsive. Gage was at his sister's side, his expression stricken. Jessica was hustled inside as another EMT called out numbers and medical shorthand regarding Tina's status. The urgency in the medic's voice shook Jessica to the core.

"Will she be all right?" she asked, looking to the EMT. When she got no response from the medic, she glanced to Gage.

His eyes met hers, and he shrugged. "I'll see you at the hospital."

When Gage turned to jog toward his fire crew, Jessica shivered, a cold fear and sense of isolation rising in her, suffocating her. After Tracy and a medic with the name Jim Carroway stitched on his uniform shirt climbed in with Jessica and Tina, the bay doors closed from outside.

Jessica tried to slide closer to Tina, tried to take her hand, but again she was nudged aside. "Sit back, please," Tracy said, "Let's finish your assessment."

With the bounce of tires over ruts and a wail of sirens, the ambulance set out for the hospital, and Jessica closed her eyes to pray.

GAGE PACED THE sterile waiting room outside the ICU where Tina lay in a coma. She'd been hooked up to a zillion monitors and IV tubes and put on a respirator. How was this happening? He'd just talked to Tina this morning, teasing her about the burned hot dogs she'd served at her cookout the past weekend.

In the future,l eave the fire work to the exp rts,T intin.

Now his younger sister was barely clinging to life.

At least she's alive. The voice in his head stopped him, stole his breath as he replayed what he'd learned moments ago from Sara Callen's family. Sara hadn't survived the wreck, couldn't be resuscitated at the river. The news of her friend's death would devastate Tina when she woke. *If she woke…*

Gage clenched a fist and slammed it into his opposite hand. *Stop that. Don't be defeatist. Tina needs all the positive mental energy and ptimism she can get.*

"Gage?"

He spun around, hearing the hoarse female voice behind him. Jessica stood a few steps away, wearing baggy blue scrubs. She had one hand on a rolling IV pole and a bleak look in her dark, bloodshot eyes. Even with her olive complexion, the only thing she'd ever gotten from her father, he saw the red facial blotches that said she'd been crying. Without questioning the impulse, he stepped over to her and wrapped her in a firm hug. The top of her head fit neatly under his chin, and he leaned his cheek against her damp hair.

"Jess—" was all he managed before his throat tightened, strangling his voice.

"How is Tina?" she asked, the words muffled as her face pressed into his chest.

He took a breath to steel himself, then levered away, pinching the bridge of his nose to battle down the sting of tears. "Critical. The doctor says the next twenty-four hours are going to be touch and go, but if she makes it—"

Jessica sucked in a sharp gasp and squeezed her eyes shut. "I'm sorry. I'm so, so sorry. This is all…it's my fault."

Gage frowned. "What do you mean? I know you were driving, but at the accident scene you said there was a guy who caused the accident, the man who approached you."

Her chin snapped up, and as she stared at him, her face turned gray. She wobbled, and he quickly wrapped an arm around her waist and escorted her to a seat in the waiting room. "Maybe you should go back to your bed. Weren't you checked into a room earlier?"

She sank onto the formed plastic seat and shook her head. "I'm just getting a round of antibiotics and fluids." She gestured vaguely to the plastic bag of clear liquid hanging from the wheeled pole. "Because of the cut on my head and the dirty river water and…" She paused, seeming to lose her train of thought. "I'll be released from the ER after that."

"Good. I'm glad you weren't more seriously hurt." Gage took the seat next to her and squeezed her shoulder.

Jessica glanced away, her chin quivering and her forehead creased. "If I could, I'd trade places with Tina, with any of them. It's not right that I survived, and they're all—"

Breaking off abruptly, she shifted her gaze to scan the other faces in the waiting room.

He assumed she was looking for her family. She had a son in college, if he remembered right. And she was still friendly with her ex-husband, Tina had said. "I don't think your people are here yet."

Her gaze flicked to him, and she pressed her lips in a taut line, clearly trying to rein in her emotions. "I asked the nurse not to call them. I'll let them know what happened later. I'll be okay, and I didn't want Eric upset for nothing. He's got tests this week and doesn't need—" Again she dropped her sentence, and with a shuddering sigh, she asked, "What do you know about Holly and Sara? I don't see the Callens or Teales here yet. Have you heard anything?"

He clenched his back teeth. Damn it, he didn't want to be the one to break the bad news to her. But she deserved to know the truth. He stared down at his feet. He'd deliver the blow to her, but how could he look in her sad brown eyes as he did it? Gage cleared his throat and blurted, "Holly's parents are in with her. I talked to them a little while ago. She's is critical, like Tina, but stable. Holly is breathing on her own, but not conscious. The doctors will be running several tests to see—" He stopped and tried again. "Her brain was without oxygen for an extended period and they want to assess—"

"She could have brain damage?" Jessica finished for him and released a half sigh, half whimper of despair. "And Sara?"

Gage swallowed hard. He'd do anything to spare her the pain of what he must tell her. But there was no way around it. "She didn't make it, Jess."

When he heard no reaction from Jessica for several seconds, he angled his gaze toward her. She stared at him with a bewildered expression, as if she hadn't understood. He placed a hand on her arm, feeling the shiver that raced through her. "Jess?"

Slowly, as if the truth had needed time to soak in, her face crumpled, and her shoulders jerked as a sob tripped from her. *"No."*

He drew her into his arms to hold her as more gut-wrenching sobs rolled through her. "Yeah. I'm sorry."

I'm sorry? What paltry comfort for a woman who'd been through a trauma and lost one of her best friends. A wave of grief washed through Gage, knowing he could still lose Tina.

Touch and go, the doctor had said. *The next twenty-four hours are critical.*

He stroked Jessica's back, offering what solace he could— and finding his own in her. She'd apparently bathed and washed her hair at some point, because her hair smelled clean. Floral. He probably stank of fishy river water, even though he'd hastily changed into dry clothes at the fire station before racing to the hospital. He inhaled the scent of her, taking the fresh aroma deep into his lungs. Something stirred inside him. Something he'd struggled for years to suppress—an affection and attraction deeper than anyone in his life knew. How could he be dwelling on his secret feelings for Jess while she was in shock and emotionally hurting?

His head knew wanting Jess, especially in this moment, was wrong, but he'd never been able to convince his heart and his libido of that truth. For almost as long as Tina and Jessica had been friends, Gage had hidden his truest feelings for his sister's *bestie*. She'd always been off-limits. First because he told himself she was too young, then she'd dated Matt and gotten married. Then, by the time Jess got her divorce, the bonds of the women's friendship had been too strong, too precious for Gage to risk. If he pursued his feelings for Jessica, he'd throw a huge rock into the equilibrium of the women's friendship. Or so he told himself. Maybe he was just a coward. Afraid of blowing up the yearslong dynamic of friendship he had with Jessica.

Besides, Jessica had never given him any hint she returned his romantic feelings. So he'd shoved the feelings aside and continued living his bachelor life. He couldn't justify settling for another woman, had never formed the same depth of feeling for anyone else. Why would he commit to second best while he had genuine feelings for another woman?

He moved his hand from her back to cradle her nape. Bending, he gave the crown of her head a kiss. In response, she raised her chin, her wet eyes meeting his.

"Gage," she started, as her gaze drifted away, taking in the rest of the waiting room. "I—" She hesitated again and drew her bottom lip between her teeth.

The impulse to kiss that abused lip kicked him hard, and he clenched his back teeth, pushing the clawing hunger down.

As if she'd read his thoughts, seen something damning in his face, Jessica tensed in his arms. Her back straightened, and her breath hitched.

Hell.

But when her face froze in a mask of fear and her body trembled, concern washed through him. "Jess, what is—?"

She met his gaze, a wild look in her eyes, as she rasped, "He's here!"

Chapter Five

Jessica curled her fingers into Gage's shirt and held tight so she wouldn't topple as her head spun. *Henry was here.*

Gage cast a brief glance over his shoulder, then narrowed his eyes as he studied her. "Who's here? What's wrong?"

"H-Henry."

Heart thundering, she peeked past Gage again. Her frantic gaze scoured the spot in the hospital corridor where she'd seen her tormenter, the man who'd caused her accident and hung around long enough to taunt her over the tragedy, to blame her.

But he wasn't there now. Her pulse ramped higher as she continued scanning the hallway, the waiting room, searching for him, panicked that he would approach her. Had she imagined him? He'd looked real enough, had met her gaze with a dark glare.

"Jessica?"

"He…he's gone." Henry's rapid disappearance bothered her almost as much as his being there in the first place. "He's gone! Where'd he go?" She heard the panic in her voice and inching closer to Gage, she actively slowed her breathing.

"Are you sure?" Gage loosened his grip and turned in his seat. "Who is Henry? Why does he scare you?"

"Get a grip," she muttered under her breath. Gage did not need to see her fall apart. No matter how devastating this night had been, she had to stay strong.

"Jessica? Who did you think you saw? Do I need to get security?"

"I don't see him now. But—"

"Hey," he said, carefully pulling her into a hug while avoiding the IV lines. "Take a breath. I got you. Tell me who you thought you saw. What's going on?"

A measure of relief trickled through her. Gage wouldn't allow anything or anyone to hurt her while he was around. Tina's brother had always been so protective of his sister and her friends. He'd always had Tina's back. And, by extension, Jessica's.

She clung to Gage and mustered an answer for him. "Henry is...th-this guy I went out with a couple times..."

Beneath her hands, Gage tensed.

She raised her head to cast a glance around. Had the doctor come out? Was Henry back? But no. No doctor with a report on Tina. No Henry.

You have only yourself to blame. I don't like being ignored or dissed! Don't disrespect me like that ever again, Jessie!

She suppressed a shudder and inched closer to Gage, more in his chair now than her own.

"Go on," Gage said, using a finger to pull her chin around and angle her gaze back at his.

She exhaled and sagged against him. "Henry kept calling and texting after I told him I didn't want to see him anymore. He wouldn't take no for an answer, and—" A shiver raced through her. "He showed up at the Mexican restaurant where we had our girls' night tonight. He confronted me. And—"

A combination of fear and grief strangled her, and she had to take a moment to choke the emotions down.

Gage's eyes, the shade of storm clouds, honed in on hers, his jaw rigid. "Is he the guy that frightened you at the accident scene?"

She bobbed her head. "He followed us from the restaurant." Jessica swallowed hard. "He was chasing us and driving erratically, braking hard in front of me all of a sudden. He's the reason I swerved. I was trying to avoid hitting him, but.I. lost control of the car and—"

A sob rose, surprising her, escaping before she could squelch it.

Gage tucked her closer, his hold strong. Secure. Just what she needed in that moment. She'd be strong later. She'd have to forge ahead with her life and face the repercussions of this night soon enough. But right now, in this moment, she drew comfort from the kindness of her friend's brother. Gage was grieving, too, she realized, and sucked in a sharp breath. "Jeez, I haven't even asked how you're doing. Tina…"

His dark brow dipped, his face grim. "I'm…managing. Holding on to hope."

Gage twitched a cheek in a failed attempt to smile, and a pang arrowed through her heart. She'd caused him this pain, this worry. She…and Henry. She sat taller, pulling away from Gage as the heat of anger poured into her cheeks. "I… I need to talk to the police. Report what happened." A sense of urgency raised her pulse. She searched the waiting room for a policeman. Hadn't there been a uniformed officer here earlier? "I have to tell them about Henry and his harassment. There were witnesses at the restaurant and—"

She stood too quickly, and her head spun, her knees buckled.

Gage caught her by the arms. "Jess. Hey, sit down a sec."

"The police—"

"Will be back by here in a bit to talk to you. The officer in charge said they'd get a statement from you after you finished with the doctor." Gage sighed and glanced away a moment before returning a penetrating stare to her. "He said they wanted a blood alcohol test on you if you were the driver."

Jessica nodded, guilt tripping through her veins again. *Yow ere the driver.*

"They told me that in the ER. Already took the sample. But… I wasn't drinking. You know we always assign a designated driver."

He nodded. "That's what I told them, but they have procedures to follow."

"Of course." Jessica pinched the bridge of her nose as a throb built in her head.

"Jess?"

She cut a side-glance to Gage. "Yeah?"

"I really think you should call Eric now."

A different sort of pain twisted through her now. *Eric.* Her sweet boy. How would all of this bad news affect him?

"I.I. lost my phone in the river."

He pulled out his phone and offered it to her. She took his cell and stared at it, hesitating.

"I can't. I—"

Gage blinked and tipped his head. "Don't you think he'd want to know you're all right?"

"But ignorance is bliss, and I don't want him worrying about the rest of it when there's nothing he can do. I'll tell him…later."

Gage twisted his mouth, as if he disagreed with her choice. "And Matt? Are you going to tell him?"

Jessica sat in silence for a minute, wavering. Maybe Matt

should know. And her ex-husband deserved to weigh in on how and when they broke the news of the accident to Eric. Finally, she nodded, tapped in Matt's phone number and drew a breath to calm the fresh surge of emotion flapping in her chest.

"H'lo?"

When Matt's voice answered her call, she reached for Gage's hand and gripped it as she said, "Matt, it's me. There's, uh…been an accident."

JESSICA SPENT THE rest of the night beside Gage in the ICU waiting room, anxiously awaiting news on either Holly or Tina. Through the long hours, she continued scanning the corridors, the concessions alcove and passing faces for Henry. She was certain she'd seen him, but as the weary minutes of the late night ticked by without finding him watching her, she began to wonder if seeing him in the hallway had been a trick of light or something her traumatized mind had conjured. And yet…every so often a tingle would nip the back of her neck and some primordial sense would tell her she was being watched. She'd snap her gaze up and not breathe easily again until satisfied Henry wasn't there.

At least she had Gage with her for company. His presence gave her a measure of security. Given how Henry had fled rather than face confrontation from another male—the rescue teams, the restaurant manager—she hoped having Gage next to her would keep Henry at bay. At least for tonight.

But every half hour or so, Gage got up to visit Tina and ask the nurse about any changes in her condition. Only family was admitted into the patient rooms, so for a few minutes each hour, Jessica was alone in the waiting room. She'd asked Gage if he wanted to stay with Tina full-time, the way Holly's parents were staying with her, but Gage refused to leave Jessica to sit alone. "I'm ten steps from her room. I've told her I'm here, that you're here. If anything happens, we'll see the nurses go in her room," he argued when she protested.

In the early hours of the morning, Holly's monitors blared and the nurses rushed into her room. The Teale family was forced to step out into the waiting room, their faces wan with fear and worry. Holly's father held a tearful Mrs. Teale close to his side as they huddled just outside their daughter's door.

Jessica's heart raced, and her stomach swooped with alarm. Unhooked from her IVs now, she rose on trembling legs and walked toward the couple. She'd not had the opportunity before then to express her sorrow and concern and was desperate to know what was happening with her friend. But even before she reached the older couple, Mrs. Teale spotted her, and a mask of anger suffused her face.

"Stay away from us!" she spat at Jessica.

Jessica pulled up short. "Mrs. Teale, I just wanted to tell you how sorry—"

"No! You did this to our baby, and I will never forgive you!" The older woman's tone and expression were hostile.

Jessica was so stunned by the woman's vitriol, she could only stare at her wide-eyed.

Gage rose and hurried to Jessica's side. "Mrs. Teale, please." He raised a conciliatory hand as if to quiet her shrieks. "This isn't Jessica's fault."

"Isn't it? We talked to the police. They told us *she* was at the wheel, that reckless driving was involved."

"But—" Gage started, but Mrs. Teale ranted over him.

"The doctor said Holly's blood alcohol was high. Very high."

"But not mine. I hadn't been drinking," Jessica said.

"Forgive me if I don't believe you," Mrs. Teale said with a sneer. "You *would* say that to stay out of jail, wouldn't you?"

Jail? Jessica's heart tripped. Were the police thinking of charging her with something? She hadn't even considered that nightmare. "I.I. —"

"That's enough," Mr. Teale said, tugging on his wife's arm. "Don't say anything else to her that could taint our case." He gave Jessica a cold glare as they turned their backs. "You'll be hearing from our lawyer."

Jessica's legs wobbled beneath her. Only Gage's supporting arm catching her elbow kept her from crumpling on the floor. Holly's parents were suing her?

The room spun as Gage led her back to a chair. Though she accepted her share of blame for the accident, she was troubled to think Holly's family considered her reckless or criminally culpable. She'd gladly trade places with Holly or Tina if she could. She was heartbroken and guilt-ridden over their injuries. Over Sara's death.

A fresh wave of grief flooded her, and she lurched from the chair and barely made it to the ladies' room before she heaved up the rest of her dinner. Tears spilled from her eyes as she let the waves of horror and loss from the night wash over her.

She was still slumped on the tile floor in one of the stalls when she heard a knock, the squeak of hinges and Gage's deep voice. "Jessica? You okay?"

"No."

Footsteps. The unlocked stall door opening. A hand on her shoulder. "You going to be sick again or do you want to get up?"

When she didn't answer, he stooped and, placing hands under her elbows, lifted her to her feet. When she wobbled, he caught her close, holding her against his broad chest and rubbing her back. He stood still, silent, with her in his embrace, until she stopped shaking. When decorum dictated she should have pushed away, she continued hugging him. Tonight, in the wake of so much turmoil, Gage had been the only thing solid and real she'd had, and she didn't want to let go.

Over the next forty-eight hours, she and Gage leaned on each other a lot as they waited for Tina to wake from her coma and take her first breath on her own. But her friend never did.

After two days of holding vigil, eating little other than burned coffee and vending machine snacks, and making do with paper towel baths from the bathroom sink, Gage convinced Jessica to go home. He promised to call her if Tina's condition changed.

"Get a shower, sleep in your own bed, get on with your life," he told her. "It could be days, even weeks, before there's any change with Tina."

"But I… I don't want you to be alone up here," she said, knowing he was Tina's only family available to visit. Their father had died two years earlier, and their mother had early-stage dementia and resided in a nursing home.

"I won't be." He inhaled deeply, his nose flaring and his gray eyes stormy. "Because I'll be going back to work tonight myself. I'll visit her when I can, of course, but… Tina wouldn't want us to stop living because of her."

Jessica caught her breath, ready to counter his assertion, but stopped. Nodded. He was right. She needed to return to work, return to some semblance of her life. And she had to prepare for what was coming. Sara's funeral.

She'd offered Sara's husband to help with meals, child care, errands—anything she could do to assist with the difficult days ahead. He'd politely declined, saying they had family in from all over. But Jessica knew the newly widowed father would need her support in the weeks ahead, even if he didn't ask.

In the ensuing days, at random moments when she'd usually text or call one of her posse—lunch breaks when she had to vent, bedtime when she wanted to reflect, odd moments when something curious or outrageous happened— she found herself calling Gage instead.

To his credit, he always acted glad to hear from her, and, with the exception of once when he was on a callout from the fire station, he talked with her for as long as she wanted an ear to listen. But while she appreciated his friendship and willingness to field her texts and sporadic calls, Gage didn't fill the hole left by the absence of her best friends. One dead. Two hospitalized and critical.

Holly's family continued to be hostile toward Jessica, blaming her for the accident despite her explanations about Henry's menacing behavior. They had stopped talking about a lawsuit at least, but the rejection of her friend's family stung. Their silence concerning Holly's condition felt like an abandonment, adding to her sense of isolation.

"Give them time. Everyone reacts to grief and stress differently," Gage said when she mentioned the family's coldness toward her. "But keep showing up. Let them know you aren't giving up on Holly or them."

She attended Sara's funeral the next weekend, held nine days after the car crash because the family needed time for a younger sister posted with the Marines in Okinawa to be granted leave and travel. Jessica sat with Gage during the graveside service, well aware of the stares other attendees sent her way. When the last words were spoken and the mourners began to disperse, Gage draped an arm loosely over her shoulders and patted her arm. The awkward comforting gesture was enough to bring fresh tears to her eyes.

Bless him for trying to bolster her, to show compassion and to lend strength as their relationship waded through foreign territory. She was as uncertain as he was about the parameters of this grief-born connection they were forging. She felt adrift, rudderless without the anchors of Holly, Tina and Sara in her life, and she appreciated Gage's attempts to buoy her more than he could know.

"Ready to go?" he asked.

Drying her eyes, she nodded.

Together, they started walking toward his truck. She tried to stem her tears, clear her throat and pretend she was doing better than she was. She could be strong. She *would be.* Falling apart simply wasn't an option. And most important, she couldn't let Gage believe she was crumbling. She knew he was kind enough to inconvenience himself to support her if he thought she was in trouble or struggling emotionally. She refused to be that woman—a needy and drifting woman like her mother. While he'd been a comfort in the earliest days of her grief, the time had come for her to show a braver face and give him permission to return to his old role. Just Gage. Tina's brother. Not the stalwart she leaned on or needed to stay sane.

Jessica covered his hand with hers, and when she angled a sad smile at him, prepared to give him an out from babysitting her that evening, she caught a glimpse of blond hair at the edge of the crowd that made her stumble to a stop.

Her heart jumped to her throat as she narrowed her eyes against the harsh spring sun, confirming what she saw. Henry.

Chapter Six

Across the cemetery driveway, Henry stood with his arms folded over his chest, staring at her…no, glaring. His presence at Sara's funeral, the woman he was responsible for killing, was an affront to Jessica. Her grief morphed into a fury and scorn that stiffened her body and churned her pulse. "That ass."

Gage studied her, then glanced over his shoulder, following her gaze. "Who do you mean?"

"The guy I went out with a couple times," she said, her voice strangled. "The one I thought I saw at the hospital. Henry."

I don't like being ignored! Her body shook as adrenaline coursed through her.

"Wait… The guy who caused the accident?" Gage's body language shifted, alerted like a hunter spying prey. His square jaw tensed, and his nostrils flared. "What does he look like? What's he wearing?"

"Um…nondescript blond hair. Wearing a blue jacket. Wire-rimmed glasses."

Henry turned abruptly and stalked away, into a stand of trees that bordered the cemetery and out of her field of view.

"Where did you see him? I don't see a blue jacket."

Gage took a step as if to go after Henry, and Jessica caught his arm. "Wait. He's leaving. Let him go."

"What?" he asked, his tone dark and incredulous. "After what he did? My sister almost died because of him. Sara is dead!"

Jessica noticed heads turning, people frowning as Gage's volume rose.

"Out of respect for Sara's family, please don't cause a scene. Not here. Not now."

Gage looked unconvinced, but he pressed his lips in a grim line and nodded once.

She continued to squint against the sun, searching the area she'd last seen him. "Do you see him? I want to know what sort of vehicle he's driving today. The cops told me to let them know if I saw him again." She pulled her replacement phone from her purse. She could at least alert the authorities that Henry had been there, give them a heads-up to his current location, should they have a squad car in the area. The funeral procession's police escort to the cemetery had left once the hearse had parked, but maybe that officer was still nearby?

Gage, who stood at least eight inches taller than her own five feet six, craned his neck, then scoffed. "No. Too many trees and people."

Jessica sighed her disappointment. "Man, he's as slippery as an eel. He snuck away that fast at the hospital, too." She shivered. "Tell me you at least saw him before he got away. That I didn't imagine him."

Gage's expression said he wanted to tell her that, but couldn't. "Sorry, I haven't seen him since he approached you at the accident scene." When she groaned, he quickly amended, "But that doesn't mean you imagined him. I believe you when you say he was there."

"Oh, good. So at least *you* don't think I'm going crazy. That makes one of us."

His head tipped to one side, and he put a hand at the small of her back as they resumed walking to his truck. "You think you're seeing things?"

"Ugh. No," she said, flapping a dismissive hand. "I'm being too dramatic. Ignore me. I just…" She continued to scan the crowd, searching for Henry. "If he was here, if he was at the hospital.I. wish I knew what his game was."

"His game?"

"Is he following me? If so, why? Does he want to apologize for the accident? Is he morbidly curious about the repercussions of the accident? Is he feeling guilty or—?"

When she didn't finish, Gage put a hand on her arm and faced her. "Are you worried that he's dangerous? That he's stalking you? That he wants to hurt you?"

Despite the warm day, a chill slithered down her spine. "Maybe. He certainly gives me the creeps. And having him pop up here, the same way he showed up at the hospital, is unsettling. And his turning up at the Mexican restaurant the night of the accident is feeling less and less like coincidence."

Gage tucked both hands in his pockets and exhaled heavily as he moved his gaze over the departing mourners. "I don't like the sound of this. And I don't like the fact that you live alone, in case he does try to cause you more trouble."

She flashed a half-hearted grin. "I'm not alone. I have Pluto."

His frown deepened. "I'm serious. Someone should stay with you."

"Oh, really? And who would that be? Not Eric. He's at school, and he needs to stay there. I won't bother him with this. His class work is too important. Besides, it's not his job to take care of my problems."

He walked the last few feet to his truck's passenger door

and opened it for her. "I don't mean Eric. I'll do it. On the nights I'm not at the fire station, I'll sleep on your couch."

She shook her head firmly. "No." Placing a hand on his arm, she amended, "Thank you, but no. I can't ask you to do that."

"Jess," he started, sounding disgruntled.

"I don't want you—or anyone—moving in with me. I don't think the situation is dire enough to require a room-mate, or a bodyguard, or whatever it is you think you'd be. My doors stay locked when I'm home, and I keep my cell phone close. I can call the police if necessary."

"All that is a good start, but I'd feel better if I knew—"

"No, Gage. I will not be a burden or responsibility for anyone else. I don't want anyone to have to move into my house, and—before you suggest it—I don't want to go to anyone else's house, either. I'd be in the way, and—just, no." She sighed, searching for the words to explain the pact she'd made with herself years earlier. "I promised myself after I divorced Matt that I would be completely self-sufficient and independent until I needed a nursing home."

Gage pulled a face and scratched his forehead. "Surely you can make exceptions."

She shrugged one shoulder. "If needed. But it's not needed in this case." To put an end to the discussion, she climbed into the truck and pulled the door closed.

Gage circled the truck to the driver's side and slid be-hind the steering wheel. He cranked the engine, adjusted the air temperature and fan settings, then gave her a long, odd look. After a beat, he asked, "Does that mean you don't plan to marry again?"

She shrank back a notch, startled by his question. "I— Why do you say that?"

"Trying to understand what *completely self-sufficient*

and independent—" he used two fingers to make air quotes "—looks like."

Why did that question, coming from Gage, unsettle her so much? For a minute, as they drove slowly out of the cemetery, Jessica said nothing, her thoughts returning to her loss of Sara, to Sara's family and the overwhelming shift her life had taken because of the accident. Would Tina and Holly recover fully or be left with brain damage? Would Sara's family, like Holly's, hold a grudge against her and cut her from their lives? How could her little posse of friends—heart sisters—have been so horribly shattered like this? She wanted to be independent and self-reliant, but her life now was…lonely.

Anger swelled in her. Her situation, her friends' injuries, the ruined lives—was all the fault of that jerk, Henry. Her jaw clenched, furious with the man whose recklessness had caused this tragedy. Anger bubbled for herself, as well, for having caved to her loneliness and gone looking for male companionship on a dating app. She hadn't needed a man when she had her best friends, her son. The tears that pricked her eyes now rose from her disappointment in herself.

As Gage pulled out onto the main road, she shifted on the seat to face him. "I'll tell you part of what self-sufficient and independent looks like."

He cast a side-glance her way, dark eyebrow lifted. "Yeah?"

"I'm done with dating. No more apps or fix-ups by friends. No more awkward get-to-know-you conversations or pretending you're having a good time with a guy, when all I really want is to curl up with a bowl of ice cream, a good book and my cat on my lap. Or hang out drinking wine and laughing with my girls." Her voice cracked as she realized she might never have a night with her posse again. She swiped at her leaky eyes and blew her nose in a tissue. "Damn it. I hate this."

Gage shot her a sympathetic glance and reached toward her, his hand hovering near her leg before apparently thinking better of it and snatching his hand back. He squared his body with the steering wheel, hands anchored at ten and two, and set his jaw. Under his breath, he muttered, "Yeah. I hate this, too."

HENRY SNUCK THROUGH the crowd of people, making his way to his mother's old beater. As much as he hated using the rusty sedan that stank of her cigarettes and hairspray, he couldn't use his truck until the heat was off following the incident at the river. He knew the cops would be looking for his truck, that Jessie would have reported it, and so he'd stashed it behind the garage at work for the time being. He knew his boss wouldn't question why or give him up to the cops, because Bill didn't want any attention anywhere near his operation. The boss had too many undocumented men working for him, too many off-the-books salaries being paid, and a critical sideline business to protect.

He'd left his mother's car far from the rest of the funeral traffic, near the back drive of the cemetery so he could get away quickly if needed. By hanging at the edges of the crowd, staying behind Jessie through the service, he'd managed to go unnoticed...until he was ready for her to see him. He'd let her spot him, just so she'd know he was keeping tabs on her.

He hadn't expected to see her draped all over another man. He recognized the guy as the same one who'd been at the hospital. He obviously had some connection to one of the women in ICU, so it wasn't unrealistic that he knew

Jessie, that he'd be with her at the funeral. His handsy familiarity with Jessie was a problem, though. He'd have to dig a bit and find out who this man was.

When he reached his mother's sedan, he dropped onto the torn front seat and sat for a minute, deciding his next steps with Jessie. She was an aggravating combination of hot woman and cold bitch. He chewed the inside of his cheek, seething over the way she'd tried to humiliate him in front of her friends. Going forward, she'd have to learn her place. His daddy hadn't taught him much before he died, but he'd showed him how to handle a woman, how to teach a woman her place. Authority, control and, as needed to earn her respect, a hand across her cheek.

Thanks to Jessie driving her car into the river and killing her friend, things were too hot to try again to talk sense into her. Too many people still were hovering around her, getting in his way. He could be patient, wait until she was alone to bring her in line. Talking to her at the restaurant had been a bad move. Her accident had set them back, drawn too many people into her orbit. But soon enough the hubbub would die down, and he'd get another chance to bring her around. He and Jessie belonged together, and one day soon, she'd see that, too. He'd make sure of it.

YOU'RE AN IDIOT, Gage.A sap.D eluded.

The chastisement played on a loop in his brain as Gage drove Jessica home after the post-funeral gathering at Sara's house. In the past several days, as they both struggled to cope with the tragedy and stress that had befallen them, he'd thought they'd found a new common ground, a new connection and—yes—intimacy.

When Jessica had started calling him at night and sharing her thoughts and fears, her regrets and longings, a spark of something he'd banked for years had flickered to life. He'd dared to hope that Jessica might come to see him the way he'd seen her for years—as more than a friend.

But her quick refusal to have him stay at her house to protect her, her assertion that she had no use for men or dating or new relationships, had doused those hopes. He scoffed and shook his head, disgusted with his quixotic delusions.

"What?" she asked, turning damp, red eyes toward him. Those dark brown windows to her grieving soul had cried copious tears even before the funeral this morning, a beacon calling him to hold her and comfort her.

He flipped a hand. "Nothing."

"Mmm," she hummed, before turning to stare silently out the side window, not pressing for any more explanation or showing any further interest in what had drawn the huff of frustration from him. He told himself he wasn't disappointed she'd dropped the matter so easily. *You* did *say "nothing."*

Apparently, he'd imagined the growing connection and deeper trust between them. Apparently, nothing had changed for her. He'd stupidly assigned her need for support and a friendly shoulder for her tears this week as some sort of awakening in her, an acknowledgment of feelings she'd denied for twenty-plus years. He'd let the scent of her shampoo, the silkiness of her hair tucked under his chin, the strength of her grip holding him go to his wishful head.

Gritting his back teeth and squeezing the steering wheel, he jammed the newly inflated feelings back into the tiny box where he'd stored them for so many years, waiting. But like any blowup mattress or beach toy, getting all of his confused feelings and hopes regarding Jessica to fit back into the safe box was going to be difficult. His raft of emotions knew how it felt to hold her, inhale her floral scent. The edges of his years-old yearnings wouldn't tuck neatly away now that he'd shared so many frank conversations and emotional exchanges with her. The shared confidences had seemed like a beginning to him, but were something entirely else for her.

"Oh, shoot," she mumbled, looking around her and in the back seat of his truck.

"Problem?"

"I left my lasagna pan at Sara's house. The last thing Cody and the kids need is another dirty dish to wash and find the owner for."

"I can turn around, go back to get it." Gage moved his hand to his turn signal, prepared to do just that.

She puckered her mouth for a moment, debating. "No. Cody and his mom were all going to lie down with the kids for a bit and try to get some rest. I don't want to disturb them. The kids haven't slept well in days and neither have the adults. For different reasons." She raked her hair back from her face. "I'm guessing that, with the funeral behind them, the adrenaline and stress they've been running on will crash, and they'll get their first sleep in days."

Gage nodded. He understood about running on adrenaline and stress. He'd done much the same since seeing Tina's limp body pulled from the river.

Jessica pinched the bridge of her nose. "I'll text Cody. Tell him to set it aside dirty, and I'll come by for it tomorrow after work." Suiting words to action, she reached in her purse for the new phone she'd bought a couple days after the accident.

Gage had driven her to the phone store, then later the same afternoon, they'd gone to pick up a rental car, since at that point, her insurance company hadn't gotten her claim processed. He'd offered to go with her to shop for her new vehicle, once her insurance settlement was finalized, and had been rebuffed.

"I can do it by myself," she'd said. "In fact, I want to. I need to."

He hadn't understood her insistence to buy her car without his help, but he'd respected it. But now she was deferring to that same go-it-alone mentality when her safety was at risk. He needed to change her mind. Or...was he just looking for excuses to spend time with her?

At Jessica's house, he escorted her inside and gave her cat a pat on the head as he walked to her front door. "You be a good guard cat, okay, Pluto? You're her only line of defense here in case of trouble." Though he'd been joking, the statement niggled. If this Henry dude was following her, he *really* didn't like the idea of Jessica being alone. "Jess, are you sure you don't want me to stay here tonight?"

She pulled a frustrated face. "I'm positive."

"I know you don't want to impose and that you have a bug up your butt about being self-sufficient, but with Henry showing up at the cemetery—"

She scoffed a laugh. "A bug up my butt?"

He dragged a hand down his face. "You know what I mean. You can be rather stubborn."

One thin eyebrow lifted, and she growled under her breath.

He gave her a measuring scrutiny. "I don't have to report to the station until tomorrow morning. I could sleep on your couch—"

She placed a hand on his forearm, her touch stirring something warm in his belly, and she shook her head harder. "Really, Gage. No need. Thank you, but no. I'm going to get a hot bath, climb in bed and read accountant reports on my laptop until I fall asleep. Nothing better for insomnia than a boring spreadsheet." She pulled open the front door, and as he moved past her he stopped to give her a hug.

"Call if you need anything. 'Kay?"

She rose on her tiptoes to drop a quick kiss on his cheek. "Thank you, but I'll be fine."

He didn't leave until he knew she had his cell number programmed for speed dial on her new phone and had secured all her doors.

Though the day had exhausted him emotionally, Gage stopped by the hospital to check on Tina before going home. Her condition was unchanged. The doctors had warned him it would be a long journey for Tina, but Gage desperately wanted some tiny sign of improvement, some glimmer of hope. Not just for Tina, but for Jessica. Despite her bravado, he could see how the fallout of the accident wore on her. While the Jessica he knew was strong, independent and courageous, everyone had their breaking point.

And he feared Jessica was nearing hers.

Chapter Seven

The weeks following the accident passed in a numb haze. Jessica went through the motions of life—getting up in the morning, going to work, being told to stay away by Holly's bitter parents, then sitting in the ICU waiting room in Gage's company. She talked to Tina via Gage's phone, held to his sister's ear, as if her best friend could hear her, because the nurses said they believed she could. But the only response Tina gave to Jessica's chatter was the lonely beeps and drones of the machines her friend was hooked to.

The highlight of her day was the brief check-in she had with Eric most nights. She used text exchanges more often now, instead of Facetime, because she feared he'd hear something in her voice or see something in her expression that would tip him off that her life was not as rosy as she painted it. She didn't want him worried about her or distracted from his studies.

On nights that Gage was at the fire station, she would text him updates from the police about the investigation into the accident and locating Henry. The process was taking a frustratingly long time. She didn't understand why they couldn't simply go to Henry's residence and arrest him for leaving the scene of an accident or reckless endangerment or involuntary manslaughter.

The only reply the police department seemed willing to offer was the investigation was still open and that they'd let her know when there was news.

The nurses were likewise unwilling to share information with Jessica about Holly or Tina, due to privacy laws, a source of ongoing frustration for her. But she'd learned to glean hints from the nurses, if only from their facial expressions as they left Tina's room.

Every time she texted Gage with these updates, he'd reply with, Thanks. And how are you doing?

Fine.

His reply each time was, I'm here for you if you need anything.

Jessica's chest would warm at the sentiment, but she knew better than to believe that Gage's offer was anything more than the polite, expected platitude it was. Gage had his own life, job and responsibilities. She couldn't expect him to be there for her in the long term, so she was better off getting her act together and moving on with her new normal.

ONE MORNING, ABOUT five weeks after Sara's funeral, Nadine, the receptionist for Jessica's employer, rang her desk phone.

"There's a gentleman here to see you."

Jessica frowned and checked her desk calendar, worried she'd forgotten an appointment. She had no in-person meetings planned until the next afternoon. "Who is it?"

She heard Nadine ask for a name, then a muffled male reply. "He says he's your boyfriend," Nadine said, her tone intrigued. Then in a singsong whisper, she added, "He brought you flowers."

Jessica's pulse hammered, dread filling her belly. "I don't have a boyfriend. What did he say his name was?" But even before Nadine pressed the visitor for the information, Jessica knew.

"Henry Blythe," Nadine confirmed. "Shall I send him back?"

"No!" Jessica blurted, even as she heard Nadine calling, "Sir, wait! You can't go back there without—"

Jessica slammed the phone down and shoved away from her desk. She rushed out to the corridor to intercept Henry, wondering what in the hell he wanted. More important, how had he found her office? Had she told Henry where she worked? She could only remember telling him she was a corporate marketing manager, so how—

"Hello, Jessie."

She stumbled to a stop as Henry rounded the corner from the reception area and grinned at her. Rather than friendly or affectionate, his grin seemed smug and satisfied, as if gloating over having bested her somehow.

"For you." He held out the bouquet of white daisies and pink carnations.

She didn't reach for them, didn't want them. "How did you know where I worked? What do you want?"

"I wanted to surprise you. Take you to lunch for your birthday."

Her breath snagged. "Today's not my birthday."

But the day after next was. And she *knew* she hadn't shared that detail of her life with him.

He shrugged. "I know. But close enough. I've got other plans for your actual birthday." Another crocodile grin that pooled dread in her core.

When he stepped closer, still trying to hand her the bouquet, she moved back a step. She raised a palm toward him and shook her head. "I don't want your flowers. And I'm not going to lunch or anywhere else with you."

Henry's mouth tightened, and he cut a glance over his shoulder where even without being able to see around the corner, Jessica knew Nadine was watching Henry with interest. He walked closer to Jessica, moving out of the receptionist's view, and she edged farther away. "You're making me look bad here, Jessie. Will you take the damn things—" he shook the flowers so hard a daisy blossom fell off "—and get your purse or whatever else so we can go to lunch?"

"You're not hearing me, Henry," she said, trying to keep her tone low and even. "We are not a couple. I do not want to see you again, and if you don't leave now and stop following me, I will file a restraining order and—"

"Following you? I just thought we'd go to lunch. How's that following you?"

"I saw you at the cemetery and at the hospital. Now you've showed up here out of the blue? I want it to stop!" When her voice rose along with her anger, she took a beat to calm herself. She didn't want to cause a spectacle in front of her coworkers. Which, come to think of it, was probably exactly what Henry was hoping for—that she'd comply rather than cause a scene.

"What's wrong with you?" he asked, his tone accusing. "On our first date, didn't you say you thought we had everything in common? We are a perfect match." He wagged a finger back and forth between them. He lowered his brow, and his eyes sparked behind his glasses. "You belong with me! Why are you fighting it?"

Jessica gritted her teeth. "Your reckless, hostile driving killed my friend! That alone is reason enough to never—"

She stopped short, realizing the opportunity Henry had handed her. If she could stall him here while Nadine or someone else called the police...

She wet her lips and tried to calculate the best way to backpedal without raising suspicion. Her heart thundered against her ribs, and after swallowing hard to moisten her dry throat, she said, "Fine. We'll talk. But not at lunch. We'll talk in my office." She took the flowers from him. "Wait here. I'll just have Nadine put these in water for me."

She strode past him, through the lobby, to Nadine's desk. She felt Henry's eyes following her. As she handed the receptionist the flowers, she leaned in, saying, "Stay calm, but I need you to call the police. Send them to my office. This is the guy who caused my car accident."

Nadine's face blanched, and her eyes widened. She shot a nervous glance to Henry.

"Don't look at him," Jessica whispered. "I told him I was going to have you put these in water for me. So smile, maybe sniff them."

Nadine gave her a strained smile and ducked her face to the flowers. An actress the woman wasn't.

With a deep breath for composure, Jessica turned and crossed the lobby back to the spot where Henry waited. His eyes narrowed with suspicion.

"What did you tell her?"

"I asked her to find a vase for the bouquet and to hold my calls while we talked."

She took a few steps toward her office, but Henry grabbed her wrist and pulled her up short. "Don't lie to me. I saw how she looked at me. What did you say?"

Across from her, Chan Woo stuck his head out of his office, his brow furrowed, and asked, "Jessica, is everything all right out here?"

Henry released her arm and turned his back to Chan.

She pasted on a fake smile. "Sure. I'm fine."

Chan hesitated a moment before he moved back into his office and closed his door.

Henry tugged Jessica out of the sight of Chan's office window and growled in a hushed tone. "You're going to be sorry you treated me this way. I deserve better, Jessie."

With that, Henry paced down the hall to the employee staircase and stormed through the door.

She chased after him, seeing the chance for the police to catch him slipping away. From the top of the switchback staircase, she called, "Henry, wait! We can talk. Come back up and—" The clang of the ground floor fire exit door slamming echoed in the stairwell.

Jessica clenched her fists and growled under her breath. Turning, she returned to the office corridor and found Nadine hovering outside her office.

"The cops are on their way," the receptionist said, her expression still anxious.

Jessica sighed and shook her head. "Too late. He's gone."

THAT NIGHT JESSICA told Gage about the incident at work as they sat in the ICU waiting room, eating the fried chicken he'd picked up on the way to the hospital. She raised her wrist to show him the new bruises Henry had left with his viselike grip. "He did this, and he probably scared five years off Nadine Holloway's life."

Gage wiped his greasy fingers on a napkin before lifting her arm to examine the bruises. His expression darkened. "Did you show these to the cops when they arrived?"

"Well, no. They hadn't really darkened then, and I was more concerned with them tracking him before he left the area."

He pursed his lips in thought. "Well… I'm not exactly sure how the law works, but I'd say you have grounds for a restraining order here." He dipped his head and gaze, indicating the fingerprint bruises.

Jessica considered that. "If he's going to keep popping up uninvited and bothering me, that might not be a bad idea. How do I get a restraining order?"

"Again, I'm not a lawyer. But… I can put you in touch with a friend of mine who might be able to help."

Jessica shrugged, knowing this was her battle, not Gage's. "Thanks, but I have a lawyer. Surely the woman who handled my divorce could put me on the right track for a restraining order. I'm betting that sort of thing comes up frequently in her practice."

"True. So you'll call her in the morning?" Gage's voice was quietly encouraging, urgent.

"I will." Jessica realized that Gage was still holding her arm, his thumb gently stroking the tender underside of her wrists where Henry had left his mark. His touch stirred a heady thrum in her core, and a sweet and languid hum flowed through her veins. Two things struck her at once— the contrast between Henry's damaging grip and Gage's soothing one, and how much she liked the soft caress of his thumb. The slow back-and-forth motion was hypnotic. Pleasant. Even…erotic.

As the word entered her mind, Jessica yanked her arm away, catching her breath so hard and fast that she choked, coughed.

"You okay?" he asked.

She forced a laugh. "Mmm-hmm. You know me. I can stumble over a painted line on the floor and, apparently, choke on air. Such a klutz." She rolled her eyes and gave him a wry grin.

Gage tipped his head. "Really? I've always thought of you as one of the most poised and graceful people I know. You know, thanks to all your gymnastics and cheerleading in high school?"

"Oh, well…" She shrugged, not wanting to dwell on her flimsy cover story. She wasn't about to tell him she'd found his touch arousing, or that she'd wondered for the briefest moment what it would be like to have him touch *other* places on her body. "So…" she continued, guiding the conversation safely away from the scandalous path that had tripped her up. "I'll call Olivia in the morning and get a restraining order in the works."

"Good. In the meantime, let me take a picture of the bruises as evidence the judge may want. And I'm repeating my offer to stay at your house for a little while. You might need a little added protection until the cops do something about Henry."

She was shaking her head even before he finished speaking. "I've been taking care of myself since I was eight years old. Maybe earlier. I've got this."

"I'm not doubting your competence, Jess. But sometimes having someone else around is an effective deterrent to a creep that is looking to bully or harass you. His track record proves he's likely to flee the scene rather than contend with someone who might challenge his presence." He spread his hands and gave her a disarming smile. "Someone at your service, ma'am."

She patted his chest and returned a grin. "I appreciate the offer. But I'll be fine."

"So you've taught Pluto to attack on command, then? Or dial 911 in a crisis?"

Just the thought of her derpy feline managing any level

of training or defensive maneuvers made her laugh. "Not even close."

Sighing, Gage folded down the lid on his meal and stowed his trash in the carryout bag. "I just want to know you're safe, Jess. I've already got a sister fighting for her life. I can't stand the idea of something happening to you, too."

He looked so sad, so pained, Jessica couldn't help but put her arms around him, lean her head on his shoulder. "I know. And you're the best of friends for being so considerate and protective of me. Especially since I'm the one who—"

"No!" He returned the embrace. "Stop blaming yourself. One person is to blame, and he will be brought to justice, one way or another."

For a moment she just took comfort from his hug, something she'd had too few of since her divorce and Eric's leaving for college. Surely just her craving for human contact had spurred her carnal thoughts of Gage a few moments ago?

When she backed out of his arms, she added her dinner trash to his, musing, "I just don't understand why the police haven't found him and taken him into custody yet. How hard is it to find a person, if you know their name and have their vehicle description?"

"Good question." He pulled out his phone and motioned to her arm. She held it out for him to photograph. "I understand they get overwhelmed with cases and a shortage of manpower but...this delay is curious." He bent his head over his phone. "I'm texting you a copy of the photos now."

"Thanks." As Jessica found the small hand wipe that came with the greasy combo meal and tore open the packet, her thoughts strayed in another direction.

How did ouk now where I worked?

She stilled. Henry had never answered that important

question. She hadn't shared more than superficial information about herself, as a matter of standard practice and safety. She hadn't even given him her cell phone number, choosing to communicate through messaging apps for their first dates. So if she hadn't told him the name of her employer, which she was 99.99 percent sure she hadn't, what sort of digging and prying had he done to locate the business she worked for? A chill wriggled through her, knowing how much personal information could be gleaned from the internet by someone willing to do the work. Knowing Henry had employed even a fraction of that kind of research to track her down was...unsettling.

A whistle cut into her thoughts, and she jerked her attention to Gage. "Huh?"

His hand was extended, and he chuckled. "I said, 'Do you want me to take that for you?'"

"Oh. Thanks." She handed him the used wet wipe to add to the rest of the trash.

"Where were you just then? You looked worried."

She exhaled and dropped her shoulders. "Just wondering how Henry found my office. He must have done some checking up on me or followed me from my house one morning or—" She gave a shudder. "It's creepy."

Gage's brow dipped. "It is."

His concerned look asked, *Are you sure you won't change your mind about having me stay on your couch tonight?*

Jessica shook off the uneasy feeling that crawled through her. "I refuse to let him cow me or make me change or restrict my life. That's how bullies win." She stood and dusted biscuit crumbs from her lap. "I'll be fine."

Despite her assurances to Gage, Jessica wished she could be half as confident as she pretended. She made a mental note to call her lawyer in the morning about the restraining order. If Henry was upping his game, she'd have to do the same.

OVER THE NEXT couple of weeks, Jessica, with the help of her attorney, filed and won a restraining order against Henry. While she couldn't tell the judge where to find Henry to serve him with the legal documents surrounding the case, her attorney had posted a legal notice in the local paper. In court, the police report from the car accident and sworn statements from the manager of the Mexican restaurant, Gage, Chan Woo and Nadine Holloway were enough to convince the judge to issue an initial temporary order. But even with the legal measures in place, she found herself looking over her shoulder, startling at noises at night and checking her rearview mirror more often than usual. And every time she did, she chastised herself for renting Henry the space in her head.

She started visiting the hospital more often and staying later, using the excuse that she owed it to her friends to keep vigil. In truth, her house seemed emptier, lonelier than usual lately, and she enjoyed knowing Gage would be at the hospital to keep her company. His presence gave her more than companionship, she acknowledged privately. He anchored her with something familiar, someone kind when her world was topsy-turvy and uncertain.

Eric came home for a long weekend in early May, and she cherished the few days with her son before he left to visit his father, then return to campus for summer semester and the job he'd secured at a Chapel Hill restaurant.

When Memorial Day rolled around three weeks later, a day when she and her posse would have traditionally held a cookout and potluck in someone's backyard, she invited Gage and Sara's family to join her at her house for grilled hamburgers, hot dogs and all the fixings. Gage accepted readily, but Sara's widower, Cody, declined, saying he planned to take the kids to his parents' house for the weekend instead. And so just she and Gage ended up having dinner at her house, a pitiful semblance of the sort of gathering they used to have. More and more, she and Gage were going it alone, and Jessica became increasingly aware of the sacrifices he was making to keep her company, check on her and give her support. His attention was exactly the kind of pity and indebtedness to him she didn't want...but which she found herself craving more with every passing day.

GAGE TOOK THE wet salad bowl Jessica handed him and dried it before stacking it with the other dishes after their Memorial Day dinner. Jessica had cooked an enormous meal, enough for twenty instead of the two that their party had been. Her abundant preparations gave him further evidence of how much she missed her friends and longed for the life that had been destroyed earlier that spring.

For nine weeks now, she'd put on a brave face, never complained, and continued to faithfully visit the hospital after work, even though Tina remained in ICU, her condition unchanged. But all the strained smiles meant to convince him she was fine and the ritual of her routine didn't change the sadness that shadowed her dark eyes or the worry that had etched tiny lines at the corners of her mouth.

"I think the rest of these will keep," he said, nodding his head toward the last few pans that soaked in the sink. "You've got to be tired after all the prep and cooking you put in today."

She rolled her shoulders and stretched her neck, even as she said, "Naw. It's no big deal."

He stepped over to her and gave her shoulders a firm

squeeze. The groan that rumbled from her throat both called her a liar concerning her fatigue and lit a fire in his belly. He all too easily could imagine that purr-like expression of pleasure as her response to intimate acts between them. And he'd let himself imagine such acts with growing frequency over the past weeks, an indulgence he'd never dared except as a randy teenager when his lust for Jessica was new. His sultry daydreams were a risk, he knew. If she learned the kind of relationship he wanted from her, the dynamic between them could implode.

He had to be careful. He refused to risk the yearslong friendship they had or destabilize Jessica's last pillar of support, when so much of her life was falling apart. Still, as they'd grown closer, spent more time together, shared more of the sort of daily chatter and commiseration that spouses might, he'd found it easier to imagine their relationship eventually following the trajectory they seemed to be on. For all the awfulness of the last few months, he couldn't begrudge the excuse he'd been given to get closer to Jess. He yearned for their increasing intimacy to become physical, for her trust of him to grow, allowing him to share his true feelings.

He moved his massage to her neck, and she allowed her head to loll forward, her raven hair spilling over her shoulders and hiding her face. Having met Jessica's mother when they were in high school, he knew she had light brown hair and a fair complexion. He'd never asked Jessica about her father, only knowing what he'd overheard Tina tell their parents when they'd asked about Jessica's absent father.

"He was a one-night stand," Tina had said, "and her mother lost contact with him before Jessica's birth."

Did Jessica know anything more than that about the guy? What had it been like growing up with that blank regarding your heritage, a whole invisible branch of your family tree?

Curiosity poked him now as the ebony strands of her hair tickled his hands. Her dark coloring must have come from her father, and he wondered how she'd felt seeing that glimpse of him when she looked in the mirror.

"Can I ask you something?" he ventured.

"I think you just did."

"Ha ha. I'm wondering…about your father."

She didn't say anything, but her chin came up a notch and she pulled away from his touch.

"I'm sorry," he said. "If that's a touchy subject, you don't—"

"I never met him, but I saw a picture of him once."

Gage slid his hands in the back pockets of his jeans. "Oh? I was under the impression from Tina that he was—" he caught himself, wanting to be tactful "—not really a part of your mother's life."

Jessica chuckled and took her unfinished glass of wine from the counter. "Hmm. So Tina told you, huh?"

He wrinkled his nose. "Sort of."

After a dismissive lift of an eyebrow, she hitched her head, indicating he should follow her.

He took a beer out of her refrigerator and joined her in the living room. Pluto was curled up sound asleep on the chair he usually chose, so he took the spot next to Jessica on the sofa, angling his body to face her.

"My dad was a casual acquaintance my mom knew through a waitressing job she had at the time. He was one of several men she'd slept with in that time frame, and she didn't know which of the men was my dad until I was born with black hair and a dark complexion."

He nodded once at her confirmation of his suspicion but let her continue without interrupting.

"He was Native American. Cherokee. At the time, my

mom lived near the reservation in the western part of the state, and he was a regular at the diner where she worked. Someone took a picture of her blowing out candles on a birthday cake, and he was in the group of people standing around her, singing."

"Cherokee, huh? I'd guessed he was from India or the Middle East. Do you know his name?"

"Mom wouldn't tell me. She didn't want me trying to find him someday. She didn't even put his name on my birth certificate."

"Did she tell him about you?"

"I doubt it," she said and took a sip of her wine. "My mom was…selfish. Shortsighted. Impractical. She didn't care about anyone's rights or happiness but her own, right up to her death by overdose. And that includes her daughter's."

Hearing the despondency in her tone, Gage scooted closer to her and drew her into a one-armed hug. "I remember that—her death when we were in college. I'm sorry I didn't make it back for her funeral."

"Pfft, do *not* worry about that. It was not so much a funeral as me, Matt, Tina and my college roommate spreading her ashes in a wildflower field outside of town." She toed off her sandals and tucked her bare feet under her before leaning against his side.

Gage hummed an acknowledgment. With the arm around her shoulders, he reached up to give her head a finger massage before leaving his hand resting lightly on her hair. "Want to watch a movie? I bet we can find *Saving Private Ryan* on some channel this weekend."

She groaned. "Wonderful piece of cinema and touching tribute to our men in uniform, but I'm not sure I can handle the gore and tension of that movie tonight. I need something light and funny. Something feel-good."

Gage reached for the remote of her television and turned the screen on. "All right. Stop me if you see something that fills the feel-good prescription." He pulled up the programming guide screen and began scrolling.

Jessica made a few noncommittal noises now and then, showing half interest but no enthusiasm for anything. When he scrolled past an airing of *Saving Private Ryan*, he chuckled and said, "Told ya."

"Your psychic powers amaze me," she deadpanned, then took the remote from him and turned the TV off. "Gage, are we old now?"

"Depends on how you define old."

"Hundreds of channels available, but I'd rather just have silence and a glass of wine."

"Naw. Quiet is…self-care, not age. I'm older than you, but despite a few gray hairs, I'd like to think I still have a little gas in my tank."

She sat up and twisted to face him. "You have gray hairs?"

"Not a lot. And not all of them somewhere the public would see 'em…"

Jessica's eyebrows shot up. "Oh."

He sent her a devilish grin. "Wanna see?"

She sputtered a laugh. "Gage!"

"Oh, get your mind out of the gutter, Harkney. I meant my chest." But his teasing, challenging grin lingered.

She moved her feet back to the floor and, after holding his impish stare for a moment, she tugged up his T-shirt to expose his stomach. "Where?"

Sitting forward, he pulled the shirt higher and found a couple of said stray gray hairs on his chest. He pointed them out. "Satisfied?"

Jessica canted forward, lifting a finger to the grays. "Well, well, well." She grasped the hairs and plucked them.

"Agh! Hey!"

She tossed him a smug look. "Problem solved."

"That hurt!"

Flattening a hand against his chest, she pulled a pouty face and gave the offended spot a rub. "Aw, did Gageypoo get an owie?"

He should have knocked her hand away and yanked his shirt down. In their younger days, when they teased and engaged in horseplay, he'd have nudged her away with his shoulder and a tickle or scared her away with an armpit or spit string. Annoying brotherly stuff like what he waged on Tina. But…

Her soothing hand on his chest felt heavenly and sparked his libido. The unbrotherly feelings for Jess that he'd been fighting in recent weeks flashed hot. His breath caught and held. His gaze locked with hers. He swallowed hard.

Jessica's playful grin froze then shifted as he stared into her eyes. He couldn't say what his face revealed, but she'd read something there. Her pupils grew. Her lips parted. And a ragged breath whispered from her.

He covered the hand she still rested on his chest with his, then curled his fingers around hers. Her attention fell to their joined hands as he lifted hers to his lips and brushed a soft kiss on her knuckles.

Was this it? Was this the paradigm-shifting moment he'd waited for all these years? Gage waged a rapid-fire debate in his head. Act on his impulses or rein in his heart as he had for so long? Should he lean in and kiss her now, giving her the truth about his feelings in one simple act of affection?

Something warm and encouraging flickered in the espresso depths of her eyes. Desire? Curiosity? Consent?

Adrenaline as potent and stirring as the day of his first house fire buzzed through his brain, his limbs, his blood. Her heated look, the beer he'd had at dinner, or some wishfulness he'd pressed down long enough prodded him. He leaned in, dropped his gaze to her lips, angled his head…

Jessica jerked back. Snatched her hand from his. Her breath as she exhaled quavered in the silent living room. She inched away from him on the couch, shaking her head, her brow creased with confusion. Maybe even consternation.

Gage's heart sank. His gut tightened. Had he destroyed everything he'd fought all these years to protect in a matter of seconds? In one foolish move?

He surged to his feet, fisting his hands at his sides, and strode across the floor. He stood with his back to her for a moment before he said quietly, "I'll see myself out."

He made it as far as her front door before her voice reached him.

"Gage?"

He paused, his hand on the doorknob. The quick patter of bare feet on carpet, then tile announced her approach. His heartbeat crashed against his ribs, and his dinner soured in his stomach. *Damn it,m an! What have youd one?*

Jessica placed a gentle hand on his back, and he flinched as if burned. "Gage?"

He turned to face her, trying not to look as guilty as he felt. "Yeah?"

Jeez, his voice sounded like he'd been chewing glass.

"Thanks for coming over tonight," she said in a quiet voice. "I.I. had a good time."

Tenderness wrenched in his chest as he heard her attempts to normalize his exit. As if he hadn't just shattered the framework of their twenty-six-year friendship.

"Yeah." He could play along. "It was good. Dinner was great. Thanks."

He opened the door and stepped stiffly out onto her porch.

"Um…call me or…text me tomorrow? You know…if you go by the hospital."

Hating the formality, the awkwardness and uncertainty now between them—his doing—he nodded. "Mmm-hmm. Be sure to lock the door behind me. Huh?"

A shadow of something flickered over her face. "Always."

Gritting his back teeth, he closed her door and sighed.

WHAT JUST HAPPENED?

Jessica leaned against her front door, her mind spinning. Had Gage really tried to kiss her? Had she imagined it, panicked for nothing? And what if he had kissed her? What would that have been like? Gage was a handsome man, no doubt about it. Charming, kind, intelligent.

And a serial dater. A commitment-phobe. Not the sort with whom she would ever consider a romantic relationship.

A snort ripped from her at the absurdity of her line of thought. Good grief! This was Gage Coleman, Tina's brother she was having these delusional thoughts about. Just because they'd grown closer over the past couple of tragic and stressful months, just because she felt isolated and alone without her posse, just because she'd failed miserably to find a match on the dating app, didn't mean she and Gage were suddenly somehow anything more than the friends they'd always been.

She returned to the living room, grabbed her wineglass and finished the dregs in a gulp. The merlot did little to calm her thoughts or settle her rattled nerves. She glanced over at her cat sleeping on the recliner. "Let's finish in the kitchen and go to bed. What do you say, Fuzzface?"

Pluto raised his head and yawned before hopping down from the chair where he'd been napping.

In the kitchen, Jessica fed the cat, put away the dried dishes and wiped the counter before heading upstairs. She would read until she fell asleep, she told herself as she performed her nightly ablutions. But her novel couldn't keep her mind from wandering—to Henry showing up at her office, to Tina and Holly still in the hospital, and to the strangely alluring pull she'd felt toward Gage tonight.

With a groan, she punched her pillow and rolled over. "Girl, you really are down the rabbit hole, aren't you?"

The next morning, after getting little sleep, she grumbled when the alarm on her phone told her it was time for work. She shut it off and flopped back, pulling the sheet to her chin and trying to muster the energy to rise and start a new week.

Sometime later, she was stirred from a bad dream about drowning by the incessant buzz of her phone. Squinting against the morning sun in her window, Jessica answered the call, noticing her bedside clock as she did. She was late for work.

"Sorry!" she told her boss as she threw back the covers and hurried toward the shower. "Horrid night. And I...overslept."

Chapter Eight

As the sun rose higher and burned off the last bit of morning fog, Gage left the hospital with a bit of a bounce in his step. He'd been summoned to the hospital early that morning to find that, after more than two months, his sister had *finally* been taken off the respirator. She'd been awake, though still quite weak and not very communicative. But if she continued breathing on her own and meeting small benchmarks, she would be moved out of ICU to a regular room in the next few days. The doctors said she still had a long way to go and would have to have physical therapy to rebuild her strength, but...

But. Gage exhaled, releasing some of the tension that had twisted him in knots for the last sixty-two days. Tina was breathing on her own, making progress at last! He wanted to shout it, wanted to hug someone, wanted to share the news with J. essica.

He didn't question why Jessica was his first thought, even before any of his colleagues or extended family. She'd been just as torn up over Tina's slow progress as he had, and he wanted to give her the good news. He wanted something, anything that could ease the guilt and grief and worry that had been plaguing Jessica since the accident. He took out his phone to call her, then hesitated. Last night's debacle replayed in his mind. She'd played it off, tried to gloss over it, but he'd not heard from her since. Not that it had been all that long. Twelve hours at the most.

He refused to let his bad judgment last night spoil what they'd had for twenty-six years. And he wouldn't let any awkwardness ruin his good news. He wanted to deliver the news of Tina's progress in person, wanted to see Jessica's face, her smile…hell, he wanted to see *her*.

Though he was still kicking himself for having nearly kissed her, he'd only make things worse if he let it change the dynamic between them. His phone said it was 9:12 a.m. He twisted his mouth, debating. She'd be at her office by now. Normally, he wouldn't bother someone at work, but this news was big. Important. He wanted her to have a report of Tina's progress to boost her day, give her hope.

Gage climbed into his pickup truck and headed toward the downtown office building where Jessica worked. Fifteen minutes later, he was at the receptionist's desk, asking to see her.

"Um, I don't think she's gotten in yet." The woman glanced to a coworker as if for confirmation. The other woman shook her head.

"She's still not in?" a third woman asked as she walked past. "I know she overslept. I called her earlier, but she promised she could be here by a little after nine." The well-dressed, gray-haired woman huffed her frustration and checked her smartwatch. "It's been almost an hour since she said she'd be here in forty."

A band of worry tightened in Gage's chest. "And that was the last you talked to her? She hasn't called to explain her delay?"

Concern puckered the older woman's brow as she told the receptionist. "Nadine, try Jessica's cell again."

Gage held up a hand. "Let me. I need to talk to her anyway." He dialed Jessica's number, and it rang until it went to voice mail. "Jess, it's Gage. Call me when you get this. It's important."

The receptionist gave him a weak smile. "She's probably in the elevator on the way up here right now."

"Let's hope so," the gray-haired woman said, her tone nervous. "We have an important presentation to make at ten."

Gage tried again without luck to reach Jessica, both calling and texting, his apprehension rising. After pacing the reception area for ten minutes, he left a message with the receptionist for Jess, in case she arrived right after he left, and then headed for her house.

She could have had car trouble. She could have fallen in her shower and not be able to get to her phone. She could be—

The fear that had niggled since the first unanswered call roared through his brain, hastening his pace back to his truck. Her stalker could have come after her again.

Gage broke the speed limit every mile of the way to Jessica's house. As he parked in the drive, he assessed the property, not immediately seeing anything amiss. But when he climbed out from behind the wheel and headed toward her front door, the sound of an engine running and the faint smell of exhaust sidetracked him. He stepped over to peer in the window of the garage door.

Jessica lay sprawled on the concrete floor while her car's engine idled, filling the space with carbon monoxide. Adrenaline jolted through him, and he scrambled to raise the main garage door. The door wouldn't give. *Damn it!* Her automatic opener must be engaged.

Spying a side door, he raced around the corner of the house. The lock around this door had clearly been jimmied, the wood frame around the strike plate damaged. New waves of worry rushed through him as he yanked open the side door, did a quick scan for an intruder and raced to Jessica. He coughed, the built-up exhaust choking him.

"Jess!" he said, crouching, trying to rouse her. When she remained unresponsive, he scooped her into his arms and draped her over his shoulder in the classic firefighter's carry. Once outside, he set her gently on the grass of her front yard and patted her cheeks. "Jessica? Jess, come on, sweetheart. Wake up. Please, Jess, wake up."

His voice cracked, and he stopped long enough to shove down the emotion and pull his phone from his pocket. He dialed 911 and gave the operator the pertinent information. Yes, she had a pulse. Yes, she was breathing, barely. Yes, he'd moved her to get fresh air. Knowing he could do nothing else for Jess, he returned to the garage to turn off the car's engine and use the wall-mounted button to open the main garage door. Fresh air flowed in, and the poisonous gas flowed out of the garage. Next, he went inside the house to open her windows and front door and to shut Pluto, who seemed fine, safely in a bathroom with the exhaust fan on.

Finally, he returned to Jessica's side and cradled her head on his lap, wishing he had his station's oxygen mask for her. He stroked her bright pink cheeks and held her hand. "Don't leave me, Jess," he whispered, his voice a croak.

Closing his eyes, Gage said a prayer for her and didn't stop praying until the ambulance arrived.

JESSICA DRIFTED SLOWLY out of a thick fog, her head throbbing, her ribs aching, nausea churning in her gut. She preferred the drowsy oblivion…let herself slide back toward darkness. Someone patted her face and gave her a shake. The motion made every pain gripping her more intense. She reached up to bat the pestering pat away, her arm weak, and encountered a plastic cup on her mouth and nose.

"Jessica, can you hear me?"

Her pulse kicked at the sound of the male voice. A thread of fear crawled through her though she couldn't say why. Her brain scrambled to sort out the reason for her sense of danger. Images flashed. Sensations. Scents.

Rising water. A hissed threat. Drowning. Can't breathe. Pain. A kick. Protect your head.

A scream rose in her throat, along with her panic. She sat up fast and blinked at her strange surroundings. Fresh anxiety swelled in her when she saw unfamiliar faces around her. A guy whose dark hair had frosted tips. A woman with glasses and a single blond braid. She heard the rumble of an engine, whine of a siren. Felt the bounce of tires over potholes.

A tangle of tubes and wires fettered her as she shrank away from the man next to her. Her sudden movement sent another paroxysm of agony through her chest, her head. Feeling her gorge rise, she gripped her stomach.

"Easy," the man said, covering her hands with his when she clawed at the plastic mask. "You're safe. Let's leave the mask on. You're getting the oxygen you need."

"Sick," she said, the mask muting her voice. But the man next to her understood. He pulled the mask off and grabbed a plastic bag to hold in front of her when she retched. She wiped her mouth on stack of gauze squares he handed her and added them to the bag of waste.

"Better?" Frosted Tips asked, and when she nodded, he nudged her shoulder, easing her back down, and replaced the oxygen mask. "We're about a minute out from the hospital and your husband is going to meet you there."

Husband? More confusion and panic spun through her. She furrowed her brow as she battled the thundering pain in her head to focus her thoughts. Husband? Matt?

"Who's coming?" she muttered.

"Gabe," the guy said.

The woman shook her head. "I think he said Gage."

Gage. She opened her mouth to deny he was her husband, but stopped. Despite the shrieking pain racking her body and head, a wash of something warm and calming flowed over her at the thought of Gage. There was a jostling bump, then the vehicle stopped, and doors opened at her feet.

And then Gage was there. The second she was unloaded from the back of the ambulance, his well-cut face and comforting strength was at her side. "Jess, you're awake! Thank God."

He grabbed her hand and strode quickly alongside her as she was hurried into the hospital. He only gave way once, so that the stretcher could be pushed through the narrow exam room door. Gage settled at the far side of her gurney, clutching her hand between his, as the medics passed her care off to the ER nurses.

She watched a nurse check monitors and get out supplies, still drifting in a sense of the surreal.

"Jeez, Jessica. You scared the hell outta me." She focused her attention on Gage when he spoke, his fingers cupping her cheek and his gray eyes as bright as silver with worry. "What happened? What do you remember?"

"I don't...know. I was going to...ask you the same thing."

His dark brows drew together. "I found you sprawled on your garage floor, the car running. You'd apparently been breathing the exhaust for quite a while. You were passed out, your cheeks red."

Jessica digested that information. She remembered a rushed morning. Juggling items to get in the car. "I was going to work," she said, but sounded more like a question.

"Did you fall? Get dizzy and faint?"

A sputter of anxiety ignited in her again. "I—I don't know."

"Sir, can the questions wait?" the attending nurse asked. "You seem to be upsetting her. Both her pulse and blood pressure just spiked. We want her calm and comfortable so we can be sure she's stabilized."

Gage pressed his mouth in a taut line as if chastened and nodded his understanding.

As much as she wanted answers about what happened, the stir of fear and panic that hovered like a mist around her told her the truth wasn't pleasant. The initial confusion and panic faded, and her muddled thoughts began to clear. But new questions rose.

She glanced at the nurse who was wrapping a cuff around her arm to check her blood pressure. "I hurt…here." She motioned to her rib cage, stomach, lower back. "A lot. And I threw up. In the ambulance."

The nurse nodded. "Nausea is common with carbon monoxide poisoning."

Jessica touched her aching ribs and gasped as she winced. The blurry image of a man hovering over her holding something…a bat? A stick? The man was angry. Yelling.

When she tensed as if to brace for a blow, her abdominal muscles objected with a throb.

"Ma'am, I need you to take slow, deep breaths, okay?" Her nurse squeezed the rubber bulb and the cuff inflated.

Jessica nodded, swallowed, and holding the nurse's

friendly gaze, took several intentional breaths—slow, but not too deep. Deep breaths hurt. Each inhale, she flinched and backed off, remiss to hold the air in when her ribs throbbed.

The cuff deflated, and the nurse read the small electronic screen. "A bit high, but that's understandable. I'll check it again once you've had a few minutes to relax, enjoy some more of that good air." She tapped the mask. "At this point, this is your best medicine. So keep breathing deep and even. Okay, ma'am?"

She nodded. "Jessica."

Both Gage and the nurse leaned closer to hear her repeat the mask-garbled word. She lifted the mask and glanced at the nurse, digging down for her sense of humor, one of the tools that had helped her survive the ups and downs of her life to date. "My name is Jessica. *Ma'am* makes me look around for someone's mother."

The nurse chuckled and helped her replace the oxygen mask. "All right, *Jessica*. Your other numbers look pretty good all things considered. You're lucky this guy found you when he did."

She angled her head toward Gage and mustered a grin. "Yeah." Careful breath. Exhale. "He's one of the good ones." Careful breath. Exhale. One of the good ones...

She shivered as a voice hissed in her memory.

A restraining order? You thought you could get rid of me?

She gasped, startled by the flash of memory, then moaned when lightning pain streaked through her abdomen.

She clutched her middle, splaying her hands over her left ribs. But it was the shadowy images teasing her brain that made her tremble. *Don't piss me off, Jessie.*

"Jessica?"

She worked to bring the rest of the memory to the fore,

but the effort wore her out, and each time an image flickered in her brain, she shied away from it, as if something inside was trying to shield her from something awful.

"Jess, what is it?" Gage brushed the hair from her forehead.

"H-he kicked me," she muttered.

The nurse's head came around sharply, and she sent Gage a wary look before focusing on Jessica. "Who kicked you?"

Gage leaned closer. "Jess, did Henry do this? Did he hurt you?"

She moaned and nodded. "Guess the restraining order didn't work."

Angling his gaze toward the nurse, Gage said, "We're going to need to file a police report."

GAGE DRAGGED A hand over his face, standing aside as the hospital staff settled Jessica in her room. He'd seen too much of this hospital in the last few weeks as he kept vigil over Tina. Now Jessica was here.

Without parents and with her son at college, he was all Jessica had, it seemed.

She had work associates, of course. Her ex, Matt, in Valley Haven. But her best friends...

He didn't finish the thought, because it led back to his own grief and the reason he knew which vending machines on which floors had the best snacks. Instead, he took a seat beside Jessica as the orderly withdrew and the nursing assistant double-checked the oxygen flow before retreating with a smile.

Jessica angled her head toward him, her eyes troubled, her brow lined. "You don't have to stay."

He shrugged one shoulder. "Where else am I going to go?"

"Home. Coffeehouse. Batting cage. I'm sure there are

hundreds of things you'd rather be doing," she said, her voice slightly muffled and her breath fogging the oxygen mask as she spoke.

"Nothing that won't keep. Besides, I have all the comforts of home right here. A hard chair—" he slapped the arm of the uncomfortable visitor's seat "—and my choice of at least six only slightly pixelated television stations." He picked up the remote wired to her bedside and flicked on the small screen on the opposite wall. "And since I had planned to spend most of the day upstairs with Tina anyhow—" He slapped his palm to his forehead. "Oh man! In all the confusion and concern for you, I almost forgot. I... have good news to tell you."

Her black eyebrows lifted, an invitation to continue.

"Tina was taken off the respirator last night. She's breathing on her own this morning."

Tears filled Jessica's eyes, and she sniffled as she gave him a wobbly grin. "That's fantastic. Oh my goodness!"

Her hand shaking, she swiped at the moisture leaking from her eyes.

Gage leaned forward again and patted her arm. "I figured you could use some good news, and I wanted to give it to you in person."

"And you ended up saving my life instead." She exhaled heavily. The edges of her eyes crinkled, hinting at her smile.

"Well..." He quirked up one cheek while he shoved down the roil of unrest over the close call. "Glad to be of service."

Her expression shifted, her gaze darkening and growing stormy. "There's something I don't understand." She carefully rolled to her right side to face him, holding her ribs as she moved.

"The doctor said confusion and brain fog, memory gaps, were normal considering your condition."

She closed her eyes and shook her head slightly in dismissal. "Not that. I— How did you know to come to my house?"

His hands fisted on the arms of the stiff-backed guest chair as his mind brought back images of her lying unconscious, curled in a ball on her cold concrete floor amid the clouds of exhaust.

"I started at your office, but when you weren't there I drove to your house to check on you."

She nodded again as if understanding. Then scrunched her nose. "So, if you hadn't had news about Tina to tell me…"

Gage sat back and frowned. He hated to think what would have happened to Jess if he hadn't found her when he did. "Yeah."

"In a way, Tina saved me today as much as you did." Her eyes sparkled with tears as she settled back in her pillows.

A knock on her door called their attention as a plain-clothes police officer stepped into her room, flashing his badge. "Ms. Harkney? I'm Detective Nick Macnally, Charlotte PD. I understand you need to file a police report? An assault?"

Gage stood and shook the officer's hand and introduced himself. Officer Macnally then took a statement from them each regarding Henry's violation of the restraining order, breaking and entering, and assault.

"Can he be charged with attempted murder? He left her there to die from the exhaust fumes," Gage said.

"That'll be up to the DA's office. I'm just here to take your statement." He flipped his notebook closed and clicked off the recording function of his phone. "And having done that, unless you have more to add to what you've told me, I'll get going and let you rest."

Jessica shook her head and offered a muffled "Thank you" through the oxygen mask.

Turning his focus back to Jessica's needs, Gage asked, "What can I do? Another pillow? Is the room warm enough? Should I call Eric or Matt for you?"

Her eyes widened, and she gave her head a vigorous shake. Tugging the mask down, she rasped, "Don't bother them. I'm going to be fine, and there's nothing they can do to change things for me, so…just let it ride. Would you call my office and tell them what happened, though?"

"Done. They send their best wishes."

She replaced the mask and took a deep breath, her eyelids drooping. "All I need now is a nap. That painkiller they gave me is making me drowsy."

He ducked his chin in a nod of agreement. "I'll let you sleep, then. I should get back upstairs and look in on Tina anyway." He moved to the side of her bed, intending to kiss her forehead, but balked, echoes of last night, the alarm in her eyes when he'd almost kissed her, replaying in his head. Instead, he simply gave her shoulder a light squeeze and flashed a grin. "I'll be back to check on you later."

JESSICA EXPERIENCED A strange pang as Gage left the hospital room. Being alone and facing the creaks and shadows, the doubts and recriminations, had been easier at home. Being in the hospital, a victim of Henry's violence, shook her to the marrow.

You aren't alone. The hospital staff won't let Henry hurt you.

But what about after she was released from the hospital? Henry had shown he could find her, that no judge's order to stay away fazed him. What would happen to her if the police continued to stall out on finding him, arresting him? And even if Henry were caught, he could get bailed out, more vengeful than ever, free to harass and stalk her, before his case ever went to trial.

She shuddered and weighed her options. While she knew Gage would stay with her, lend his presence as a deterrent to Henry, how could she justify asking him to do that?

The oath she'd made on the last day she'd darkened her mother's door played in her mind like a video on rewind. When her mother learned of Jessica's plan to attend college, using money she'd squirreled away for years, one acorn at a time, she'd gone ballistic.

"You're not going anywhere! You can't just abandon me!" her mother had screamed. "After everything I've done for you, feeding you and putting a roof over your head, how dare you think of running out on me when I need you most?"

Eighteen-year-old Jessica had wavered for a moment, guilt tugging at her. What would become of her mother after she left?

But then her mother had narrowed a heated glare on her and screeched, "You always were an ungrateful bitch. You've taken everything I've done for you for granted!"

And Jessica had felt slapped out of her sympathy for her mother. Not only had her mother essentially ignored Jessica most of her childhood, Jessica was the one who'd taken the initiative to work weekend and summer jobs, earning just enough to keep them from getting evicted when her mother couldn't pay their rent. Jessica had worn a hand-me-down uniform for cheerleading, skipped meals, cut corners and kept them afloat. She'd managed all this while maintaining her grades, winning scholarships, and putting pennies in an account that, after five years, had barely been enough for her first semester's tuition.

Her mother, meanwhile, had drifted from one boyfriend

to another, playing the victim and acting helpless, growing increasingly dependent on men and on Jessica. The thought that her mother would try to block her from pursuing her education and shame her out of following the dreams she'd sacrificed for, all while she cursed and blamed and guilted her daughter, had galled Jessica.

Anger had burrowed to her core, and she'd grated out a promise, an oath to herself and her mother as she stormed out of her mother's home for the last time. "You have a very warped and selfish view of history, mother. I will not stay and enable you any longer, and I will never be like you, surrendering power over my life, my survival or my self-worth to anyone, especially not a man."

She'd kept that promise to herself through the years, no matter the cost. How could she give in now? She refused to let her fear of Henry make her dependent on Gage.

Her resolve wavered, however, when Gage brought her home from the hospital the next day, and she found a message spray-painted in black on her garage door.

I'll be back.

ON A RAINY evening in June, Jessica had just finished her microwave dinner and was rinsing the tray for the recycling bin, when through the window over her kitchen sink, she spied a car pulling into her driveway. She didn't recognize the dark sedan, and her heart stilled. Anxiety squirmed in her gut as she dried her hands on a towel and hurried to her living room window for a better look. She'd spent the last several weeks since getting discharged from the hospital looking over her shoulder and jumping at her shadow. The arrival of a car she didn't recognize rang enough alarms to chill her to the core.

When a tall, raven-haired figure climbed from the back seat, Jessica caught her breath.

Eric!

Her son's unexpected arrival brought tears of joy and relief to her eyes—but also concern. She flew to the foyer, unlocked the door and snatched it open before Eric had even reached the porch steps.

"Hi, Mom." Eric flashed a lopsided smile that said he knew he'd surprised her and was proud of himself for keeping his arrival a secret.

"Oh, honey! What are you doing home? I'm thrilled to see you of course, but—"

"No reason. I had a free weekend and..." He flipped up a dismissive hand.

She opened her arms, and, dropping his bag of laundry and his suitcase, he stepped into her embrace. His hug was long and strong, and she cherished every second. "Oh, Eric, you give the best hugs."

Whether her compliment or the warble in her voice influenced him, she didn't know, but he gave her an extra squeeze before stepping back and retrieving his belongings. "We have no class Monday for Juneteenth, and since I worked double shifts earlier this week at the restaurant, the boss gave me a couple days off. So I thought I'd drop in as a surprise."

"I'm so glad you did!" She held the door for him as he bustled inside and dumped his bags in the foyer. The sight of her son, even after only a few weeks away, filled her with such joy she couldn't even bemoan the smelly sack of laundry stinking up her entry hall.

Eric rubbed his hands together and gave her a speculative look. "I haven't eaten yet, and I'm starving. Want to order a pizza?"

She cleared the lump from her throat so she could speak. "I would love nothing more."

Over dinner—she nibbled a slice of pizza without telling Eric she'd already eaten—Eric told her all about his summer classes, his coworkers at the restaurant and the plans he'd made to take a study semester abroad. "Dad said he's okay with it if you are."

"A semester abroad? Wow. That sound fantastic!" She tried to hide the sinking feeling that diminished her genuine excitement for her son's opportunities. Having Eric four hours away was bad enough without him being an ocean away—or farther. "Where are you planning to go?"

He shrugged a shoulder as he stuffed the last bite of crust in his mouth. "Not sure." He chewed a minute, then said, "There are great programs in Switzerland and Japan, but the program in Paris would count toward my premed work. So, does that sound okay to you? It's not too late to sign up for French in the fall. I have to show a proficiency in the language for the programs in Switzerland and Paris. I can swing it if I knock out my Poli Sci requirement second session this summer."

She nodded, unable to speak as unbidden emotion tightened her throat, and she realized she'd been counting on Eric's presence, his company, his protection later this summer from Henry's lingering menace. That expectation was wrong in so many ways, it was no wonder she hadn't allowed herself to examine her feelings as she anticipated Eric's homecoming. Sure, she was happy to see her son and thrilled to hear about his life at UNC, but putting anything else real or perceived on her son's shoulders was unfair, inappropriate and just...wrong.

"Hey, I saw a white Camry in the garage when I came in. Is that another rental or could they not fix whatever was wrong with your old car?" Eric asked and helped himself to another slice of the pepperoni pie.

When Eric had been home in May, she'd only told him she'd had a car accident that required the rental she'd been driving, and he'd mercifully asked few questions, once he'd been assured his mother was unharmed.

"Oh, right. That one's mine. The insurance company finally paid up after my accident, and I bought that one a couple weeks ago." She pressed a hand to her stomach to quell the quiver that memories of the accident still stirred, then forged ahead. Eric needed to know the truth…or *some* of it. And so, as succinctly and gently as she could, she caught her son up on the key events of the past months, carefully avoiding mention of her dates with Henry Blythe and his continued harassment. The full extent of the car accident and its fallout were tragic enough.

Eric's face grew still and pale as she explained about the night she and her friends had ended up in the river, trapped, drowning. She hated dumping the sad news on him, soiling this golden time in his life.

"Aunt Sara is dead?" Eric had called the members of the posse his aunts in a nod to the close relationship the women shared with his mother. *Like sisters.*

She answered his questions about the accident, about Holly's and Tina's conditions, and her own health. Tina, she told him, remained stable with small improvements to her blood pressure and amount of oxygen she needed, while all she knew of Holly were the bits and pieces she'd gleaned the night of the accident. She reassured him as best she could, keeping a stiff upper lip, not wanting to add her own fragile state to the worries she was unloading on her man-child. But her composure slipped when he asked, "And what happened with the guy who caused the accident? Did they catch him? Is he being charged with manslaughter or anything?"

Jessica fisted her hands on her lap. "He has not been taken into custody yet, but...the police are working on it." She forced a smile. "They'll get him."

Eric tossed down the crust he held and leaned back in his chair, his expression stunned. "Damn, Mom. I'm so sorry! Why didn't you tell me when it happened? I could have come home—"

"Which is why I didn't tell you. You didn't need the distraction from school, and there was nothing you could have done here to change anything. I was unhurt...essentially. Physically. You were where you needed to be, so I chose not to tell you."

He exhaled harshly and narrowed his gaze on her. "I'm not a little kid anymore, Mom. I can handle bad news. And I want to be there for you." He sat forward and leaned on his arms as he drilled her with a dark gaze so like her own. "Don't shut me out again. I want to be in the loop on things like this. Okay?"

Her heart warmed with pride for her only child. So mature, so grown-up, so precious to her. "I hear you."

"Do you promise?"

Not a chance. She would never stop protecting her boy, trying to shield him from the brunt of life's pain, and sparing him from his desire to flip their roles and take care of her. She crossed her fingers under the table and lied, "I promise."

Eric returned to Chapel Hill two days later, and Jessica felt his departure deeply, as she did every time he left.

This empty nest business is...for the birds! She gave a wry chuckle at her lame joke as she watched his Uber take him away.

She had only been back inside her quiet house for a few

minutes before she heard a knock at her front door. Assuming Eric had forgotten something and puzzled why he would knock instead of using his key, she hustled to answer the door.

But it wasn't Eric.

Chapter Nine

When she answered the door, she found Detective Nick Macnally, the officer who'd taken her police report at the hospital, on her porch. His hands were jammed in his pants pockets. His expression grim. A heavy throb pulsed through her, and she could feel the tensing of her neck, her muscles bracing for bad news.

After a terse, perfunctory greeting, she showed the detective into her living room and motioned for him to sit.

Macnally perched on the edge of her couch and propped his arms on his thighs as he leaned forward. "I wish I had better news for you, but the truth is, our search for Henry Blythe has hit a dead end."

Jessica's stomach plummeted. "How so? Can't you just look him up in the DMV records or tax files or—"

"Of course, we could. And we did search all the usual records and databases." Macnally shook his head. "No Henry Blythe exists in Charlotte or any other part of the state. At least not anyone that fits the physical and demographic description you gave us. Not even close."

"That's...not possible!" Jessica gripped the arm of her wingback chair, her head spinning. "What about the truck? The license plate—"

"The plate was stolen. The owner had reported it missing from their car three days earlier."

Jessica sat in stunned silence for a moment, staring at her lap, goggling at what she was learning. "So he...used some sort of alias or something? And changing license plates makes it sounds like he intended something nefarious and wanted to cover his tracks."

The detective ducked his chin slowly. "Appears so."

A new thought occurred to her, and she jerked her head up. "What about his profile on the dating app?"

Macnally spread his hands and twisted his mouth in a discouraging frown. "Deleted, apparently. We found no Henry Blythe, H. Blythe, or any variation of spelling on the app you mentioned—"

"What about—"

"Or any other dating or meetup app our techs could find."

Jessica furrowed her brow and plowed her fingers through her hair, wincing when her fingers met the tender spot where Henry had hit her. "This is crazy! So—" she exhaled harshly, her frustration and fear roiling in her chest "—how do we find him?"

"We'll try other resources, keep the case open." He cleared his throat. "I'm sorry I don't have more to offer." He paused and tipped his head as he regarded her. "Given the lengths this guy has gone to in order to avoid being found, it might be a good idea for you to have someone stay with you for a while. Or stay with family or a friend. This amount of preparation and planning doesn't say ordinary stalker to me. My gut is telling me he's planning something more drastic."

Jessica flopped back in her chair. Her head pounded, and the ragged edges of despair crowded in on her. "More drastic? Like what?"

He twisted his mouth. "I don't mean to alarm you, but he could escalate. Kidnapping is a possibility. More violence. Like I said, he's gone to a lot of trouble to avoid detection. That reeks to me."

"Well…" She lifted a trembling hand to her mouth. "You may not mean to alarm me, but…you have."

"I'd be remiss if I weren't honest with you. I really think you need to stay with someone. Being here alone, where he knows you live, is asking for trouble."

Jessica chuffed a harsh sigh. "But where? My three best friends are either dead or in the hospital still because of Henry—or whatever his name is. My son is at college. I don't know my father, and my mother is—" she sighed, choking down the lump in her throat "—dead."

Macnally gave her a look of regret. "Then…get out of town. Get a dog. Buy some pepper spray at a minimum. Men like this guy stalking you don't typically just go away, even with a restraining order."

"As he's proven."

"My best advice to you is to make a change of some kind for your own protection. We'll continue to do everything we can to find him, including added drive-bys to watch your house, but until we catch him, you need to take extra measures to stay safe."

Jessica nodded her understanding. She didn't like the truth bombs Macnally had dropped on her. In fact, she hated the idea of leaving town or hiding from Henry—for lack of his real name. She'd never been one to run from her problems, even if it meant making difficult choices.

But was leaving the area avoiding her problem, or was it the hard choice she had to make to stay safe? If Detective Macnally was advising she lie low somewhere away from Charlotte, caution said she should heed his recommendation.

She walked with the detective to the front door, thanked him again, and locked up tight in his wake.

That night, she got no sleep. She jumped at ordinary sounds—the ice maker cycling, the wind rattling her loose shutter, Pluto jumping onto her bed. She couldn't live like this. Her blood pressure had to be through the roof.

But if she left, where would she go? She could hardly move into the men's dorm at UNC with Eric. The expense of a hotel room would add up quickly.

Gage? She weighed and discarded that idea for the same reasons she'd turned down his help in earlier weeks.

Cameron Glen. Just the name of the vacation retreat property owned by the family of her ex-husband's new wife filled her with a warmth and comfort that beckoned to her. The times she'd been invited to Cameron Glen for family functions, she'd reveled in the bucolic setting, soaked in the peacefulness and savored the beauty of the landscape. The Cameron family's hospitality and genuine affection toward her had been an unexpected and cherished bonus. Each trip, by the time she would return to Charlotte, she'd feel refreshed and empowered to take on the daily grind again.

But just as she wouldn't impose on Gage, she couldn't be a burden to her ex-husband and his new family, no matter how kind and welcoming they were. She'd also have to make arrangements with her boss to take a leave of absence or to work remotely. Henry had shown that her office was on his radar same as her house.

She was on her third cup of coffee when she finally convinced herself she had to follow Macnally's advice. Her first call was to her boss, who was understanding, if stressed by how they'd cover Jessica's workload while she was out.

"Look, that's my problem, not yours," Carolyn said. "You have enough on your plate. I'll get a temp to cover for you, and I promise your job will be here when you get back. Just...be careful and come back in one piece when you can."

After finishing the call with work, Jessica gathered her composure for her next call. She chose to ask her ex-husband's wife, since Cameron Glen belonged to Cait's family and it was more within her purview to grant or deny Jessica's request. She and Matt had parted amicably, both realizing several years earlier that their lives had diverged and neither was happy in their marriage anymore. But they'd made an effort to remain friendly for Eric's sake.

For several years, they'd navigated separate lives, sharing custody of their son without quarrel. And then, quite unexpectedly, Matt had found Cait and remarried. Jessica had been truly happy for her ex, and in a more serendipitous twist had found a friend in Matt's new wife. Cait Cameron had been both generous of spirit and warm toward Jessica, and her family genuinely welcoming of Jessica for Cameron family gatherings and special occasions like Eric's birthdays, his high school graduation, even Thanksgivings when Jessica would have otherwise been alone. Cait and her family made what could have been awkward and strained seem the most natural and happy of events.

Over the last three years, Jessica had bonded not only with Cait, but with all of the Camerons. In fact, last year, when a corrupt man tried to blackmail the family into selling the family's property at Cameron Glen, Jessica had been included in a scheme to protect the land from that and future hostile buyouts. Jessica had pulled together the funds to purchase a tiny share of Cameron Glen, the sizable retreat property in Valley Haven, near the Smoky Mountains, that had been in the Cameron family for generations. In addition to the vacation rental cabins, several members of the

Cameron family had homes in Cameron Glen, including Matt and Cait and their young daughter, Erin.

"Hi, Jessica! How're you doing?" Cait's chipper voice greeted her and instantly a measure of relief and the sting of tears swelled, telling Jessica she had made the right choice in calling.

She squelched the automatic and polite response of "Fine," choosing to be honest. She could with Cait, which was one of the reasons she'd decided to call. "Not so great. Rather a mess, in fact."

"Oh, Jessica," Cait said, her tone full of sympathy. "What's going on?"

"I'm…being harassed by this guy I had a couple dates with."

"Harassed how?"

Jessica curled her free hand in her lap to stop the trembling. "He keeps…showing up. At my house. At my office. Following me and…trying to hurt me." Her voice did squeak then. "Remember my accident this spring? He caused that. He's responsible for killing my friend Sara and putting Tina and Holly in comas."

"How horrible! You've…told the police, I'm sure."

"Mmm-hmm," Jessica affirmed, her throat tight.

"So why is he not in jail?"

"I… I've tried a restraining order against him, except… he ignored it." She paused again when her voice threatened to crack. "And the name I gave the police, the name he used on our dates…doesn't exist. That is, when they ran his name, the men that came up through government records were all wrong. Wrong age. Wrong race. Wrong physical description." She sighed her frustration, the breath shuddering. "Cait, I'm scared. I don't feel safe here. He's gotten into my home, my garage and was lying in wait for me."

Cait gasped.

"He attacked me and…left me for dead."

"What!"

"He's threatened me. Cursed at me. Vandalized my home."

"Jessica! I— What are you going to do? How can I help?" The urgency and concern in Cait's voice heartened Jessica.

"I know it's a big ask, but…"

"Doesn't matter. Ask. You're family, Jessica. We'll do whatever we can for you. You know that."

Tears of gratitude leaked onto her cheeks. "I need to get out of town. Now. For the rest of the summer possibly. The detective working the case thinks I'm at risk, and he advised me to move out of my house for a while. I need to go somewhere safe until the cops can catch him, somewhere I can have some peace of mind and…find my way forward. So I was hoping…could I—"

"Yes. Come here. Come to Cameron Glen," Cait said before she could finish the question.

"Thank you. So much. But…where would I stay? I don't want to impose, and I hate to take up a cabin that could be rented and earn income for your family. I mean, I can pay rent—"

"You're a part owner. You came through for us when we needed help, and that grants you privileges. You won't pay rent."

"Are you sure the rest of the family will agree to that? I…" Jessica bit her bottom lip, already feeling significantly better about her situation. Still, guilt nagged at her. The Camerons weren't broke, but neither did they need to lose income during the height of vacation season.

"I'm sure they'll be fine with it when I explain the circumstances. Besides, I've been given the authority as the rental manager to make decisions regarding the cabins without constantly conferring with the family. They trust my judgment."

"If you're sure…"

"I am. In fact…" Cait's voice held a note of inspiration. "I may have an idea that benefits us both, if you're game."

Chapter Ten

"So the Juniper cabin is undergoing renovations that had been put off in previous years, but became mandatory after a pipe burst and flooded the kitchen late this past winter," Jessica told Gage later that evening when she called him about her plan. "As long as the cabin was getting those repairs made, the family decided to do a complete upgrade and remodel, including adding a second bedroom/bathroom suite."

"Okay," Gage said, sounding wary. "Why do I feel like you're leading up to a big announcement of some sort?"

She took a steadying breath. "Because I worked out an arrangement where I will live in the cabin throughout the stages of repair in exchange for keeping tabs on the carpenters, electricians and plumbers that would need access to the cabin."

"What about work?" he asked, and she could hear a note of regret or disappointment in his tone that made her pause. As much as he'd been her support in the past few weeks since the accident, had she been his? He had buddies at the firehouse, friends from school still in the area, but…clearly he'd chosen to spend time with her over them. Was that by choice rather than a sense of obligation?

"Well, summer is the busiest time at Cameron Glen for cabin rentals and making reservations for autumn, so I offered to help out at the rental office part-time. With an almost-two-year-old underfoot, Cait welcomed the chance to pass off bookkeeping, cabin maintenance and daily guest requests to me."

"Uh-huh. I meant your job here."

"Oh, right." She picked at a loose thread on her bedspread. "I'm not resigning, if that's what you mean. I will work on a few things, finish up a couple current projects remotely. I can use Zoom to attend meetings. But Carolyn was understanding and promised my job would still be there when I got back."

"That's great. So...you do plan to come back?"

His hopeful tone triggered a pang in her chest. She'd miss seeing him regularly. She was surprised at how quickly he'd become a fixture in her life, an anchor but also a confidant.

"I do," she said. "I just...don't know when."

"Hmm." He was quiet for a moment. "When do you leave?"

"Tomorrow."

"That soon?"

"No point in stalling. Especially if Henry is, in fact, lurking and dangerous."

Gage gave a low whistle. "You always were a woman of action. What can I do to help?"

"I don't need help."

"Do you have a plan for how to get out of town without being followed? If this bastard is stalking you, he could have eyes on your house or be keeping tabs on you going to work, or—"

"Damn. I hadn't thought of that." A shiver crawled through her. "Do you have a suggestion?"

He grunted again, a sound that said he was thinking. "The key is to not let him know you're relocating, so he can't see suitcases leaving your house. And if we could somehow get you in my truck without him noticing, that'd be good, too. He's less likely to follow me out of town."

"Gage, you don't need to drive me—"

"If it will keep you safe, get you away undetected, I do. I'll be there early. Say, six, seven?"

"Good heavens, Gage. I have to pack still. Make it ten." She chuckled, then sobering, added, "And thank you. You're a good friend."

She heard another low hum, then a small sigh. "You're welcome."

LATE THE NEXT DAY, Jessica and Gage arrived at Cameron Glen and were met by a large contingent of the Cameron family. They circled the truck as Gage parked at Jessica's home for the summer and greeted them both with smiles and hugs and expressions of concern for Jessica's recent traumas and the prolonged hospitalization of his sister.

Gage shook her ex-husband's hand. "It's been a while. How are you doing? I hear congratulations are in order. A wife and baby since we last talked."

"Yes. Thanks." Matt's answering smile was bright, though tinged with something awkward, as if he felt guilty for having so much happiness and good fortune while Gage remained single, childless and coping with his sister's illness. "I understand you're still with the fire department."

"I'm so glad you've come to stay here this summer," Cait's mother, Grace, said, pulling Jessica's attention away from the men's pleasantries. "Please make yourself at home, because, in a way, it *is* your home, too."

Jessica nodded and flashed a lopsided grin. The gracious

welcome from the Camerons soothed the jagged emotions that had been seesawing in her for months. The beautiful landscape of Cameron Glen put her at ease, as well, and she knew she'd made the right choice in coming. "I do have one special request, which I hate to impose, but… I brought my cat, Pluto, with me. While he'll be fine with me at night, do you mind if I take him with me to the rental office during the day? All the construction work noise would be scary for him, and the nails and loose wires and things would be dangerous—"

"Of course," Cait said before Jessica could finish. "Or bring him to our house. Unless you think an overly enthusiastic toddler would terrify him."

Jessica shrugged. "I guess we won't know until we introduce them. He's generally laid-back, so I think he'd be fine." She opened the truck's back door and pulled the travel carrier out.

To camouflage her escape, Gage had pulled into Jessica's garage, and they'd closed the door to hide their activity as they loaded the few clothes and belongings she was taking to Cameron Glen. Jessica had hidden on the floor of his extended cab, until they'd driven several miles out of town.

"Speaking of introductions," Jessica said now, "Gage needs to meet everyone."

Grace nodded but said, "What if we save those for tonight. I've planned a family meal, and we want you both to join us."

Jessica smiled and heard her stomach growl as if in anticipation of good food. "Thank you. Let me see what Gage thinks. I'd hate to answer for him. Right now, I need to get Pluto out of his cage so he can explore his new digs."

Gage saw her holding the travel carrier and hurried over. "I'll get that for you."

Following Gage's cue, the men, including Matt's brothers-in-law, carried all her bags and miscellany from the truck inside the small cabin.

"So, what did you tell your boss in Charlotte? She just let you take leave for some unknown months?" Cait's sister Isla asked, her own toddler propped on her hip. CeCe, born the same day as Cait and Matt's daughter, held a fistful of Isla's long red-gold hair, and Isla winced when her daughter pulled too hard.

"Well," Jessica said, "my boss knew everything that happened recently, from the car accident and my grief over my friends and...other stuff. She was completely sympathetic to my situation, and while her hands were tied regarding corporate rules that limited paid personal time, she promised my job would still be waiting in the fall, even if I'm not getting a salary all summer."

Isla pivoted toward Cait. "Can't we pay her something for helping in the rental office?"

Jessica shook her head. "You're already giving me lodgings rent-free. I can't accept anything more."

"But—" Isla fumbled her daughter's fingers free from her hair again "—you helped us out financially when we were in a pinch. I just want to repay the favor."

"You have. You are." Jessica touched Isla's arm and gave her a grateful smile. "I'll be fine. I have some savings. It's just for a little while." *I hop* .

Detective Macnally had tried to be encouraging at first, but Henry's apparent use of an alias had thrown sand in the gears of the investigation. The detective couldn't honestly say when she'd be safe to move back to Charlotte.

Jessica balled her hands and battled down the swell of anxiety that thought stirred in her. Exhaling and jamming down the agitation, she straightened her shoulders with determination. She'd take things as they came, one bridge, one decision, one challenge at a time, as she had her whole life. She'd found the strength and courage to take care of herself when her mother couldn't. She'd handled being both mother and father to Eric while Matt was deployed overseas for months, and she'd adapted to the life of a divorcée, relying on herself alone to deal with the messes life threw at her.

Her current mess might be bigger, scarier, murkier, but she'd grope day by day to feel her way through, determined not to show any weakness or depend on anyone for her survival.

The men emerged from the cabin again, and Gage moved to her side. "So, do you want time to unpack or shall we go grab a bite to eat before I head back?"

"If I may," Grace interjected, "I'd like to have you both to join us for dinner. We're having our weekly family gathering tonight, and since Emma and her family are out of town, there's more than enough for you two to dine with us."

Jessica glanced at Gage, measuring his interest. His returned look clearly deferred to her choice.

"It sounds wonderful to me. Cameron family dinners are something to experience, according to Eric," she said.

"All right. Then we accept," Gage said. "Thank you."

Grace bobbed a nod. "Good. You take an hour or so to unpack and relax, and we'll see you at our place—" she turned and pointed to a large house up the hill from the Juniper cabin "—which is right there, at six thirty. Sound good?"

"Sounds great," Jessica said.

Cait gave Jessica a hug, and Matt shook Gage's hand again as the Camerons dispersed. Gage and Jessica entered the cabin and went in search of Pluto. She found the cat sniffing around the bedroom, exploring all the new smells. Reassured that her cat was okay and settling in, she returned to the front of the cabin. Gage stood in the kitchen, unloading a few items she'd brought over in a cooler into her refrigerator.

She did the same for the box of dry goods she didn't want to go stale before she returned at the end of the summer, filling the pantry shelves with crackers, instant oatmeal and granola bars.

Those small tasks done, she eyed her suitcases, but Gage caught her hand and led her to the den. "The rest can wait, can't it?"

She lifted a shoulder. "I guess. Why?"

He perched on a recliner and propped his arms on his legs, raising a somber gaze as he addressed her. "I just wanted make sure you're going to be all right here."

She smiled and settled back in the recliner angled next to his, tucking one foot under her. "You'll meet most of the family tonight. But you've already seen how kind and gracious they are. That wasn't fake or for show. They've always been incredibly warm and welcoming toward me. I'll be fine."

He nodded, but his expression remained serious. "I'm sure they'll be accommodating and kind. But I mean…will you be *safe*? You're still alone in this cabin."

A thread of unease wound through her, and she rubbed her palms over the goose bumps that rose on her arms. "I suppose we'll see. The doors have locks. I believe the cabins have security cameras outside. And I'll have a number of protective Cameron men close by. While here, I'm out of Henry's sphere, in theory. That's the best I can do."

"Unless I stayed here with you."

A jolt of surprise—and unbidden longing—coursed through her. She leaned forward, dropping her foot back on the floor as she gaped at him. "What?"

"If you want me to, I—"

She held up a hand, cutting him off. "You can't just up and move over here for the summer. You have a job—"

"I'll ask for leave."

She blinked. "What about Tina? You can't leave her alone over there in the hospital."

He frowned. "Yeah. I don't like being away from her, but…" He clamped his mouth in a taut line for a moment. "I can commute to Charlotte a few times a week to check on her."

She gave him a dubious frown. "She needs you more than I do."

His brow creased. "Does she? She's not the one with a lunatic harassing her, potentially trying to kill her. I don't like leaving you here alone."

Jessica shook her head, and pushed down the tiny voice in her head screaming, *Yes! Please stay!* "Gage, no. I've told you so many times, I can't ask you to—"

"I'm volunteering. I can ask the station chief for a few weeks of time off for a family emergency."

She chuckled, a bittersweet pang tugging at her core. "I'm not family."

He took her hand in his and held her gaze, his own piercing, intense. "Aren't you? Family doesn't always mean blood relations."

A tingle rushed from where his fingers touched hers, crackling through her body like an electric charge. Her heart pattered a staccato rhythm as she studied the strong, masculine cut of his jaw, his straight nose, his magnetic gray eyes with a thick fringe of lashes.

Good grief! Holly and Sara were right. He is *a gorgeous man.* Maybe she'd always known it, but in that moment, she saw her best friend's brother in a new light—one that made her tremble to her core with a purely feminine desire. Catching her breath, she snatched her hand from him, confused and rattled by her unexpected lust. What was wrong with her? This was *Gage*, for crying out loud!

The same guy who'd had no fewer than ten different girlfriends since she'd become Tina's best friend in high school. The same guy who'd tossed her in the freezing swimming pool at Tina's New Year's Eve party last year. The same guy who'd been an usher at her and Matt's wedding.

She shoved to her feet, stepping away from him, and his expression fell. "Jess, what's wrong?"

He rose, too, moving toward her, even as she put more distance between them. She needed the physical distance in order to put the emotional space back in place. "I… I think I'll go check on Pluto."

She scurried from the room, fighting to calm the rapid-fire beat of her heart. Maybe this was some strange mental or emotional backlash because of Henry's attack in her garage and the car accident.

Since Memorial Day and what she'd interpreted as an almost kiss, she'd spent an inordinate amount of time thinking about the odd pull she'd felt for him that night. Had recent events so rattled her composure and shaken her world that she was imagining romantic feelings toward *Gage*? She scoffed an ironic laugh and shook her head. Ludicrous. All the more reason to spend the summer away from Charlotte, regaining her equilibrium and inner strength.

She found Pluto in the bedroom, sniffing the bedspread and her suitcases. The cat glanced up as she walked in and meowed. Jessica sat on the edge of the bed and stroked her cat's beige fur and soaked in the solace of Pluto's rumbling purr. "Everything will be fine, Pluto. We just needed a break from the turmoil, a little distance from the bad man."

She didn't know if Pluto bought her line, but Jessica had to believe it, because the alternative was unacceptable.

"OKAY," MATT SAID with a grin, lacing his fingers, inverting his joined hands and stretching his arms in front of him as if preparing to do a major task, "are you ready?"

Gage wiggled the fingers of both hands in a "bring it on" gesture. "Do it."

Jessica's ex-husband moved to his wife and daughter, where he motioned with his hand. "You've already met my wife, Cait, and our daughter, Erin, who'll be two this summer."

Gage offered Cait a small smile and salute of recognition.

"This is Cait's younger sister, Isla, and her husband, Evan." He pointed to a strawberry blond and the dark-haired man holding a toddler with reddish blond hair next to her. "Their daughter, CeCe, shares a birthday with Erin."

"Isla, Evan, CeCe," Gage repeated. "Nice to meet you."

"Grace and Neil Cameron, the parents-slash-grandparents of this brood—no, *clan*—" Matt said with a nod to an older woman in a wheelchair, whose white hair showed hints of red. "And the matriarch of the family, Flora Cameron, who prefers everyone call her Nanna."

"A pleasure, Mrs. Cameron," Gage said with a little bow to the frail older woman.

"The pleasure is mine, lad. But you heard Matt. Call me Nanna. Please." The woman's voice held a Scottish burr. She reached a gnarled hand for his, and he grasped it. Her grip was remarkably firm. "We Camerons don't stand on ceremony. *Ceud mìle fàilte.*"

"Um, pardon?" Gage asked.

"Nanna grew up in Scotland," Cait said, "and has done her best to teach us all a bit of Scots Gaelic. She wants to keep Scottish traditions and foods alive in the family. She said, a hundred thousand welcomes."

"Thank you, Nanna," Gage said with a flirtatious grin. "I look forward to learning more."

"Yeah," said a light-skinned Black teenager leaning against the door frame. He pulled a wry grin. "We Camerons have the best Burns Night celebration in town."

The family chuckled, and Matt said, "The jokester over there is Daryl, the youngest of the Cameron siblings, who was recently accepted to Westpoint and will leave for basic training this fall."

Gage blinked. "Westpoint? Wow! Congratulations!"

Daryl lifted a hand in thanks and greeting as he grinned.

The front door opened and another couple with a baby hustled in. The man, whose bright blue eyes and chiseled cheeks marked him a Cameron, called, "Sorry we're late. Ravi slept late, and we hated to wake him. What'd we miss?"

"Just introductions," Matt said, waving the couple in. "This is Brody and his wife, Anya."

The petite South Asian woman smiled broadly over the baby's head. "Hello. You must be Gage. Welcome! This is our son, Ravi Neil, named for his two grandfathers." She pried the baby's clutching hands from her shirt and turned him to face the room. Ravi's dark eyes took in the crowd. His face crumpled, and he quickly buried his head in his mother's chest again with a whine.

Grace rushed over to Anya, arms outstretched. "Oh, Ravi. Will you come to Grammy?"

The baby shrank away from his grandmother, his whimpers increasing.

"Sorry," Anya said, patting her son's back. "He's going

through some rather significant separation anxiety. Only mommy will do these days."

Matt clapped his hands together once. "Let's see. Who'd I miss?"

"Where are the all the Turners?" Jessica asked.

"Right," Isla offered, "our sister Emma, her husband and their daughters are out of town for a speaking engagement and mini vacation in Washington, DC."

Gage nodded. "The oldest daughter is Fenn? Eric's friend?" He cast a glance to Jessica for confirmation. "The one who was kidnapped a couple years ago?"

"Yeah," Jessica said. "She and her parents founded S.T.O.P., which teaches sex trafficking awareness and prevention in high schools."

Gage's eyes widened. "Impressive." He turned to the family. "I'm so glad she was returned to the family safely. Jess told us about it when it happened. My sister, Tina, and I were praying hard for all of you."

"Thank you. We appreciated every bit of support we got during that time. And we're so proud of our girl Fenn. She's been so brave and come back so much stronger these past couple years."

"So that's everyone," Matt said, his chipper tone dispelling the more serious turn the conversation had taken. "Shall we eat?"

Grace laughed and waved everyone toward the dining room. "You heard the man. Supper is served. Daryl, come help pour drinks. Neil, show Gage where he can wash up."

As Gage followed Neil to the front bathroom, he admitted to a tug of jealousy. The large, multigenerational Cameron family, all living so near each other, seemed an ideal situation in an idyllic setting. No wonder Jessica, an only child whose mother had never been supportive, loved this place so much. And how could he compete?

THE LIGHT BANTER and friendly debates around the dinner table were a welcome distraction for Jessica. She was heartened to see how well Gage got along with the family, as well, though why that seemed so important to her she didn't want to examine.

I just want him to feel comfortable here tonight.

The justification was enough to appease her conscience, and the hearty meal, replete with fresh vegetables from Grace's garden and the fluffiest biscuits she'd ever eaten, proved a balm, as well. Maybe there really was something to that old *comfort food* expression.

"First thing Monday morning, after I get Erin her breakfast," Cait said, casting Jessica side-glances while cutting up small bites of cantaloupe for Erin. "We can meet to go over the current occupancy list and check in/check out schedule for the cabins. And the electrician should be at the Juniper cabin around eight a.m. to wire the new addition, so if you'd let him in to start working?"

Jessica nodded. "Sounds good. Will do."

The conversation turned to Daryl's to-do list before he left for Westpoint, which the teen took in stride. Young man, really, Jessica thought. Eighteen was old enough to vote and join the military, and his broad shoulders, cut jawline and stubble-dusted cheeks bore little resemblance to the kid she'd first met four years ago. Surreptitiously, she studied Daryl anew. He was handsome. Obviously a good student if he'd been accepted at Westpoint. Funny, in a dry wit sort of way. She could well imagine Daryl breaking hearts all over the place in the years to come—although, she amended, he also seemed the sort who'd be careful not to toy with a girl's emotions. Grace Cameron would have taught him that for sure.

"Well, dinner was delicious. Thank you again, Grace," Gage said, wiping his mouth with his napkin and pulling her attention away from the Camerons' adopted son.

"Not so fast. We have dessert. A family favorite. You don't want to miss it," Grace said.

"Tempting, but I should be getting on the road back to Charlotte." He angled his head toward Jessica, adding in a low voice, "Unless you've changed your mind about me staying on your couch."

Jessica's stomach swooped at the thought of Gage leaving, even if she was surrounded by friends as kind and welcoming as the Cameron family. Gage had been her rock for these past weeks. At the accident scene. During those difficult and emotional visits to see Tina in the hospital. In those late-night texts when she felt overwhelmed. And he'd saved her life when Henry had left her to die in her garage. His reassuring presence at her bedside as she recovered from the terrifying incident meant more to her than she could express, maybe more than she wanted to admit.

"You're driving home at this hour?" Nanna asked.

"Well, yeah. That was the plan."

"All right. You can stay on my couch tonight and drive home tomorrow," Jessica blurted before she'd considered the implications of what she was saying.

Neil faced her and lifted an eyebrow. "As I recall, your cabin currently only has one bedroom and no couch in the den."

"Oh," she said, her cheeks heating as the weight of the family's inquisitive and speculating stares fell on her. "Right. Of course."

Why had she asked him to stay? She'd shown her vulnerability, her fear like a child who couldn't let go of her parent's hand on the first day of school.

"Mom and Dad have an extra room you're welcome to use," Isla volunteered, sending her mother a meaningful look. "Don't you, Mom?"

Gage chuckled uncomfortably and lifted a hand. "I couldn't impose."

"No imposition," Grace assured him. "You're more than welcome. In fact, I insist."

Turning to Jessica as if to consult her, Gage lifted his eyebrows in query. Was he asking her advice or permission? Her pulse thumped, and in return she merely gave him a shrug.

"I think y'all are missing the point," Daryl said, lifting his glass for a sip. "She asked him to stay *with her.*"

A few of the younger Camerons tittered and grinned, and Grace gasped, "Daryl, for Pete's sake! Mind your manners." Then to Jessica and Gage, she said, "I apologize for my son's cheek."

Daryl grinned unrepentantly. "Just saying..."

Jessica, face flaming, chuckled awkwardly. "You're not wrong. That had been my intent, though not for the reason you're thinking." She gave Gage a side-glance. "But the Camerons' offer works, too. Keeps you off the dark road and traveling late."

Gage placed a hand on her shoulder and squeezed. In a playful voice, he added, "Gosh, Jess. If I didn't know better, I'd think you cared."

A laugh rose around the table, easing the awkward truth of the situation. She did care about Gage. More than she wanted to admit. He'd been a better friend than she'd imagined he was prior to the accident. Before, he'd just been Tina's big brother, someone fun and safe to flirt with, because neither of them was actually looking for a relationship. He'd always been just…there. Just… Gage. Now the simple weight of his hand on her shoulder sent a crackling awareness through her veins. Her body hummed like a struck tuning fork. Why, as she considered the idea of him being hours away in Charlotte for the next several weeks, did she suddenly sense an odd attraction to him? Was it real or a strange manifestation of the unwise reliance she'd formed this spring?

As the conversation at the table moved on, she pitched her voice low, so that only Gage could hear over the guffaws and giggles around the table, and leaned toward him. "Stay."

His expression sobered a bit, and he nodded once. When Cait finished asking her mother to pass the basket of rolls, Gage said, "All right, Grace. I accept, on the condition that you allow me to treat you, your husband and Flora—er, Nanna—to breakfast at Ma's Mountain Diner. Jessica tells me their waffles are not to be missed."

Daryl spread his hands and cocked his head. "Ahem?"

Cait swatted at the teenager. "Like you'll even be out of bed for breakfast."

"You're welcome, too, of course," Gage said, then met Jessica's eyes and lowered his volume. "As are you."

A strange ripple of something sweet and intimate flowed through her, as if he were whispering endearments during sex instead of inviting her to breakfast at a country diner. Jessica took a moment to quell the odd thrum in her belly before smiling and saying, "Thank you. That sounds nice. But be forewarned. I'm known for my appetite at breakfast."

"True story," Matt said from across the table, "I've seen her eat as much at breakfast as Eric when he was a teenager. It was impressive."

Gage's gray eyes twinkled as he grinned at her. "Intriguing. I look forward to seeing this appetite in action."

Jessica felt a heat rise in her cheeks along with a surge of pure pleasure. Dipping her chin, she bit the inside of her cheeks to hide the sappy smile that tugged her mouth.

Why was she acting so giddy and ridiculous? Sheesh! She was reacting like a goofball over breakfast with Gage. No, not the breakfast invitation per se, but—she swallowed hard—Gage himself. His attentive and flirtatious gaze. The sexy timbre of his voice. His playful teasing. Nothing she hadn't shared with him in years past, and yet...

She gave her head a subtle shake. When she thought she had her smitten-schoolgirl reaction under wraps, she raised her head, and her gaze immediately clashed with her ex-husband's inquisitive and suspicious stare. Matt cut his eyes to Gage and back again before raising his eyebrows as if to ask, "What's the story? I know something's up."

Jessica frowned and gave Matt a subtle and dismissive shake of her head. But her heart thumped like a trapped rabbit. If her feelings had been so transparent to Matt, had Gage noticed the flush in her cheeks, heard the nervous quaver in her voice, seen the twitch of her giddy grin?

Through dessert, she studiously avoided Matt's knowing gaze and worked to tamp down the disconcerting flutter that accompanied each interaction with Gage, whether hers or a Cameron's.

Dessert—a raspberry, oat and whipped cream confection the family claimed was a traditional Scottish treat called cranachan—passed in a blur for Jessica. She got lost in her own thoughts as she tried to sort out her strange reaction to Gage and her growing despondency at the thought of his leaving tomorrow.

After dinner, the family invited her and Gage to stay for

a few rowdy and competitive rounds of Trivial Pursuit and Pictionary. The laughter and games served as a welcome distraction, but when the play wound down and Gage offered to walk her back to her cabin, the strange buzz of attraction returned.

You're just grateful for all the companionship and support he's offered you since the accident, she rationalized as they strolled across a grassy lawn twinkling with fireflies and moonlight.

"This place is beautiful. I can see why you would want to buy a share of it." Gage's quiet baritone voice cut into her musing.

A smile bloomed on her face. "Isn't it, though? And each season brings a new kind of beauty. You should see the azaleas and rhododendrons in the spring. And in autumn, the hardwood trees are a breathtaking counterpoint to the Christmas trees on the hills." She paused and sighed contentedly. "But the main reason I invested in Cameron Glen isn't because it's so heavenly here. The Camerons have always been so good to me, and they welcomed Eric into their family so warmly, even before Matt married Cait, that I was determined to repay their kindness. So when they needed to raise a bit of cash and divide the ownership to protect the property from poaching developers, I was all in." She slapped at a mosquito and laughed. "Ow. Stupid biters are the serpents in this paradise."

He gave a soft, humored grunt and fanned away a bug in his own face. "They are ubiquitous, huh?"

She elbowed him and chuckled. "Well, listen to you using a ten-dollar word."

"Excuse me," he returned, his tone playfully insulted, "which of us scored higher on the SAT in high school?"

"What! Good grief, who remembers that? I can't even remember what I made, much less you."

She crowded closer to him to avoid a rut in the ground, and he caught her elbow, steadying her as she stumbled a bit over the uneven ground. His touch fired fresh sparks inside her.

"I remember, because I was psyched to have done as well as I did, considering my grades didn't compete with yours or Tina's straight A's."

"So competitive!" Jessica shook her head. "But we established that well enough during Pictionary tonight, huh? Honestly, I thought you were going to burst a vein getting Cait and Matt to see a bird in the mess of squiggles you drew."

"Touché." His low chuckle rumbled from his throat and resounded like a pleasant thrum in her blood. "A guy doesn't play sports most of his life and not develop a competitive streak."

Dang it, what was wrong with her? Harboring any kind of ill-conceived attraction to Gage—Tina's brother, for crying out loud!—was a recipe for disappointment and future awkwardness. She needed Gage, the yearslong friend, the man sharing the same grief over Tina's injuries and slow recovery, her sounding board and support during this difficult time, far more than she needed a boyfriend or a lover.

Lover? Gadzooks! She really was down the rabbit hole.

She quivered deep in her core and freed her arm from his steadying grasp. Surely a few weeks' distance and calm here at Cameron Glen was all she needed to get herself in order and remind her libido that Gage was her friend and nothing more. That he couldn't be anything more without shaking the foundation she'd built her friendship to Tina on. That she had no desire for a man, especially a serial dater like Gage, in her life.

A gentle breeze stirred, carrying the scent of roses from the flower bed beside one of the cabins they were passing. Jessica inhaled deeply and held the sweet scent in her nose for a moment before letting it out. With each passing tranquil moment and lighthearted hour spent with the Camerons, she became more convinced that taking refuge at Cameron Glen had been the right move. Even if she would miss Gage.

The tag-on thought pierced her chest, and a despondent hum of resignation slipped from her, unbidden.

"Something wrong?" he asked.

Only that I've grown too attached o you.

She shook her head as the gravel of the driveway to her cabin crunched under her feet. "Just tired, I guess. So forgive me if I don't invite you in?"

"No problem. Sleep well, and I'll be around to get you for breakfast at—" He hesitated and ducked his head a little as he eyed her speculatively. "Seven a.m. too early for you?"

"Most days it's not. Though I'm not saying I *like* getting up before eight."

He chuckled as they reached the small porch where rocking chairs were positioned for the best views of the nearby ridge of the Smoky Mountains. "Then we'll make it eight… or even eight thirty."

She keyed open the cabin door and faced him. "No, I have a feeling Grace and Neil are early risers. Cait said her parents like to be up at dawn to work in their garden and walk the property before the day heats up. Seven is fine."

He bobbed his chin once in agreement, and in the dim porch light, she saw his gaze shift to something behind her. Before she could turn, his hand reached out, jutting past her ear as he closed his hand around…something. She gasped quietly, startled.

He brought his hand back in front of her chin and opened it slowly to reveal a blinking firefly. "Make a wish."

"You caught it. You make a wish."

His expression turned serious as if contemplating a difficult math equation instead of a childhood superstition. Then, as the small lightning bug flew away, he leaned close and kissed her lightly on her mouth.

She stilled, blinked at him, her body humming like the night frogs singing in the trees and water. "Was that your wish?"

She hoped her tone sounded light and amused rather than stunned. Or choked by an onslaught of desire...

The corner of his mouth twitched as he took a step back from her. "Maybe."

"Um." She curled her lips in, pressing her hand to her mouth and undecided whether she was savoring the tingle left by his kiss or trying to purge the lingering memory of it. Furrowing her brow, she whispered, "Gage, I don't think..."

He cleared his throat, and his expression darkened. "Don't. I...apologize. I guess I got caught up in the allure of the setting, the moonlight. The romance of this place. It..." He exhaled harshly. "It won't happen again." He took another step back before turning and hurrying off the porch. "Good night, Jess."

She opened her mouth to call him back or, at least, return his parting wish, but no sound came out.

It won't happ n again.

Was that what she wanted...or what she feared?

Chapter Eleven

Hellfire. Why had he kissed her like that?

Gage gritted his back teeth as he walked back up the hill to the elder Camerons' house, his gut churning. The startled look on Jessica's face had been a cold slap of reality. Whatever else had changed in the past three months since the accident, her feelings for him clearly had not.

"Idiot," he muttered, watching the unfamiliar road at his feet for ruts as he stewed.

"I hope you don't mean me."

Gage jerked his head up to see Matt and Cait walking toward him, their sleeping toddler on Matt's shoulder. "Oh, no. Of course not. I'm the idiot."

"Why is that? I thought you were pretty darn smart at Trivial Pursuit tonight," Cait replied, grinning.

Gage hesitated, and in the silence, Matt asked, "Because you kissed Jessica?"

"Uh—" Gage sputter-coughed.

Cait elbowed her husband and gave him a *"Really?"* look.

"So…you saw that?" Gage plowed fingers through his hair and frowned.

"We weren't spying," Cait said, "But the porch light was on, and, well…"

Gage sighed and nodded. "Yeah. That's why."

"Why is kissing her such a bad thing?" Cait asked. "You two clearly have chemistry. That was easy enough to see tonight."

Gage jolted. "It was? I—"

Cait tipped her head. "Am I wrong?"

Grunting, he shoved his hands in the pockets of his jeans. "I don't know. Apparently, I misread some signals. Jess looked at me like I had two heads just now when I kissed her. I may have just ruined twentysomething years of a perfectly good casual friendship."

"Well…" Cait wrinkled her nose sympathetically. "You don't know that. Maybe you just caught her off guard."

"Oh, I did that at a minimum." He dragged a hand down his face, knowing the memory of the surprise on Jessica's face would haunt him well beyond tonight. Guilt kicked him. "Me mucking up things with Jessica is the last thing she needs right now. Since the accident, she's been in turmoil. She's had so much to deal with, beyond Sara's death and Holly and Tina being in the hospital. I was, kind of by default, her main support."

He glanced up at Matt and Cait, adding quickly, "Not that you haven't been kind and a good sounding board for her, but… I was local. I was who she called at night when things felt overwhelming. I guess I was kinda a substitute for Tina."

"Yeah," Matt said. "She mentioned how much you've helped her out. That you went to Sara's funeral with her. She has appreciated everything you've done." Matt shifted his daughter slightly in his arms, angling a look at her when the little girl stirred. Once Erin quieted again, he asked, "When you say she's had so much to deal with beyond

Sara's death and her other two friends in the hospital, you mean her stalker?"

Gage raised his chin, narrowing a startled look on Matt. "Yeah. I knew she'd told you about the guy, but I wasn't sure how she framed it. She's…a little bit in denial about how dangerous this guy might be, even after the incident in her garage. I keep offering to stay with her. You know, an added layer of protection, but she's so stubborn, so determined to go it alone."

Cait and Matt exchanged a quick look, and Matt asked, "How dangerous is this guy?"

Twisting his mouth, Gage debated how much he could share. Henry Blythe's behavior, the threats he'd made, was Jessica's story to tell. But if Jessica was going to be safe this summer, she needed the people around her to be aware of everything Detective Macnally had said.

When he continued debating, Matt's expression hardened, and he took a step closer. "Gage, tell me. This is my son's mother we're talking about."

Gage tipped his head back and stared up at the stars, the winking fireflies, the yellow moon that had slipped behind a thin cloud. What the hell? Jessica was already mad at him for kissing her. If she wanted to be ticked off about his sharing the truth of her situation, so be it. The bottom line was, whether she liked it or not, Jessica needed every bit of protection possible.

Returning his gaze to Matt, he said, "All right. And for the record, Eric doesn't know about the stalker. Jess only told him a fuller truth about the car accident a couple weeks ago. About Sara's death. Tina and Holly in the hospital. She didn't want him worried about her or distracted from his class work. She pretended she was fine while Eric was home before summer semester started."

"Yeah. She asked me not to tell him the whole truth, but Eric's no fool. He sensed something was up. He's told me his mom seemed tense. Had been unusually tightlipped about her life. Not calling as often as she normally would. I think he deserves to know what's happening."

"What is happening with Jess, beyond the mess we already know?" Cait asked and grunted, "Which is bad enough."

Gage scuffed his shoe on the asphalt road, kicking at a pine cone. He capsulized the confrontation in her garage and how Henry had left her unconscious on the floor. "She breathed carbon monoxide for a good while before I found her."

Cait gasped.

Matt scowled. "How badly did he hurt her?"

"Cracked rib, goose egg on her head. I don't think killing her was his intent. But by the time I found her—and it was a miracle I had reason to go by her house looking for her—she'd already breathed a great deal of carbon monoxide. She spent a day and a half in the hospital, but the doctors don't think she has any long-term damage."

"Good Lord!" Cait pressed a hand to her mouth, clearly stunned. "Why wouldn't she have told us this? Doesn't she know how much we care about her?"

"That's probably why," Matt said, turning to his wife. "Jessica has never liked to accept help from anyone and hates to think she's inconvenienced or burdened anyone. During the times I was deployed overseas, she took on single parenting like a lone wolf. She refused help from neighbors and denied herself time off for self-care. It's honestly pretty amazing that she agreed to stay here this summer."

"If she didn't feel she was contributing by working in the office and assisting with contractors on the cabin renovations, I doubt she would have," Gage said. He tucked his hands in his pockets and puffed out his cheeks as he exhaled. "So…do me a favor and keep an eye on Jessica this summer."

"Of course. Definitely," Matt said.

"I plan to check in on her regularly. My twenty-four on, forty-eight off schedule at the fire station will allow me to pop over now and then. I offered to stay full-time, but she refused. Of course." He grimaced. "And now I've gone and thrown a monkey wrench in things by impulsively kissing her." He huffed. "What was I thinking?"

Cait angled her head and grinned. "Maybe that she's more than a friend to you?"

Gage grunted softly and glanced away. "Unfortunately, it's not mutual."

"I was watching her with you tonight, man," Matt said. "I know my ex-wife. And… I wouldn't be so sure it's not mutual."

JESSICA SETTLED EASILY into a new routine at Cameron Glen. The mountain air, the change of scenery, the ample company of loving friends all provided a balm to her tattered soul. Pluto, too, seemed thrilled about the change of venue, chattering through the window at the chipmunks, bunnies and ducks that passed the cabin windows at various times throughout the day. When her need for her own car became obvious, she and Gage schemed a way for him to get it to her. Jessica hired a wrecking company to haul her car from her garage, as if it were in poor repair, and meet her and Cait at a rest stop along the interstate, after which she drove it the rest of the way to Cameron Glen.

As the late June days passed and July arrived, she spent more time conversing with Cait and her sisters the way she used to with her posse. Through those discussions, she began to gain some clarity on some matters regarding Eric, Henry…and Gage.

Eric, they reminded her, was an adult who didn't need to be shielded from the ugliness of life. She'd raised a strong, resilient and intelligent son who would only resent being kept in the dark.

Henry, they warned, wasn't likely to give up and go away. The Cameron women all agreed with Detective Macnally that her stalker's obsession with Jessica could easily become more volatile. They kindly suggested that now was not the time to put her pride in front of her safety. She needed extra protection, even at Cameron Glen. And as long as he was volunteering…

Gage, the Cameron ladies agreed, was the perfect candidate to protect her. And, oh, by the way, why wasn't she doing something about that hot firefighter who clearly adored her?

At night in her bed, in quiet hours strolling the retreat property, and when she should have been reconciling financial books at the rental office, Jessica found herself thinking about Gage. She thought about what should have been an innocent, playful firefly kiss, about the strange new stir of feelings he evoked, about the comfort their friendship had given her through the years. And about the risk of losing that friendship if the delicate balance between friends and lovers was disturbed.

The only thing she could say for sure was that she missed Gage. Phone calls, texts, even Facetime didn't take the place of seeing him in person, having his steadying presence beside her when she visited Tina, being close enough to smell the crisp combination of soap, pine and coffee that clung to

him, having him take her hand or squeeze her shoulder at
the end of a long day.

So when he asked if he could come stay with her over
the weekend in mid-July, she eagerly accepted. She even
found an unused single bed mattress that she dragged to the
Juniper cabin for him to sleep on in the living room, rather
than have him bunk with the senior Camerons again. She
wanted him near, wanted their privacy, wanted…

With a subtle shake of her head, she dismissed the rest of
that thought unfinished. It was enough that Gage was coming to visit, to bring news of Tina, to fill the lonely place
inside her that only he could fill. She could examine the
ramifications of that curious dynamic later.

HENRY, WEARING A new disguise today, lurked near the jani-
tor's closet watching Gage Coleman talk to his sister's doctor in the hospital corridor. The usual conversation. The
sister was making small improvements. Full recovery would
take time. So grateful to the medical team for all they'd
done. Yada yada.

Big deal. Who cared? What was more important to Henry
was that he hadn't seen Jessie visit her convalescing friend
since late June. Neither had he seen any activity at her house
for the past three and a half weeks. Whenever he'd called her
office, he'd been put on hold before the receptionist asked
to take a message. Clearly something was up. Not knowing
what that something was infuriated Henry. The idea that Jessie had gone MIA made him restless. He'd been so careful
to avoid detection before, but he needed a plan to find Jessie.

He was stewing over what action he needed to take when
Coleman said something that caught Henry's attention.

"I'll be out of town this weekend visiting a friend. Please

ask the nurses to call if anything at all changes with Tina's condition. They have my number."

Visiting a friend out of town? Was it possible Coleman knew where Jessie was? Could the friend he was seeing be Jessie, holed up somewhere hiding? He decided immediately that he couldn't let this opportunity to possibly track Jessie down pass. When Coleman strode toward the elevator, Henry hit the stairs and reached the ground floor before Coleman did. He kept the other man in sight as he hurried to his truck, then tailed Coleman out of the parking lot. He kept a good distance between them, not wanting to tip off Jessie's friend. When Coleman hit the interstate headed west, Henry followed. A tingling sense told him he'd caught Jessie's scent again.

The hunt was back on.

Chapter Twelve

When Gage arrived at the Juniper cabin that afternoon, Jessica rushed out to greet him and flung herself into his arms for a long, tight hug. Neither of them said anything for long moments. They only broke apart to go inside when the voices of a family staying in another cabin wafted to them from the road. Jessica stepped back from Gage and gave the strolling family an awkward wave and greeting.

Gage picked up the duffel bag he'd dropped at their feet for the embrace and cleared his throat. "I've missed you, Jess. More than I thought I would."

"Same here," she admitted, ducking her chin so he couldn't see the extent of that reality in her eyes. Pivoting on her toes, she hitched her head toward the cabin. "I hope you're hungry. I've got lasagna in the oven and all the fixings in progress. Salad, garlic bread, and your favorite pie for dessert."

"Wow. That sounds terrific. Is it my birthday?" He scrunched his nose as if trying to remember. "No…that's not for a couple months. So, what's the occasion?"

She held the screen door for him as he carried his bag inside. "Just because I had the time to cook. And I wanted to thank you for everything you've done for me these past months."

He shook his head. "Not necessary." He paused when he stepped inside to inhale deeply. "Dang. That smells divine, Jess."

She refused his offer of assistance in the kitchen, directing him to get comfortable and watch whatever ball game or movie rerun he wanted while she put the pie in the oven.

The last minutes of the lasagna's cook time were spent relaxing together, laughing, sharing a bottle of pinot noir and enjoying a moment to just *be*. Gage caught her up on Tina's condition and a morsel of surprise good news.

"I ran into Holly and her parents in the hall outside Tina's room a couple of days ago."

"Holly? She's awake? Walking?"

Gage nodded and grinned. "Walking slowly. Able to recognize me. She asked about you. Her mother shut that down pretty quick, and after we went our separate ways, her father stopped me to tell me Holly has no recollection of the accident. Remembers nothing after leaving the restaurant. They plan to leave it that way and want your word you won't say anything to her."

Jessica goggled at him. "That's a horrible idea! She's going to remember at some point. I won't lie to her!" She huffed and balled her fists. "What did they tell her happened?"

"Just that she was in a car accident. No details about who else was involved or how it happened."

"She must feel abandoned by her friends. They won't let me see her, Tina can't and Sara's..." Her sigh was ragged and frustrated. "I have to fix that. When I get home, I have to talk to her parents again, convince them to let me see Holly. I know what it's like to feel abandoned by someone you love."

Gage drew her into his arms and held her close. He kissed

her forehead and stroked a hand on her arm. The cuddle was far more intimate than she'd have been comfortable with even a few weeks ago, but somehow, now it seemed…right. *Because we're better friends.*

Even as she justified the nearness, the touches, a nagging voice whispered that she wanted more. This wasn't the Gage she'd known since high school. Not the guy who'd crashed her sleepovers with Tina and made fart noises with his armpit to drive them nuts.

This was the courageous firefighter who entered burning houses, who'd saved her from the poisonous gas in her garage, who'd been her ride-or-die since the accident. Yeah, they had grown closer as they coped with trauma and grief. Nothing wrong with that. And she savored his affection, his nearness enough to silence the jangling in her mind that told her to back off. He'd be leaving for Charlotte again soon, and she wanted the comfort of his body beside her, his soft laugh tripping down her spine, his enticing caress on her skin.

Only when the jarring buzz of the oven timer sounded did she drag herself away from him. Her body hummed pleasantly as she returned to the kitchen and set the strawberry pie and lasagna on the counter to cool. She turned off the oven and put the garlic bread in to warm in the residual heat. As she carried the salad to the table, she called, "Will you pour the wine, Gage? Everything else is just about done."

He helped her set the table and serve plates, then tuned the television to an all-music channel that played soft rock. Gage paused as he headed into the dining room, a strange look on his face.

"Gage? Is something wrong?" Jessica crossed the room to him, angling her head in query.

He chuckled wryly. "No. I just realized what song this is." He aimed a finger toward the TV.

She glanced at the screen and read, "She's All I Ever Had" by Ricky Martin. "Do you remember dancing to it at my senior prom?"

"Um." She tried to think back. His senior prom would have been her junior year, and she'd gone to prom with... Mark Shane. "I remember one dance with you, but not the song." She wrinkled her nose. "I'm surprised you remember. You're sure it was this song?"

He nodded and took her hand, tugged her into his arms and began to sway. "Positive."

She swayed absently with him as she tuned her ear to the poignant words and melody, letting the music pull at her emotions, soften her mood. It felt natural to melt against Gage and move slowly as he rocked her gently. While she was surprised Gage would remember something as trivial as the song they'd danced to so many years ago, she found it sweet. She'd rarely seen this sentimental side of Gage.

She canted back in his arms to tell him such, but the words stuck in her throat when she saw his expression. The desire in his eyes puddled inside Jessica, leaving her breathless and her heartbeat scampering. She thought back to the grazing kiss he'd given her the night she'd arrived at Cameron Glen, excusing it as a firefly wish.

The impulse to kiss Gage now, not just a quick brush of lips but a true kiss, a deep and passionate kiss, blindsided her. Before she could overanalyze the yearning, she stood on tiptoes and pressed her mouth to his.

In response, Gage tightened his hold on her with one arm and cradled the back of her head with his other as his lips drew greedily on hers. The cabin fell away, the changing song on the television faded and only that moment between them existed. Raw and real and earthshaking.

Relationship-altering.

Some zap of reality restarted her brain from whatever short circuit had temporarily overcome her. Tearing her mouth from his, she ducked her chin and mumbled, "Good grief. I'm sorry. I don't know what came over me."

A groan that sounded almost angry rumbled from Gage's chest, and she peered up at him, unsure what she'd find in his expression.

His jaw tightened, and his gray eyes pierced to her core. "Don't apologize. And please, Jess, don't retreat from me again."

She blinked. "Retreat?"

"Like you did on Memorial Day and the day I brought you here to Cameron Glen. I know you felt the pull between us both of those times, and I saw you shut it down and walk away from it."

She wiggled free of his embrace, putting distance between them so she could think. Facing him again, she shook her head. "I don't know what you mean," she lied.

Her pulse beat in her ears, a panicked whooshing, as she scrambled for a way to right the situation, to grab back the sure footing she'd had with Gage just five minutes earlier. If things changed, if she lost his friendship, where would she be? The notion terrified her.

He took a step forward, holding a hand out to her. "Can you honestly tell me that over these past few weeks you haven't thought about kissing me? What it would be like to make love to me?"

Jessica stilled, pinned by his bright, penetrating eyes, while inside her emotions were in turmoil, her thoughts scrambling, her pulse a living creature she could feel kicking in her veins. "Are you saying you have?"

He chuffed a soft laugh. "Damn right. I'd have thought that was obvious." His expression sobered as he took another step toward her. "Have I messed this up? Read things wrong? I was under the impression that you'd begun to feel the same way. Isn't that why you just kissed me?"

Her body hummed as he took one more step toward her, moving close enough for her to feel the heat of his body around her, like a blanket he'd drape over her shoulders. "I feel...something. I can't define it, but—" *Can't or won't?* a whisper in her head asked.

He brushed her hair off her cheek, his fingertips grazing her face and shattering her train of thought. With a tremulous exhale, she leaned into his hand, let him cup her chin, smooth his thumb along her jaw. His gentle caress lulled her, made tiny sparks crackle in her core. How easy it would be to give herself over to the primal call howling in her soul. Need clawed at her, battling reason and practicality and...fear.

"But?" he prompted, his voice low and intimate.

Firming her resolve, she rasped, "But it doesn't matter. I can't."

"Why can't you?" he asked, his tone patient.

"It wouldn't be smart. I can *want* any number of things, but that doesn't mean I can have them. Following my impulses or whims would only give me a few moments of pleasure in the big picture."

"Is that such a terrible thing? Aren't you allowed to do what you want instead of what your brain says you should all the time? Isn't it possible that those nudges toward spontaneity are your subconscious or a higher power showing you the right path?"

She moaned her frustration. "My mother was spontaneous and flighty and undisciplined, and it ruined her. She had a string of bad, sometimes abusive relationships and died penniless and addicted to painkillers."

"I'm aware. But you are not your mother."

She swallowed hard, feeling the lump that rose in her throat. Taking a beat, she lifted her chin, hoping to manifest the confidence she needed to push her temptation away. "I will not go down the slippery slope of momentary pleasure."

"What if the pleasure wasn't momentary? What if that inner voice you're shouting down is trying to lead you to a lasting happiness?" Gage caught her closer, wrapping his arms around her waist.

She put her hands on his chest, meaning to push away, but somehow curling her fingers in the soft flannel of his shirt. She was having more and more difficulty sorting her reason from her yearning, finding the practical in the maelstrom of heady longing sucking at her, making her tremble.

"For once, let yourself have a moment that's yours. Follow your heart," he whispered, the pinot noir–scented tickle of his breath taunting her. "Give yourself a chance to savor, like you would a fine wine or decadent chocolate."

Just once…

A moment to treasure…

As he ducked his head to kiss her, she closed her eyes and let herself just…*feel*. No thinking. No analyzing. No second-guessing or projecting what might happen tomorrow or next week if she…just. Let. Go.

HENRY EMERGED FROM the bramble-dense woods and crept along in the shadow line of the trees until he spotted Coleman's pickup truck. *Bingo.* He had Jessie.

Henry curled up a corner of his mouth in a gloating smile. *Thank you, Mr. Coleman, for your services. I'll take it from here.*

After Coleman had turned in at Cameron Glen, Henry had continued into the small town of Valley Haven to do a bit of research. He'd found a pamphlet about the vacation rentals at Cameron Glen and studied the map of the property. He asked questions about the rental cabins at the gas station as he filled his tank and learned a bit about the family, the property and the security measures in place.

After getting some food at a local diner, he'd headed back toward Cameron Glen and parked on the side of the road. He'd made his way onto the rental property on foot, then scanned the property around the cabins, making sure no one was around, taking a moonlit stroll. He hadn't come this far just to have some nosy bystander report his presence or interfere with his plans.

All clear.

Sprinting to the back wall of the cabin, he sidestepped around a pile of scrap lumber and other construction debris and moved to the nearest window. Peering inside, he discovered what was apparently the bedroom Jessica was using, though the lights were out and he couldn't make out much detail. Light illuminated the hall outside the bedroom like a beacon leading him to the next room. Easing along the cabin's outer wall, careful not to kick any construction trash or step on anything sharp, Henry moved around the corner to the next window. The lit window gave him a golden view into the den where he found Jessie and Coleman—*kissing*.

Rage flashed through Henry like a windswept wildfire. The chick at the hospital had lied to him. Coleman wasn't just a family friend to Jessie, he was her *lover*. The shock of the revelation left him shaking, seething. A sense of betrayal and disgust pounded in his skull. And just that fast, his plan changed.

He patted his jacket pocket, glad now that he'd brought his Glock. Forget scaring Jessie. If he was going to convince

Jessie they belonged together, job number one was eliminating the competition. Permanently.

But not here. Not now. Too public. He needed to get Gage Coleman somewhere remote where he could leave all evidence of Jessica's lover behind. He ground his back teeth together and weighed his choices. Could he disable the guy and drag him into the woods? No. Even if he thought he could move the probably almost-two-hundred-pound man, the woods were still too near the cabins. The rotting body would be found too soon.

Henry's gaze shifted to Jessica's car, parked next to Coleman's truck. And a plan took root.

Chapter Thirteen

The warmth of Gage's lips was a siren call, luring Jessica deeper, nearer. And like a sailor ignoring the imminent danger of a rocky shore and caught in Gage's thrall, she canted forward and let her body go slack. She melted into him, circling his shoulders with her arms. His mouth tested hers, a tentative touch, then parted slightly as he drew on her more deeply.

A sweetness like thick honey flowed through her, making her head, her limbs feel languid, sated…impatient. Drawing a shaky breath, Jessica sealed her lips against his, capturing his mouth and opening to him.

Gage smoothed his hands up her back, burying his fingers into her hair, then trailing his fingers back down her spine to start again. Savoring the intoxicating taste of his kiss and the heady magic of his exploring hands, Jessica lost herself, letting the rush of pleasure blot out everything except this man, this place, this exquisite kiss.

His fingers cupped and squeezed the curve of her bottom, pushed her hips forward, a silent invitation. Hungry, untamed noises rumbled from him, and she felt the vibration from his chest against her own. She freed several buttons on his shirt and slipped her hands inside to feel his hot skin against her palms. He answered by untucking her blouse from her shorts and dipping his fingers under her waistband to massage the sensitive skin at the small of her back.

When she let her head fall backward, exposing the tender arch of her throat to him, he moved his kiss to the pulse point there. With a tiny nip of his teeth, he stirred a fresh surge of electricity from her core, charging her need, amplifying her pleasure. A small moan escaped her, and he answered with his own feral growl. With tiny backward steps, he walked them toward the new couch, the closest horizontal surface besides the hardwood floor.

Her hands continued roaming across his muscles, tugging at buttons, rumpling his hair as she baby-stepped with him. She caught his face between her hands, taking his mouth again in a savage kiss, and tugging on his bottom lips with her teeth.

"Oh, Jessica…" he mumbled, his tone thick with desire, "finally. *Finally.*" He slanted his mouth to kiss her deeply, then paused long enough to yank his shirt over his head without unfastening the last several buttons. "I have wanted this, wanted *you* for so long. So many, *many* years…"

His words, like a shard of ice, sliced through the muzzy heat of her passion. A jolt of sobriety snatched her back from the edge of the dangerous cliff where she teetered. Every muscle inside her tensed as she flinched back from him, replaying his words in her head. Surely she misunderstood. Perhaps in her rush to slake her hunger she'd imagined his confession.

"Jess?" Gage said, his brow beetling. "What's wrong?"

"Wh-what did you just say?"

Gage straightened his spine, and a smile split his face as he met her eyes. "I said, I've wanted you for a very long time. And I have. But now…" His smile brightened, and he reached to draw her close again.

But Jessica jerked away, stumbling back a step. Two.

Her pulse, thrumming with desire a moment ago, now thudded heavily in her skull—dissonant gongs reverberating and filling her head with a nerve-splitting cacophony.

Gage's smile fell. "That bothers you?"

She struggled for a breath, seeing the past decades she'd spent as Tina's best friend and in Gage's orbit in a whole new light. Their entire past relationship had been a lie? "How long? Since…when?"

"I don't know exactly. I've always thought you were beautiful." He reached for her again, and she knocked his hand away.

Her head spun. Her chest prickled, then her neck, as the heat of anger climbed higher and settled on her cheeks. "You've…been living a *lie* with me the whole time I've known you?"

"Not a lie. That's harsh. Look, don't overreact—"

She barked a hard laugh. "Whoa! Do *not* tell me how to feel about this!"

He held up a hand, wincing with apology. "Sorry. I didn't mean—"

"Does Tina know?"

"I…don't know." His frown said he knew he'd messed up and was looking for a way to backpedal. "I never—"

Jessica's temples throbbed as one new and humiliating thought tumbled after another. Hadn't she sworn, after seeing her mother live with the carnage of liars and their lies, that she'd never accept dishonesty in her own relationships? How was it possible a man she'd thought dependable, had welcomed in her closest social circle, had been hiding secrets from her? Was she that bad a judge of character? Could she not trust her own perceptions of men?

Gage exhaled heavily and spread his palms in appeal. "Can we just…take a minute. Take a breath before we say or do something that we'll regret."

"You mean like, 'Oh, by the way, I've spent the last twenty-three years pretending to be someone I'm not'?" she said sourly.

"I thought I was doing the right thing keeping it to myself," he returned with just as much salt.

"Lying is never the right choice."

He blew out a frustrated breath and furrowed his brow. "I never lied to you, Jess!"

"Oh, really? Isn't omission its own kind of lie?"

"I— Not in my book. Not when the truth would have caused problems."

"Problems? Ya think?" She growled and curled her fingers in her hair. Her thoughts were too scrambled and poisoned with a brew of emotions to sort out what was what.

Spinning on her heel, she stomped to the cabin door and snatched her keys from the side table.

"Jess, where are you going?" A note of concern sharpened his tone.

"I don't know. I need air. I need…space." Without looking back, she rushed from the cabin and scurried to her car. The driver's door was unlocked, and she climbed behind the wheel. Her hand shook as she tried several times to get the key in the ignition.

Movement and a loud knock on the side window sent a jolt of adrenaline through her. She yelped and cut a startled look to Gage.

He opened the driver's door and frowned at her. "Jess, come back inside. Please. We'll talk and—"

"No. I clearly can't think straight around you. Just—" She put a hand in the center of his chest and pushed him back. Closed the door. Turned the key in the ignition. The engine rumbled to life.

When he tried to open the door again, she gripped the handle and dragged it back. "No, Gage. I need some time by myself. Please!"

Still unaccustomed to her new car, she squinted in the dark to find the door lock button on the armrest. Instead, she hit the window open button. The mirror adjustment.

The passenger door opened before she found the door lock, and Gage climbed in the front seat with her. "Look, I'm not sure what just happened or what upset you, but can we please just go inside and talk?"

Tears puddled in her eyes, and she shook her head. "I'm not sure I can explain it. I… I just…need to get away for a bit."

He sighed. "Jess, running away isn't the answer. Besides, you're not in a good state of mind to be driving."

She opened her mouth to argue when a strange clicking sound came from the behind her.

"Actually, driving is exactly what you should do now," a cold male voice said.

As she and Gage whipped their heads toward the back seat, Henry snaked his arm around Gage's throat. He drew his grip so tight across Gage's neck that her friend gasped for breath. Pinning a dark glare on Jessica, Henry shoved a gun to the base of Gage's skull. "Drive us away from here, now, or pretty boy lover gets a bullet in the head."

Chapter Fourteen

Icy fear slithered through Jessica. For a fleeting moment, she thought of opening the car door and running. But doing so would mean abandoning Gage to a madman with a gun and an agenda. Meanwhile, in the back of her brain, the message of safety videos she'd seen at college scrolled through her mind. *Never let an attacker take you to a second location. If you get in a car with a kidnapper you are as good as dead.*

Bile rose from her gut, hot and bitter, as her brain scrambled for what to do.

Clawing at Henry's arm, fighting for air, Gage flung his head backward. But Henry anticipated the move and dodged the blow. "Nice try, Coleman, but I wasn't born yesterday." Angling the gun, he poked it at Jessica. "Why aren't we moving yet? Drive!"

Panic flooded her gut, and without a better idea, she put her car in gear and backed out of the short gravel driveway. Once on the narrow road leading out of Cameron Glen, they passed other vacation cabins where guests were cozied in for the night. Then they approached the small farmhouse that was Isla and Evan's home. Her gaze angled toward the yellow glow of their front porch light, and she calculated.

If she pulled in their driveway, if she blasted the car horn, if she—

"Be smart here, Jessie," Henry growled. "If you rouse your friends out of their house, I'll shoot them the minute they step on their front porch."

Was he serious? Would Henry really shoot innocents because of his obsession with her? Could she really presume he was bluffing, and risk her friends' lives?

Gage was gasping louder, clearly desperate for air, and he finally got his head turned enough that he could duck his chin behind Henry's arm. As Jessica rolled slowly past Isla's and toward the property exit, Gage sank his teeth into Henry's arm.

With a roar of pain, Henry jerked his arm away.

Gage folded forward, coughing and sucking in deep breaths, but before he could right himself and make any defensive move, Henry retaliated.

Slamming the butt of the gun down on the back of Gage's head, he snarled. "You sonofabitch! I should kill you now and be done with it!"

"No!" Jessica screamed, stopping the car and reaching for Gage. He lay slumped against the passenger door, not moving. Horror slithered through her, and tears dripped onto her cheeks.

"Drive!" Henry roared. "Or there's more for him where that came from."

Anger and fear curled together in her belly, vying for top spot. She wrenched around to glare at Henry and shove a finger in his face. "Don't you touch him! Your beef, your perverted fascination is with me. Leave him out of it!"

"I wish I could, darlin'," he said, "but he became a part of this the minute he put his hands on you. I saw you two kissing and groping each other like dogs in heat. So obviously I have to get rid of him if you and I are going to move forward."

The contents of her stomach curdled. She wanted to argue the fact that she'd never have anything to do with Henry, but riling him further while he held a gun didn't seem advisable.

Gage still hadn't moved. The idea that he could be dead sliced painfully through her chest. She lifted a hand toward him again, and Henry made a hissing noise through his teeth as he waved the black gun at her.

"Just...let me see if he's breathing. Please?"

Henry's jaw clenched, and he grabbed Gage by the hair and pulled his head back. Jessica gasped in dismay at the rough treatment, but held her hand under Gage's nose until she felt the soft tickle of his breath. She gripped his wrist, as much taking solace from the connection as looking for a pulse.

"That's enough." Henry jabbed the gun at her again. "Go!"

"Which way?"

"Which way is town?" he asked.

"Right."

"Then go left. Take us out into the boonies, the mountains. The farther from people the better."

Quaking inside, Jessica pulled the car onto the highway. She sent up a silent prayer that she could figure out an escape, some means to rescue herself and Gage. Before it was too late.

HENRY GREW SILENT as she drove, sitting behind her with the gun aimed at Gage's head. The clear message was if she tried anything that didn't align with his plans, Gage would pay the price. When a bluish glow filled the dark car, she looked in the rearview mirror to watch Henry. With one hand, Henry was flicking through screens and scrolling on his phone. What in the…? Did he really think the middle of a kidnapping was the best time to check his email?

Could she use this moment of his distraction to her advantage? Maybe. But how? Drive the car off the road into a tree or sign post? If they'd been closer to Valley Haven or another town, maybe. But not knowing how far they were from civilization, how soon another vehicle might come by, she decided stranding herself and Gage on the side of the road, miles from help, with an enraged Henry wasn't a good idea. How far had they come?

Time felt elastic, both stretching out, tense and fragile, and retracting as the miles between them and Cameron Glen rolled on. She hadn't paid attention to road signs at first, preoccupied with Gage's condition and Henry's gun. She was all too aware that it had been her fit of anger and confusion that had sent her bumbling outside to her car and into Henry's snare.

If she hadn't left the cabin, what would Henry have done? A moot point, she acknowledged. Better to focus on the reality of her plight instead of the what-ifs and self-recriminations.

They passed a sign indicating a junction with another rural highway, but being unfamiliar with the smaller roads in this part of the state, she learned nothing about their location.

"Take the next left," Henry said.

She met his gaze in the mirror. "What? Why?"

"Because I said so!" He aimed a finger, pointing out the road as they approached the reflective signs marking the turn. "Here."

She did as he said, scanning the roadside for any landmark that might help her if she was able to get away from Henry. A side-glance to Gage's limp form put a hole in that fantasy. She could not, *wouldn ot* abandon Gage.

"So you've…" Her voice was thick with anxiety, and she paused to clear her throat, wanting to sound calmer, more in control. "You've been following me? Watching my house?"

"What of it? You wouldn't talk to me, so I had no choice."

She noticed he'd turned the facts around, putting the blame on her, but she didn't argue with his screwy logic.

"And how…how did you know I was at Cameron Glen?"

Henry grunted. "I didn't for a long time. But I'd seen you so often this spring with *him*—" he motioned toward Gage with the muzzle of his gun "—so I started watching him when you disappeared. I knew he made frequent trips to the hospital to visit the vegetable."

A fresh wash of fiery anger flashed through her at his callous reference to Tina's earlier condition, but she clamped down on it.

"So today, I heard him tell one of the nurses he would be heading out of town to visit a friend for the weekend and asked her to call him immediately if anything changed. I figured the *friend*—" Henry said the word with so much sarcasm and loathing that Jessica felt a chill "—might be you, so I followed him." He paused. "Tell me, Jessie. Do you think the vegetable knows her husband is cheating on her with you?"

Jessica sputtered a startled laugh. "What?"

Henry jabbed her with the gun. "What's so damn funny?"

"The woman in the hospital is Gage's *sister*. Not his wife. And I've told you, we're not a couple."

"Liar. You were kissing him. I saw you."

"That was—" What was it? Earthshaking. Divine. Intensely intriguing. Something that needed to be further explored?

She shook her head. That answer wasn't helpful in dealing with Henry. "It wasn't planned. It was nothing. He's a *friend.* Just a friend." If she could drive that point home, convince him Gage wasn't a rival, would it de-escalate the danger for Gage?

She sent Tina's brother a side-glance. Why hadn't he woken up yet? How long did it take people who'd been knocked out to recover consciousness? Was something more seriously wrong with him?

She had her answer roughly ten minutes later when Gage stirred with a groan. She sucked in a sharp breath of relief and cut a glance toward him.

Gage caught Henry's attention, as well. He smacked the gun into Gage's temple, and Gage slumped again.

"Hey!" Jessica cried, irate. "I told you not to do that!"

Henry only snorted. "Yeah. You did. But I never agreed to those terms. *I'm* in charge here. *I* make the rules. And rule number one is, lover boy stays out until we get where we're going."

Maybe she should be thankful Henry hadn't shot Gage and dumped his body, but she couldn't work up any gratitude, considering he'd kidnapped them and brutally knocked Gage out twice.

"Where *are* we going?"

"Found us a place to stay for a few days through a rent-a-house app. Real private so nobody will bother us."

Private. As in remote. Her chest squeezed as she imagined why he would want to be far from civilization and other neighbors. Her mind dwelled on this detail when a deer bolted out from the edge of the road, right into their path. She gasped and cut the wheel hard, narrowly avoiding the animal, but causing the car to fishtail as she corrected.

Henry cursed at her, which did nothing to help the jolt of adrenaline charging through her. "Are you trying to kill us?"

"Did you want me to hit the deer? That wouldn't have ended well for anyone!" she shouted back.

Henry reached up from the back seat to smack her cheek. He hit her hard enough that she bit her tongue, tasted blood.

"Do not speak to me that way. Ever. Again," he grated. "Understood?"

"Or what?" She'd seen her mother cower to bullies too often to stand down, to submit without at least a show of defiance. While her head said it was foolish to argue with an armed and unpredictable man, neither did she want to go out with a whimper instead of rebellion.

Henry leaned forward, putting his mouth right beside her ear. "Or I can make your life miserable, make lover boy wish he was dead." His breath was hot on her skin and smelled like morning breath times ten.

More miserable than you've already made me? She bit the inside of her cheek to hold the snipe back. Defiance was one thing. Unnecessarily poking the angry bear was another.

Forty minutes and several more turns onto increasingly more pothole-riddled roads, Henry directed her to turn in at a weed-choked dirt driveway. The twin beams of the headlights illuminated a double-wide trailer on cinder blocks that had seen better days…a long time ago.

"This?" Jessica asked, aghast. She hadn't expected a Holiday Inn, but she found it difficult to believe the owner of this hovel thought anyone would pay money to rent it. Except maybe for a meth lab. Or a serial killer's lair.

And yet Henry had. She hesitated before turning off the car's engine. Cutting the motor was resigning herself to going inside this dump. She didn't remove the keys from the ignition, though. Maybe if she stalled long enough…if Henry climbed out first…

"Give me the keys," Henry said, as if reading her mind.

He held out his hand and waited until she complied. "Now get out. Leave the headlights on for now, then come around this side and help me get lover boy inside."

"He's *not* my lover." Her relationship with Gage was none of Henry's business, but clearly his misconceptions about their relationship fed Henry's choler toward Gage. If she could convince Henry she hadn't slept with Gage, maybe he'd feel less threatened by him. Maybe she could keep Gage a little safer. "We're just friends."

Henry slapped her again. "Stop lying!" A darkness filled Henry's tone, a fury. "Friends don't claw at each other's clothes like that and stick their tongues down each other's throats." He made a growling sound deep in his throat. "If I didn't need him alive to keep you in line, I'd whack him right now, just to be rid of him."

Keep her in line?

"Go on! Get out!"

Heart sinking, she shouldered the door open and climbed out into the humid night. Around her in the darkness, unseen cicadas, crickets and tree frogs filled the air with night song. A mosquito whined in her ear, and she slapped at it. The vegetation tickled and scraped her calves as she waded through the unkept grasses and burr-laden weeds. She prayed there were no worse booby traps or vile creatures lying in wait, hidden by the darkness.

By the time she'd circled the front fender and reached the passenger side, Henry had climbed out and was unceremoniously dragging Gage from the front seat, his arms hooked under Gage's. She hurried forward, wanting to protect Gage from Henry's rough treatment. Even as she caught Gage's feet, Henry allowed Gage's lolling head to bump hard on the ground as he dropped him in the dirt. She set Gage's legs down gently and scowled at Henry. Not that he saw it with only the headlights to illuminate the night.

Henry took a moment to tuck his gun in the waist of his jeans at the small of his back. A shiver chased through Jessica. That gun was the difference between their captivity and having the upper hand. If she could wrangle control of the weapon from Henry, the tables would be turned. But how could she get it from him?

"All right." Henry nodded his head to Gage's feet. "Let's go."

Bending, she lifted Gage's legs again and staggered over the ruts and rocks of the yard to the concrete-block steps to the trailer door.

Henry jerked his chin, telling her to go first. "Owner said it was unlocked. Go on in."

Unlocked. What did that say about the property and the owner's disregard for the condition of the place?

She juggled Gage's right leg while she twisted the pollen-coated doorknob and shoved the door open. The scents of mildew, old cigarettes and something more rank and organic slammed into her immediately, and she gagged at the fetid smells. "Good grief! It's ripe in there."

Henry clearly caught a whiff, too, because his nose wrinkled. "Well, I wasn't expecting the Ritz. We'll open some windows and air it out. Now go on. Coleman's getting heavy."

Taking a last gulp of outside air, she edged inside, moving slowly, blindly, in the unlit room.

"Get the light," Henry said.

She set Gage's legs down and groped until she found a light switch. When she flipped the lever, a light fixture came on, and one of the two bulbs popped loudly and blew out. The one lit bulb was enough to see the disaster of their lodgings. Cockroaches skittered across the cracked and curled linoleum. What furnishings were available were soiled and water-stained. The couch cushion had a rip with the stuffing spilling out and had previous tears that had been repaired with silver duct tape. Animal droppings of all sizes were littered across the floor, and based on the chattering noises from the overhead, she'd guess either a squirrel or raccoon had nested in the ceiling. Black mold grew on the walls and human trash, beer cans, cigarette butts, old syringes and fast-food wrappers cluttered every surface. Darker stains soiled the shag carpet and countertop that might have been dried blood.

Jessica felt her gorge rise. If she had a week and ten gallons of bleach to clean this place, she doubted she'd feel it was sanitized and safe yet. And Henry expected them to sleep here tonight?

"This is disgusting!" she said, her tone reflecting her horror. "You can't be serious about staying here!"

Henry put Gage down on the filthy floor and braced his hands on his hips as he turned slowly, surveying the cesspool. "It is nasty." He grunted. "But functional. And cheap. It'll serve my purpose for now." He sniffed again and shook his head. "Once I get you two secured, I think I'll sleep in the car."

Before she could ask what he meant by secured, Henry unbuckled Gage's belt and slid it out of the loops of his khaki pants. He wrapped the belt around Gage's ankles and drew it tight. Pulling a folding Swiss Army knife from his jeans pocket, he set about making a new hole in the leather where he could buckle the belt and keep it tight and secure on Gage's legs.

Jessica hugged herself despite the summer heat, wanting to curl in a ball, shrinking inward as much as she could to protect herself from the filth around her. She tried to breathe shallowly through her mouth to avoid the worst of the stench. How did she get out of here? She had to set aside her shock at the condition of her surroundings and focus her brainpower on saving herself and Gage.

Despite the recurring impulse to run, to save herself even at the risk of being shot at, she always shied from that instinct when her conscience reminded her she couldn't leave Gage. Her heart bumped at the notion that Gage would be safe at home if not for her. He should never have been caught up in her predicament with her stalker. And yet...

She sighed. Selfishly, she was glad Gage was here on some level. That she wasn't going through this horror alone. Gut churning, she swore to herself that no matter what it took, she'd get them both out of this mess—literally and figuratively. She owed that much to Gage.

She eyed the black gun at Henry's waist. Could she snatch the weapon while he was bent over Gage's legs, cutting a new slit in the belt for the buckle? If she did get it, would she be able to use it? When they'd been married, Matt had taught her to use a military-issue pistol they'd kept in their house, but that didn't mean she'd be able to figure Henry's weapon out before he seized it back. Another idea formed as she watched Henry roll Gage to his stomach and pulled his arms behind him. If Henry could knock Gage out, she could return the favor. She glanced around, looking for something heavy enough to wield as a weapon. But she saw no lamps, no empty liquor bottles, no frying pan.

Henry pulled the laces out of Gage's boots next and used one of the thin cords to bind his wrists. Jessica's breath came quicker as she sensed the clock ticking. If she didn't act soon, Henry would tie her up, as well, and leave her defenseless. Her own shoes, pitifully lightweight canvas tennis shoes, may be comfortable for knocking around the house, but were useless for knocking someone out. As her frustration and fear grew, her hands jiggled at her sides and her gaze darted from one corner of the trailer to another. Nothing but filth and useless detritus. Damn!

Jessica fisted her hands so hard her fingernails bit into her palms. *Her fingernails...*

She might not be able to knock Henry unconscious, but she'd be damned if she'd stand by and do nothing. Taking a ragged breath for courage, she edged more directly behind her captor and mentally counted to three.

Lunging at Henry from behind, she jumped on his back. With a feral roar, she curled her fingers and gouged at his face, knocking his glasses aside and aiming for his eyes. Henry jerked upright, battling her clawing hands, cursing a blue streak. All too easily, he flung her off, knocking her to the floor.

He turned to her, his face suffused with red, brow line taut and jaw clenched. "You will be sorry you did that, Jessie. Very sorry."

She scrambled to get to her feet, but he caught her by her hair before she could get out of his reach. With a hard tug that shot needles of pain from her scalp and made her eyes water, he drew her close enough to glare at her, nose to nose. "I'd planned to leave you unrestrained as a courtesy. But seeing as how you're not being nice, looks like you'll be tied up like Coleman."

She fought to free his hand from her hair, grabbing at his wrist and trying to pry his fingers loose. "Let go, you animal!"

With his free hand, he seized her wrist and twisted it behind her before untangling his other to wrench her free arm behind her, as well. With one large hand, he was able to clamp her wrists together and pin her against the nearest wall, while with his now available hand, he scooped a discarded plastic grocery sack from the floor.

Jessica's cheek was flat against the mildewed drywall, her field of vision limited, but she heard him ripping the bag. Despite the biting grip of his hand holding her arms and the weight of his hip shoving her belly first into the wall, Jessica bucked and writhed and struggled. She wouldn't submit quietly to this cruelty. She almost twisted free once, but he slammed his free hand into the back of her head, making her skull crack hard against the wall. The crinkle of plastic gave her only warning before he looped the sack around her wrists several times and tugged a tight knot.

Discouragement and dread balled inside her. Henry grabbed her arms and turned her to face him. He wore a gloating grin that soured her mood further. "You're a heartless bastard. How can you think I'd ever want to be with you?"

His grin dimmed briefly, before he cocked his head to one side and adjusted his glasses. "And yet here you are. And here you'll stay until you see reason. We were meant to be together, and together we will be. One way or another."

Without warning, he grabbed her face between his hands and slammed his mouth on hers. She struggled and wrenched her head aside, tearing away from his assault. Ducking her head, she wiped the remnants of his kiss on her shoulder, trying not to gag. When he went in for another try, she stomped hard, aiming for his foot.

But her lightweight tennis shoes were worthless for inflicting the kind of pain that would help her cause. All her kicking and stomping accomplished was to tick him off again. Fisting his hand in the front of her shirt, he dragged her, stumbling, to the ripped and stained couch and shoved her down on it. Casting his gaze about, he zeroed in on an empty set of plastic six-pack rings and folded it three times crossways. Pulling off her shoes, he shoved the plastic rings over her feet until the rings circled her ankles.

"A rather ill-prepared kidnapper, aren't you?" she taunted.

He glared at her. "This was not my original plan. Finding him—" he thrust a finger toward Gage "—groping you changed things."

For a moment, Jessica's mind flashed back to the heated kisses she'd shared with Gage.

I have wanted his,w anted〉 oyf or so long.

Yeah, that moment had changed things for her, too. She still hadn't had a chance to process Gage's confession. Jessica opened her mouth to deny an intimate relationship with Gage again, but Henry had seen what he had seen. They had been kissing. At this point, she couldn't predict what tact was best for ensuring Gage's safety. Disputing the truth of what Henry had witnessed would anger him. Confirming the truth would make Gage a more certain target of Henry's jealousy. So she said nothing, choosing instead to try to negotiate with Henry. Test number one…after more than an hour of driving, she needed to use the bathroom.

She took a slow breath through her mouth, still trying to block the worst of the trailer's stench. In as calm a voice as she could muster, she said, "Henry, would you please take the plastic off my hands and feet. I need to use the bathroom."

An involuntary shiver chased through her. She didn't want to think about how nasty the bathroom in this cesspit would be.

He snorted. "Nice try. The restraints stay on until *I* say they come off."

She worked to show him an earnest face rather than a

frustrated or hostile one. "I honestly need the restroom. Please. Don't make me have to soil myself."

He lifted one eyebrow as if realizing how that might, in fact, play out. He'd have to be accommodating or...

Huffing his disgust, he removed the plastic at her ankles and walked her to the bathroom. After checking that there were no windows in the bathroom she might use to flee, he stood back and let her enter. "Hurry up."

"And my hands? How am I supposed to do this with my hands bound behind me?"

"That's your problem. The hands stay tied." He jerked his head toward the bathroom, where the fluorescent light flickered.

Jessica sighed and stepped in the small room, trying not to look too closely at the stains and debris in this room. With effort and some awkward contortions, she managed to take care of her business. When they returned from the bathroom, Gage was groaning and beginning to stir.

Relief surged in Jessica. She darted to Gage's side, dropping on her knees next to him, before Henry could stop her. "Gage, thank heavens! Can you hear me? It's Jessica."

She wanted to touch him, to soothe him, to hold him and tell him how sorry she was for involving him in this train wreck.

"Jess?" He angled his head toward her, his gaze reflecting a dullness and confusion. His arms twitched and his frown deepened as he realized his hands were tied. "What happened? Why—"

She saw Gage's attention shift, sensed Henry moving up behind her.

"Well, look who's back with us. Enjoy your nap, Coleman?" Henry chuckled, the tone smug and grating on Jessica's nerves.

Gage's jaw tightened, his glare darkening as he tested the bindings on his arms and legs with abbreviated tugs and twists. "You sonofabitch! If you've hurt Jessica—"

Henry scoffed as he crouched beside Jessica and leaned close to Gage's nose. "You should be far more worried about what I might do to you."

Chapter Fifteen

Gage's head throbbed and his vision blurred, but his greater concern at the moment was what this cretin had in mind for Jessica. And his uselessness while trussed up like a Thanksgiving turkey.

"Jess, are you hurt?" He drank in Jessica's gaze, assessing her well-being and state of mind as best he could without a chance to hold her, talk privately with her.

"I—"

"Come on. That's enough." Henry grabbed her arm and yanked her to her feet. Her arms were bound behind her, as well, it seemed. Fury burned in Gage's core, the spike in his pulse making his temples pound, and a fresh rush of hatred for the guy pumped through him.

Henry rolled his shoulders and surveyed his captives. "Clearly, I'm gonna need something else to hold y'all. What have we got around here?" He strolled into the kitchen and dragged open drawers, checked cabinets.

Gage used the moment to meet Jessica's eyes and ask quietly, "Are you all right? Has he hurt you?"

She hesitated, then shook her head. "Nothing to worry about. How's your head? I'm so, so sorry about—"

"Bingo!" Henry called from the kitchen and returned,

twirling a mostly depleted roll of duct tape on his finger. "You first, Coleman." Henry crouched as he peeled a strip of tape from the roll with a nerve-splitting *strrrppp*. When Henry moved to wind the tape around Gage's ankles, Gage rocked backward. Lifting his legs, Gage landed a flat-footed kick from both of his heels in Henry's face.

Jessica gasped.

Henry howled in rage and pain, grabbing his bleeding nose and cursing. The returned kick, which landed in Gage's ribs, while not immediate, wasn't entirely unexpected. Worth it, Gage decided, to have given Henry at least a taste of his wrath.

"No!" Jessica cried. "Please, both of you stop this! Pummeling each other gets us nowhere!"

Henry shook off the blow and wiped the blood from his nose with his sleeve. Then, grabbing Gage's bound legs, he flipped Gage to his stomach and, with rough motions, reinforced the binding on his hands. Gage used all his strength to keep his hands as far apart as he could, hoping to keep even a smidgen of slack in the binding. When Henry stepped back, Gage rolled to his side to glare up at their captor. "If your intention is to win Jessica over, you can bet you're scoring big points with this cluster bomb. Nothing says 'I love you' like kidnapping and brutalizing a girl and her friend."

Henry took Jessica by the arm and dragged her to the filthy couch. He continued dabbing blood from his seeping nose as he faced Gage. "Either shut the hell up, or I'll shut your mouth for you."

Before Gage could reply, his cell phone, which was somehow still in his pocket, rang.

Henry tensed. Frowned. Stepped over to snatch the phone from Gage's pocket.

Gage's heart sank. If he'd had any chance of later using

the phone to call for help or find their way back from wherever they were, that chance was now gone.

After checking the screen, Henry turned Gage's phone
off and jammed it in his own pocket. "Oops, looks like you
missed a call from the hospital," he said with an ugly sneer.
"Hope your sister's okay."

Rage boiled in Gage's gut, competing with concern for
why the hospital was calling. What *had* happened with Tina?
"If she dies," he growled, "her blood is on your hands."

"On my hands?" Henry snorted and jabbed a finger toward Jessica. "She's the one who overcorrected and drove
into the river. Any blood to be claimed is hers." He straightened and arched an eyebrow. "Which reminds me," he said,
walking closer to Jessica, who glared from the couch. He
peeled a fresh strip of tape from the roll. "I broke your
car window and got you out before you drowned. You still
haven't thanked me for saving your life."

Jessica looked ill. Her normally tanned complexion
leeched of color, her expression a toxic mix of revulsion,
guilt and pain. "I wouldn't have been in a flooding car if
you hadn't forced me off the road! Your reckless driving,
your intentional harassment of us on the road is what caused
that accident. Sara's blood is already on you, and because
of you, Tina and Holly will probably never be the same!"

Henry shrugged and knelt to wrap tape around her ankles. "You're wrong."

"You could have saved them when you pulled me out,
and you didn't!" Tears choked her voice, and her dark eyes
blazed with contempt.

"We'll just have to agree to disagree on that. Besides,
you were the only one I cared about. Although, if I'd known
how much trouble you were going to be, maybe I'd have let
you stay in that car."

Jessica shook her head, her heavy breathing a sure sign of her upset and turmoil. "Why would you save me at the river, only to knock me out and leave me to die from carbon monoxide in my garage days later?"

Henry propped both hands on his hips and frowned at her. "Letting you die was never the plan. You made me mad in your garage when you wouldn't hear me out, wouldn't talk to me, wouldn't give me a chance. After I left, I realized you'd need help, and I went back to save you before anything bad happened." He cut a sharp look at Gage, his tone growing resentful. "But then he was already there. Had you on the front lawn with the ambulance workers."

Gage wanted to shout at the pissant, tell him something bad *had* happened to Jess. That she'd had enough carbon monoxide in her system to require a few days' treatment in the hospital. But Jessica spoke first, and her need to vent, to have her say took precedence over his.

"Henry," she said, her voice taut and low, "let me make this *p rfectly* clear. I didn't want to talk with you then, because there is nothing to discuss. I want *nothing* to do with you. Ever. I have never felt anything for you and never will. The restraining order I got should have made that obvious."

Henry shifted his weight and narrowed his gaze on Jessica. A prickle of alarm skittered through Gage. While Henry had to know the truth, Gage feared what her brutal assessment would do to his temper. Would he retaliate by hurting Jessica?

Henry sniffed and looked away for a moment before exhaling harshly. "Once again, you are wrong. You picked me out of all those men on the app, because you liked what you saw. We had *everything* in common. And when I asked for another dinner with you, you said *yes*." He leaned close to her and shouted in her face, "Because you liked what you saw and wanted me!"

Jessica shuddered but met his glare boldly. "You agreeing with everything I say and pretending to like everything I do is not a real connection. It was forced and fake, and I knew it from that first night. I could have said I like eating dog poop, and you'd have agreed with me. The truth is, even before you showed your evil, depraved and irrational side, I was certain there would *never* be anything between us. Your cloying, desperate need to make yourself seem so agreeable was a big red flag."

Henry's hands were shaking, and his face grew red. "Liar! We went out again. You kissed me good-night. You let me think you were in love with me."

"You showed up unexpectedly, and I gave you the benefit of the doubt. Those subsequent dates were as big a mistake and a failure as the first. Then *you* kissed *me,* and I told you *no.* If I was too polite in saying 'go to hell,' then let me correct that now. *Go to hell, Henry!* You are a hateful, sick man who has caused me nothing but grief and heartache. I don't want anything to do with you!"

Henry paced across the room and back, shaking his head. "Nope. Nope. That's wrong. That's all wrong."

"Henry, don't do this. Untie me. You have to let me and Gage go!"

Their captor continued to grouse and shake his head. "I can't. It's too late for that now." He fisted his hands as he glowered at Jessica. "You're either mine or you're no one's."

Gage's heart sank, realizing how truly deluded Henry was. If Jessica couldn't get through to him with the truth, he'd have to find another way to get himself and Jessica free. As he racked his brain, trying to tamp down the tumult inside him and find the calm to make a new plan, Henry snorted loudly.

"This place is a dump. I'm sleeping in the car." With that, he stomped across the floor, shut off the lights and slammed the trailer door behind him.

ONCE SHE HEARD the car door slam and knew they were alone, Jessica turned her full attention to Gage. "The truth, Gage. How bad is your head? You were unconscious for a long time."

"Actually, I roused a little before we arrived but played possum so I could listen and plan. Unfortunately, the bump to the head as he dragged me from the car put me out again, just as I was about to spring into action."

"Do you think you have a concussion?" she asked into the darkness. "Before he dragged me away I saw a bump on your head. That's a good sign, isn't it? That the wound is swelling out instead of pressing in on the brain?"

He chuckled without humor. "Listen to you. When did you go to medical school?"

"I raised an active little boy. You pick things up. All mothers are nurses by the time their kids move out. So how bad is your head? Any nausea? Blurry vision?"

He grunted. "I'll be all right. Did he hurt you? Did he…" He fell silent before exhaling loudly. "Did he *do* anything to you?"

"Nothing overly grievous." Then, realizing her answer wouldn't calm his worry, she added, "I'm fine, Gage. Really."

For several minutes after that neither of them said anything. Fatigue battled with her need to figure a way out of their situation. Given his silence, she figured Gage was working on that problem, as well, until he said, "I wish I could hold you right now."

A shiver chased through her despite the sticky heat inside the trailer. Being in Gage's arms sounded pretty wonderful, now that she thought about it. His solid presence, his comforting smile, his reassuring strength had gotten her through the past four terrible months. The need to be near him, even if their bound arms didn't allow them to embrace, roared through Jessica so powerfully her head spun.

"I think I can make it to you." She tested the theory by flopping onto the floor and wiggling like an inchworm to scoot across the floor. She breathed through her mouth, trying not to inhale the stench of the carpet or think about the filth she'd seen before Henry turned the lights off.

"Jess, did you fall? What was that thump?"

"Like I said, I'm coming to you. Keep talking so I can find you."

"What am I supposed to say?" He groaned. "Besides I'm sorry, that is."

"What do you have to apologize for?"

"Considering you hadn't seen or heard from Henry since moving to Cameron Glen, it's pretty obvious that I led him to you today." His heavy sigh voiced his frustration. "All I've wanted to do since I learned about this creep is keep you safe, and instead, I…brought danger to you."

She bumped into a warm, solid body and used her toes to inch higher, so that her body was aligned with his. "Let's not assign blame or start down the what-if path tonight. We have bigger issues to solve. Namely, how do we get back home?"

He placed a kiss on the top of her head, and she laid her

cheek on his chest. His heart beat steady and strong beneath her ear, and it soothed her like a lullaby.

"I don't know," he murmured, "but I swear that I will get you out of this. One way or another."

Chapter Sixteen

Jessica spent a restless and uncomfortable night on the floor beside Gage. Though they both dozed, she made sure to wake Gage every couple of hours and check on him, in case he had a concussion. Not that she could do anything for him if he did.

Fortunately, he roused easily, could answer her questions and said his head hurt less as the hours passed. "I think we dodged a bullet," he said sometime around dawn. Without her phone, her only sense of time was the weak light peeking through the blinds and the twitter and chirp of birds greeting the day. Despite her circumstances, Jessica took a moment to focus on the birdsong. The peeps and trills calmed her, and she imagined herself in a meadow, by a babbling brook—

She moaned. Maybe not the brook considering her full bladder.

"You okay?" Gage asked.

"Define okay."

He chortled. "Can I do anything to help?"

"Tell me you've come up with a foolproof plan to get us out of here." When he grunted, she continued, "Okay, not foolproof, just…possible."

"Well, obviously, step one is getting out of these constraints. I've spent most of the night trying to free my wrists, but all I did was tighten the knots."

Struggling to a seated position, she glanced around the trailer. Shifting to her side, she again wiggled her way back toward the sofa and an abandoned soda can. "We need something sharp. Maybe if I flatten this can, the sides will rip and I can—"

The trailer door opened, and Henry appeared, looking rumpled, half-asleep and grumpy. He switched on the overhead lights and moved into the living room, saying nothing. He stopped in front of Gage, glared at him and nudged his feet as if to check that they were still bound. Turning, he gave Jessica an up-and-down scrutiny. Apparently satisfied his prisoners were still secure, he headed to the kitchen. Through the cutout section of the wall over the breakfast bar, Jessica followed Henry's progress as he moved from one cabinet to another, opening and slamming doors closed. Each shelf Henry checked appeared to be empty, or at least not yielding anything that satisfied their jailer, because his huffs of irritation grew louder and each slam of a door more forceful.

Finally, Henry bit out a sour curse and jammed his hand through his hair, leaving it all the more mussed. "I'm starving, and there ain't diddly squat in this place to eat!"

"You were expecting a breakfast buffet?" Gage asked.

Returning to the living room, Henry glowered at Gage. "You can shut up!"

Finding the roll of tape he'd discarded last night, Henry tore off a strip—the end of the roll—and slapped it over Gage's mouth.

Henry tossed the now-empty roll aside and paced the

dirty shag carpet, his expression dark. "Damn, I'd give my left nut for a cup of coffee."

Yes, coffee! Jessica thought. Her stomach growled just at the thought of food. Last night, they'd never gotten to eat the dinner she'd made for Gage. Her mouth watered, picturing the lasagna and pie sitting on her cabin's kitchen counter. And then an idea struck her. "So…what's stopping you? You have my car, my keys. I'd love a coffee and breakfast biscuit myself."

Henry glanced at her, clearly suspicious.

Jessica snorted and wiggled her bound feet. "We're not going anywhere, but nothing is keeping you from driving back into that little town we came through last night. I remember a couple fast-food places and a diner there. Maybe a small grocery where you could stock up on snacks for all of us."

Suspicious of her motives or not, she'd clearly gotten Henry thinking, craving. He rubbed one hand on his chin, then pressed the same hand to his stomach as it audibly rumbled. With a nod of his head, he said, "I am gonna need supplies if we're going to stay here for a while."

Jessica sent Gage a quick look. His eyes met hers, and he ducked his chin in an almost imperceptible nod.

"Then you'll bring me back a coffee? And a sausage and egg biscuit? No, make it bacon." She saw Henry swallow hard as if salivating at the idea of bacon and eggs, and she piled on. "Lord, I love bacon. And hash browns if they're crispy. Chocolate chip cookies for snacks. And peanut butter filled pretzels. Maybe some fruit. And diet colas. Some pastrami and Swiss cheese for sandwiches. Taco-flavored chips."

Henry finally snapped, "That enough! You'll get what I give you." He dug out the keys from his front pocket and bent close to taunt Gage. "And as my mother used to say, you'll get nothing and like it." With a low chuckle, Henry crossed back to the trailer door. "Y'all stay here. I'll be right back. Maybe…" He laughed then, as if he'd told the best joke, closing the door behind him.

Jessica heard the snick of the door locking and met Gage's eyes again. Next came the car's engine, the crackle of the tires on gravel. Then silence. She exhaled heavily, and let a small laugh out herself. "Thank God."

Gage's eyebrows rose as if to say, *Now what?*

She rolled her shoulders, loosening the muscles there and said, "Okay. We're on the clock." She rolled the can closer and, lifting both bound feet, stomped the can. Instead of flattening, it slipped off her canvas tennis shoe and spun away. She growled her frustration. "This would be so much easier if I could just—" She paused as an idea came to her.

Gage grunted from behind the tape and lifted his eyebrows in query.

"Let's see if I'm still as flexible as I was as a cheerleader in high school, shall we?" She wiggled and scooted her cinched wrists as low as she could behind her. Hunching her shoulders and inching her hands under her bottom, she slowly scooted backward, an inch here, a centimeter there. Little by little, she scrunched her hands under her thighs, then brought her knees to her chest. With some more inching and wiggling, she stepped through her linked arms, bringing them out in front of her.

Relief spun through her, and she flashed a broad smile at Gage. "Ta-da!"

A muffled chuckle tumbled from his throat, and the dip of his chin said, *Impressive!*

Gage's approval burrowed deep inside her, warming her. After all the ways she'd cost him, burdened him, landed him in danger, she'd finally done something right. With a cleansing breath, she bent over and used her bound and numb hands to pick at the tape around her ankles. Because her hands were still bound, her progress was slow, but bit by bit, she loosened an end of the tape on her ankle. After what felt like hours, she finally had a large enough piece to unwind the strip.

Next came the plastic six-pack rings, which, over the next few minutes, she stretched and tugged off over her feet. With her ankles freed, she stood and stretched and shook the ache from her leg muscles. Turning her attention to Gage, she hurried over to him and grasped the edge of the tape covering his mouth. "Fast or slow?"

He cocked one eyebrow, and she rolled her eyes at her goof. "Nod for fast, shake for slow."

He nodded, and she ripped the tape from his mouth with one quick motion. He yowled in pain and squeezed his eyes shut for a moment. His jaw muscles flexed as he gritted his back teeth before exhaling and meeting her gaze. "That smarts. Especially since I haven't shaved in two days."

She winced in sympathy. "Sorry."

He lifted a corner of his mouth. "Necessary. Don't sweat it. What's next?"

She raised her arms. "I have to get this off somehow." She studied the plastic bags tied around her wrists. "With my teeth I guess."

He shrugged. "I guess."

She moved back to the sofa and nibbled at the grocery bag Henry had torn and knotted to bind her wrists. Again, the task was a practice in patience, in micro progress and backtracking when she tugged the wrong piece and tightened the knots again. She groaned her frustration.

"Hey." Gage hitched his head. "Bring it here. My turn."

She crossed to him, kneeling to be at his level on the floor.

He chomped his teeth and teased, "You know the saying—two mouths are better than one."

"Is that a saying?" she returned wryly, but held her wrists to his mouth where he squinted at the knots then began his own nibbling and tugging. When he worked a strip of the bag loose, she bit it from the other side and pulled it free. Her forehead grazed his as she worked a newly exposed knot on her side. She sensed more than saw his eyes lift to meet hers. A breath away. Nearer than she'd ever been to him…except when they'd kissed. That knowledge snagged the air in her lungs. She stared, her heart thudding so loudly she knew he could hear it.

His right eye had a small patch of green set against his gray iris. Why had she never noticed that before? And this close she saw the tiny creases that fanned from the corner of his eyelids. Laugh lines.

Jessica jerked her gaze away. She had no business noticing such details. Those were intimate observations lovers made, the kind of details one only saw up close.

Even as she worked to calm the flutter in her veins, Gage worked the last strip of plastic free from its knot. The grocery bag fell away. Her hands were free.

Jessica tossed the bag aside, then rubbed her sore wrists and wiggled her fingers, stimulating the blood flow. Pinpricks of pain sparked in her hands as the numbness receded.

"Excellent," Gage said, smiling. "Now me. I have a small utility knife in my pocket. Can you fish it out?"

She gaped at him and scoffed. "You have a knife? Why didn't you say so before?"

"How would you have used it while your hands were bound?" He lifted his brow and gave her an even look.

She returned his look with one of her own. As she studied him, the morning sunlight peeked through the cracked blinds and lit his face with buttery rays. In his face, she saw the fatigue of a restless night. The lingering pain from Henry's blows to his temple. And the kindness and affection of a yearslong friendship that for him had been more. Deeper. Respectfully silenced. Unrequited.

I've wanted you for a very long time. His words, spoken after a kiss that had shaken her to her core and had been hot enough to melt her bones, whispered through her again. She'd answered his confession, his honesty, by running away. By landing him in the grips of a dangerous man. Gage had never been anything but kind and protective and thoughtful. Even when, through the years, he'd included her in his brotherly teasing and antics, he'd respected her and respected her marriage to Matt.

As she continued to stare at him, he arched a dark eyebrow. He thrust one hip toward her. "This pocket. Time's a'wasting."

Without stopping to second-guess the impulse, she framed his face with her hands and leaned in to kiss him.

Chapter Seventeen

Beneath her palms she felt Gage jolt, heard his sharp intake of air. She'd surprised him, surprised herself. But he didn't pull away, and neither did she. She savored the heat of his mouth, the light scrape of his two-day-old beard, the silky caress of his tongue tangling with hers. The kiss was every bit as tantalizing as she'd remembered from last night. Jeez, had it just been last night? But this kiss held a hint of something new and fragile, something precious and poignant. When she finally canted away, her eyes searching his, she whispered, "Sorry."

He twitched a grin. "Don't be. That was nice."

Jessica cleared her throat, gave her head a small shake. "No... I mean, yes, it was. But... I got you into all this. I—" She swallowed hard. "I freaked out last night when you said you—"

"Uh, yeah," he interrupted. "About that. Can we...forget I said that?"

She blinked, stung. "You didn't mean it?"

"I meant it, but... I shouldn't have said it. I shouldn't have laid it on you when you're already dealing with—"

She silenced him with another deep, lingering kiss. Then, resting her forehead against his, she released a slow exhale and closed her eyes. "Let's save this conversation for…later. Like you said, time's a'wasting."

Gage nodded. "Right."

Sitting back on her heels, she pointed to his hip. "This pocket, you say?"

He leaned back and angled his hip toward her. "All yours."

Evidence of what their kiss had done to him strained against his fly, and she gave him a wry grin. "A knife is not all you have in your pocket."

His smile turned sultry. "Your fault."

Holding his gaze, she slipped her hand in his front pocket until her fingers found the slim knife and curled around it. After extracting it, she flipped open the tools until she found a small blade. Crawling behind Gage, she sawed through the duct tape at his wrists. "Brace yourself. One, two—" She ripped the tape free, yanking several black hairs from his arms.

"Augh! Jack bless a milk cow!"

She chuckled at his nonsensical expression, one she'd heard Tina use, as well, and flung the sticky bindings aside. After freeing his ankles, she rose to her feet and offered him a hand up.

Gage worked through a series of stretches and shoulder rolls, groaning as he relieved his muscle kinks and soreness. "Okay, so what's the plan? Are we lying in wait for Henry to ambush him when he gets back or hoofing it out of here, not knowing where we are or how far it is to someone with a working phone?"

Jessica smoothed her hands over her shorts, debating. "I'm not keen on the idea of trying to ambush an unstable man who still has a gun in his possession."

Gage hiked up an eyebrow. "It's not ideal."

She cast her gaze around the filthy trailer and chewed her

bottom lip. "I just want to get out of here. Everything about this place disgusts me and creeps me out. It feels…evil."

"And then what? He has your car."

She nodded. "I'll get it back when the police catch up to him. What matters to me now is not being here when he gets back, even if that means we go on foot."

Gage's brow creased, and he twisted his mouth, clearly analyzing the situation for himself. Bobbing his head once, he said, "All right, then. We'll hike outta here. But we're kinda far from civilization. We should grab a thing or two from here before we bolt."

"Like what?"

"Like…" He strode across the room and collected one of the plastic grocery sacks from the floor, along with an empty soda bottle and the pop-top lid from an unknown can.

Jessica eyed him skeptically. "We need trash?"

He wagged the soda bottle. "For carrying water, after we rinse it out. This pop-top lid is metal and will reflect sun a bit like a mirror." He paused before adding, "In case we get really lost and have to signal for help."

"How lost can we get if we just follow the road we drove in on?" she asked.

"True enough, but do you really want to be on the same road Henry will be driving back up here on in a few minutes?"

"No."

"We can keep the road in sight, but until we are a good ways from this trailer…" He shook his head. "Let's not make it too easy for him to find us again, huh?"

Next Gage collected both his shoestrings and hers, peeling them away from the tangle of duct tape they'd become enmeshed in.

"What are these for?" she asked, taking over the separation of tape and her laces.

He gave her an odd look. "To lace our shoes."

She slapped a hand to her forehead and burst out laughing. "Oh, my word. I can't believe I asked that. My only excuse is, I haven't slept. I was on a different thought path. I just—"

Gage's laughter joined hers, and he wrapped her in a hug. "Oh, Jess, I'm *so* not going to let you forget this."

She cringed. "Ugh. Rightfully so."

They were still chuckling over her brain fart a few minutes later as they re-laced their shoes, and she carried the soda bottle to the kitchen sink. The water that poured from the tap was rusty brown, and Jessica wrinkled her nose. "Gross."

"Let it run for a while," Gage said, glancing over her shoulder. He turned to start opening cabinets, much the way Henry had. And like Henry, he found nothing of use. "It could just be from disuse. I still think anything we get out of the pipes here is better than not having anything to drink in this heat."

The color of the water slowly cleared, and she rinsed and filled the soda bottle, trying not to think about who might have drunk from that bottle before. They weren't in a position to be picky. She handed the water to Gage, and he placed it in the grocery sack. He also added a can of roach spray he found in the cabinet and an empty beer can from the floor of the bedroom to their oddball collection.

She wrinkled her nose in confusion as he looped the bag handles together for easier carrying. "You'll explain the reason for those things later? Right now, we need to make tracks. Henry could be back any second."

"Agreed, and I will." He moved to the trailer door and

opened it slowly, peering out to scan the yard before stepping through.

A dense fog hung in the air, making the morning humid
and shrouding the woods around the trailer. The gray veil
spiked Jessica's trepidation about their escape, as if Mother
Nature was hiding potential threats.

Gage held a hand out for Jessica as she stepped down
the wobbly cinder block stairs from the door to the ground.
They'd only made it a couple of steps toward the line of trees
when the whir of tires on damp pavement, the rumble of an
approaching car engine sounded from the road.

Jessica turned an anxious look to Gage. "Do you hear
that?"

Gage's mouth tightened, and he nodded as they both
looked to the cover of the woods. "Run!"

Chapter Eighteen

Matt stood on the porch of the Juniper cabin, waiting for Jessica to answer his knock. Her car was gone, but Gage's truck was in the drive, so he presumed they were together. Maybe gone to breakfast in town?

Except that Eric had texted him this morning asking if Matt knew why Jessica was not responding to her son's texts. He'd texted several times last night and again this morning. He'd even *called* her phone, which Eric let him know was tantamount to emergency measures for his generation. Jessica hadn't answered. The lack of reply from Jessica counted as an emergency in Matt's view. She might ignore a text from her ex-husband for a day or so, but she'd *never* ghost her son for even an hour.

Matt knocked a second time, and when no one answered again, he dialed Jessica's phone. The faint sounds of a familiar ring tone played from inside the cabin. Matt frowned. Wherever she'd gone, she'd not taken her phone with her? That was extremely out of character for his ex-wife.

He dragged a hand down his cheek, debating. While he wasn't one to worry under normal circumstances, recent circumstances weren't normal. Jessica had a man stalking her. Matt took a seat in one of the rocking chairs on the cabin's porch and thumbed through his contacts. When he found Gage's number, he hit the dial icon. The line rang several times, then went to voice mail.

"Gage, it's Matt. I'm looking for Jess, and she doesn't have her phone with her. I was hoping she was with you and that you could tell me she was okay. Call me when you get this. Thanks."

He disconnected and clenched his back teeth, not happy with this turn of events. For Gage to not be answering his phone either hiked Matt's concern up a notch. Shoving back to his feet, Matt tested the front doorknob. Unlocked. After Jess had promised to keep her doors locked always, whether she was home or not. Whether she had company or con-struction workers present. Breaking that promise was also not like Jessica.

"Jess?" he called into the cabin as he let himself in. No answer. Matt moved deeper into the quiet cabin, checking the rooms with a sweeping gaze. He edged from the living room through the kitchen, where dirty pans were stacked in the sink, past an uncut pie that waited on the stove. He smelled something like burned toast and opened the oven. Though the oven was cool, overtoasted garlic bread slices sat on a cookie sheet, forgotten. He remembered Jessica's trick of heating bread for a meal in the residual heat of an oven she'd turned off. Scowling, he moved into the dining area. On the table was an uneaten meal, a lasagna by the looks of it. An open bottle of wine. Half-full glasses. Jes-sica's phone lay next to one plate. Jessica would not have left food out to spoil, dishes unwashed. His ex-wife hated loose ends, was compulsive about order and housekeeping. She'd never been spontaneous or rash.

A chill of dread filled Matt's gut, because wherever Jessica was, she'd left the cabin abruptly, unprepared. And that boded all kinds of ill.

SPINNING TOWARD THE WOODS, Jessica sprinted across the weedy yard. Gage, ever protective, stayed even with her, though she knew he could easily have outpaced her. Over her ragged breathing and thudding steps, she could hear the car getting closer. The rumble louder. She pumped her arms and pushed herself to run faster. Faster…

She reached the woods and plunged into the morass of fallen leaves, underbrush and low branches. Gage darted past her, leaping over a rotting tree trunk, and leading the way into the shadowy forest. Jessica shot a glance over her shoulder as the grumbling engine noise crested.

An old pickup truck sped past on the highway, spewing exhaust. Relief spun through her. Not Henry. They were—

Jessica stepped in a leaf-camouflaged hole. When her foot stuck, she sprawled on the ground. Her ankle wrenched to an unnatural angle. Pain came, quick and intense. A cry of agony ripped from her throat. One look at her crooked ankle told her the damage was significant. Critical. Disastrous.

Gage was at her side in an instant. "Jess! Are you o—" His question dropped off as his gaze landed on her ankle. He plowed a hand through his hair and muttered a bad word.

Tears of pain and frustration filled her eyes. "No, no, nooo!"

"Hey," Gage said, his arms circling her, "it's going to be okay. I'm going to take care of you."

His words, meant to comfort and calm, stirred a different ache in her chest. A devastating reality sliced through the haze of pain and the pulse of adrenaline. With an injured ankle immobilizing her, she was dependent on Gage for the foreseeable future. Her injury ruined their plan of escape. She had to rely on Gage, to whom she was already so indebted, to rescue her from a situation she'd just made a hundred times worse.

Her anger, frustration and loathing turned inward, roiling and climbing her throat. Tipping her head back, Jessica loosed a feral howl from the depth of her soul. Balling her hands in fists, she pounded the ground and shouted a guttural "Aaagh!"

Gage stroked her hair and cradled her face in a cupped hand. "Hey, hey…easy. You're gonna be okay. I know it hurts, but I'm going to help you."

She gritted her teeth, swallowing hard as the sharp throbbing of her ankle and deep disappointment in herself churned nausea in her stomach. Raising damp eyes to his, she snarled, "That's exactly what is wrong."

"Um, what?"

She squeezed her eyes shut, determine to hold back the rising tears. "Oh, man, could I be any more of a cliché?"

Gage gave her a puzzled look as he scuttled closer to her foot and gently gripped her heel. "This may hurt. Hang on." He eased her foot free from the hole, and the movement shot new waves of pain up her leg.

Jessica hissed, clenching her teeth, but choking down the wail of pain that swelled. She took a few deep breaths, trying to ride out the incredible ache blazing from her ankle. The foot and joint were already swelling, and she knew she'd be hiking nowhere today. She was stuck here, with Henry due back any moment. "You should go on without me."

Gage, still gently probing her ankle in full first responder mode, cut an incredulous look over his shoulder. "What? Not a chance."

"Gage, I can't walk on *that*!" She thrust a finger toward

her injured foot with a glare of disdain. "But you can still save yourself."

A sternness she'd never seen in Gage before firmed his face, and he pivoted to grasp her shoulders. "There is no way in hell I'm abandoning you, so drop that narrative right now. We're getting out of this together. I promise. Trust me to take care of you, Jess. Okay?"

"But I can't—"

"I'll carry you." The resolve that blazed in his eyes burrowed into her, and she could easily believe that he would move mountains and swim oceans for her. The assurance should have comforted her. Instead, it rankled. Knowing how dependent she was on him sat uneasily, like a rock in her shoe. She didn't want to cost him so much. Cost him more than she already had.

One traitorous tear escaped her eyelashes and tickled her cheek. When she lifted a hand to dash it away, her fingers bumped his as Gage wiped her cheek with the pad of his thumb.

"I'll be right back," he said, then rose to run back toward the trailer.

Jessica watched the road anxiously as she waited for Gage to return. The first vehicle they'd heard hadn't been Henry, but the next one easily could be. She grimaced. If only they'd known that truck wasn't Henry. They could have flagged down the driver and been on their way to town, a phone or the police for help right now.

But what about another car? How long would it be if they waited for someone else to drive by? She chewed her bottom lip, trying not to think of how much her foot hurt, trying to reason out their options. While hoping to catch a ride with a passing car seemed a good choice, hitchhiking along on the side of the highway made them sitting targets for Henry. And yet *she* would be hiking nowhere fast. She would slow Gage down.

The trailer door squeaked, and Gage emerged, holding something blue balled up in his hands and casting a wary glance toward the road before running back across the yard to her. When he reached her, he handed her what proved to be a bed sheet. "I can tear this in strips to bind your ankle in a minute, but right now I want to get us out of view before Butthead gets back. You're too visible here." He gathered the plastic sack they'd filled earlier and handed her that, as well. "You're going to have to hold all this. Okay?"

"I... Yeah. But what—" She swallowed the rest of her sentence as he stooped and placed an arm behind her knees and another under her arm and across her back.

Jessica gasped as he scooped her up. She clutched the items in her lap with one hand while throwing her other around Gage's neck. Cradled against his chest, she clung to him as he set out, striding quickly into the misty woods.

"Gage, you can't carry me all the way to...wherever," she said, although at the moment, held in his arms was exactly where she wanted to be. The position was as close to a hug as they had time for at the moment, and if she were honest, she really needed a hug right then. She was scared. She hurt. She hated how much of this disaster fell squarely on her shoulders.

"I won't be carrying you this way...the whole way," he said, sounding winded already. "Just a bit. Just 'til I think... we'll be safe enough...to stop for a minute...while I wrap your ankle."

Her bad ankle bumped a low hanging branch, and she yelped softly as pain juddered through her.

He cursed. "Sorry. I'm trying not to jostle you more than I have to."

"No. Don't apologize. I'm—" she gritted her teeth, forcing down another gasp as her injured ankle knocked her good one "—fine," she finished on a wheeze.

"Know what I wish?" he asked.

"That a Boy Scout troop with cell phones and a premade travois would magically appear out of the woods right about now?"

He huffed a short laugh. "Boy Scouts and working phones… would be helpful. Not what I was thinking, though."

"What do you wish?" she asked, overwhelmed by a desire to give him anything he wanted, to make up for everything she'd put him through, in any way possible.

"You remember that dinner…we had with Tina…and my friend Robby…last New Year's Eve?"

She did remember. The food had been divine. They'd all stuffed themselves and sworn they'd be frequent customers at that restaurant in the future. "The nice steakhouse in Concord?"

"Yeah."

Her stomach growled. She definitely could go for a meal like that right now. "Yeah."

"Remember how I talked you into splitting the cheesecake with me?" he asked.

Her mouth watered. "Mmm."

"Yeah, I'm kinda wishing now I hadn't done that."

She furrowed her brow. Angled a look up at him. "Are you saying…?"

He flashed a devilish, lopsided smile.

"Hey!" She poked him with her elbow, and he chuckled between heaving breaths. "Fine!" She sputtered a half laugh, secretly pleased to have him baiting her this way. "Put me down then, if I'm so all-fired heavy!"

This teasing-Gage was the Gage she knew. The Gage she

understood. The Gage she'd pushed from her mind when she kissed him this morning.

She'd *kissed* him this morning. And it had been such a good kiss. *O h man!* She couldn't think about that now.

"Watch your head," he said, and she bent her chin to her chest to avoid a frond of something with thorns. A few steps further into the cover of the trees, she heard another car. This time the whoosh of tires on pavement slowed.

Gravel crunched. The engine cut off. A door slammed.

Jessica locked eyes with Gage, her breath frozen in her lungs. "Henry!" she mouthed.

He nodded, then kept moving with a quicker step, less mindful of the slapping branches and clawing vines. She tucked her face into his shoulder to avoid the worst of the battering foliage and whispered a prayer for help, for protection, for success in their escape. At this point, with her ankle likely sprained at best and possibly broken, praying was the best she could do for them.

Her thudding heart and Gage's pounding steps counted the seconds until she heard the distant slap of the trailer door, then Henry's furious scream. "You're a *dead man*, Coleman!"

Chapter Nineteen

Matt headed back to his cabin, already working through contingencies. He knew through research for his suspense books and the recent misfortunes of the Cameron family that the police didn't consider an adult "missing" until they'd been gone for a much longer time than in the case of a child. An adult had the free will to go off alone and not communicate with family or friends if they chose. Unless specific suspicious circumstances were established—witnesses to violence against the individual, physical evidence of a serious crime—the police weren't going to do much in the next few hours. But Matt had an ace up his sleeve. He had a phalanx of Camerons who could search and make phone calls to jump-start the process of finding Jessica and Gage.

As he neared his cabin, his head lost in thoughts of next steps, a familiar car pulled up beside him and stopped. He scowled as he stepped to the driver's window of his son's Honda. "Eric, what are you doing here?"

In that moment, with the morning sun highlighting his chiseled face and dark features, his son looked so much like Jessica it made Matt's chest squeeze. "I was worried about Mom. This business with the guy harassing her, then not being able to reach her has me kinda freaked. When she didn't answer my calls this morning, I got in the car and started driving. I called you from the road."

"Why didn't you tell me you were on your way?"

"Because you'd have told me not to come, not to worry."

Matt nodded. "You're right about that."

"And you should know me better than to think I can write off this kind of anomaly with Mom. What kind of asshole knows his mother could be in danger and does nothing about it?" Eric gave him a level look.

"Not my boy," Matt said, reaching through the open car window to ruffle Eric's hair. "All right. Let's go to the house and talk."

Once Eric had parked, and Cait had greeted her stepson with enthusiastic hugs, Matt and Eric gathered in the living room of their family's cabin. Matt explained what he'd found at the Juniper cabin and his reasons for holding off on calling the police. "In and of itself, an uneaten meal and forgotten phone are not evidence of foul play. They're out of character for your mom and suspicious to us, but I don't think the police would see it the same way. I didn't see any blood or signs of a struggle to indicate they'd been taken by force."

"That's good. Right?" Cait said, clearly trying to buoy Eric's spirits. "Maybe there's a perfectly innocent explanation for all this. Huh?"

"I guess," Eric returned, his tone and expression glum. "But Mom knows better than to worry us. Especially when we all know this guy she met through the dating app has been making trouble."

Eric's watered-down description of the problems Henry had caused let Matt know Jessica had likely not given Eric the whole picture. That fit. Jessica would have wanted to shield Eric as much as possible. He exchanged a look with

Cait when she shifted in her seat and wrinkled her brow. Cait, too, sensed that Eric's understanding was limited, he could tell. Matt gave his wife a subtle headshake that said, *Leave it for now.*

In the silence of their mutual brooding, the soft pad of bare feet signaled the arrival of the resident two-year-old. Erin's face lit when she saw her older brother and she squealed, "Ewic!"

Eric grinned and rose from the couch to sweep his sister up into his arms. "Hey, Pipsqueak!" He blew a loud raspberry on her cheek, winning peals of laughter, before pretending to drop her, then immediately caught her again. Erin's happy squeals grew louder as her big brother repeated their favorite game.

"Mowr!" the toddler demanded, but Cait got up and took Erin into her own arms.

"Maybe later, Butterbean. Let Eric talk to Daddy right now while you get dressed," Cait said, escorting Erin back to her bedroom.

"Okay." Eric returned to the couch and pinned a hard look on his father. "I'm not going anywhere until I know Mom is safe. So…what are we going to do to find her?"

GAGE DIDN'T SLOW his pace for several minutes. Goal number one was to be not found by Henry, so he pushed on, deeper and deeper into the woods. He followed no particular vector other than getting Jessica away from Blythe. His head still ached from the blows Henry had delivered last night, but he ignored the pain. His plodding steps became automatic, allowing his mind far too much time to think. About their next move. About Jess's injury. About her kiss.

She'd stunned him with that lip-lock this morning. But what had brought it on? Gratitude to be escaping? Apol-

ogy? Or…just maybe…a change of heart? They hadn't really talked about his confession to her since it happened. Or
her freak-out over it. In hindsight, he could see why it had
been so shocking to her, so paradigm-shifting. She'd seen
him as one thing for more than twenty years, and suddenly,
at a moment in time when her world was already crooked
on its axis, he'd dropped his little truth bomb on her.

Great timing, man. He gritted his teeth and grunted his
frustration with himself.

"If you need to rest, I think we're far enough from the
trailer now that you can stop to catch your breath," Jessica
said.

"I'm fine. I'm just…" He shook his head and immediately regretted it. "Never mind. But we are overdue to wrap
that ankle." He glanced around for the best place to stop. He
found a fallen tree where she could sit, and he set her down
beside it. She let the bundle of supplies fall into a nest of
leaves and eased herself onto the log. Her ankle had swollen
to twice its normal size and was an angry red. Gathering the
bedsheet he'd taken from the trailer, he used his pocketknife
to start a few slits spaced evenly. He tore the sheet down the
middle and handed half back to Jessica, then ripped a few
strips. When she started to tear the other half, he stopped
her. "Let's not rip that part up yet. We don't know what we
might need it for."

She shrugged. "You're the boss."

Did he hear a note of frustration behind her reply? Brushing the question aside, he knelt in the leafy detritus of the
forest floor and carefully grasped the heel of her injured
foot.

She hissed in pain, and he glanced up at her. "Sorry.
There's no way to do this that won't hurt."

She nodded and flapped a hand at him. "It's okay. Do

what you must. I'll…bite a stick or something if I have to."
She flashed a lopsided grin, which he returned.

All things considered, she was still in pretty good spirits, so…there was that. He found the end of the first strip of sheet and started winding it around her foot, tugging it tight and moving upward with each circle. Eyes shut and teeth bared in a grimace, Jessica endured his manipulation and the squeezing pressure of the wrap on her injury nobly. When he finished, tying off two ends in a simple knot, he noticed her complexion was a bit wan.

"You okay?"

She gave him a tight, jerky nod.

He brushed the hair back from her face. "I wish I had some Advil or something for you."

"It's okay. I'll live." She swallowed hard. "Hey, I survived thirty hours of back labor without painkillers when Eric was born. I can do this."

"Attagirl."

She took a deep breath and blew it out slowly through her pursed lips. Gage's attention snagged on her puckered mouth, and heat skittered through him. Jamming his palms against his eyes, he battled down the bump of lust and rose to his feet. Rolling his shoulders and flexing his back, he worked the fatigue from his muscles, preparing to carry Jessica again. He found the bottle of water and drank before passing it to her. She sipped then recapped the bottle.

"Want me to ride piggyback now? You know, the way Eric used to do when he was a kid?" she asked, while loading their supplies and the rest of the sheet into the plastic bag.

"You'd probably prefer that to the firefighter's carry, huh?"

"The one where you drape a person over your shoulder

so that their head is dangling down your back?" She arched an eyebrow. "Uh...*yeah*. Nice as your ass is, I'd rather ogle it from right side up than upside down, all the blood rushing to my head."

"You think I have a nice ass?" He shot her a cocky grin.

She snorted. "Not the point, Coleman." She wiggled her fingers at him. "Hand up?"

He grasped her palm to help her get to her feet...or rather to her *foot*. She hung the sack from her arm and held her injured foot at an angle as he crouched for her to clamber onto his back. He hooked his arms under her legs, and she clasped her arms around his neck, riding on his back. He'd always thought "turtleback" would have been a better name for the hold than "piggyback" since the passenger clung to you like a tortoise shell.

In this position, Jessica's chin was right by his ear. As he walked, jostling her, her breath hissed and caught, whispered and exhaled, hot and tickling the fine hairs of his neck. He tried not to think about the way she was squished up against him, the way the ragged pants in his ear reminded him of the sounds of making love.

Instead, he concentrated on problem-solving. They needed to find their way to a phone, to someone who could drive them to the police and get Jessica to the hospital.

"Since I was unconscious for most of the drive to the trailer, I have no clue where we are. What can you tell me about the closest town and direction we need to head?"

Jessica sighed. "Not too much. I don't know this part of the state well, and the mountain roads were so dark and twisty I lost my sense of direction." She paused a beat then added, "Sorry."

"Stop apologizing. None of this is your fault."

"All of this is my fault." Her tone dripped dejection.

"Bull. It's Henry's fault."

"But if—"

"I mean it, Jess. I won't have you shouldering any blame." He stepped over a rill of runoff from the surrounding slopes and surveyed the way ahead, looking for the clearest path. "It is not your fault this maniac latched on to you and started harassing you, and I refuse to let you beat yourself up over the way things have transpired."

She said nothing for a moment, then murmured, "I'm responsible for the way I reacted—or overreacted—after our kiss at the cabin. If I hadn't bolted out there and climbed in the car where Henry was hiding—"

"Or if I hadn't blurted a rather huge admission without preparing you. I climbed in that car blindly, too. If I had done a better job protecting you, if I hadn't led Henry to your refuge—"

"Stop," she said, slapping his chest lightly with her palm. "I get it. There's blame enough to go around."

"Right. So now let's move past the blame game and put our heads together to get us home and put Henry behind bars."

"Okay. So I know the highway is a risky move. Henry could be patrolling it, searching for us. But if we hid out of sight of the road and waited for another driver—"

"Uh… Jess, would you stop to pick up a guy who bursts out of the woods at the last second, running out to flag you down?"

She rested her chin on his shoulder and groaned. "No. That reeks of crazy person."

"I'm okay with walking, carrying you. Our fitness program with the fire department requires us to stay in shape and be able to carry heavy equipment or an unconscious fire victim. But…" He slowed his pace and turned a full three-sixty, assessing their progress and their options. "I don't want to wander aimlessly."

Jessica lifted a hand to point. "It looks like there's an outcrop over there. Maybe we'll be able to get a sort of bird's-eye view of the terrain? Or see a house in the distance we can target?"

"Works for me." Gage trudged through the brambles and cleared a path with his foot through the slippery fallen leaves. He trekked over roots, rocks and ridges to the large granite rock that jutted out over a dense green valley. He set Jessica down carefully, and she clasped his arm as she stood on one foot to appraise the vale of yellow birch, rhododendron and hemlock.

"I don't see any houses or signs of a town."

"Me, either." He placed his hand over the one she'd wrapped around his arm and nodded toward a flat spot on the rock. "Let's rest a moment, huh?"

Jessica hobbled with his help to sit down and dug the water bottle out of the bag.

He motioned to her. "Ladies first."

Jess angled her head. "I'm not the one doing all the work." She thrust the bottle toward him. "Drink. 'Cause if you go down, we're sunk." She followed the observation with a frown and a mumble.

"What's that?" he asked, wiping his mouth with his arm after taking a swig of water.

"Nothing. You...wouldn't understand." Her gaze dropped to her hands, which she'd balled in her lap.

"You sure about that?" He offered her the water again, and she took a small sip.

"It's...complicated."

He took a seat beside her and nudged her with his shoulder. "Well, I may not have been a straight-A student like you, but I'm pretty good at figuring stuff out. Why not try me?" When she stayed silent, glaring at her hands, he added, "Jess, I just want to help."

Her head pivoted toward him then, and she heaved a dramatic sigh. "That's the thing, though. You're already doing everything! Thanks to my stupid ankle, you're having to carry me like a child. Do you have *any* idea how much I hate feeling useless and dependent and at the mercy of other people?"

He gave her a wry glance. "Sure I do."

"Really?"

Her dubious tone irritated him. "Really."

She scoffed. "Did *your* mother spend your childhood putting one loser boyfriend after another ahead of your welfare? Did you miss meals because your mom couldn't get her act together, or did you get left stranded at school because your mom was drunk and passed out with her latest bad choice?"

"I—"

"Did you have to raise yourself because your mother couldn't even take care of her own crappy life? That's feeling helpless. And that's when I learned not to depend on other people."

Gage had heard bits of Jessica's backstory before, but the pain behind her rant stung him anew.

"No, I didn't have that experience. You know what kind of parents Tina and I had."

"Mike and Carol Brady."

"Well, maybe not that saccharine, but…yeah. We had a good childhood." He paused, twisting his mouth. "And while we knew some of what you were dealing with at home, I guess I never knew all of it. I'm sorry."

She waved off his regret. "I kept a lot to myself."

"Still…what we knew…that's why we wanted to include

you in our family stuff. Dinners, vacations, game nights. We knew you needed family, and we wanted to be your support. But—"

Her shoulders drooped. "And I appreciated it more than you could know."

"But..." He shifted to face her and drilled her with an un-flinching stare. "Here's what I know about feeling helpless. I know how it feels to wake up after being knocked out to discover that you're in the middle of nowhere."

Her brow creased, and her dark eyes grew sad. Or maybe guilty?

He touched her knee. "Then you realize your hands and feet are tied, that you're being held by an unpredictable man, and that you are unable to protect or defend the woman you lov—" He cut himself off, swallowing the words he knew she didn't want to hear right now. Maybe ever. He shoved down the sting he'd known last night when she recoiled from his admission.

Retraining his focus on what he'd been expressing, he exhaled and started again. "Knowing that you're useless to help a good friend who is at the mercy of an obsessed and dangerous man." His gut clenched as he remembered the frustration and disgust he'd experienced last night and again this morning.

"I've watched a family's home burn to the ground be-cause the fire had spread too far before our crew could get there. I've seen an accident victim die because I couldn't stop their femoral bleed fast enough. And as bad as it's been sitting by my sister's hospital bed, knowing how eas-ily I could lose her and knowing I couldn't save her, last night was worse. You were at Henry's mercy, and I could do nothing to save you. So yes, I know how powerlessness feels, and it's not a feeling I'll soon forget."

"Oh, Gage…" A heart-wrenching sympathy passed over her face, leaving her eyes damp. Her nose flared as if she were fighting tears.

"It sucks to feel helpless, Jess. I get that." He framed her face with his hands. "But I know this, too. You are *not* helpless in this situation. You're strong, and smart, and capable. And if your ankle keeps you from walking, there is nothing wrong with accepting help from someone who cares about you until you're back on your feet. Literally and figuratively." His mouth twitched in a half grin for the unintended pun.

Her gaze dropped, and he nudged her chin back up. "Receiving help doesn't make you weak or vulnerable. It makes sense. It's the smart choice."

She rolled her eyes and gave a small nod. "Maybe. I can't say I agree, but I won't argue the point with you."

"Jess, I—"

A rustling in the woods behind them yanked his attention from any further discussion. Had Blythe tracked them? The trail of disturbed leaves would have been easy enough to follow. He pressed a finger to his lips, telling Jessica to stay silent as he rolled to a crouch and peered deep into the shadowy trees. He squinted against the early rays of the sun as they cut through the lifting fog. Movement drew his gaze. A dark figure moved through the woods.

Chapter Twenty

"I'm riding with you," Matt said as he climbed in the passenger seat of his son's car.

"We'll cover more ground if we split up, take more cars," Eric countered.

"True." Matt buckled his seat belt. "But you've been known to be a bit rash when you get emotional. I want to make sure you don't end up in jail today if things don't go our way."

Eric glared at him. "Rash? What are you talking about?"

Matt scoffed. "Well, besides the numerous incidents in high school of underage drinking, truancy and general acting out, I remember a time when you ran away from home in sixth grade, once when you encouraged my wife's niece to climb out her bedroom window in the middle of the night to share ill-gotten booze, and once when you broke into an unoccupied cabin—"

Eric snorted as he backed his sedan onto the private lane. "I was a kid then and still dealing with a lot of stuff I have a better handle on now."

"Yeah. You've come a long way, and I'm proud of you. But your dad knows you have a hot head, so I'm riding shotgun, just in case."

Eric sighed and headed out of Cameron Glen. He pulled onto the highway headed toward the business area of Valley Haven.

"Besides, now that you're in college, I don't get as much time with you. Maybe I just want—" Matt fell silent as they passed a silver truck parked just off the side of the road. The Ford F-150 was tucked largely out of sight in the woods that bordered Cameron Glen. "Stop the car!"

"Huh?" Eric sent him a dubious frown but complied.

"That truck back there. Did you see it? The silver one." Matt unfastened his seat belt as Eric slowed to a stop on the shoulder of the road.

"What about it? Did you recognize it?"

"Not specifically. It shouldn't be there, for starters. That's Cameron Glen property. But…" He frowned as he racked his brain for the details Jessica had told him about the night of her car accident. "I think the truck her stalker drove was silver."

Eric's eyes widened. "Stalker? How bad has this guy been bothering Mom?" His expression grew darker. "How much danger is she in? Do you think this guy has her?"

Matt shouldered open the passenger door and swiped a hand down his face. "I've said too much. We didn't want you worried."

Eric scoffed and raised a hand as if to say, *What the hell?*

Matt jerked his chin as he climbed out of the car. "Keep a cool head, and let's go have a look at that truck."

Eric followed Matt, and they peered in the windows of the truck. An open box of pistol cartridges sat on the front seat along with a Cameron Glen brochure.

"Dad," Eric said. "Isn't this enough to amplify Mom's missing status?" He waved a hand toward the truck, his eyes wild with fear. "Doesn't this qualify as reason to believe Mom is in danger?"

Matt took out his phone. "It does for me. I'm calling the police."

JESSICA FROZE, HEARING the same crunch of leaves and snap of twigs Gage had clearly heard. She twisted at the waist as far as she could. Having any sort of threat at her back sent chills through her blood. When she tried to shift her injured leg, pain snaked up her calf and throbbed in her foot. Although she bit back the yelp, the catch in her breath and scuff of her pivot on the rock might as well have been a shout.

Gage held up a hand, telling her to be still. He slipped his pocketknife out of his pocket and unfolded the tiny blade. Not much of a weapon, but all they had.

Moving to his feet, he crept closer to the trees, his eyes narrowed and one hand shielding on his brow to block the sun. He sidled toward the nearest tree trunk of any size and stood behind it. An instant later the rustling became a crashing. Gage's body tensed along with her gut. But in the next instant, his shoulders dropped, and he exhaled loudly. "A deer. A nice-looking buck, in fact. Guess he finally smelled us and bolted."

He snapped the knife blade back into the handle and crossed to her.

"Can we get moving again? It was just a deer this time, but the longer we delay…"

"Sure. But first…" He gathered a few small stones and took the empty soda can from the bundle of supplies. "It was a deer this time, but…next time it could be a bear. This—" he rattled the can so that the rocks clattered and clanked "—will let bears know we're coming, and hopefully, scare them from our path. They don't want to tangle with us any more than we want to tangle with them."

He extended a hand to help her up, putting his shoulder under her arm as soon as her good foot was under her. Once she was steady, he squatted, allowing her to climb on his back again. She did, both savoring the feel of her arms around his wide shoulders and regretting the burden she was for him. He grunted as he hoisted himself up, and she tucked her face in the curve of his neck. "I swear I will pay for your PT or chiropractor to get your back in shape again after this."

"I'm fine," he said. "I am."

Though his tone was earnest, her continued helplessness and dependency on Gage sawed in her gut. She'd spent her life not wanting to need anyone, learning the hard way how to be self-sufficient...

Fate really had an ironic sense of humor.

Trust me to take care of you, Jess.

Scary as it still was for her, Gage had certainly proven himself in recent months and especially in the past several hours. As she rested her cheek against his ear, a wave of calm washed through her, knowing she could rely on Gage to get them through this crisis.

A tickle in her gut asked, *And what about beyond this debacle? What about that kiss?*

Gage was infamously commitment-phobic. He changed girlfriends like Mother Nature changed seasons. He claimed he'd had feelings for her for years, yet he'd never acted on them. How did he explain that? And why was she so reluctant to bring that subject up again? Maybe because it seemed too soon to lay his admission open and study it. Everything about their new dynamic felt so new, so hopeful and so fragile. He'd kept a bombshell secret from her for years,

and she feared what other land mines she might encounter
if she ventured down the path of the past with him.

THE CAN OF bear-deterrent pebbles rattled and clanked
against his hip as Gage put one foot in front of the other.
He tried not to think too hard about anything except the
next step. And yet he knew his paced had slowed. They
weren't making nearly the progress they had earlier in the
day. But then, he *had* been trekking through the woods for
several hours now. His back hurt, and his arms were tired
from carrying Jessica.

He quickly shoved the complaint from his mind. He didn't
care about tired arms or feet. He'd happily endure far worse
discomfort, if it meant saving Jessica. He doggedly trained
his thoughts on something other than his own plodding
steps and aching muscles. But the notion that popped into
his head was equally upsetting.

The hospital had tried to call him. Did that mean Tina
had taken a turn for the worse? Man, he prayed not. He gritted his teeth, determined he wouldn't dwell on that, either.
Stay positive. Jessica needs your optimism.

He knew the topic that gave Jessica the most joy and
promise, the most determination to fight and survive. The
beacon that had carried her through Matt's long deploy-
ments, her divorce and years of solitude. Her son. "So when
will Eric have another chance to come home? He will have
a week or two off before the fall term starts, right?"

"Yeah." He heard the brightness in her tone, just as
he'd hoped he would. "His exams are at the very end of
July, then he gets two weeks off before fall classes start...
hmm, around the middle of August. Don't remember the
exact date."

"He is planning to come home then, right? Not go to the beach with buddies or anything?"

"Last I heard he'll come over to Cameron Glen. Especially since both Matt and I are there. Assuming I'm still there and not back in Charlotte or—"

"Hey. Listen," he cut in, coming to a stop and raising his gaze from the overgrown path. A low rumble rolled through the woods, confirming what he'd suspected. "Did you hear that?"

Jessica's grip tightened on his shirt. "Sounds like a car engine."

"Sorta. But deeper. More like a diesel truck."

Gage perked his ears and held his breath, listening, turning slowly to decipher from which direction the sound had come. The rumble they'd heard was joined by a familiar, piercing beep. The warning signal of a large vehicle in Reverse. "Well, unless Henry has stolen a fire engine or concrete mixer to search for us, that's not him. I'm following that noise."

He altered his path slightly, headed toward the grumbling engine. The noise didn't fade like a passing vehicle on the highway, but grew louder as he walked nearer to the spot where the sound originated. Encouraged by the first signs of civilization and help in hours, Gage picked up his pace, adrenaline and hope fueling him.

"There!" Jessica released her grip briefly to point through the trees to the flash of a bright orange construction vehicle in the midst of a clearing.

A tension he hadn't realized he'd been holding in released in his chest like the opening of a hydrant. Relief flowed out, and he marched the final yards through the forest with a grin spread across his face.

THE FIRST THING Jessica noticed as they emerged from the trees and waved down the workers at the construction site was the logo on the side of the bulldozer and backhoe.

Turner Construction.

A giddy laugh escaped her. "Gage, look! It's Jake's company!"

"Well, I'll be damned."

Their appearance had roused the attention of a man in a hard hat who stood with his head bowed over a blueprint. He conversed with a second man in terse shouts in order to be heard over the grumble of the diesel equipment. Having spotted them, the man in the hard hat strode across the uneven, upturned earth, frowning.

Gage met the man halfway, stopping by a pickup truck bearing the Turner Construction logo.

"Can I help you?" Hard Hat asked, his gruff tone at odds with the friendly question.

"You can if you have a working phone we can borrow or someone who can drive us to the nearest emergency room," Gage said, helping Jessica slide off his back. "We're stranded, and my friend has an injured ankle."

She stood on one leg beside him, bracing her hip and one arm against the truck's tailgate. Hard Hat dropped his gaze to Jessica's wrapped foot and rubbed the scruff on his cheeks. "We can spare someone for a while to drive you to the hospital up the road, I suppose."

"Is Jake Turner here, by any chance?" Jessica asked.

Hard Hat raised his eyebrows, clearly surprised she knew his boss's name.

Jessica smiled. "He's a friend of ours. Sorta family. Finding one of his work crews out here when we need rescue feels like providence."

"Naw. Mr. Turner's not here."

She shrugged. "It was worth a shot, huh?"

Hard Hat gave a grudging smile.

Gage pointed to the cell phone clipped to the man's hip. "Any chance that thing's got a signal out here? We'd like to call Jake or someone in the family to let them know where we are and that we're safe. They're bound to be worried."

Hard Hat unclipped the phone and passed it to Gage, who handed it to Jessica, saying, "After you call Matt, I want to call the hospital in Charlotte and check on Tina."

She squinted in the sunlight to see the screen of the cell and tapped in Matt's phone number. The call was answered with a dubious, "Hello?"

Jessica almost sobbed in relief. "Matt, it's me. Long story, but…we're safe, and we need a ride home."

She heard her ex-husband speak to someone else followed by a voice she'd know anywhere. "Mom? What the hell? Where are you?"

Tears filled her eyes. "Eric? What are you— Why—"

Then Matt came back on the line. "We're on our way, Jess. Where are you?"

She gave a small, hiccupping laugh. "I honestly don't know."

TWO HOURS LATER, after the construction foreman had dropped them off at a small-town hospital, the local police had been summoned and an initial interview given, Jessica was reunited with her ex and her son. She and Gage were still in the waiting room doing paperwork when the two burst through the doors of the tiny ER like avenging angels, and Jessica fell happily into her son's embrace.

"Damn, Mom. We were so worried! What happened?" When she hesitated, deciding how much to tell her son, Eric held her by her shoulders and frowned at her. "Don't sugarcoat it for me. I'm not a child. I don't need protection from the bad stuff in this world. I want the whole truth."

Jessica looked at the young man scowling at her and goggled, realizing how much her boy *had* grown up. At nineteen, Eric was the age Matt had been when they got engaged. She nodded reluctantly and launched into the whole story, from the beginning. When she was finally taken to a curtained-off space in the exam area, Eric went with her to hear the rest of the disturbing tale. She described for the attending doctor and Eric how she'd stepped in the hidden hole and wrenched her ankle.

"I'm pretty sure it's broken," the doctor said, "but I'm going to send you for an X-ray before we decide what sort of cast you'll need. I'll go write up those orders, and someone from Radiology will come get you in a moment."

No sooner had the attending stepped out than a deputy from the sheriff's department peeked behind the curtain of the exam room. "I know you gave the city department a general rundown of what happened, but I have some more questions, if this is a good time."

She learned Gage had already given his account of events, and the deputy updated her on developments he'd already learned from the city police.

"A car matching the description of your sedan was found abandoned on the side of the highway, and a resident that lives about a quarter mile from the abandoned car reported their minivan stolen. So we're looking for the missing van and have put out a rough description of the man you say kidnapped you and Mr. Coleman." The deputy consulted his notes. "Henry Blythe."

Jessica sighed. "Except that's not his real name. That's just how I know him. The police department in Charlotte already ran that name and came up with nothing. Henry Blythe is an alias."

The deputy scratched his ear and grunted. "That's what Mr. Coleman said, as well. I've made a note of it. Can you come to the station when you finish here to help our artist create a rendering?"

"Happy to," she said. "The sooner that man is off the streets the better."

"Can't that wait?" Eric protested. "You've been through enough today. You need to rest, prop that foot up."

"I'll rest when Henry is off the streets." Turning back to the deputy, she said, "Tell your artist I'll be there as soon as the hospital discharges me."

HENRY PROWLED THE cheap motel room like a caged lion, seething at his miscalculations and the latest turn of events. He'd been sure Jessie and Coleman had been secure, and he hadn't been gone *that* long. His first mistake had been not building a better plan before taking Jessie, but when she'd climbed in the car where he'd been hiding, it had seemed like fate.

Now she was gone, in the wind—with Coleman. He clenched his teeth harder. Knowing he'd had his chance to kill that bastard to get rid of the competition and hadn't caused his gut to burn. But he'd thought he could use the firefighter to bend Jessie to his will.

He growled under his breath and dropped heavily on the edge of the sagging mattress. If he were Jessie, where would he go? She might be hiding in a hotel somewhere, or believing herself protected by Coleman, she might have gone back to Charlotte. Coleman's truck was still at the cabin in Valley Haven, at the vacation place... Cameron Valley or Colton Hills or some such.

Before he drove all the way back to Charlotte, it made sense to look for Jessie in Valley Haven first. Mind made up, Henry shoved to his feet and stalked to the motel room door. He peered out cautiously, checking for cops before heading to the van he'd snagged. Frowning at the behemoth, he decided he'd make a quick pit stop to trade for a less conspicuous vehicle. Then he'd find Jessie and make her pay for humiliating him. He no longer wanted anything from the troublesome bitch except revenge.

Chapter Twenty-One

Unfamiliar with using crutches, Jessica hobbled into the cabin that evening and dropped more than sat on the couch once in the living room. Her X-ray had confirmed a hairline break at her ankle, and she'd been given a walking cast along with crutches for extra support for the first few days of healing.

Noticing a citrus scent in the air, she gave Cait a puzzled look. "Do I smell lemons?"

"Oh, that's the cleaner I used to freshen the place up before you got here. I cleared up the food from the table and dishes from the sink and gave the place a general wipe-down. The last thing you needed was to come back to a day-old mess."

Jessica pressed a hand to her chest. "You're so thoughtful. How can I ever thank you? Not just for the cleaning help, but for everything this summer."

Cait shrugged. "It's what friends do."

Friends. Jessica's heart gave a bittersweet tug. While she was grateful for Cait's friendship, she missed her posse. The reminder of losing Sara fisted in her stomach. And what about Tina and Holly? Would she ever be able to share dinner and laughter with her best friends again?

"Special delivery!" Isla called as she bustled in with two

large sacks from Ma's Mountain Diner. "I got a variety of vegetables since I wasn't sure of your favorites and plenty of fried chicken for that hungry man of yours."

Jessica opened her mouth to tell Matt's sister-in-law that Gage wasn't her man, but the words stuck in her throat. An instant later the moment was gone, as Gage, Matt and Eric trundled in after giving the area around the cabin a thorough search.

"No sign of the boogeyman," Matt announced, and little Erin, playing on the floor with her cousin, giggled, repeating, "Boogie!"

"Boogie, boogie, boogie!" Eric said and swept his laughing sister up for a playful tussle before tucking her under one arm and Isla's toddler under his other. "I'll take the pip-squeaks back to our place so y'all can talk."

Jessica shook her head. "I'm talked out. That sheriff's deputy and artist were nothing if not thorough."

"And I'm famished," Gage said, peeking in the bags Isla had set on the kitchen counter.

"Message received," Cait said, tugging at the sleeve of her husband's shirt. "We'll get out of your hair." She embraced Jessica and whispered, "I'm so thankful you're all right."

Jessica chuckled and swallowed the lump in her throat. "That makes two of us."

Once Matt, Eric and the Camerons had said their goodnights, Jessica helped Gage explore the varied offering of homestyle goodies Isla had supplied. For several minutes, neither said anything as they tucked hungrily into the spread of fried chicken, mashed potatoes and four different vegetables.

Only after he'd finished one plateful and was helping himself to seconds did Gage say, "You know, being back here at the cabin, having dinner with you, reminds me…"

His lead-in was enough to tell her where his thoughts were, and her pulse jumped. "Gage—"

He set his plate down and raised his gaze to hers. "It's kinda where we left off before—"

Jessica put her fork down and nodded. "I know."

"And since then, we haven't really addressed the elephant in the room."

"I suppose not." Feeling suddenly fidgety, she clasped her hands together in her lap to keep them still. "Listen… I'm sorry I freaked out. I don't want you to think—" She hesitated, sighed. "It's not that I don't care about you. Of course I do. But you flipped more than twenty years of friendship on its head, and it was…a lot to digest."

"I get that. I realize I shouldn't have blurted it out like that." Gage pushed his plate away and angled his chair to face hers more directly. "However…what I said was the truth."

"But how…? Why didn't you say anything for so long?"

Gage dragged a hand over his face and gave her a sad half smile. "Because I couldn't. At first, I struggled with the fact that you were so close to our family, Tina's best friend. It felt…*wrong* somehow. You'd been like a sister. I tried to convince myself I didn't feel what I felt. Then you met Matt and…man, was I jealous of that relationship." He gave a wry chuckle as he glanced away. "I *had* to keep quiet then. I wasn't going to spoil your happiness. And I thought, maybe this is for the best. I couldn't tell you I loved you when you were married to another man. I told myself your being with Matt would force me to move on and put my fascination with you behind me." He returned his gaze to her, his eyes full of an ancient pain that speared her soul. "But I didn't move on."

She ruminated on his confession for a moment, then

asked, "I don't understand. You've dated a lot of women through the years."

He chuckled without humor. "Dated, yes. Fallen in love with? Nah. I couldn't commit to another woman when I was still in love with you."

Her heart thrashed in her chest like a wild rabbit fighting to get free. "I always thought you didn't get married because you didn't want to settle down or have kids. That you liked being a bachelor and playing the field."

He blew out a sigh and rubbed his cheek. "Of course I wanted to settle down and have a family. With you. And when that was not possible, I chose not to settle for second best. That's no way to start a marriage."

Jessica's lungs felt leaden, and a deep sadness dragged at her. Gage would have been a terrific husband and father. "So *I'm* the reason you never had kids? Never had a long-term relationship with a woman?" Her voice cracked as she saw the past twenty-plus years through a new lens.

He must have seen something in her expression of how that knowledge weighed on her, because he reached for her hand and pressed it between his own. "I'm not saying it's your fault. Don't take that on yourself, Jess. I made that decision, and I can live with it."

"But, Gage, I— If I'd known…" She let her words trail. What *would* she have done if she'd known his feelings? Certainly it would have been awkward at best. And how would it have changed her relationship with Tina if she hadn't been comfortable around Gage at the family events? *Tina…*

"You said earlier you aren't sure if Tina was aware of how you felt."

Gage's eyes grew round. "Well, I sure didn't tell her. I knew she wouldn't have kept it a secret from you, and I wouldn't have asked her to try. If she ever suspected, she never said as much to me." His brow dipped, and his silver gaze sharpened. "There was just too much at stake for me to toss a stink bomb into the mix. Your friendship to Tina. Your marriage to Matt. Our friendship." He paused and narrowed his eyes on her in a heartbreaking way. "We are friends, aren't we, Jess? Have I spoiled that by telling you my truth?"

Tears pricked her sinuses, and emotion clogged her throat. "Of course. But…"

His chest swelled as he drew a breath, as if bracing to hear what followed. "But?"

"I'm not sure what else we are. I know I've come to see you differently over the past several weeks. And the past few days, I—" She squeezed his hand and swallowed hard to clear her throat, choose her words. A breathy half laugh escaped. "You're definitely a good kisser."

He tugged up one cheek. "Just good?"

She cocked her head slightly to the side. "Fine. A great kisser. A mind-blowingly amazing kisser. Which only makes it harder for me to figure out what's happening. What I want."

His frown said that wasn't the answer he was hoping for. He sat back, releasing her hands and flattening his palms on the table in front of him. "I see."

"Gage, it's still new to me, this seismic shift between us. I…have questions."

"So ask. I want a clean slate with you."

"Well, what about after I divorced Matt? Why didn't you say anything then? I've been single for eight years now."

He lifted one eyebrow and nodded. "True. But do you remember what you told people after you divorced Matt?"

She paused and rewound her memories to the days

after she split from Matt. "I probably said a lot of things I shouldn't have. What is it you remember?"

"That you were done with men, done with relationships, and only wanted to be a mother and have your independence from then on."

"Hmm. Right. That *was* how I felt. Even friendly divorces are hard."

Though her split from Matt had been amicable, it stung to see the relationship dissolve. Her reasons for going solo, her disappointment in what she perceived as Matt's unavailability and growing distance had only reopened the scars her mother left. Matt's months of deployment meant she'd essentially been a single mother for long stretches. And when Matt had been wounded in action and medically discharged from the military, he'd had demons of his own to fight.

They'd struggled to reconnect, each having grown in a different direction. Though intellectually she knew Matt hadn't truly deserted her, the ghosts of her childhood whispered to her that Matt hadn't been there for her when she needed him, just like her mother and absent father.

"So," he said, turning up a palm. "In the wake of a declaration like that, what chance did I have in the months after your divorce?" He fisted his hand then and bumped it lightly on the table. "And then... I kept waiting for the right time to tell you how I felt. And kept pushing the conversation down the road because—" he lifted a shoulder and waved one finger between them "—of this. I didn't want to wreck our friendship or yours with Tina."

Jessica wrapped her arms around herself, nodding. "I get that. I do."

"You're important to me, Jessica. More important than I've let on through the years, because I didn't want to scare you away. But I decided, at some point, that having a little of you in my life was better than blowing everything up and losing what I did have." He drew his brow into a deep V. "I'm sorry if my silence feels like a deception. That was never my intent."

She sighed and gave him a gentle smile. "I know you well enough to know that's true. I shouldn't have accused you of that. I was in shock. Confused. Reeling."

He became still, and his eyes more intense. "And now? Where are we? What do you want?"

She pushed away from the table and stood. Rubbing her arms, she clomped in her boot cast to the window to look out at the long shadows as the sun sank behind the mountains. "I don't know. I have a lot to think about and things have been so nuts…"

"No pressure. I don't want to rush you." He gave a humored chuff. "Lord knows I've been patient long enough. A few more days or weeks isn't going to change things for me."

She faced him and lifted a cheek in a soft smile. "Thank you." With another glance out the window, she said, "I think I'm going to go out for a bit. It's a pretty evening, and I have a lot to consider."

He arched an eyebrow. "In your cast? Aren't you supposed to keep your foot elevated?"

She chuckled. "I didn't say I was going for a run. I'll use the crutches and stay close to the cabin. But the outdoors helps clear my mind and center me. I need that right now."

"Let me come with you," Gage said, "You can lean on me when you're navigating the rough or uneven spots."

She shook her head. "Please, don't. I need…time to think. Some time alone to wrap my head around what's happening between us."

Gage pressed his mouth in a taut line and folded his arms over his chest. "It'll be getting dark soon."

Jessica chuckled wryly. "You sound like me when Eric was a kid and wanted to ride his bike after dinner. He used to say in his too-smart-for-his-own-good style, 'That's what streetlights are for.'"

Gage lifted a corner of his mouth. "I suppose. Still…"

"I'll just be at the fishing dock. You can see it from the front window." She tucked her crutches under her armpits and crossed to the front door. She flashed a wry grin. "If you get bored waiting for me, you could do the dishes."

He exhaled as if in concession. "Just…be careful. Remember the boards on the dock are uneven and—" He stopped himself and swiped a hand over his mouth. "Just… be careful."

She nodded. "Of course."

Setting out across the grassy lawn, which was easier to traverse than the gravel drive, Jessica took a deep breath of the fresh evening air. She walked slowly, even after making it to the paved road that wound through the glen. The last thing she needed was another tumble, and the hill down to the dock was steeper than she remembered.

Through a lit window, she saw the family renting the Pine cabin sitting down to dinner, and she heard the giggle of female voices coming from the direction of the Turners' house. She smiled, imagining the Turner girls, Fenn and Lexi, playing on the tire swing she'd seen earlier that summer.

The crutches thumped loudly as she hobbled to the far end of the wooden dock that extended well into the lake, affording fishermen better access to the deepest part of the stocked pond.

After some awkward gyrations, she was glad Gage hadn't witnessed, Jessica sat down on the end of the dock. She wished she could dangle her feet in the cool water, especially her already hot and itchy casted leg. Instead, she simply watched the dragonflies skim over the surface of the small lake and the first hints of the sunset cast a pink glow around the black silhouette of trees. A soft breeze sent ripples across the water, but soothed her soul.

Turning her head slowly to take in the whole setting—the fishing lake, the hillside striped with the crop of fragrant Christmas trees, the yellow glow of lights in cabin windows, the flower beds offering their splashes of color—she sensed a sweet peace that had been all too rare recently.

If she were honest, she couldn't credit the idyllic retreat setting for the whole of her calm and contentment. Her talk with Gage had been productive, given her insights and answers that settled the stormy seas inside her. Sure, she saw Gage in a new light, but she no longer felt the same shock that had initially rocked her equilibrium. What did it mean for their relationship going forward?

"That *is* the question," she muttered to herself as she leaned back on braced arms. Staring across the small lake, she watched one of the ducks that lived on the property nibbling plants in the shallows and allowed her mind to start sorting, analyzing, shuffling.

Initially, Gage's confession had terrified her. But why? She didn't shy away from telling the people who meant the most to her she loved them, and she treasured expressions of love from Eric, her friends, even Matt—though the words meant something different now. She'd probably even told Gage she'd loved him before—in the same breath she told Tina the same. So why had this felt different? Why had it scared her?

Was it Henry's obsession and twisted use of the word *love* that haunted her, tainting the words? She shuddered just remembering her stalker's misuse of the expression. No,

Henry wasn't anywhere near the same category as Gage. She saw no cross contamination there.

Hadn't she already sensed her own feelings undergoing a shift toward Gage? She'd turned to him following the accident, texting him, confiding in him, sharing reciprocal support, understanding and grief over Tina's condition. She—

With a shake of her head, she stopped that line of thought. Her hesitation, her fear wasn't about how she felt toward him. That realization startled her. She exhaled, turning this discovery over in her head. She trusted her own feelings, but could she trust Gage's? She'd been viewing Gage as a womanizer, unwilling to commit. She'd used the same wary standard to judge him that she'd learned watching her mother's poor choices. But hadn't Gage proven himself reliable, loyal, genuine?

He'd rallied to defend and protect her when Henry's behavior became more threatening. He'd never backed down or walked away in the face of her continued pushback, her stubborn independence.

And he'd gone above and beyond to get her to safety, to literally carry her on his back to save her when she'd hurt her ankle. He'd patiently waited in the wings for decades, loving her, respecting her needs, her marriage, her independence. Gage had been one of the pillars of her life since high school. Like the petals of a flower sequentially unfolding or dominoes falling, each realization led to another, illuminating her life, her fears, her feelings. Gage's steady faithfulness. His unselfish dependability. His—

The dock vibrated, and the thud of heavy footfalls told her she had company.

His insistence that he needed to protect her, she added semi-peevishly to her growing "Gage list."

"I told you I wanted some time alone." She huffed with frustration as she twisted at the waist and looked behind her.

And froze.

"And I've told you, I'm tired of your games," Henry groused as he stalked down the dock, the wooden planks shuddering with each stomping step toward her. "This ends now, Jessie."

Chapter Twenty-Two

"Either you're coming with me, or you're never going any-where again." Henry's tone and expression were hard, cold. "I warned you not to humiliate me. I've given you chance after chance. But I'm done. This is your last chance."

Limbs weak with fear, Jessica fumbled for her crutches, burdened by her cast as she tried to stand. "Stay away from me! Why can't you leave me alone?"

He spread his hands, his voice cracking. "I can't stay away. I love you, Jessie."

"No!" she shouted, finally pushing unsteadily to her feet. She edged back a step, mindful she was at the end of the dock with nowhere to retreat. "You don't know what real love is. Love doesn't hurt and harass and torture. You have to stop this!"

Realizing she couldn't defeat Henry alone and injured, that she had to rouse back up, she screamed, "Someone help me! Gage, hurry!"

Henry's pleading face soured quickly. He surged forward and, knocking the crutches from her grip, grabbed her by the arms. "*Gage?* Seriously? What is it with you and that bastard?" He shook her so hard her teeth clicked and her head whipped violently. "If I shake you hard enough, maybe I'll rattle him loose from your head."

His hostile shaking rocked her already precarious balance. Without her crutches for support, she stumbled, teetered. Her walking cast slipped off the wooden planks, the sinking weight of it further destroying her equilibrium. Jessica gasped and clutched at Henry to break her fall.

But the heavy cast and laws of gravity won.

Jessica splashed into the lake, and her panicked grip on Henry pulled him in, as well. In a tangle of his limbs and hers, Jessica sank beneath the surface. Her heavy cast, quickly sodden, pulled her down like an anchor. The murky pond rushed into her sinuses, spiking her panic. She struggled to surface, but Henry's floundering on top of her and the deadweight of her injured leg hindered her.

With her lungs burning for air, Jessica kicked her good leg and spread her arms, trying to right herself, battling to break the surface. The muddy water and fading sunlight made it hard to see, to orient herself. Memories from that spring, of her car entering the river, of being trapped as the water rose around her, flashed in her mind. The helplessness, the agony of being unable to save her dear friends.

Finally untangling herself from Henry, she pushed off from the muddy bottom of the lake. She broke the surface long enough to gasp a mouthful of air before Henry's grasping hands dragged her back under.

FOR LONG MINUTES after Jessica left the cabin, Gage had stood at the cabin window and watched her on the dock. The sinking sun cast her in a rich golden light, and he wanted to burn the image in his brain, wanted to drink in the beautiful picture she made. The peaceful setting, the evening glow, her serenity had mesmerized him.

But Jessica had asked to be alone, and in respect for her privacy, he'd forced himself to walk away, to turn his attention to cleaning up the kitchen. He could at least do something useful while he waited for her return. His pulse thumped, and anxiety spun through him as if he were waiting for a jury to come back with a verdict on his future. Would Jessica be a part of his life? Had he done irreparable harm to their relationship after all these years of biding his time and waiting for her?

He cracked open the window over the sink, letting the evening breeze refresh the kitchen. From his position at the sink, he had a tranquil view of the distant mountains and, directly behind the cabin, a hillside lined with two-foot-tall Douglas and Fraser firs, destined to be Christmas trees in a few more years. A wild rabbit hopped between the rows of firs, pausing to nibble the long grass. Gage studied the rabbit, deep in thought, until something startled the bunny, and it scampered away.

He craned his head, looking for what had spooked the shy creature, but saw nothing.

But then a scream sounded outside.

Jessica.

Like the rabbit, Gage ran. Out of the kitchen. Through the front door. Across the yard toward the lake.

At first he didn't see her. She wasn't on the fishing dock anymore. But sunlight glinted on a disturbance in the water. He saw two people struggling, flailing, splashing. And icy horror filled his veins.

"Jessica!" He sprinted down the grassy hill toward the lake. His speed didn't slow as he leaped onto the dock, and his feet pounded down the wooden walkway. He spotted Jessica's crutches, discarded at end of the dock, and his anxiety ratcheted up. As he toed off his shoes preparing to dive in the lake after Jess, he recognized who was grappling in the lake with her.

Anger twisted in his gut. *Enough* of this jerk coming after Jess! If the cops didn't do something about this guy, he would. He was a microsecond from jumping into the lake to help Jessica when he heard a shout. "Gage!"

He shot a glance over his shoulder to Matt and Eric. The father and son were across the lake on the Harkneys' back deck. "It's Blythe! Call the cops!"

Without waiting to see if they complied, he estimated the best place to land and jumped in the lake.

JESSICA SHOVED AGAINST Henry's grasping hands. Between his grip and the sinking heft of her cast, her energy and her air were quickly draining. She wasn't sure if Henry was pulling at her trying to save himself or if he was intentionally holding under the surface.

Until his hands closed around her throat and squeezed. A new level of panic flooded her limbs, her heart, her lungs. Fueled by fear and adrenaline, she clawed at his grip around her neck.

His fingers were unyielding. Henry was too strong. She couldn't pry his hands away. But her hands were free to attack him. She tried to bash his nose with an upward strike of her palm. Resistance of the water drastically cut the power of her punch, virtually nullifying the effect. Fast, powerful strikes weren't possible. So she curled her fingers and clawed at his eyes.

She heard his lake-muted growl as she dug her fingernails into flesh and raked his face. He thrashed his head to the side, but she kept swiping, digging at any vulnerable place she could reach.

Her lungs screamed for air, and darkness was creeping

in from the edges of her vision. She was losing the battle. Slipping away.

Profound sadness washed through her. Regrets. She'd never see Eric get married. Never see the sunrise again. *Never get to tell Gage she loved im.*

The last thought sent a sharp pain through her.

At the end of her held oxygen supply, she gasped. And choked as pond water filled her mouth.

She had only an instant to realize Henry had released his hold on her before strong hands seized her arms and propelled her to the surface. She coughed, sputtered, then vomited dirty water. Blinking, she tried to clear her vision. Water and hair blinded her to all but a blur of activity beside her. Grunts. Splashing. Too soon, she was sinking again. She gasped a ragged breath just before her head went under.

GAGE GRAPPLED IN the water with Henry. The struggle was more of a wrestling match than a fistfight in the water. His attack had startled Blythe briefly, shifting his opponent's attention from Jessica long enough for Gage to grab her up, out of the water for a breath.

But Henry latched on to him from behind, an arm around his throat. Gage wrenched his head aside and chomped down on Blythe's arm. Hard. Drew blood.

Henry released him, shoving him away as his dark, angry growl rumbled in the splashing waves. Gage had only a moment to scissor-kick, suck in air and pivot to face his foe before Henry came at him again. As he braced for Blythe's attack, he saw Jessica sinking again, her arms flailing weakly.

He deflected the assault of Henry's grabbing hands as best he could while reaching for Jessica. He stuck his hand toward her, praying she saw it, could grasp it before she hit bottom. Their fingers brushed—and slipped apart.

Henry climbed Gage like a ladder, propelling himself out of the lake to get a new lungful of air, even as he pushed Gage deeper below the surface. Gage took the opportunity to wrap his arms around his opponent's legs, trapping them, hindering Henry's ability to kick or to stay upright. Gage savored having the upper hand, if only briefly, before realizing how much trouble Jessica was in. No matter how it pained him to forfeit his advantage, Jessica was his priority. Now and always.

He twisted and thrust out, buying some distance from Blythe. With a kick, he turned. Circling his arms, he propelled himself toward the bottom of the lake, toward the dark blur of Jessica's hair.

Her groping hand touched his foot, clutched weakly. But it was enough for him to reach her, grab her wrist, tug her upward. When he could wrap an arm around her back, under her arms, he flutter-kicked and brought her to the surface once more. He inhaled a restorative breath, but Jess only gagged and wheezed.

"Here!"

The voice called his attention to the dock, where Eric lay on his stomach, arms outstretched. Gage lifted Jessica's arm within her son's reach. Eric seized hold of her and dragged her onto the fishing dock, rolling her onto her side.

Before he could register more than that, Henry had attacked him again, taking a fistful of Gage's hair and bending his head backward. A thousand pinpricks of fire blazed on his scalp. Fresh fury fired and fueled his fight. Gage dunked and performed a backward roll like the ones he'd perfected at summer camp years before. His feet flipped over his head, and he jammed his heel in Blythe's nose.

The fist yanking Gage's hair released, and Gage righted himself in the water, already preparing his next move—a move he never got the chance to deliver.

Chapter Twenty-Three

Jessica lay on her side, coughing and gasping like a fish on land. Despite the tremble of fatigue and fear in her limbs, she struggled to sit up. When hands reached for her, she flinched away, until she swiped sodden hair from her face and blinked Eric and Matt into clarity.

"Where's Henry?" she rasped, her anxious gaze darting from side to side to find the source of her terror.

"Gage is handling him," Eric said, a note of hero worship in his tone.

"Yeah, I need immediate police and ambulance presence at Cameron Glen. The fishing lake pier…" Matt said, a cell phone to his ear.

As Eric shoved to his feet, his eyes rounded. "Dad, look out!"

Jessica twisted in time to see Henry levering himself up on the edge of the pier, arms braced, a malevolent glare on Matt.

Eric snatched up one of her crutches and swung it like a baseball bat. The crutch caught Henry across the temple, and her stalker's eyes rolled back. Jessica sagged as Henry toppled into the lake again. They had a moment's reprieve, but—

"Where's Gage?" Pulse thrumming, Jessica scrambled on her hands and knees toward the end of the pier. As she spotted him in the water, unmoving, a cry ripped from her throat. "Gage! No!"

Eric spun to find Gage, and quickly tore off his shoes. "I'll get him." He pulled his cell phone from his back pocket and shoved the device into Matt's hands. When Eric jumped in the lake, fresh waves of horror crashed through Jessica. If anything happened to her son—

No! The mere thought strangled her. Not her baby, her only child! She squeezed the edge of the wood planks, searching for Henry to gauge the threat he posed. He, too, floated in the lake, his body still. A tremor crawled through her. How hard had Eric hit her stalker? Was he...dead?

A splash and grunt called her attention back to her son. To Gage.

Still panting for restorative oxygen, she watched Eric grab Gage's unmoving body under the arms. Her son hoisted Gage enough to keep his head above water as he scissor-kicked and pulled Gage closer to the dock. Setting his phone, line to the emergency operator still open, onto the dock, Matt sank awkwardly onto his good knee. He braced himself, trying to lift Gage out of the water. Jessica hurried to help, taking one arm, grabbing the waist of Gage's jeans.

While Eric pushed, Jessica and Matt pulled. The effort wasn't pretty, but they dragged him onto the dock.

"Gage? Say something! Wake up, please!" Jessica stroked his cheek with her palm, then gave his face sobering pats.

Soon, Gage groaned and raised a hand to wipe his eyes as Matt and Jessica rolled him on his side. Spitting out a mouthful of water, Gage slowly turned onto his stomach and pushed up to his hands and knees.

Seeing Gage rally, Jessica turned back toward the lake.

She heard a swish of water but didn't see Eric. Her heart climbed into her throat. "Eric!"

"Easy, Jess. He's right here," Matt said, once again reaching toward the water.

Jessica left Gage's side to assist in extracting Eric from the lake. But it was Henry's lolling head that rose above the edge of the pier. Her heart tripped, and she physically recoiled as her ex and her son maneuvered Henry's limp body onto the dock.

Eric hoisted himself up and climbed out of the lake with the skill of the young athlete he was. But for all his newly acquired maturity and manly physique, her son's eyes were those of a frightened child's as he gawked at Henry. He lifted his stricken gaze to Matt, then turned to Jessica. "Did I... kill him?"

Jessica rushed to embrace her son, cradle his head against her shoulder. "Oh, Eric. My brave boy. You saved me, you saved Gage."

"But I—" Eric levered away from her hug to shift his attention to Henry.

His face tense, Matt pounded Henry on the back, and Gage, still sucking in air between coughs, crawled over to the other men. "Get him...on his back."

Jessica kept her arm around Eric, needing him for support as much as she guessed he needed hers. She watched Matt and Gage begin CPR on Henry—flipping him on his back, checking for breathing, for a pulse, then starting chest compressions.

She bit her bottom lip, choking back the sounds of distress that bid to rise. As much as she'd prefer for Henry to die, a fit consequence of his terror campaign on her and just karma for his part in Sara's death, she also couldn't wish the man dead when Eric had dealt the blow that knocked him unconscious, caused him to slip under the water.

Eric didn't need a front-row view of the lifesaving procedure. Nor did she. With a nudge, she tried to coax Eric to leave the scene. "Walk with me? Please?"

Probably only because she appealed to his protective and caring instincts where she was concerned, Eric moved stiffly down the dock toward shore. He cast repeated glances over his shoulder to the other men, his expression troubled.

When they reached the end of the pier, she veered away from the stairs and found a spot on the grassy hill to stand and keep vigil. She put an arm around her son's waist in a side hug, and he reciprocated with his arm across her back at her shoulders. The chirp of crickets and nocturnal frogs surrounded them as they stared back at the activity on the end of the pier.

Sensing a new presence beside her, Jessica cut a glance toward the new arrival and met Cait's worried eyes. Cait draped a blanket around Jessica and Eric, then rubbed a comforting hand on Jessica's back, no words necessary. Another stir of movement in her peripheral vision drew her attention to the crowd forming at the top of the hill by the head of the steps that led to the dock. Guests to the retreat had clearly heard the ruckus and were drawn out to see what had happened. Camerons, young and old, also assembled, ready to offer help. Cait sent a hand signal to her sister Emma, who turned and ran, as if silently dispatched on a mission.

The distant wail of a siren signaled the approach of the emergency assistance Matt had called for. She spotted Matt's daughter, Erin, in Grace's arms, Cait's mother ever ready to quietly assist and provide backup to her family during good times or crises.

The whole Cameron family was steadfast. Loving. Reliable in a way Jessica's mother never had been. A tug of jealousy besieged her until she realized the Camerons' loving loyalty extended to Eric.

The envy morphed to gratitude. Eric had been embraced by this inspiring family. And…so had she. The Camerons' compassion and generosity were not limited to blood ties. Their hospitality toward Jessica throughout the summer gave evidence of that. Cait's warmth and friendship had been a surprising serendipity when Matt remarried. And like concentric waves, the acceptance and devotion rippled out. Cait's siblings, parents, brothers-and sister-in-law—Jessica had been welcomed into the family, wrapped in the same familial love and support, adopted by their clan.

Tears sprang to her eyes as the truth penetrated the layers of protection she'd erected around her heart. Because of this family, she was not and would never be truly alone. Just as she'd never truly been alone for years, thanks to the constant and encouraging presence of her posse—Holly, Sara, Tina…and Gage.

Her focus returned to Gage, hunkered over the man who'd tried to kill her, the man who'd savagely knocked Gage out and bound them both, the man whose reckless disregard for life had cost Sara hers. Gage compressed Henry's chest over and over, unrelenting. A rescue professional in action. When Matt placed a hand on Gage's shoulder and shook his head, Gage shook it off. Continued working to revive his patient.

He was wholly committed to his calling as a first responder. Honorable to a fault. And had proven time and again his devotion and loyalty to her. The truth warmed her from the inside, filling her with light and hope like the sun brightening a new day. She stared at Gage, studying him with her new perspective. He'd said he'd never married anyone else because he'd been in love with her. He'd never forced his feelings on her, waiting patiently through her marriage to Matt, through her post-divorce healing.

Her attention only shifted again when an ambulance arrived and a stretcher was carried down the stairs and out the long dock. And only when the EMTs pushed him aside and took up the compressions did Gage stop rendering CPR.

"Mom," Eric said softly, a quaver in his voice, "if the guy dies—"

Jessica turned to her son, her stomach dropping when she saw how pale and frightened he looked. She knew where his mind had gone. "Oh, Eric, don't—"

"It will be my fault. I hit him with the crutch."

She grabbed her child into a bear hug and squeezed him as if she could crush the guilt and worry from him. "Don't go down that path, baby. You've done nothing wrong."

"But.I. killed him."

"No. Maybe. It's not… Oh, Eric." She swallowed hard. "Even if Henry dies, you did the right thing. It was self-defense. You were protecting me and helping Gage. You did nothing wrong."

But even knowing the truth of the circumstances did little to quell the trip of fear down her own spine. What if the police didn't believe their account of the facts? And even if no charges were filed against Eric, how did he grapple with the trauma of what had happened today? With his part in Henry's death? Because she had a horrible suspicion the EMT wouldn't have any better luck reviving her stalker than Gage had had.

Chapter Twenty-Four

By the time the police finished questioning everyone and Jessica had a new cast put on to replace her waterlogged one, a new morning was dawning. Jessica was beyond exhausted, but she wouldn't sleep until she'd assured herself Eric was all right.

"Will you drop me off at Matt's house?" she asked Cait's brother-in-law. "I need to check on my son."

Gage gave her a skeptical look across the back seat of Emma and Jake Turner's minivan. Cait's older sister and her husband had won the debate over who would stay at the hospital to drive Jessica and Gage home. Cait, Isla and Brody had young children to put to bed. Matt needed to stay with Eric, whose interview with the police had taken longer than the others. And Neil and Grace were chosen to calm the retreat guests and reassure everyone Cameron Glen was safe.

"I will," Jake said. "But Matt texted to say they're fine. Daryl went over to sit with Eric and give him moral support."

Jessica smiled tiredly, happy to hear Eric had someone near his own age to lean on. Her son's friendship with the Camerons' adopted son had strengthened in recent months. Just one more blessing the Camerons had been to her family.

"Just the same," she said, "I need to see him. Hug him."

Emma turned to smile at her. "I understand *completely*."

When they entered Matt's cabin a few minutes later, Eric surged from the couch where he was talking to Daryl and rushed over to give Jessica one of his wonderful bear hugs. She held her boy for long moments before finally rasping the question she'd been fretting over for hours. "What did the police say? Are they charging you with anything?"

He shook his head. "Based on our description of events and Henry's history of stalking and kidnapping you at gunpoint, they believed it was self-defense. And because they found no evidence I meant to kill him, they said I was free to go."

"Oh, thank heavens!" She captured Eric's face between her palms and kissed his forehead.

"Do you want to tell them what *you* learned from the police a little while ago?" Gage prompted.

Eric pulled back to eye her curiously. "Mom?"

Jessica took a deep breath and nodded. "We already knew Henry was using an alias, so the police ran his fingerprints and submitted a DNA sample searching for hits. And while it's too early for DNA confirmation, they got a hit with his fingerprints in the FBI's national system, called AI—" Her weary brain faltered.

"IAFIS?" Matt supplied.

"Yes, that." She exhaled and reorganized her thoughts. "Henry's real name it seems is Henry Cavendal. He was wanted in Ohio for killing his mother and another woman that he'd been dating."

"The dude killed his own mother?" Daryl asked from the couch. "Cold. Ice-cold."

"He'd been on the run, evading Ohio authorities for three years," Gage added.

"Eric, man," Daryl said. "You're a hero. You rid the world of one bad apple."

But Eric didn't look relieved. His brow still furrowed with guilt.

"Eric?" Jessica said, tipping her head, trying to make eye contact with her son.

He took a step back and forced a smile. "I'm okay. I just… need time to come to terms with everything."

When he returned to the couch, she tried to follow, wanting to do something, *anything* to relieve her son from the turmoil she knew he was suffering. Gage caught her arm, though, and murmured, "You heard him. He needs time. And you need sleep."

Even as she pivoted to argue the point, she wobbled on her crutches and her head spun. Gage caught her around the waist and nudged her toward the door. "You've seen him. He's not going to face charges. Either come willingly, or I will carry you out of here." His cheek twitched with humor. "You know I can…and I will."

With a final glance toward Eric, Jessica nodded and let Gage take her home.

HOURS LATER, SUNLIGHT peeked through the curtains of the Juniper cabin's bedroom, nudging Jessica reluctantly from sleep. An arm draped over her from behind, its owner snoring softly at her back.

She remembered little of last night from the time she left Eric at Matt's cabin and hobbled on her crutches to fall into bed. Except…

"Stay with me. Hold me. I don't want to be alone tonight."

Too tired to fight or question what her heart craved, Jessica had only to whisper the request as she drifted to sleep, and Gage had cuddled behind her, his arms wrapping her in a secure embrace.

Now, feeling more rested but with muscles aching in places she'd never imagined existed, Jessica turned to face Gage, a process that involved untwisting the sheet from her cast and using a hand to help move the extra weight around her foot. The stir of activity woke Gage, of course, and she wrinkled her nose as she muttered groggily, "Sorry. I'm not too graceful or stealthy at the moment."

"Everything all right?" he asked, rubbing his eyes with the heels of his hands.

She opened her mouth to answer, then hesitated.

He sat up, frowning when she didn't answer. "Jess? What is it?"

"A pat response didn't feel right, and I realized I hadn't really processed everything that happened yesterday." Raking the hair from her face with her fingers and lying on her back, she stared up at the ceiling. "Henry is dead. He can't threaten me anymore."

Gage placed a warm hand on her thigh. "Yeah. You're safe, sweetheart."

Her gaze darted to meet his when he used the endearment, but before either of them could comment, his cell phone rang, and he turned to check the screen. His face sobered, and he held up a finger signaling, *Just a minute.* "The hospital in Charlotte."

He swung his legs out of the bed as he answered the call and listened carefully. "This is he. Yes?"

Gage carried the phone with him as he left the bedroom, and Jessica used the moment alone to send up a quick prayer that Tina was all right, was improving. She struggled to sit up and retrieve the crutches from beside the bed, then glanced down at the oversize T-shirt she wore like a nightgown. She found her bathrobe, used the bathroom and followed the scent of coffee and the low rumble of Gage's voice to the kitchen.

He handed her a steaming mug of coffee, fixed just the way she liked it, as he finished up his phone call. "Thank you for calling. I'll be there in a few hours to sign the paperwork."

He disconnected the call and stared at the blank screen for a moment, his brow furrowed.

Jessica's pulse kicked up. She was *so* tired of bad news and grief. "Just…tell me."

He exhaled long and hard as he met her gaze. "Tina's doctor is discharging her from the hospital today."

Jessica set her mug on the counter with a thunk that sloshed her hot drink. "What?"

A stunned smile grew on his face. "Her vitals have continued to hold steady, and he says she's ready for the rehab center. He's optimistic that with hard work and time, she can make a full recovery."

Jessica clapped a hand over her mouth to catch the sob of relief.

"I have to go back to Charlotte today and sign papers regarding the transfer, but…" He stopped and narrowed his focus more sharply on Jessica. "I hate to leave you in the lurch, so soon after—"

She waved him off. "Go! Go! This is great news. Tina needs you. Not me."

His eyebrow shot up, and she realized how harsh the words sounded. "All I mean is, Tina is the priority now."

He nodded once slowly, his eyes still locked with hers. "You're sure?"

She hitched her head toward the back porch where they could drink their coffee from the rocking chairs that boasted a view of the rising sun. Once she'd taken her seat and propped her crutches against the cabin wall, she inhaled the fresh air deeply and gathered her thoughts.

"Before you leave for Charlotte, I owe you some answers."

Gage's hand visibly tightened around his cup, and a spark of curiosity and wariness lit his gray eyes.

"Before Henry showed up last night, I had enough time to decide some things about us."

Gage stilled, seeming to hold his breath.

"I thought a lot about what you told me about how you feel, how you've felt for years without me knowing. Knowing that truth and considering everything that has happened in the past few weeks…" Her hands started trembling, and she set her coffee on the wobbly wooden table between their chairs. "I don't think we can be *friends* anymore."

He jerked his chin up, his eyes wild with confusion and hurt. He sprang up from his seat and paced to the edge of the porch, his hands clenched. "Jess, I don't—"

Pushing with her arms, she hoisted herself from the rocker to clomp the two steps to him.

Framing his face with her hands, she stroked his cheeks with her thumbs and took a breath for courage. No, not courage. She didn't have anything to fear. Not where Gage was concerned.

"Because," she said and crooked a grin, "I'd rather be your lover. Your life partner. Your *wife*."

He stared at her without responding for a moment as if replaying her words in his head, double-checking his hearing. "Um…"

"I've always been so scared of being vulnerable, of letting myself become that scared little girl whose mother wasn't there for her again. I told myself I had to be self-reliant at all costs. And…it has cost me. My marriage to Matt, my ability to trust most people…" She grasped his chin and blinked back the tears that filled her eyes. "But I don't want it to cost me *you*. I was so scared when I felt my feelings for you changing. But you have proven in so many ways that you have my back. That you are loyal and dependable and patient and…more important to me than my next breath. I want you in my life, in my bed, in my heart for the next twenty-five years and beyond!"

His eyes widened, and he swallowed hard. "So what are you— Um…"

She laughed and smacked a kiss on his mouth. "Gage Coleman, I'm asking you to marry me! And you'd better have something better to say than 'Um!'"

A tremor rolled through him, and a bright grin lit his face. "How about lover, life partner, wife *and best friend*? I don't see why we have to lose the friendship."

She slipped her arms around his neck and leaned into him, reveling in the sexy warmth of his smile and the strength of his embrace. "I'm good with that, but…who's going to break the news to Tina that she's got to share her *bestie* title with you?"

"Ooh," Gage said, grimacing. "I'd take a bullet for you, love. But I'm remembering a time when I asked Tina to share the last piece of pumpkin pie at Thanksgiving. It got ugly. Mom ended up telling us neither of us got it. And you're an even better prize than pumpkin pie."

Jessica threw her head back as she laughed. "Are you saying you're scared of your little sister?"

Gage raised his eyebrows. "A little. But for you, I'd pick up the gauntlet."

Jessica smiled broadly and pressed a kiss to his lips. "Yes, love, I believe you would."

Epilogue

Six months later

Jessica chose an ivory silk suit for her second wedding. Her attendants, Cait, Tina and Holly, were resplendent in jade green dresses that captured the spirit of the Christmas season and set off the red poinsettia blossoms in their bouquets.

Tina still suffered headaches on occasion, but through physical and occupational therapy, had made an almost full recovery over the past six months. Holly was still working to regain mobility, and though she might never recover her full dexterity and muscle coordination, she was alive. Holly retained her sharp wit and kind heart, and she had stood up to her parents when they tried to keep Jessica away.

"She is not just a friend," Holly had told her family with a steady voice when Jessica visited her at the rehab center. "She is my heart sister. A member of my posse. Do *not* get in the way of that."

Jessica had never felt more loved, more grateful, or more blessed…until that moment as she walked down the aisle toward Gage and met his bright, loving gaze.

He'd asked Eric to be his best man, an honor that had humbled her son and cemented the men's bond. And so, her two favorite guys in the world stood side by side, smiling their dashing smiles and mirroring the deep love she had for each of them.

The first two rows at the Valley Haven church were lined with four generations of Camerons, from Nanna to Cait's nephew Ravi. The family had declared Gage and Jessica part of their clan at the rehearsal dinner the night before, when Cait presented the couple with a Scottish wool scarf in the color pattern of the Cameron tartan.

Jessica wore the scarf now, draped across one shoulder and pinned at her opposite hip, the red and green tones the prefect complement of Christmas colors.

Taking her place at the altar, Jessica felt a happy tear drip on her cheek as she faced Gage. Never had anything felt more right in her life. She was marrying a man who'd proven to be her most ardent supporter, a smokin' hot lover, and—with Tina's willing and joyful acceptance of second place—her best friend.

Gage took her hands in his and returned a broad grin through the vows and exchange of rings, and even before the minister pronounced them man and wife, Gage tugged her close and placed a long, deep kiss on her lips. As he broke the kiss to the cheers of their assembled family and friends, he whispered, "I've been waiting a long time for this."

She stroked his cheek and answered, "Turns out, so was I. And I couldn't be happier."

* * * * *

COMING SOON!

We really hope you enjoyed reading this book.
If you're looking for more romance
be sure to head to the shops when
new books are available on

Thursday 21st November

To see which titles are coming soon, please visit
millsandboon.co.uk/nextmonth

LET'S TALK
Romance

For exclusive extracts, competitions and special offers, find us online:

- **MillsandBoon**
- **@MillsandBoon**
- **@MillsandBoonUK**
- **@MillsandBoonUK**

Get in touch on 01413 063 232